WHISPERS OF THE ELIXIR

ORDER OF THE EMBER, BOOK 1

C.P. SILVER

YELLOW THEARCH ENTERPRISES

This is a work of fiction. Names, characters, places, and incidents are products of the author's imagination or are used fictitiously and are not to be construed as real. Any resemblance to actual events, locales, organizations, or persons, living or dead, is entirely coincidental.

Cover design by 100Covers

Map by C.P. Silver

First Trade Paperback Edition: October 2025

First Hardcover and Ebook Editions: October 2025

Published by Yellow Thearch Enterprises

Print ISBN: 978-1-0682450-1-5

Ebook ISBN: 978-1-0682450-0-8

Hardcover ISBN: 978-1-0682450-2-2

Contents

Dedication

For Luc,
the kindest and best of men,
wellspring of my happiness.

And for Eva and Sylvia, in
whom my happiness finds its
completion.

Hoto Watani
Lost Sea
JENG TERRITORIES
Felken
Ghenzan
OUTLANDS
Ren
SHUDON
Kiir
Ghenzan
Sea
Hanmar
Greenstalk
Village
MIN TERRITORIES
Fox River
Sea of Yarin
Fyeng
Silver Fox Springs
Hachen
Namun
Tey Zuben
Tenisha Ko
WORLD OF ARIZAN
Pearl Sea

IMPERIAL LINEAGES

MIN EMPIRE (Southern Shudon)

The House of Min

Descendants of Yanai Sumi, who united the southern queendoms

Empress Zinchen — Reigning sovereign of Min

Princess Tori — the Min Daughter, heir to the throne

Lord Yan of the House of Min — Younger brother of Empress Zinchen

Lady Yuchi of the House of Min — Daughter of the late Lady Ko-li, deceased younger sister of Empress Zinchen

The Min-kezu — A lesser branch of the dynasty, residing chiefly in Jeng

JENG EMPIRE (Northern Shudon)

The House of Jeng

The ancient empresses of the north, extinguished by the Antiquital Emperor Zanith

House Thana

Once vassals of The House of Jeng, ascended to rule following Zanith II's fall

The Jeng Emperor — Nineteen years of age, sovereign in name, yet not permitted to govern until reaching the age of imperial majority

The Crown Prince — Son of the emperor, two years of age

Prince Filo of House Thana — Half-brother to the emperor and second in line to the Jeng throne

Lord Tam of House Thana — Late royal consort of Empress Zinchen, descended from a lesser Thana line

House Shazori

Regents who wield authority until empresses and emperors attain majority

Regent Loreshi of House Shazori

Vice Regent Caliss of House Shazori — Wife to Loreshi

The Shazori Regent's Council

The Hymn of Ketuan

Belovéd daughter, radiant one,
Lady wrought from stony ground,
Her bones alight with elements,
With elegance and power crowned.
Arizan's resplendent queen,
Ketuan of twilight, dawn,
She breathed and loosed her breath again,
To bless the world she breathed upon.

Her swelling womb held hidden life,
Then lights within, the elements,
Poured forth in water and in flame,
Their birth a solemn sacrament.
She made the sun and stars and moon,
A boon for those six born to her,
And as a mountain tall she rose,
To shield the children drawn to her.

Verses I & II — ***The Hymn of Ketuan***
Third Age, circa 1,000 B.U.,
From the Archives of the Loremasters
— Author unknown

Chapter One

TAILU SPRING FESTIVAL

Tori fought the feeling of being on a leash. She raised a hand halfway to the feathers fastened around her neck, hesitated, then let it fall.

"Is it itching, Princess?" Lady Elnora said, watching her.

"Like all insanity, but no point fiddling with it."

Her gentlewoman adjusted the feathered ruff anyway, providing no relief whatsoever. It didn't matter. Collared or not, today she would prove she was not her mother's lapdog.

She struggled to see above the red filigree rail of the Imperial Observation Pavilion—where the royal family sat, far above the masses—the weight of her ceremonial robes resisting her every effort. Imperial decorum, it seemed, had not been designed with mobility in mind. It was times like these that she regretted her small stature; her mother, no doubt, could see perfectly.

Once she finally shifted forward, however, her three-story vantage point allowed her a perfect view of the float parade winding through the city of Silver Fox Springs in a ribbon of color and sound.

"I still don't see them," Tori said, craning her neck forward.

Elnora's smooth brown finger pointed the way. Blending seamlessly with the sculptures of giant mythical creatures adorning the streets, Tori's pantomimists balanced on their stilts, waist pouches packed so tight with skades that the little stones stretched the seams. Pantomimists had never been seen before at the Tailu Spring Festival—and would remain hidden, until her plan required it.

Elnora's brow creased beneath her dark curls, but Tori cut her off before she could object.

"It's the right thing to do. I'm doing it."

The crease between Elnora's brows deepened, a sign of that well-meaning, overdeveloped sense of caution Tori so often found herself trying to assuage.

"Every festival day, there are children eating scraps off the streets," Tori said. "Here, in Min!"

"She said you couldn't." Elnora's gaze darted briefly to the empress, seated ten paces away. "I just don't want you scuttling your own ship."

Elnora was right, of course.

But Tori lifted her chin, projecting a confidence she didn't feel. "It has to be today. The time has come for my mother to admit she doesn't control me."

She tilted her head to one side, then the other, stretching out tight muscles. It had been a trying morning—her lead pantomimist had taken ill at the last moment, forcing her to replace him with someone less capable.

The sight of the new man among her other pantomimists made her tap her heel to try and release her tension. As she studied his smiling, painted mask, a cool gust of wind swept through the pavilion, blowing a straight black lock of hair into Tori's face.

She pushed it aside just as a colorful cloth float, two stories high, rolled into the main square. Tori shielded her eyes from a glare—the float had been waxed so well, it reflected sunlight like fine porcelain.

The painted image of "Infinite Sword," one of the seven historical warriors, stared at her with a fearsome expression. In one hand, he held the head of a humanoid creature with red eyes and jagged teeth—a vanquished Antiquital. In his other, three swords.

The Tao Ti artists, musicians, and hulking floatsmen that pushed the float all bowed to her as Min Daughter, heir to the throne. They repeated the gesture to the chief equitess, Tori's great-grandmother and the chief judge of the land, bowing lower still.

But when they turned to Tori's mother, the Empress Zinchen, this time they lowered their bodies to the ground, foreheads pressed against the white stone.

"Min is the empress, the empress is Min!" they proclaimed with one voice.

Then, after a dip of the empress's chin, the float veered on its massive wheels and rolled down Main Street.

The lithe, white-robed men accompanying the float resumed their performance of the ancient martial form of Tao Ti in flowing unison, spinning in the air to land light as cats, then twirling their swords with perfect, coordinated timing. A chorus of feminine squeals rose from the crowd.

In about the time it would take a candle to burn, the float parade would be finished and the execution would begin. After that, it would be time for Tori's surprise.

She set her jaw, forcing down the doubt before it could show. For the better part of the morning, she had been sending messages to the new man, struggling to make him understand what she expected of him. As her servant boy handed him yet another message, he swayed precariously on his stilts trying to read it, nearly tipping into the crispy hop stand beside him.

Determined not to let him rattle her, Tori pulled her gaze away, focusing instead on a small girl in rags standing barefoot a little ways from the crowd. She was obviously an Ant—the half-race of part-human, part-Antiquital—as could be seen from the soft whiskers fanning outward around her black triangular nose.

Warmth lit Tori's chest. For once, every child here, no matter how poor, would be able to buy at least one generous portion of festival food. It was going to be a great day for everyone.

She looked around at the food sellers, wondering what the children would buy. The aroma of *elloku* filled the air—her personal favorite, fried dough balls with tiny pieces of crab—their fragrance mingling deliciously with the spicy, earthy scent of crispy hops.

A cluster of people waited eagerly at the crispy hop stand, watching an elderly man lower a metal basket filled with grasshoppers into a huge vat of boiling oil. Customers held their pink or blue skades high, each person willing him to serve them first.

When he lifted the basket out, the grasshoppers had been transformed into a mouthwatering treat, which the seller scooped into rice-paper cones in exchange for a skade or two, depending on the cone size. She imagined a swarm of children there instead.

"...as the Great Tailu descended upon Yanai Sumi," the orator's voice boomed, announcing the arrival of the tailu-bird float, "blessing her as the first empress of the Min Territories." As the official narrator of all festivities, the man had a voice that carried, but Tori had tuned him out.

The orator's tower stood diagonally across the square from the Imperial Observation Pavilion, mimicking its color and design, with crescent-moon eaves, gilded scrollwork, and shiny red paint. However, whereas the pavilion was large, the tower was merely tall, just wide enough for the orator and two of Her Majesty's archers, who scanned the crowds constantly.

"And so, the House of Min, through the power and might bestowed by the Great Tailu, liberated"—he emphasized this last word dramatically—"the people from the evil Antiquital Emperor Zanith and the maleficent wielders who placed him in power. Thus, the Peasant Revolt ended, bringing peace and prosperity to all!"

The crowd cheered. Whistles shrilled. Horns blew.

Maleficent wielders.

The words hit Tori like a slap. She kept her face smooth, unblinking, and reached absently for a broken clamshell in her pouch, running a finger over its time-worn edge. That word had nothing to do with her—she was cured. Now, she just needed to forget.

Clouds gathered in the distance, dark against the bright spring sky, and the scent of rain hovered in the air.

Dancers in glittering bird costumes gyrated and shimmied around the tailu-bird float to the sound of flutes, hand cymbals, and drums. The float stopped before the Imperial Observation Pavilion, its golden beak and talons gleaming. The outstretched wings were painted in sparkling red, white, and black, as well as blue, burned earth, and green—the same colors as Tori's ruff, the tailu-bird being the symbol of the House of Min.

On the other side of Tori's mother, her great-grandmother—a gifted conversationalist—chatted with her entourage, no doubt giving a discourse on history, while murmurs of delight wafted up from behind Tori and Elnora, where Tori's other two gentlewomen sat.

"Oh, Princess!" Lady Anlin looked on, eyes bright. "The wings really do look like jewels."

"Exquisite," Tori said.

And it was. Still, it was hard to feel excited about something that, like everything here, was simply a carefully orchestrated tribute to her mother's greatness.

Except the pantomimists, she thought, and repressed a smile.

Throwing money to the children would not cause her mother to lose face—Tori couldn't afford that risk—but her message would be clear: a ruler's greatness is not measured in tributes to herself, but in how well she cares for the most vulnerable.

Her shoulders tensed again. What would her mother's response be to the veiled criticism? Tori barely saw the tailu-bird float's performers as they made their bows.

Three more floats to go.

The orator's theatrical voice announced the next two floats, which came from the longevitists. The first belonged to the Silver Cloud Mountain Sect. A group of disciples in blue-and-white robes walked serenely before a giant silver cloud. Dull, at best.

Her feathered ruff felt scratchier when there was nothing to distract her, and she hooked a finger into it briefly, creating a momentary relief.

The new lead pantomimist jerked up his head, straightening to full height on his stilts and reaching for his waist pouch—he had mistaken her idle gesture for the signal. Her stomach knotted.

She gave a firm shake of her head, and cut her hand through the air—*not yet*. Her fingers were steadier than she felt. He finally settled down, somehow managing to look confused despite his mask.

Simpleton. The signal was that she would touch both earrings at the same time. Clearly she would have to be more careful—timing was everything.

She needed something to keep her mind off the possibility of failure. Past the tiresome silver cloud, the penultimate float should be arriving on Yanai Avenue soon, before making its turn onto Main Street. It was the only float she had been looking forward to seeing, the last of the longevitist floats. If her sources had been correct, a senior sect member would be riding on it—a man rumored to be over 130 years old.

As she waited for the float to roll down Yanai Avenue, her gaze landed on the people lining the street: children perched in trees, chewing candied hawthorn, and people ringing little bells. Others waved flags painted with colorful designs that evoked the logograms for the numbers twenty-four and four: the twenty-fourth day of the fourth moon, the day of the annual Tailu Spring Festival.

Something at the entrance to the avenue caught her eye: beyond the crowds, a man sat on horseback, partly hidden by the trees. His straight black hair was pulled into the ponytail typical of the Varanaken tribes, and the sword on his back, along with his braided leather chest guard, marked him as one of the Varanaken warriors.

What in the name of the Six was he doing there? And was that a sack tethered to the saddle, dragging on the ground? She squinted, trying to get a better look.

But the dancers and musicians turned the corner, startling his horse, and the Varanaken steadied his mount, pulling back behind the trees.

He had given her an unsettled feeling, but she looked away, scanning the crowds once more, only to find her lead pantomimist wavering on his stilts. He swayed back and forth for several endless breaths, trying time and again to right himself, then finally slipped, falling headlong into the street.

Tori's stomach pitched. Onlookers pointed and gathered around him, forming a semicircle. She darted her eyes to her mother. If the empress sent someone to investigate, Tori's plan would be foiled.

The empress narrowed her eyes, apparently noticing the commotion.

Tori scanned the pavilion, searching for a solution, nervous sweat trickling down her back despite the servants' constant fanning. Her servant boy was ascending the stairs, holding a tray with golden bowls on it—ordering festival food had been her way of sending him with messages into the crowd.

When he came to her, she grabbed a bowl, then motioned to one of the fanning maids. "Quick. Give this to the empress before it gets cold."

The girl took the bowl of crispy hops, visibly confused.

Straining to see through the corner of her eye, Tori watched as the maid held out the bowl to the empress. She responded with an incredulous look, then flicked her fingers, sending the maid away.

When the empress turned her face back to the crowd, however, the pantomimist had already gone.

Tori blew out a long breath and dabbed her brow. Then she lifted her fan to her mouth as though eating, and spoke to her servant boy. "Get him out. I'm ordering the number two pantomimist to take the lead. Go."

He dipped his head, then ran.

Her muscles were painfully tight. Her entire plan now rested in the hands of the number two pantomimist, and she couldn't fathom whether he was up to the task.

Seeking a distraction, she focused again on Yanai Avenue, where the float from the Bridge of Heaven Sect was finally rolling into view. On a chair between two golden bridges at least sixteen handspans high sat a man with flowing hair and a long beard, both snowy white.

Tori had always been impressed with the vigor of her mother's longevitist adviser and Speaker, yet that woman was forty-five—only a third of this sect member's age; Tori had never seen a sect elder before.

The float entered the square, revealing the old man's bright eyes and upright posture, evidence of the vitality dawn-essence cycling was said to produce. Dawn-essence was the energy that ran through everything, created at the dawn of the world by the first woman's breath.

When the float stopped, the disciples and floatsmen bowed to Tori, then to the chief equitess, the elder doing likewise from atop his bridge. But when the time came to pay respects to Tori's mother, the elder descended the float in two quick hops, then lowered himself easily to the ground.

Tori's eyebrows lifted; she had been prepared for vitality, but this was something far beyond. The empress dipped her chin.

Two hops had him back on top of the float again, and Tori tracked him with her eyes all the way down Main Street.

One more float to go.

She tapped her heel again as the little Ant girl came to mind. Her mother had denied Tori's request to quietly gift money to the children—what would she think of this display? What if she was so furious she banned Tori from accessing the imperial treasury? Tori's secret rice donations to the Ant slums would be cut off.

Or what if her pantomimists hit the children in the head with the skades, leaving them unconscious? Tori stilled—she hadn't thought of that. The stones were small, but then, so were children.

She wiped sweat from her palms and took a long, slow breath, eyes wandering to the execution area on her right, where the main square abutted the forest; the Imperial Observation Pavilion had been carefully designed to allow its occupants a perfect view of it.

Two executioners sat on logs, waiting for their moment to shine. Both were Ants, naturally. One had round eyes with inner eyelids that blinked vertically like a bird's, pale yellow with no whites, betraying the heritage of his Air Antiquital ancestors. His gaze followed some passing musicians as he nodded in time with their music, foot tapping to the beat of the drums. The other Ant was shirtless, and he leaned back on the upward-sloping forest floor, staring at the sky. He showed signs of Water Antiquital blood, with iridescent red scales running up the sides of both arms from wrist to shoulder, but otherwise he looked like any normal man.

The empress's soldiers guarded the prisoner's cage. Backs straight, swords at their sides, they were the model of discipline. They must have been baking in their steel helmets on a sunny day like this.

The prisoner's cage sat out of the way, but still had a full view of the street. Part of his punishment, after all, was to watch the festivities taking place, knowing that his death would add to the entertainment. A man-sized saw had been set up for the occasion.

Tori grimaced inwardly at the thought of the blood and innards that would soon soil the square, but she stopped herself. The harshest punishments were necessary when dealing with the harshest crimes—this murderer had taken several lives in a dispute over a well. And the executioners wouldn't drag it out—people were looking forward to the firework display at the end; her mother had promised something more extravagant than they had ever seen.

The last of the floats made its lumbering way up Yanai Avenue, where two mermaids with seaweed hair and milk-white eyes lounged on their sides, back-to-back, hands stretched outward to the crowd. The execution would take place shortly.

Tori found the number two pantomimist, who now wore the mask that designated him as leader, and she made a hand signal, letting him know to get ready. He looked confused.

She exhaled sharply through her nose. Now, of all times, was not the moment for confusion.

Just then, the same Varanaken she had seen at the entrance to the avenue trotted on horseback past the mermaid float. A man in rags stumbled behind him, his bound hands tied by a rope to the back of the horse's saddle. They made their way toward the square.

As they neared, the man's feet came into view: dried blood caked his soles, a testament to the distance he must have suffered over rough terrain. The mermaid float stalled halfway up the avenue, and people in the surrounding crowd looked at each other in confusion.

The Varanaken approached the pavilion, proud and erect on his horse. He dismounted smoothly, almost arrogantly, then pushed the bound man to his knees before bowing low himself.

Tori glanced at her mother. The empress tapped a fingertip against her armrest, then stopped—she was puzzled.

With a flick of the wrist, her mother's fan glided open to cover her mouth, imperial lips too exalted to be seen moving before common eyes. The Imperial Speaker—the empress's voice to the commoners—leaned forward, inclining her ear close to her sovereign's face. The Speaker bowed her head in acknowledgment, then stood and looked out onto the square.

"Her Majesty bids you make your business known," she said, her voice sonorous as a bell.

The Varanaken bowed again, then responded in a deep, haughty voice, "While patrolling the lands in Her Majesty's name, I discovered an evildoer of the vilest sort. I humbly request Her Majesty to permit these charges to be read and justice administered." He stood with his legs apart, chin up, eyes fixed on the Speaker as he handed a scroll to a page boy, who ran with it to the orator's tower.

Tori studied the criminal's face, then his rough-spun peasant's tunic and trousers. He wasn't old, but sun and fatigue marked him.

Yet something wasn't right. Tori tilted her head. The man seemed almost...relieved.

She took in the criminal's downcast eyes, his bound hands, the Varanaken's words replaying in her mind: *an evildoer of the vilest sort*.

As she looked at the man's wrists again, a sinking feeling settled into her chest—she knew what he was accused of. His wrists were double bound with atha rope, something only done to wielders.

Tori started, pressing a hand to her stomach. No vibrations. He wasn't a wielder; she would have felt the vibrations otherwise. Cold dread ran through her as the implications of this settled in, and her gaze snapped to the saw.

The orator was already reading the charges: "...that one Lee Ren Shiven, of Redfin village, in Her Imperial Majesty's province of Waterwheel, did use the forbidden and degenerate art of wielding to call forth fire from heaven, and further did use such forbidden and degenerate art to knowingly and maliciously burn, destroy, or otherwise desecrate the barley fields of Her Majesty, the serene and majestic Empress Zinchen, and, in accordance with the laws of the Min Territories established by Her Majesty's decree"—his voice picked up intensity here—"it is hereby requested that Her Majesty administer the full penalty of the law—death by saw!"

Tori cursed behind her fan. The Varanaken was using the public occasion to gain prestige by bringing a supposedly dangerous criminal to justice.

She swiveled toward her mother, swallowing against the tightness in her throat. She couldn't tell anyone how she knew the man was innocent—not without endangering herself. But as the executioners sharpened the massive blade, guilt shot through her, and before she could stop herself, she was speaking.

"Your Majesty," she called in a loud whisper.

Her mother pretended not to hear.

Tori spoke louder, though still too low for anyone outside their respective entourages to notice. "Your Majesty, I cannot allow this to be done. I must insist the man be imprisoned and questioned, as usual."

The empress's eyes tightened above her fan. "The Varanaken have the right. Settle down."

Two hundred years ago, the Varanaken had vowed to eradicate wielders—then seen as the greatest threat to the throne and society. Since that time, the old law had allowed them to appear before the empress at any time to demand judgment on an accused wielder, though it was usually done in private.

Tori looked beyond her mother to the chief equitess, searching her lined face. Surely the chief judge of the Min Territories would stand against such a grave injustice. "Please, Grandmother."

Her great-grandmother nodded slowly. "Equity demands he offer a defense, Your Majesty."

The empress swept her gaze over the crowd, and in the space of a breath, she had read their mood. She returned her eyes to Tori and responded with a shake of the head.

The chief equitess would not oppose her, for although she was sworn to administer the law equitably, the empress *was* the law. Tori was alone.

"With respect, Your Majesty," Tori said, "the right to offer a defense is a bare minimum for anyone."

"Wielders are no one—and they are certainly not just anyone." Her mother calmly returned her gaze to the crowd. The conversation was over.

Tori's mind raced. The empress might not be willing to speak out, but why shouldn't the Min Daughter? Her mother would be livid, but it would work.

Elnora seemed to sense Tori's thoughts. She gripped the corner of Tori's sleeve, whispering behind her fan in a voice so soft only Tori's ears would hear. "Please, Princess. There's nothing you can do."

The empress must have sensed it, too, because she lifted a finger, and instantly, her mother's gentlewomen shielded her mother from public view.

The empress lowered her fan. "Whatever you are considering, you will restrain yourself." Her tone held all the authority of her position.

Tori fought for the courage to defy her openly. The empress had the power to restrict Tori's movement, her funding, her very lifeblood it seemed.

Squaring her shoulders, she stood, her legs as unstable as pillars of water.

Murmurs blew through the crowd, and the people gazed up at her, their faces a mix of expectation and curiosity.

Tori's hands were cold and clammy; addressing the crowd directly was unheard of for a member of the imperial family. She straightened to full height, such as it was, dwarfed by her mother's majesty, but she kept her gaze straight ahead.

"This is a day of celebration!" Tori said, thankful her voice didn't crack. She didn't have the Imperial Speaker's training, and strained for volume. "In celebration of the Imperial House of Min's valiance in liberating the land of Shudon from the Antiquital Emperor Zanith, the Imperial House will show mercy!"

A child in the crowd cheered and rang a bell. His mother swatted his head, and he stopped.

Tori's gaze flicked briefly to the side, where her mother sat perfectly composed. Only Tori noticed her clenched jaw, her flashing eyes.

But the people seemed awed by her voice—it was going well. She would find a way to release the man quietly.

"As guardian of equity, I undertake to ensure this man will be imprisoned and thoroughly interrogated until such—"

Vibrations in her belly caught her off guard.

"Until...such time as..." The vibrations intensified, like a thousand loose pearls ricocheting off her stomach floor. Her mind went blank. She groped for her words, but all she could think of were the pearls. Total confusion engulfed her. Her eyes shifted to her mother, who was studying her now with a curious expression.

Tori tried again, mouth dry, unable to understand why this was happening. Then the bound man looked toward Yanai Avenue, moving his lips and shaking his head, as though trying to convince someone not to do something.

"Until such time as justice is—"

A hysterical female voice broke in. "He ain't no wielder!"

A young woman ran up the avenue and into the square, her tunic and hair soaked with sweat and dirt, like she had run all day along dusty roads.

She hunched over, gasping for breath. "We was clearin' the dry fields, is all. I swear it. And it weren't him! It were me!"

One of the guards shoved the woman back, while the Varanaken swept out his foot, tripping the bound man to the ground. She rounded on them, scowling, but the bound man stumbled back to his feet, shaking his head frantically at her.

The pearls inside Tori's stomach exploded. "Oh no."

A fireball leaped from the woman's hands onto the guard and two others behind him. They hollered and clawed at their helmets as smoke poured out.

Arrows flew at her, then disintegrated into ash, the arrowheads tinkling on the ground. People screamed and ran.

The Varanaken hopped onto his horse and reached back for his sword, then dropped it with a curse, shaking a burned, red hand.

The woman hurled another fireball, and the horse reared, hooves thrashing in the air, throwing off the Varanaken. He rolled and sprang to his feet, sword raised.

Heaving from exhaustion, she spun, facing the pavilion, contempt twisting her face as she raised a trembling hand. The empress slipped a red stone from her sleeve and turned it toward the woman, the motion hidden from all but Tori. A pathetic yellow flame sputtered to life in the woman's hand, then fizzled, vanishing. She raised the other.

But an arrow sang through the air, lodging in her eye. For a heartbeat, her body stood frozen, then she buckled at the knees and toppled over, the contempt on her face now permanent.

In the space of two long breaths, it was over.

The bound man let out a heartrending wail, then slumped to his knees, head to chest, weeping.

In the hush that followed, the pearls in Tori's stomach went quiet, and she stared dumbly, lips parted.

The guards who had formed a wall around the empress now moved aside, and she quickly slid the mysterious red stone back into her sleeve. She gave a hand signal, and the captain shouted orders to his men. The injured soldiers were carried away on stretchers, others calmed the crowd, while still others moved the murderer's cage into the forest for him to be executed another day.

The orator's wig sat tilted to one side of his bald head, but he bellowed, "Never fear, Her Majesty has restored order!"

The wide-eyed crowd settled, so great was their confidence in their sovereign's protection, though many still cast glances at the weeping man's double-bound wrists.

A few of them looked up at Tori, then a few more. Soon, every eye was on her. She only then realized she was still standing—they were expecting her to speak.

She forced herself to think. Saving the man now was out of the question—he might as well have attacked the empress himself.

Her eyes stung. A quick death was the best she could do.

Feigning confident serenity, she lifted her chin. "As I was saying, the House of Min will show mercy today! This is a day for celebration, not needless blood. Just as Infinite Sword beheaded the Antiquitals, the criminal shall be beheaded!"

The air grew thick with tension as people exchanged unsure glances, or furrowed their brows, clearly unhappy. This was turning against her.

"And skades for all the children!" she blurted out, pawing on both earrings.

For a few beats, the number two pantomimist just stared. Finally, he jerked up and signaled to the others.

The sound of a fiddle awakened the last of them, the fiddler weaving his way through the crowd as planned, hopping and dancing to the tune of "The Merry, Merry Berry Girl."

Pantomimists threw skades to the children, the little stones catching the sunlight like pink and blue raindrops. Other fiddlers echoed the tune on Yanai Avenue and Main Street, and soon skade-throwing pantomimists were everywhere.

Laughter and shrieks of joy came from children scrambling to catch their skades in the air, or snatch them off the ground, while the adults looked on with expressions of guarded amusement.

Her mother's gaze swept the crowd again, then it landed on Tori, where it lingered icily for half a breath before she lifted her fan to her mouth.

A moment later, the Imperial Speaker announced, "But first, death by arrow!"

The last vestiges of doubt left the people's faces, and they cheered, setting off horns, bells and the wild beat of a drum.

A woman in the crowd shouted, "All hail Her Imperial Majesty, the great and merciful Empress Zinchen! And blessings on the Min Daughter, the princess with the common touch!" Others joined in.

The prisoner was shoved forward. He grunted as an arrow caught him in the arm, then he doubled over as successive arrows caught him in the chest and back, each one raising exuberant shouts from the crowd. An arrow in the temple drove him to the ground.

Tori's stomach twisted violently at the sight, all her efforts crumbling like sun-dried clay, but she kept her face a smooth, unblinking mask.

Finally, the Ant with the scales on his arms raised a curved blade and swept off the prisoner's head, lifting it in the air to a crescendo of cheers. When the other executioner had taken off the woman's head, Tori raised her hand to quiet the crowd.

"Now let the festivities continue! The blessing of the Six and of the Great Tailu be always on the people of Min!"

Everyone clapped, some honoring the empress by touching their foreheads to the ground. Musicians and dancers again filled the streets.

Tori sat, her feathered ruff choking her.

The heads of the accused wielders, arrows still protruding from them, were mounted onto the hands of the milk-eyed mermaids that lounged on the final float.

As the float passed onto Main Street, one gruff voice yelled, "Scatter their ashes to the nine winds!"

Others echoed the sentiment. "May the filthy wielders never find rest!" Some spat and raised their fists.

Tori waited until protocol no longer required her presence, then she rose and bowed deeply to her mother. The empress stiffened, her mouth a flat line. After a long moment, she gave a tight nod.

At that, Tori and her ladies descended the back steps of the pavilion into the forest.

Fireworks erupted across the darkening sky, great birds made of red, copper, and indigo light. Their wings unfurled to the sound of thunderous cheers—all, of course, in praise of the empress.

As this was happening, she heard her mother speak.

"Hear my decree," she said in quiet tones. She would be addressing the Imperial Speaker.

"I, Zinchen, in light of the grievous assault upon my August Person, do hereby decree: henceforth, anyone found to be a wielder shall be seized and shown no mercy. The right to a trial is hereby revoked. They shall be brought before me and put to death by saw without delay."

Tori stiffened, turning the words over in her mind. Then, with a queasy feeling, she mounted the waiting carriage.

Chapter Two

KAZANI

Tori spent the ride home in a daze. She didn't notice the passing forest, or even the noise of her ladies' nervous chatter. The only thing she was really aware of was the rain, which streamed down the clear mica pane of her carriage window, blurring the scenery into a haze of greenish-gray.

The carriage veered right, beginning the slow ascent to the palace at the top of the hill.

"Stop!" Tori rapped twice on the wall.

They slowed to a halt, and an instant later, her driver poked his head through the door beside his seat. Two Varanaken pulled their horses next to her window—her bodyguards, Dan and Bokoon. She avoided their gazes.

"Turn around and take me to Kazani," Tori told the driver. She couldn't bear to see her mother—not tonight—and longed for her quiet country home. She felt like an animal licking its wounds, vulnerable and smarting, searching for a place to hide.

Elnora looked at her. "You'll miss the Tailu Feast, Princess. The empress won't be happy."

True. But by the time she noticed Tori was missing, it would be too late to summon her back for the feast.

Tori stared resolutely ahead and said no more, a signal her driver understood.

He bowed. "Very good, Princess."

Though they were soon traveling away from the palace, unease tugged on her mind. Dan and Bokoon wouldn't report to her mother, would they? She resisted the urge to check if they still followed. No—they were loyal. To her.

Just like their fathers had been.

She closed her eyes, shutting out the thought.

It wasn't until they had traveled a distance of thirty-five fen—about the time of a stone's warming in the sun—that Tori finally relaxed: the front gate of Kazani had come into view. She leaned back and blew out a long, tired breath.

The gatekeeper's son rang the bell wildly, announcing her presence, and the massive outer gate labored open. Just inside it, her two Kazani house guards stood in the rain, dripping wet.

The carriage stopped beside the garden stream, which burbled loudly now from the rain, cheerful and melodious. Thankfully, she would be able to stay for some days. Though she was required as Min Daughter to accompany her mother to court once per week, Tori's next court session was still several days away.

She and her ladies exited the carriage, then crossed over the stream on a small, arched bridge. Dan rode through the water, passing them, his horse trotting toward the fishing pavilion by the lake. The unease she had buried pushed through again—where was Bokoon?

She tried to suppress the thought. Nothing would disturb her peace of mind while she was at Kazani.

Her house peeked at her through the trees. All pale wood and gently sloping crescent-moon roofs, it stood raised on stilts, as though eagerly pushing up on its toes to see her, while the hallways connecting the main house to its wings spread out on either side like open arms. The residence had been given to her eight years before, when she was twelve, to celebrate her successful completion of the equitess examinations.

She tilted her face to the sky, letting the rain wash her mind.

Kazani had been meant for a small household: it had been expected that she would have at least two lawful intimates by her present age. As Min Daughter, her duty was to make political alliances—something every noblewoman with a son seemed to know. But she had managed to resist her mother's efforts in that regard, leaving Kazani as her sanctuary of defiance.

"I'm never trusting the weather almanac again," Elnora said, covering her head with her arms to protect her curly hair, water streaming off her smooth brown skin.

Anlin chuckled. "Lady Elnora, I promise the sky won't fall on your head before the maids get here."

Up ahead, maids poured out of the east wing and down the hallway's veranda, then exited into the garden with waxed cloth umbrellas, their gauzy, light green robes grazing the ground, becoming muddy at the hem.

While the maids held the umbrellas above Tori and her ladies—Elnora, Yumay, and Anlin—they made their way through the carefully planted trees and shrubs that so beautifully mimicked the arbitrariness of nature. When she was younger, this garden had given Tori the feeling of adventuring in the wild. Now, it only evoked bittersweet memories of happier times.

She crouched over a small collection of herbs, its strict organization out of place in its surroundings, and brushed her fingertips over the circle of mismatched stones enclosing it. Wan, her late mentor, had planted them years before, in order to teach her botany—for a short while. She stood, chest aching, and breathed in the comforting smell of wet earth.

Her eunuchs greeted her at the tops steps of the house, exchanging her wet shoes for dry silk slippers, and in half the time it would take a candle to burn, Tori had shed her heavy costume in favor of her usual soft, silk robes.

She and her ladies sat outside on the veranda, around a table laden with a teapot, a wine jug, and gold-rimmed dishes. Elnora, who wasn't hungry, sat apart, taking up her crochet two paces away from the stream of rainwater trickling off the eaves.

As Tori surveyed the food, the face of the innocent man as he wept on his knees flashed in her mind, and her stomach turned. But her ladies would never eat if she didn't, so she picked up her chopsticks and lifted a small vinegared fish to her mouth to signal the beginning of the meal.

Yumay watched Elnora between mouthfuls, a twinkle in her brown eyes. Lighthearted Kazani was having its effect—on everyone but Tori. The glow of the birth charm around Yumay's neck cast a conspiratorial light under her face as she leaned toward Anlin.

"It appears our Lady Elnora isn't eating. Could it be lovesickness, I wonder?" Yumay's teasing tone made it clear that she knew the answer—she always did. As the closest thing Tori had to a spy, Yumay's network of informants was nothing short of impressive.

"Do tell," Anlin said eagerly.

Hiding a half-smile, Elnora clicked her tongue, then pointedly eyed her tangle of crochet and moved the hooks more quickly. Though Elnora held the senior position in Tori's service, none of her ladies stood on protocol between themselves and took turns teasing each other, depending on the day.

"Well, rumor has it that a young soldier has his eye on her," Yumay said.

"Wait—is it the one with the mustache?" Anlin asked.

Yumay raised a meaningful brow. "Apparently her young admirer found out she likes crispy hops, and he made it his mission to keep her happy. He bribed the servants to pour cone after cone into the golden bowls for her, till there were no bowls left."

"Ooh, I do like a resourceful man," Anlin said. She grinned, flashing the charming, tiny space between her front teeth.

Tori tried to smile, but couldn't clear away the face of the weeping man.

Elnora put down her crochet. "First of all, there were only two cones. Small ones. Second, I have no interest in him, and I told him so," she said, in her musical Tenisha-ko accent.

"Come now, Lady Elnora. You can hardly expect us to believe that." Anlin's small black eyes glittered mischievously. "I happened to notice the young man in question, and I have to say, you're completely justified in encouraging his attentions—I would."

"But I *didn't* encourage him." Elnora tried unsuccessfully to tuck her dark curls behind an ear—her hair had doubled in volume because of the rain.

Anlin raised an eyebrow. "You ate his crispy hops." She drew out the words, somehow managing to make them sound illicit. "Believe me, that's all the encouragement most men need."

She smiled a wicked smile, drawing a blush from Elnora. Yumay laughed.

Her ladies' bright chatter finally broke through Tori's gloom, and she chuckled. "Leave her alone."

Feeling her appetite return, Tori looked down at her plate—but the headless fish turned her stomach again.

As though reading her mind, an elderly servant approached and bowed. Being too low in rank to address Tori directly, she looked instead at the gentlewomen. "Something for the princess," she said, holding out a cloth-wrapped bundle to Yumay, who passed it to Tori.

The smell of fried dough and crab wafted from two small elloku, triggering a memory: this servant had bought elloku once to cheer up Tori when she was a child. Tori had wanted to play on the floor by her mother's feet at the Tailu Spring Festival, and her mother had scolded her for it. By consoling the princess with snacks without permission, the servant had shown unseemly familiarity toward Tori—and the empress had demoted her.

The woman's gesture—both then and now—touched her profoundly.

"Thank you," Tori said, picking up an elloku and taking a bite, feeling renewed promise for a time of refreshment at Kazani.

The woman grinned and backed away.

Anlin pointed to the sliding screen behind them, where Tori's letter table sat. "It looks like more came."

Through the latticework of the screen, a basket peeked out, filled with paper cut into strips—excerpts from love poems sent by Tori's suitors. She and her ladies made a game of scrambling the ridiculous phrases to make truly laughable poetry.

Tori smirked. "We'll have a poetry competition later. First, let's take a stroll by the stream. Now that the rain has stopped, the sounding stones will sing beautifully."

Before they could rise from the table, however, a small side gate opened forty paces away.

"Her Imperial Majesty's messenger has arrived!" the gate guard announced.

Tori's stomach dropped.

A messenger in black-and-gold palace livery ran forward and, spotting Tori, bowed.

"A message for Her Imperial Highness," he said to Elnora, proffering a carved scroll case.

Elnora dismissed the man and handed Tori the scroll.

The red wax seal had been stamped hastily, something her mother did when angry. She broke it.

Tori,

As you appear incapable of sound judgment, you will be banned from Kazani until further notice. You will return to the palace at once and remain confined to your rooms unless granted my permission to do otherwise.

Furthermore, you will take your place in court tomorrow—and every day thereafter. This is not a request.

For several beats she could only stare at Wan's mismatched stones.

Was she so powerless over her own life? Powerless to help those who needed her? Powerless even to take the time she needed to reflect?

After reading the summons again, she crumpled it and threw it into the grass. Then she inhaled slowly through her nose, trying to maintain her composure, which felt as fragile as the crumpled paper.

"Give me a few moments alone," she said, and went inside the house, sending the maids and eunuchs out.

She retreated to her bedroom, flung aside the curtains of her bed, and sat, angry heat prickling her neck. She would not give her mother the power to disturb her peace.

Trying to push the summons from her mind, she focused instead on the black velvet pouch filled with spirit stones for the game of Umbrage, Wan's first gift to her. But the wielder's face appeared, eclipsing the stones—one moment, alive with fear, anger, confusion; the next moment, snuffed out like a lamp. A weight pressed on Tori's chest.

Her eyes drifted unwillingly to the corner of the room where Wan's cane rested against the wall, silver handle gleaming, the jeweled eyes of its eagle's head staring back at her reproachfully.

More images flashed in her mind: the bound man weeping. The wielder's severed head. Suddenly, it wasn't a stranger's head she saw anymore, but her own. Tori's stomach heaved.

A wind blew through the house, snuffing out the lanterns—even though all the doors and windows were shut. Tori's pulse thumped, and she gripped the silk sheets into fists.

More images flashed. Fireballs. Soldiers clawing at smoking helmets.

A dark forest. Lightning. Wan's black hair, streaked with white. She blinked away stinging tears.

Her breath came short, her rib cage tightened, and she clenched the sheets till her fingernails bit into her palms, overwhelmed by pain and rage and helplessness.

For a long while, she sat, breathing hard, her mind turning the contents of her mother's scroll over and over. She would have to go back; there was no other choice.

But she wasn't going to go back and do nothing.

She returned to the veranda where her household was waiting. Her ladies looked at her anxiously.

"Get everything ready," Tori said, not meeting their eyes. "We return to the palace tonight."

When everyone else had left, she took Yumay aside and spoke in low tones. "My mother likes to make a show of following protocol—she won't let the Varanaken execute wielders in the streets. Even though there are no more trials, she'll still lock them up in that maze of dungeon cells till they can be publicly put to death. I need your people to find where they are."

Yumay nodded. "What are you planning?"

Tori studied the mismatched stones of Wan's herb garden, hoping for an answer. None came.

One thing however, was perfectly clear.

She set her jaw and met Yumay's eye. "I'm going to see to it that equity is done."

Chapter Three

GREAT DEEDS OF OLD

Black and red robes poured through the doors at the opposite end of the Royal Court Hall as Zinchen cast an eye on the missives spread across her desk. She was careful not to linger on the longest one—very little escaped her daughter's notice.

Tori was still sour over the events at the Tailu Festival two days before, as though her poor behavior had been Zinchen's fault. Slumped defiantly in the small throne to Zinchen's right—no doubt a silent protest against her house arrest—Tori feigned indifference to the court proceedings. Zinchen knew better, and she couldn't afford to have the girl oppose her today.

As the black-robed ministers and red-robed scholars lined up according to rank, Zinchen's eyes drifted to the paintings on the cream-colored wall panels, inspiring scenes set against a backdrop of cloud-covered mountains, surrounded with shiny black frames.

The women prostrated themselves on the ground before the dais—a single green robe bowing among them—and raised their voices: "We, the officials of Min, greet the serene and majestic Empress Zinchen, the all-powerful and all-wise. May you live forever and ever!"

Zinchen studied the woman in green. She was the governor of Kiir Province, from whom the long missive had come.

"Rise."

The officials split into ranks, scholars on the right, ministers on the left.

"Who will present their report first?"

The governor of Kiir stepped forward.

Excellent. The woman's vague missive had reported that people resembling the legendary Arun clan had appeared in Kiir Province. The knowledge the Arun were said to possess was the very thing Zinchen needed to make her dream a reality—their skills could make her invincible. If these really were the Arun, she needed to find a way to bind them to her service today.

Yet it was crucial that the suggestion come from the court officials. If the Minister of the Left realized what Zinchen wanted, she would manipulate everything to serve her own interests. Zinchen would have to play this carefully.

She picked up the missive from the polished darkwood table and nodded to the governor. "Speak."

"Your Majesty, I am appearing on behalf of Countess Amarin to request grain relief for the province of Kiir. The countess regrets that she could not come personally, but has, as you know, just given birth to her fifth child."

"Why would the grain capital of Min need grain relief?" Zinchen asked, for the benefit of the listeners. Even though she always read the missives, petitioners were nonetheless expected to elaborate.

"Flooding, Your Majesty. And what little grain we did manage to produce this year was stolen."

Zinchen waited for her to mention the Arun, but the woman merely stood wringing her hands.

"Stolen by whom?"

The governor dabbed her brow. "Well, the thieves appear to be"—she cleared her throat—"the Arun clan."

One of the scholars spoke up. "The legendary smiths?"

The governor nodded, provoking a round of whispers.

"Ridiculous," another scholar said. "The Arun died off centuries ago."

"Not having been seen for hundreds of years is very different from not existing," the first scholar responded.

They began to debate painfully whether an entire clan could really hide itself, and in support of their arguments they would have gone on to cite every historical text known to humanity if Zinchen had not interrupted them.

"What makes you think it might be them?" she asked the governor.

"They fit all the descriptions, Your Majesty. Some wear the crest of a lioness on their tunics. They have wild hair and shaggy, goatskin clothes; the sight strikes fear into the hearts of the citizens of Kiir." She shuddered. "Countess Amarin's soldiers were stretched thin trying to keep the province clear of them."

"Your report mentioned proof," Zinchen said. "Did you bring it?"

The woman dabbed a sleeve to her glistening brow. "Yes, Majesty, though I hesitate to call it *proof*, exactly." She motioned to the wings of the hall, and a eunuch appeared, carrying a long, cloth-wrapped bundle. He unwrapped it to reveal a bow and arrow.

Zinchen's heart shrank. With all the tales she had read of the Arun's crafting skills, she had been imagining a fine weapon made of noble wood—red, maybe—and adorned with silver embellishments. In her mind, it had also glowed with an otherworldly light.

This, however, just looked like any ordinary bow, one that had seen better days. The arrow was worse, with dingy black feathers, some missing.

The governor extended the items toward the dais, palms up. "These were found in Kiir three moons ago. They have markings on them that match the descriptions of etched metal in the histories. Only we don't know what the etchings mean, so we can't rightly test them."

The items were placed on Zinchen's desk. They were even less impressive up close. But carved into the arrowhead were strange signs. The same ones appeared again on the metal tips fixed to the ends of the bow. One sign consisted of three parallel, upward-slanting strokes, each tapering sharply at one end, with the bottom stroke bound by a horizontal bar. The other was a coiled line enclosed by four evenly spaced ticks, positioned at the cardinal points.

Warmth spread in Zinchen's chest. Though she had never learned to read them, she recognized their form—ancient logograms.

If these could be seen in action, she had no doubt the court would recommend bringing the Arun into her service. She thought of summoning the palace huntsman to test them, but she first had to know what they were testing for. Though the markings seemed almost pictorial in comparison to modern logograms, the pictures were an enigma.

She folded her hands and adjusted her expression to one of bored disinterest. "Can anyone identify these etchings?"

The bow and arrow was passed around the court. Her real hope, however, rested with Tori. With the girl's knowledge of Min's people, she was bound to know something.

The ministers and scholars examined the items, shaking their heads. Last of all, the eunuch brought them back to the dais for Tori. But Tori merely studied them silently and returned them to the eunuch without comment.

So stubborn.

Zinchen had tried to be tolerant. Tori was young, after all. But her sullenness was becoming most inconvenient.

A heavily pregnant minister stepped forward. "Your Majesty, so far we have no proof of anything except that these people are thieves. If such acts are tolerated, criminals all over Min will become bold."

Tori straightened in her seat.

The Minister of the Left, Zinchen's so-called left hand, stepped forward as well. Zinchen's muscles tensed.

"Quite right," the Minister of the Left said. "Your Majesty should send soldiers to round up these bandits and execute them publicly. This will discourage lawlessness."

Zinchen studied the woman's gaunt, pale face and marveled at how much she and her son, Lord Varu, resembled each other. Yet whereas he was striking, this woman was plain.

Six years ago, Zinchen took Varu as her lawful intimate. While the majority of her seventy-seven intimates had been chosen for the political strength they brought, Varu she had taken simply to keep his dangerous mother close. *Keep your enemy within reach*, the ancient sages had said.

The Minister of the Right stepped forward, and at the sight of her "right hand," Zinchen felt a glimmer of hope.

The woman's round face creased into a frown. "The guilty will never escape in the end. Such a demonstration of force will solve nothing. Your Majesty should instead focus resources on providing relief to the people of Kiir."

"Sending grain to Kiir won't stop these criminals from devouring other provinces," the Minister of the Left said. "The only thing that stops people like this is their heads on pikes."

Murmurs of agreement rippled through the court.

Anxiety gnawed at Zinchen. She pressed the edge of the missive between two fingertips to keep herself from fidgeting and glanced at Tori, who sat rigid, gripping the arms of her throne. If this scene had happened before her house arrest, Tori would have already jumped up to defend the underdogs.

Then the idea came. *Of course.*

Tori was the one person in the room with the influence to sway the officials, without risk that they would feel cowed into agreement. Her voice was just what Zinchen needed.

Zinchen's jaw tensed. If she miscalculated her next move, all would be lost.

As she mentally tried out various phrases, her eyes roamed over the cream-colored wall panels again. Most of the scenes painted on them depicted ancient queens holding court. One, however, showed Ishairo the Sunderer as he split the land of Shudon with his sword, banishing the lizard Antiquitals that had plagued the world in those days.

A yearning arose within her. Such were the great deeds of old.

She smoothed her robes. "Those who break my laws must be made to pay for their crimes," she said, then tapped a finger to her lips, as though pondering her course of action. "A hundred soldiers should be sufficient to root out these criminals and bring them to justice."

A satisfied expression played on the Minister of the Left's pinched face. Other ministers praised the empress's wisdom.

Zinchen's stomach churned. *Come on, child.*

Then, like a warhorse breaking through a stall, Tori bolted down the dais stairs to stand with the ministers. Zinchen let out a silent breath and thanked the Six.

Tori addressed the governor. "You mentioned the bow and arrow were found three moons ago. Was this the last time you saw these people?"

"Just so, Princess," the governor said, dipping her head.

"And am I correct in saying these people have otherwise committed no violence?"

The woman looked surprised. "Well, yes, Princess. That is to say, no—they didn't, unless you count the sheep. Some of my own were torn open at the stomach and eaten." She mopped her brow.

Tori faced Zinchen. "Your Majesty, the histories tell us that the Arun clan were not bandits in the usual sense—they only stole to feed themselves and took no human lives. This has not changed, as you have just heard. Putting their heads on pikes is beyond unnecessary. It's wasteful."

The Minister of the Left stiffened. "What knowledge could a young girl have of such matters?"

"Same as you, Minister," Tori said. "I know these reports are three moons old. The Arun are long gone from Kiir. Would you waste Her Majesty's resources hunting down a handful of nonviolent nomads? Furthermore, as you should know"—she flashed the minister a wry look—"the Arun bloodline is the only one in all of history that can nurture etching essence. It would be foolish to execute people who have the ability to create things that haven't been seen in generations."

The Minister of the Left responded with a quiet *tsk*. "Murder isn't the only form of violence. The people of Kiir wouldn't be terrified of nonviolent nomads. Furthermore, there's no real proof that these are the Arun."

Tori looked around. "May I see the weapon again?"

When it had been brought to her, she studied it, then said, "This is etched metal, both on the bow, and on the arrowhead. The markings here are for speed and homing."

Whispers erupted among scholars and ministers alike.

"We've all heard of etched metal," Zinchen said, "but how exactly does it work?" An explanation of its advantages was just what she needed.

"With Your Majesty's leave, I suggest your question be answered with a demonstration," Tori said.

Zinchen smiled inwardly. *Perfect.*

Tori scanned the court, as though searching for someone to assist. Her eyes came to rest again on the sneering woman next to her.

"I propose the Minister of the Left be the one to put this to the test."

The minister looked indignant. "I'm no lowly huntsman. I've never touched a bow in my life."

"Which is why you are the perfect one to demonstrate," Tori replied, clearly delighting in the woman's discomfiture.

Zinchen could have laughed. The girl showed a distinct lack of judgment in whom she chose to antagonize, like a child plunging its hand into an adder's nest. Still, one had to admire her boldness.

"I will allow it," Zinchen said.

Soon the Minister of the Left stood holding the dingy bow and arrow, visibly seething. For the target, Zinchen chose the standing lanterns flanking the doors at the opposite end of the hall. A single candle was fixed as the mark onto the crescent-moon roof of one.

The minister drew back her bowstring and let the arrow fly. The shot was weak, her aim off by several degrees.

But then, amid gasps from the officials, the arrow shifted midair, picked up speed, and hit its mark with such force and precision that it pinned the candle to the back wall.

Zinchen's skin buzzed with excitement. Exclamations filled the court.

Tori turned her gaze back to the dais. "To answer your question, Your Majesty, etched metal is sentient metal that has been awoken. This happens when those with etching essence carve it with ancient logograms. The logograms infuse the metal with the qualities described in the etching—in this case, speed and homing."

The Minister of the Left scowled. "That is even more reason to cleanse the land of these people. They are a danger. Your Majesty should not let thieves who possess such weapons roam free."

Tori's voice rose. "They're a nonviolent people merely trying to survive!" She turned to the other officials. "Justice may demand that thieves be executed, but equity requires that the punishment fit the circumstances. Starving people should not be killed for stealing food." She looked at Zinchen. "Your Majesty, with the skills they have, the Arun can pay for their crimes by rendering service to the empress."

Zinchen dropped her gaze to the desk to contain her smile.

"This is good advice," the Minister of the Right said. "Such talent should not be wasted."

Other officials praised the suggestion, and before long, the majority was in agreement.

The governor wrung her hands. "But, Your Majesty, I don't see as we have space for them in Kiir."

Zinchen nodded thoughtfully, then turned to Tori. "What does the Min Daughter think?"

"Having studied all the Min lands," Tori said, "I will personally see to it that these people are relocated and settled somewhere far from Kiir. Only let them be given their own livestock and the resources necessary to rebuild their forges."

Zinchen steepled her fingertips for several breaths, as though considering the matter carefully. But her pulse raced. The sooner the forges of the Arun were relit, the sooner her plans could move forward.

Her eyes again found the scene of Ishairo the Sunderer, and a feeling of weightlessness took her. Her day would come.

"Very well," Zinchen said. "It will be done as the Min Daughter suggests."

To show she was giving the matter no more thought, she picked up the remaining missive—it was from the Minister of the Right. Zinchen bade her speak.

"Your Majesty, with all the new executions, the wielders' blood is pooling in the town square. Wolves have been coming in from the forest to eat the entrails. The people are concerned."

"Your recommendation?"

"Your Majesty should send additional Ant slaves at night to ensure the area is promptly cleaned. And an archer to deal with the wolves. Then the people will feel safe."

Zinchen waved a hand. "So be it."

As she prepared to dismiss the court, she noticed the governor of Kiir staring at the floor. She had forgotten to address the woman's original request.

"Governor, Countess Amarin's infant is a girl child, is it not?" Zinchen was feeling lighthearted and generous.

"Just so, Your Majesty. Her first."

"Then gifts shall be sent to her, such as befits the birth of an heir."

"Thank you, Your Majesty."

"And grain relief shall be granted to Kiir. Present your numbers to the court administrator before you leave Silver Fox Springs."

The woman bowed, thanking her over and over. Then, with the other officials, she backed away from Zinchen for several steps before turning to leave.

Tori left last of all. As Zinchen watched her disappear through the doors, she couldn't help but feel grateful. Tori's arrival in her life had secured Zinchen's throne back then.

She smiled. Soon, the girl would do it again.

Chapter Four

THE MOON ROOM

Tori plodded down the wide steps of Her Majesty's court building, legs weary. She felt as though she had just run a race far above her skill level.

The court session had been close. Her mother's usual heavy-handedness had almost ruined everything.

Almost.

Thank the Six for the Minister of the Right.

Now Tori could notify the Arun that they didn't need to move again. She could send them more livestock, too. Legally, this time.

According to her sources, they had settled down well in the land she had found for them two moons ago, before her current house arrest predicament.

As though to underscore the precariousness of her situation, Dan and Bokoon waited at the bottom of the stairs. They accompanied her everywhere now, even within the palace compound.

Before she was halfway down the steps, her servant boy appeared and ran up to meet her, offering her a sealed note.

It was from Yumay. Tori opened it.

When the moon peaks, it said.

Her heart thumped: Yumay's visit to the guardhouse today had succeeded. Though she would see her gentlewoman shortly, Tori had told her to send a note the moment things were confirmed.

She casually slipped the note into her sleeve.

Since the moon would be full tonight, it would peak around midnight. Tori would need to sneak out, unnoticed, before then if she was to make it to the dungeon in time.

She had to get her guards to leave their post on her front porch. The problem was, they knew her only way out was the front gate, and her porch allowed a perfect view of it.

When she reached the bottom of the steps, Tori exited the court gardens, now filled with the chatter of birds settling in to roost, then turned right onto a white gravel path. In the time it would take to drain a cup, they would arrive at her residence. She needed to figure out something fast.

Before long, they approached the Houses of Healing on their left, its red lanterns already lit and swinging in the evening breeze.

Light poured through its open door. Two Varanaken, one tall and one short, stood just inside. They held a stretcher between them, with a third man lying on it. He groaned and clutched at a black, oozing hole in his side.

Midra, the palace healer, worked frantically on a wooden cabinet top, crushing herbs with a mortar and pestle, while her assistant, Sugi, stirred them into a bowl of steaming water.

Bokoon jogged up to the red wooden pillar that supported the roof.

"What happened?" he asked, looking in.

"Venom," the shorter Varanaken replied.

Bokoon spat on the ground. "Filthy wielders."

The two exchanged quiet words until the man on the stretcher writhed and cried out.

"He needs more!" the taller Varanaken barked at Sugi.

The woman rushed forward with her steaming bowl. Noticing the open door, she shut it, closing out the night, and Bokoon.

"The wielder had venom?" Dan asked when Bokoon had rejoined him.

Bokoon confirmed with a grunt. "But he cut the wielder down, so even if our brother dies, he has already been avenged."

Their callousness sickened her; she loathed her two guards in that moment. But remembering how their fathers had died in her service, guilt snuffed out her contempt, and she dropped her eyes to the ground.

The sky darkened as the walls of her residence came into view, and the round moon rose. The constellation of Ishairo the Sunderer twinkled brightly, his raised sword untouched by the clouds that covered most of the sky.

Tori glanced over her shoulder. "You two should stay with your tribesman." She smiled wryly. "I'm fairly certain I can find my way back home unaided."

The slow crunch of footsteps was the only reply.

"It's the full moon," she said, pointing to the sky. "I'll just be drinking in the moon room with my ladies."

"Our orders are to never leave you," Dan said.

Tori stopped and faced them. "Really? Do your orders include coming with me to the privy?"

Dan looked away.

"We're guards, not nursemaids," Bokoon said. He sounded annoyed.

"Well, I'm glad I've retained at least some autonomy." She decided to stop before her motives became too transparent. There was another way.

When they reached her house, Dan took his post on one side of the front door, but Tori stepped in front of Bokoon before he could do the same.

She smiled. "Listen, you've both been working hard. You deserve a break. You drink vrath, right?"

The two exchanged glances at the mention of the strong burning drink.

"How about this: since I'll be making merry, I'll have some vrath sent out to you in the back garden."

To her immense relief, they actually agreed and trotted around the side of the house. Tori pursed her lips. She hoped she actually had vrath. She detested the stuff.

She made her way to the moon room at the opposite end of the house. Her ladies sat at a low table, waiting, wine jugs warming in a brazier at one end.

The circular moon gate that opened the room onto the terrace gave her a perfect view of the garden, its paths and willow trees now silver with moonlight. On the terrace itself, the Jo dancers were already setting up their drum among the jittery chirps of crickets.

Tori scanned the room for her eunuch and found him standing by the moon gate's lattice frame, half hidden by shadows and an ornamental shrub. She motioned him to her.

"Please tell me we have vrath."

"We have everything, Princess."

"Good. Send a bottle round to Dan and Bokoon."

His eyes flicked to the Varanaken, who had taken seats in the garden, then bowed and turned to leave.

"Wait," she said. "Make it two."

Sensing Bokoon's eyes on her, she sat next to Yumay and grabbed the bumpy, braided surface of the stool, sliding herself closer to the table. Then she drank from her cup of warm blossom wine. Everything needed to seem completely normal.

Soon, a maid approached the Varanaken, carrying a tray with two cups and two bottles. She set the tray down on a small stone table, then poured.

Dan and Bokoon looked at Tori and raised their cups to her. She lifted her own in reply and took another sip of the sweet, flowery wine.

By the time the performance started, the vrath already seemed to be taking effect. Dan was laughing hard at Bokoon, who gesticulated wildly.

The evening meal was served as the Jo dancers performed. They were handsome and well-built, and wore trousers and shirts that displayed their physiques to advantage. Jo dancing was vaguely reminiscent of the martial forms, forceful and rhythmic. But Tori's mind was elsewhere; she kept one eye on the moon as it made its slow ascent, waiting for the moment Anlin would be drunk enough for her to have a word with Yumay—no need to involve more people than necessary.

Anlin hooted and clapped as one particular dancer performed solo, her birth charm glowing on her wrist. Coming out of a turn, the dancer made eye contact with her. Anlin lifted her cup to him and emptied it, then grinned, revealing the tiny gap between her front teeth.

During the distraction, Yumay leaned in and whispered, "It's time."

She pressed something cold and hard into Tori's hand. A skeleton key. It would soon be the changing of the guard at the dungeon.

"The documents and that other thing are in the wall panel," she whispered.

"Good. Keep the dancers dancing and the guards drinking," Tori said, "no matter how long I'm gone."

She tucked away the key and stood, just as a musical number came to an end. "I'm going to the privy, if anyone wants to come," she said, loudly enough for Dan and Bokoon to hear.

Bokoon cocked an eye at her, then, with a shake of the head, went back to his drink.

Anlin didn't need to go, thankfully, so when the music began again, Tori and Elnora left the moon room together and walked into the main house.

Tori opened a secret panel in the wall and pulled out a stack of papers—the charges against the prisoners. She scanned them—each was an ink drawing of the accused, followed by the evidence of wielding that had led to the arrest.

"Half of these charges are false, I can feel it. And I'm certain some of the prisoners aren't even wielders."

"Why would they accuse innocent people?"

"The Varanaken have been griping about their land allotments for decades," Tori said, sliding the papers back into the wall, "but lately they've been pushing harder, claiming Min's safety depends on them.

I'm guessing the more supposed wielders they hand over, the stronger their case that they're the only ones capable of rooting out the threat. And now that trials are gone, there's no way for the accused to prove they didn't wield."

"But they're just ordinary people."

"No one knows that," Tori said, reaching past the stack of papers to take out the other thing Yumay had left for her. "The testing implements are only ever used for official purposes—some of them, not at all." She held up a flat lancet in the shape of a tailu-bird, its enamel tail feathers red, white, black, blue, burned earth, and green. "Yumay's people only got this one because no one cares about it."

"You're bringing that? I thought you could tell on your own," Elnora said, holding out a gray servant's cloak.

"I can't risk anyone knowing that—not even Yumay. And especially not the prisoners," Tori said, putting the cloak on. "Is everything else in place?"

Elnora nodded, fastening another gray cloak about herself and raising the hood. She held up a silver lockpick. "I scoped out the guard gate earlier; my Tey Zuben pick can open it. Bless Granny. I've always wondered why she gave this to me. But we still have to be quick."

She took Tori's hand, wrapping a band of protective white cloth around it.

"We'll be a lot quicker now that I've read the charges," Tori said.

Elnora wrapped Tori's other hand, eyeing her dubiously. "You've never climbed a wall before, Princess. Are you sure about this?"

"This is my only chance before they're executed. I have to try." Tori raised her hood, covering her face, then slipped out the unguarded front door.

Now, instead of turning right outside the garden gate and taking the path to the Houses of Healing, they turned left, then left again into a narrow corridor flanked by two stone walls. It was a path no one used, as it led to nowhere—except the dungeon.

The palace complex was built in three concentric circles. They followed the corridor down from the upper circle to the middle, then continued to the lowest, where the maids and food suppliers lived. Ahead, where the stone walls ended, a narrow oak guard gate blocked the path.

Elnora made short work of the lock, and they soon found themselves standing in a wide, dark space, devoid of any buildings but one.

About eight hundred paces away, a forbidding stone building sprang from the outer wall of the palace complex and loomed over it, dark and stern in the night shadows. Her Majesty's dungeon. Beyond it was a dense, dark forest.

Elnora looked at Tori. "Ready?"

Tori nodded, then ran forward, conscious of the guard towers on the dungeon roof. As soon as she reached the wall, she gripped its thick stones, shoved a foot into a nook, and tried to climb, the way she had seen her servant boy do a thousand times.

But her foot slipped, forcing her back to the ground. She searched for a better foothold, and once again hauled herself upward as best she could. The rough stone scraped her hands, even through the protective cloth.

On her third attempt, she started to feel desperate. She swore.

How does anyone do this?

"Apologies, Princess," Elnora said, then pushed on Tori's buttocks, hoisting her upward. Tori scrambled to the top and sat facing the dungeon, hands and knees smarting. The wall was surprisingly wide, enough for four people to sit shoulder to shoulder.

Clouds covered the moon, leaving everything in relative darkness, allowing her a moment to orient herself. On her left, the gate they had just exited disappeared into shadow, while above it, the crescent-moon eaves of the houses in the second circle shone dimly, their roof edges curving upward in honor of Ketuan, who first shaped the moon as a crescent. Silhouettes of lower-ranked ministers and scholars moved around in their second-circle gardens.

Above them in the upper circle, the empress's palace towered over the other buildings, among which the wall of Tori's back garden was faintly visible.

A cloud shifted and moonlight shone through. Tori ducked instinctively, then clumsily slid onto her belly and climbed down the forest side of the wall.

Again her foot slipped. This time, however, she was unable to find another foothold. She scrambled to grip the rocks as she plummeted to the ground, scraping her skin. A sudden landing on her tailbone made her wince and groan.

She stood painfully, then studied the back of the dungeon on her right.

"Can you manage?" she whisper-shouted to the top of the wall. Hopefully Elnora wouldn't be long.

But Elnora swept over the wall and scampered down like a lizard, landing far more lightly than Tori had, despite her curvier frame. Tori spared a moment to marvel at the woman.

"We'd better move," Tori said, and headed off.

In about the time it would take a candlewick to catch, they found themselves staring at the back of the dungeon. All was solid stone, apart from a drain that stood shoulder-high to Tori, covered with a thick iron grate.

Elnora pushed it, straining. It didn't budge.

"Now what?" she said.

"Yumay said this is the way in, so it must be," Tori said. She leaned on the rusty bars. "Help me."

They rammed the grate with their shoulders over and over. All at once it gave way, and they stumbled into a dark tunnel, its ground covered in foul-smelling water.

Backs bent under the low ceiling, they sloshed toward a faint light at the end of the tunnel, coming at last to a dim stone corridor that stretched from left to right in front of them.

"Yumay said it was this way," Tori said, turning left.

A short while later, her nose burned from the reek of urine and excrement. There appeared in the darkness an enormous cell with iron bars a few paces back from the wall. It was filled with dozens of people, many bruised and lying down, as though they had been beaten.

Elnora's eyes filled with pity. "Why are wielders so hated?"

Tori looked away. "Wielding does terrible things. But not everyone here deserves death. Now, stand watch while I find out how many are innocent."

She refused to let her mother execute people simply for being wielders, she had to know if they'd committed an actual crime. But it would take too long to interrogate them all. She first had to set the non-wielders aside.

As she crept forward, people began looking up. Whispers filled the cell, then some of the prisoners kneeled and broke down, sobbing, whispering, "Min Daughter."

Tori froze. She had dressed as a servant—she hadn't counted on being recognized. If she was caught, her mother might suspect she was a wielder. Worse, she might test her. Nothing Tori said or did would be able to save her then.

Pathetic faces looked up, and she forced herself to move forward—she was the only one who could save them.

The pearls in her stomach started vibrating, but with so many people around her it was impossible to tell who was causing it.

"Please," one woman said when Tori arrived at the bars. "I swear we didn't—"

Tori held up a hand. "Not now. Come closer."

The woman obeyed, and Tori took her hand. The vibrations stopped. It was as she had suspected. There were non-wielders among them.

Just for show, Tori pricked the woman's finger with the razor-sharp beak of her lancet. The tailu-bird sucked in the blood, which shot up through its six feathers, but nothing else changed.

"Stand over there," Tori said, pointing to the empty space on the right side of the cell. The woman went, weeping, apparently believing she had somehow been proven guilty.

Tori called to the person behind her. She knew from touch he was a wielder, and the lancet of course confirmed it: the moment his blood reached the feathers, they glowed white.

She quickly moved on to the next person, then the next, until the group was separated into wielders and non-wielders.

"Thirty-five prisoners," she whispered to Elnora, "and only six are actually wielders." Her hands curled into fists.

Elnora looked around nervously. "The guard is changing, Princess. They'll check on the prisoners soon." Though no wielder had ever shown the ability to do much damage, occasionally one would manage to start a fire in the dungeon. Guards were therefore obliged to check on them whenever the shift changed.

But the words of the Minister of the Right at today's court session returned: *The wielders' blood is pooling in the town square.* Tori would not let tonight be a repeat of the Tailu Spring Festival—she would not be responsible for the deaths of more innocents.

The dungeon passage leading away from the cell shone with a dim light, and shadows shifted threateningly.

"Give me a signal if you hear a guard coming."

Elnora looked horrified. "We can't stay any longer—we might not be back in time. If Dan and Bokoon find you gone, the empress will know for sure you were breaking out prisoners from her dungeon."

"I can't leave the innocent, and I won't free the guilty. I have to ask questions. But if I leave now, they'll all die."

At her command, the first of the wielders came to her: a bent, white-haired man. She didn't recognize his face—they hadn't even bothered writing charges against this one. He had probably been betrayed by a neighbor.

His gentle eyes met hers and he shook his head. "I don't know what I did. I was sitting on my porch, watching the birds fly when they came for me."

She knew immediately he was telling the truth. As equitess, she interrogated so many people she could practically smell a lie. This man had the air of someone who had never done any harm in all his life.

He was better than she was.

"Stand over there." She directed him to quickly join the non-wielders and hurried the next person along, a weaver woman from the village of Oxtail. Her fourteen-year-old wielder son was with her.

"I wielded water," the woman said, sniffling. "I shouldn't have, I know it. But the rope snapped and my bucket fell into the well. I had nothing to draw with, and—"

"Over there," Tori said, sending her to follow the old man. "Next!"

The next two wielders had the same kinds of stories. She was able to judge quickly who was telling the truth by noting where their stories aligned from one moment to the next, and also with the charges made against them. People here had barely used their wielding, if at all. They probably wanted nothing more than to forget what they were.

She understood.

"Guards are filling the end room," Elnora said.

"Quickly! What about you?" Tori said to a man with a surly face.

"I ain't done nothing."

Tori rattled off the charges she had memorized. "The records say you killed a Varanaken. There were witnesses." She sincerely hoped he could say something to persuade her otherwise.

Instead, he crossed his arms. "All right. I seen one of them Varanaken riding past the village. I set the scum on fire." His eyes were defiant. "And I'd do it again."

The memory of the Varanaken on the stretcher at the Houses of Healing came back to her. His wound had been terrible, but what had he done to get it? The Varanaken were slaughtering anyone who fought back, and those who didn't, they delivered to the saw. They deserved this. And yet...

"You attacked and killed someone in cold blood," Tori said, feeling a stab of regret. "Which makes you no better than them. You must face justice."

The man stood at the back by himself. "Didn't have to send the Min Daughter to tell me that," he muttered. "That's why we're here, ain't it?"

"I hear footsteps," Elnora said.

Tori's hand rattled and she fumbled with the lock as she pushed in Yumay's key. She spoke to the group of innocents. "All of you, follow me."

Weeping and pleading broke out, reverberating off the walls, echoing down the hall. They thought they were going to the saw immediately.

"Please, please," the weaver woman said, dropping to her knees. "I'll go with you, but spare the boy!"

"Quiet," Elnora whispered.

But it was too late. The thump of footsteps sounded down the passageway, followed by the flicker of a lamp.

Tori flattened herself against the cold stone wall across from the cell, pulse pounding in her ears. Elnora ducked into a shadow and curled into a ball.

"Quiet, filth!" a voice boomed. "Or I'll give you something to cry about."

The prisoners choked down their sobs.

An endless moment of agonizing silence followed. Finally, the guard's footfalls receded back down the passageway, along with the flickering light.

Tori pressed her hands to her knees, trembling, and recovered her breath.

"Listen to me," Elnora said to the prisoners, turning the key. "If you don't want to die right here, then come quietly."

The people shuffled out, sniffling, and Tori locked the cell door on the one who would face justice.

"At least you'll face the saw first!" he called out to the others.

She led the prisoners back the way she had come, through the tunnel of foul water. Once they were outside the grate, they stared at the open sky, then at her, a question written on their faces.

"All of you are innocent," Tori said. "And I will not let the innocent be slaughtered. Not if I can stop it." She sent up a silent plea that their gratitude would ensure their silence.

The weaver woman dropped to her knees, kowtowing. "Thank you! Thank you, Princess." The others followed suit.

"Stop it," Tori said. "There's no time. Go, all of you." She pointed to the forest. "Don't tell anyone I freed you. And above all, do not go back to your homes."

"Where will we go?" the old man said, with fear in his eyes.

Tori tried to think of who in Min would shelter escaped prisoners. No one came to mind. They would be in danger everywhere.

"Take Fox River into Ma'yanar Forest," she said at last. "The riverboats are slow, but they'll keep you hidden. You'll be safe, at least for a time."

The old man's eyes grew wide. "Stories say the old forest is haunted."

"The Varanaken will have heard those stories, too," Tori said. "That's why it's your best hope. They'll only enter it as a last resort."

"But what will we do there?" the weaver woman asked.

Tori looked around at their frightened, tired faces. "Survive. Now go."

They shuffled off and disappeared into the night.

Elnora grabbed the grate and pulled it shut, then turned to Tori. "The Jo dancers might already be finished. Dan and Bokoon will be looking for you."

They raced back, Elnora hoisting Tori over the wall. But as before, Tori was unable to find a foothold, and once again she scraped painfully down.

This time her robe tore, and as she dropped to the other side, she landed badly, twisting her ankle. She clamped a hand over her mouth to muffle her own cry.

Elnora hopped down beside her. "Put your arm over my shoulder," she said.

Tori hobbled back to the gate, leaning heavily on Elnora, then climbed the upward-sloping path in excruciating pain.

When she reached the front gate of her residence, however, relief washed over her—the music was still going.

With Elnora's help she limped up the stairs to her front door and through the house, wincing with every step. It was then that she realized she smelled not only like she had gone to the privy, but had also fallen into it. She needed to change her clothes.

Yumay rushed in. "Thank the Six! I can't hold them off any longer, Princess. You have to come now," she said, and rushed back out.

There was no time to change. They whipped off their servant's cloaks, and gritting her teeth in pain, Tori walked back into the moon room on her own, just in time to see Dan and Bokoon heading toward them through the garden.

Tori straightened her robes, while Elnora looked her over and plucked something out of her hair. At the same moment, the Jo dancers finished with a flourish. Anlin winked at one of them and poured another drink.

Yumay eyed Anlin's cup. "Should you really be drinking so much?"

"What? Blossom wine is light as air." She turned to Tori, then sniffed the air, wrinkling her nose. She seemed then to realize the odor was coming from Tori's direction, and stopped, looking embarrassed.

"Are you all right, Princess?" Anlin asked. "You missed the whole thing."

"Bad dumplings," Elnora said quickly. "I felt funny, too."

Anlin grimaced. "I'm glad I had the chicken."

"You should lie down, Princess," Elnora said. "I'll bring you some digestion tea."

Just then, Dan and Bokoon marched past the Jo dancers, who were packing up their drum. Tori backed into the shadows, pulling her robe close in an attempt to cover the rips and dirt.

"Time for bed," Bokoon said, his voice the slightest bit slurred.

His eyes weren't glazed over, exactly. Varanaken were too fond of their drink to be overly affected by a few bottles of vrath. But he seemed unusually calm.

"Good idea," Tori said. Then, turning to her ladies, "Sleep well. We'll breakfast late tomorrow."

Dan exited again through the moon gate, and her ladies left, with Elnora promising to bring Tori's tea as soon as it was ready.

But as Tori turned to follow, Bokoon's eyes sharpened on her. With a hint of a frown, he stepped closer, scrutinizing her hair and robes. Tori lifted her chin and met his gaze, but every muscle in her body tensed.

He peered at her, his expression unreadable, as crickets chirped in a frenzied song. Then, silently, he turned and left.

Her nerves felt frayed as she stood staring at the empty moon gate for a long while after, then finally limped off to bed, the persistent jitter of crickets in her ears.

Chapter Five

GOLDEN FIGURINE

Zinchen stared at the yellow silk canopy above her. The cascading sound of a harp filled the room, but instead of putting her to sleep, the music made her brain ripple miserably.

She sat up. "This isn't working."

Lina, her Imperial Speaker and closest advisor, waved a hand, and the harpist hurried out. Then she gave Zinchen a look of patient concern. The woman's vow of chastity made her as committed as any eunuch. "Shall I bring in one of Your Majesty's intimates to serve you?"

"Not in the mood. I just need to figure out what to do about Shelan. That woman does nothing but slow me down." Zinchen stepped off the low platform that held her canopied bed and went to sit in a cream-colored settee. "How long before she returns?"

"If she could travel normally, she'd be at the palace tonight, but her internal injuries make it dangerous for her carriage to roll quickly. The slightest bump could kill her."

"Why did she have to go and get herself injured?"

"I don't think that was her intention, Your Majesty. She was caught in a landslide."

Zinchen sighed in frustration. "I know. But the longer she takes, the longer the Minister of the Left has to discover my plans. I need to move fast. She is so determined to see her son named as royal consort, she will do anything to achieve it. I can't afford that risk." She leaned on the arm of the settee and rested her forehead on her fingertips. "On top of everything else, I cannot be sure Shelan will even do her part."

"Lord Yan's work in the Jeng Palace will take care of the Min-kezu, if Shelan doesn't."

Zinchen shook her head. "Without Shelan's letter, my brother's efforts may all be for nothing. The Min-kezu value the chief equitess's opinion, or her successor's. If Shelan chooses to be obstructive, it could ruin everything. And unfortunately, as you know, she cannot be bought."

A servant arrived at the door and bowed. He was one of the men in Lina's network of spies and informants, which she operated with tremendous efficacy.

"What is it?" Lina said.

"There's been an incident with the wielders, my lady. The guard hadn't checked on them since last night, and tonight when he went to bring their bread and water, he discovered all but one was gone."

Zinchen's eyes narrowed. If this incident got out, she would lose face—a problem that had cost many a ruler their reign.

"Interrogate him under torture," she said.

"Yes, Your Majesty." The man left.

"With this kind of disorder going on under my nose, Shelan will never support the cause," Zinchen said, getting up to pace the floor.

The fact that she needed Shelan at all was the real reason Zinchen couldn't stand her cousin. The woman's very existence was a constant reminder of her own failure—Zinchen should have been chief equitess-in-waiting.

When Zinchen was a child, her mother had believed Zinchen would become the first Supreme Ruler of Min since Yanai Sumi—both empress and chief equitess, and would be the one to unite Shudon under the Min banner, the dream of their foremothers.

Her gaze fell on a massive wall painting of her distant ancestor Yanai Sumi, rendered in vibrant tones and inlaid with gold leaf. Overshadowed by the colorful outstretched wings of the Great Tailu, Yanai Sumi stood on top of water, a symbol of her exploits at sea. Shafts of golden light streamed down from the bird onto the woman's bowed head, endowing her with wisdom and power.

Along one side of the painting, a beautiful script had been carved from top to bottom. It read: *The most august empress Yanai Sumi, for whose glory it is sufficient merely to name her.* On the other side, was Yanai Sumi's most famous quote.

A prickle of shame ran through Zinchen as she remembered failing the equitess examinations long ago. She could still see the disappointment on her mother's face as clearly as if she stood in front of her now.

"What will people remember me for, Lina?"

Lina, who was preparing tea, looked over her shoulder. "Your Majesty?"

"I have reigned for twenty years, yet what have I accomplished?"

"A great many things," Lina said, bringing the tray and setting it on the table beside Zinchen. "You've built moats and fortifications, you've expanded trade routes, built monuments." She handed Zinchen a steaming cup. "You built the Grand Processional Way from Kiir all the way to Fyeng—no ruler in history has dared such a feat."

Zinchen nodded, but her heart remained a hollow cavern.

"Those things were all-consuming once," she murmured. "Now they seem pitiful." Why was nothing ever enough?

The day she had completed the Grand Processional Way had been one of the best days of her life—did anyone even remember that day now?

She inhaled the fragrance of jasmine and sipped the tea. "My mother died thinking I would never ascend the throne," she said, thoughts drifting to a forbidden place.

Zinchen had almost lost her right of succession due to her long-standing barrenness. She had been on a year-long diplomatic mission in Tey Zuben when her mother died, returning with an heir just in time to stop her treacherous sister's coronation. Memories of Tori's infant face filled her with a momentary warmth. Tori's timely arrival had secured her throne.

"But you did ascend," Lina said gently, "and now you are the greatest ruler Min has ever known."

Yet when the end came, would her life have left any mark?

"I have done nothing worthy of the *Chronicles of the Queens*." She met Lina's eyes, her mask momentarily lowered. "Uniting Shudon under the Min banner is the only thing of true significance."

Lina dipped her head. "And Your Majesty will accomplish that, too."

The doorkeeper entered, bowing and apologizing. "Bokoon of the Varanaken has requested permission to speak to Her Majesty. He says it's urgent."

Zinchen's face tightened. "This time of night? What is it with these Varanaken? Tell him I am sleeping."

The eunuch looked uncomfortable. "He says it relates to the escaped wielders." He paused. "And the Min Daughter."

Zinchen's fingers stilled on her teacup. "Send him in."

Bokoon entered moments later and bowed.

"It is late," Zinchen said. "Be brief."

"Yes, Your Majesty. I wanted to be sure the princess was sleeping before I came." He cleared his throat. "Last night the princess went to the privy—or so I thought. She came back a long while later, too long, and dirty, smelling terrible. Then I heard about the wielders."

"So, she went to the privy, came back smelling like it, and from this you deduced"—she pinned him with her gaze—"what exactly?"

"Nothing, Your Majesty." He shook his head. "I wouldn't dare. But she's unmanageable. She defies you. No one in our tribes would ever defy a clan matriarch. Except on your orders," he added quickly.

Zinchen folded her hands. "If it turns out she has gone anywhere...unsavory, your own negligence will be the cause. I will treat it accordingly."

He blanched.

"Dismissed."

But as she watched him leave, a feeling of disquiet unsettled her.

"What do you make of this, Lina? Would my daughter be so brazen?"

"Dirty robes are poor evidence, Your Majesty," Lina said softly.

Zinchen pressed a finger to her lips, thinking. "Assuming she did, though, what would be her motivation?" She frowned—Tori couldn't be a wielder, could she?

Lina gave her a sympathetic smile, as though guessing Zinchen's thoughts. "Wielders manifest at the age of twelve, Your Majesty. It would be impossible to hide it this long. The Min Daughter simply has a misguided sense of justice."

"But why go to such lengths?"

"For friends, perhaps—or a lover?"

Zinchen nodded slowly. "Yes. Lovers make young people reckless."

As she considered the implications, a small golden elephant on the table caught her eye. It had belonged to her father, a gift from his mother, the current chief equitess. He had treasured it his whole life. It was said that, whenever he was naughty as a boy, his mother would take it from him.

"A wielder lover could be useful," Zinchen said. "Fear of his exposure would bring the princess in line. And his death would be an apt punishment for her disobedience."

The next time she saw Tori, she would imply she knew her secret and watch her reaction. From then on, the girl would be as meek as a lamb.

Her gaze fell on Yanai Sumi's famous quote: *A wise mariner anticipates the storm while the sea is yet calm.* It was a maxim known by all, applied in situations where waiting to act could result in disaster.

Zinchen's shoulders relaxed. She knew exactly what to do.

"Lina, something must spook Shelan's horses tonight. They need to race the carriage back to the palace."

"Yes, Your Majesty." Lina looked like she would say more, but hesitated.

"Speak freely."

"The chief equitess, Your Majesty..."

Lina was right. Shelan's death would affect their grandmother.

As she considered possible solutions, she traced a finger over the intricately engraved blanket on the elephant's back, where a tiny gold man sat. It had been meant as a symbol of a boy sitting high in his mother's esteem. Of the chief equitess's two children, Zinchen's father had been the undisputed favorite. His mother had loved him as much as any daughter, far more than she did Shelan's father, her second son.

Zinchen held out the elephant. "Be sure the chief equitess hears of the incident the moment it occurs. Then, when she has had time to absorb the news, have this sent to her residence, with a sympathy note from me."

The elephant would remind her grandmother that those in her favorite son's line were still here. It would be a comfort to know her legacy lived on.

"It will be done, Your Majesty."

Lina snapped her fingers, and a servant materialized.

A pang of regret rose up in Zinchen as she watched the whispered exchange, and she reminded herself she was only doing what was needful.

But when the servant left with the elephant, her regret vanished, and a feeling of invigoration took its place. Tonight was a night for wine and celebration—tomorrow, her ideal chief equitess-in-waiting would be named.

She yawned and stretched. "Lina, send in Lord Varu. I think I would like some company after all."

Chapter Six

THREE DROPS OF CRIMSON

Tori jerked awake, waves still rolling in at the edge of her vision.

She hauled off the silk coverlet and stepped on something soft and moist—the herbal compress Elnora had made. It must have fallen off Tori's head while she slept.

Though the images from her dream faded slowly, a sick feeling remained. She picked up the broken clamshell from her bedside table, her fingers tracing the ridges along its back, a lump in her throat.

If only I could talk to Wan.

She padded through the sitting room and onto the wooden veranda outside, following it to a set of double doors. Inside, against the back wall, a stone altar stood with a single spirit tablet on top, an incense burner on either side of the rectangular darkwood block.

Tori lit the incense, then knelt, contemplating the birth charms in the spirit tablet. Wan had no birth charm, because he hadn't been born a noble, so Tori had chosen several substitutes.

At first, she had liked that they glowed, unlike the birth charm of a deceased person. They had made her feel he was still alive somewhere. Lately though, the light just seemed like a mockery. He was in the labyrinths. Nothing could change that.

She bowed her head. "You gave your life to free me, but I can't escape what I am." She clenched the broken shell in her fist.

Suddenly, Wan's incense flared at the end, the fire consuming it, reducing it to a pile of ash in the space of a breath. Tori froze, remembering the mysterious wind that had blown through Kazani.

"Princess?"

Elnora, who'd been in the doorway, came and knelt beside her. "Do you want to tell me about your dream?"

Tori looked at her, feeling drawn. Yet she couldn't bring herself to tell her what had just happened. "What if Wan's seal breaks?" she said instead.

"It wasn't his seal, Princess," Elnora said in her musical accent. She rubbed Tori's back. "The Door of Golden Ash sealed your stone kernel. Don't you worry now, you hear? Tell me about your dream."

But if Tori told her, it would be harder to forget. "I'm fine now. I just need more medicine."

Back in the sitting room, Tori watched as Elnora crushed herbs with her mortar and pestle, tipped them into a terrine, and filled it with boiling water.

"There," she said, handing Tori a steaming bowl.

"You have a gift," Tori said, and sipped from it.

Elnora pursed her lips the way she did when she was embarrassed. "I don't know half of what I should. Granny was a good teacher, but I always had my mind on other things."

"Well, it might not look like it, but the nightmares have lessened."

Elnora turned away to hide her pleasure.

They sat undisturbed until nearly midday, playing a game of Disdain, shifting the black and white stones on the board in soothing meditation. Yumay and Anlin knew not to come in when Tori closed the sitting room doors.

A shuffling sound outside announced what Tori thought were the maids bringing the noonday meal, and Elnora left to get it. But then an unusual number of footsteps approached the sitting room, accompanied by Elnora's agitated voice.

The door slid open and a line of maids and eunuchs filed in.

"Answer me," Elnora said, rushing in after them. "You can't just stroll into the princess's residence whenever the mood strikes!"

Tori looked at them. "What's the meaning of this?"

They all bowed, and a eunuch stepped forward. "Her Majesty requires us to dress you, Princess."

"Dress me? For what?"

But they merely shuffled forward in a flurry of clothing boxes and hairpins.

"I said, *for what*?"

Two of the maids bowed, eyes lowered as they held up elaborate green robes embroidered with all the colors of the tailu-bird.

Elnora stared, incredulous. "You dare ignore the Min Daughter?"

One of the eunuchs dropped to his knees before Tori and kowtowed. "Please forgive us, Princess. Her Majesty has forbidden us to say."

Tori peered at the robes. They were the kind reserved for special occasions, but there was nothing on her schedule. What would her mother possibly need her for that she wouldn't have been told about in advance?

While Elnora continued to protest, the maids undressed Tori down to her under-robe and slipped one layer of clothing after another over her shoulders, while others pulled and tugged at her hair, twisting it into elaborate coils on her head and securing it with pins. She took in the eunuchs' lowered eyes, then remembered the strange look Bokoon had given her the other night.

He wouldn't have said something to her mother, would he? She furrowed her brow. Had her mother ordered that she be dragged before the Hall of Equity?

She held out her feet as the maids pulled on her stockings and shoes. One of them took special care with her makeup.

Could they somehow prove she had freed the wielders? What would happen if they could?

Unless they were trying to make a spectacle of her for some other reason...some greater crime. Her stomach squeezed.

Mother knows.

Something must have happened—a fire when Tori didn't realize, or a wind.

She cast a pleading glance at Elnora, who seemed to understand. Immediately she was digging through her medicine chest, then shoving maids aside, blocking their view. In a flash, she pulled out a tiny knife and sliced Tori's finger, then her own, dripping her blood onto Tori's wound, sealing it with a dollop of ointment from a black porcelain box.

As the eunuchs led her outside, Tori stared down at her left forefinger, which now looked like it had a small blood blister on it, unsure what Elnora had done, or why.

A carriage draped in flowers waited at the bottom step. The eunuchs took her stiff, shaky hands and helped her into it.

Tori shivered. So this was how a Min Daughter was executed, dressed in her finery. Yet her entrails would spill out like anyone else's.

Would she scream? She hoped not.

Her chest heaved. Of course she would. Everyone screamed.

As the driver closed the door however, his expression made her pause. He bowed with respect, muttering something. *Blessings?* No one did that with someone about to be executed.

Tori collapsed back against the wall, squeezing her eyes shut to keep tears of relief from forming. She was being ridiculous. No one was going to execute her. Her nightmares had put her on edge.

But moments later, they pulled up in front of the Hall of Equity, and her doubts returned.

Its gleaming white stone, surrounded by crowds of cheering people, shone in the early-afternoon sun.

Tori squared her shoulders as the doors opened and her great-grandmother's chief assistant led Tori in.

The hall was lined with courtiers who bowed with respect as she made her way toward the dais, where her great-grandmother sat in the seat of the chief equitess, the empress beside her.

On the other side of the dais stood a woman in black robes embroidered with interlinking circles—the High Scholar of Fyeng, the only person in Min with the authority to address heaven on behalf of an empress.

What in the name of the Six was going on?

Tori was brought onto the dais to kneel before her great-grandmother.

Then the High Scholar spoke. "A new chief equitess-in-waiting is presented for your approval."

Tori's eyebrow arched sharply. "Where's Shelan?" she whispered to her great-grandmother.

The old woman's rheumy eyes met hers, filled with grief, and a heavy feeling sank into Tori's chest.

Lina, her mother's Speaker, held up a paper. "Hear the words of the empress. At dawn this very day, fate claimed Lady Shelan, chief equitess-in-waiting, as her carriage entered palace grounds. This grievous loss lies heavy upon all the people, and upon the empress herself, who cherished her as a sister. By imperial decree, when her body is borne on the funeral barge downriver to the sea and committed to the flames, she shall be attended with emblems of her rank and given full ceremony, as befits her lofty station."

Tori bowed her head. Shelan had been a woman of integrity, a rare gem.

Lina continued. "And now, as Min law demands the land never be without a successor to the chief equitess, Princess Tori, Min Daughter, is hereby named as such."

She said more, but Tori could no longer focus on the words, and before she knew it, a eunuch was mounting the steps carrying a golden hair ornament on a cushion.

The pin was in the shape of a tailu-bird, with multicolored jewels forming the wings and eyes, and pearls dangling from its tail feathers—the token of the chief equitess-in-waiting.

It must have been taken from Shelan's body. Gooseflesh rippled up Tori's back.

The eunuch presented the hairpin to the chief equitess, who nodded her acceptance.

"She will now perform the test," the High Scholar said. The chief equitess, face filled with grief, raised a crystal bowl in the air with both hands—a tester of wielder's blood.

Tori stiffened, all her earlier terror returning. She would go to the saw today after all.

"Your finger, child," the chief equitess said, holding a gleaming knife.

Tori fought down the urge to vomit.

But then she remembered the blood blister Elnora had made and she quickly pushed out that finger, hoping whatever Elnora had done would help. Her great-grandmother's grief-stricken eyes registered nothing as she went through the motions woodenly.

Tori's body was so tense the blade burned. She watched in silence as three drops of crimson spilled into the crystal bowl.

Any moment, the crystal would glow bright white and the hall would be in an uproar.

One breath. Then another. The moments stretched into an eternity.

Then the chief equitess held up the bowl with two hands for everyone to see—the crystal was sparkling clean. It had absorbed the blood, declaring it untainted.

Tori stared at the bowl, her mind warning her not to believe her eyes.

"The new chief equitess-in-waiting," the High Scholar proclaimed. Applause filled the hall. "The chief equitess and her second will now make their rounds through Silver Fox Springs."

Someone lifted Tori to her feet and soon she was walking again through the hall toward her carriage.

Just before she exited, she turned to look behind her. Her mother stared back, a faint smile on her lips.

Chapter Seven

DICTATES AND DEVOTION

Koren scanned the floor of the old forest for the sign described in the elder's scrolls. *Shadowy golden light.*

In his 225 years, he had never been able to puzzle out how light could be shadowy, yet that was the description the scrolls gave of the phenomena they called *Golden Umbrage*. And it was not his job to question, after all, only to find. The sooner he performed the elder's request, the sooner he could return to his day's work. Did the elder appreciate that in calling him away from it, her dictates were actually putting lives at risk?

Both in the shadows of the trees and in the sunlight that filtered through them, nothing stood out from the ordinary. Just the usual plants, animals, and general decay of the world outside his village, which permeated even the relatively clean air of Ma'yanar Forest.

He would have never left Peach Blossom Grove if he could have helped it. But the elder always seemed to find reasons to send him out.

As he circled back over his steps, a golden gleam flickered among the fallen leaves. Koren squatted and leaned forward, reaching over his shoulder to sweep away the portion of long hair that hung down his back to keep it from disturbing the ground.

Only a beetle.

He straightened, scanning the leaves again. Another flash. As he leaned forward a second time, something pulled at his topknot—a branch, by the feel of it. He jerked free, unintentionally causing the bronze topknot clasp to pop open. A straight black curtain of hair fell into his eyes.

"There were no low-hanging branches a moment ago," Koren said, standing and turning in a slow circle.

Shimmering wisps of light, some green, some yellow, darted past him, then swooped round and round. *Forest lomi.*

Some had actual faces, but even for those who didn't, Koren could still read their expressions—if something without a face could be said to have an expression. These were gleeful, happy to have disturbed him.

"Behave," he said. "You're the reason mortals believe this forest is haunted."

Giggles rippled through the air.

The nature guardians of Ma'yanar weren't evil, but they certainly were mischievous. Being so close to the Veil of Ayenashi made them more animated than most lomi in other places.

He had no time for their antics today.

"*Kaing zhu gou!*" he commanded in the Old Speech. Though they understood any language, the ancient tongue was the only one they obeyed. Immediately they ceased their flittering and shifted gently around the plants and trees, as they should.

"Worse than children," he muttered.

His thoughts drifted then to the children he had left behind in Peach Blossom Grove, a feeling of concern growing on him. When the elder had summoned him, it had seemed reasonable to leave the children in charge of Little Flame, rather than cancel their training session. Now he was having second thoughts. Sentient fire was sometimes more mischievous even than lomi.

He tried to work faster, scanning large patches of ground as he strolled instead of focusing solely on the area around his feet.

The sound of rustling and whispers came to him on a breeze, then stopped. He glanced at the lomi; they were still behaving.

It had almost sounded like a group of people. He tilted his head, straining to listen, but no further sound came.

Mortals rarely set foot in Ma'yanar. It was ridiculous to think a whole group of them would. Clearly his concern over the mortals of Peach Blossom Grove was playing on his mind.

In the shadows under one of the trees, almost at right angles with the entrance to the Veil of Ayenashi, a strange sight caught his eye. It resembled gold dust glimmering in the sunlight, sprinkled on the ground, not hanging in the air like the lomi.

Coming closer, he peered intently at it, and the gold dust shadowed over, as though hidden in a dark cloud, then reappeared again and flashed.

"Golden Umbrage," he whispered, relief washing over him. Now he could report to the elder and finally get back to his work.

He scored a small line into the tree to mark the spot, then hastened back to the Veil's invisible entrance. The familiar sensation of passing through a curtain of water met him as he stepped into another forest on the other side.

Jogging through the trees, he breathed in deeply, glad to be back where the air was fresh. A short while later, he reached the flowering village of Peach Blossom Grove.

After rushing through the village, he finally arrived at the wide swath of land holding the spirit-fruit trees that so needed his attention.

The spirit-fruit trees didn't look sickly. Their slender branches still shimmered, silver bark still smooth, making them look more like the sculptures of a skilled craftsperson than natural flora.

But it was their barrenness that was the problem. It was the entire reason he had moved the children here today, instead of staying on the training grounds. The lack of spirit-fruit had already caused the death of one mortal in Peach Blossom Grove. If Koren didn't solve this problem quickly, more would die.

Well, disappear forever, at least. No death ever touched the Veils. But that didn't make the situation any less serious for the sweet grandmothers and grandfathers whose lives wholly depended on eating the spirit-fruit daily. His devotion to these people meant that he saw their need as far more immediate—and therefore more pressing—than the matter of the elder's scroll. That had waited three thousand years, after all.

A hundred paces before the spirit-fruit trees, a thicket of old oaks stood, and between them, a stream that sparkled like a thousand white jewels in the sun. In the middle of them, the stream bent sharply and flowed away in an odd direction, instead of following what should have been its natural course to the spirit-fruit trees.

Children stood by the banks of the stream, going through their forms as Koren had instructed, while a yellow flame the size of a small plum skipped around the oaks' protruding roots without kindling them.

Koren's shoulders relaxed. Everything was still under control. He would go to the elder and be back quickly.

He made to walk past, but one of the children called out, "The oaks haven't moved at all, Master."

Koren used his immortal senses to probe the oaks. Sure enough, they were still sucking hungrily at the crystal streamlet. Such a treasure could not be wasted even on sentient trees such as these. If only he could move the streamlet himself—yet the streamlet chose its own course; any outside interference might cause it to leave the land entirely, with unknown consequences. It was said that the streamlet emanated from the Celestial City of Jade; it wasn't bound by this world's laws.

He whispered to the oaks in the language of trees. "Stop blocking the streamlet. The spirit-fruit trees need to drink. Shift outward, so the water can flow again."

He felt their defiance. Among creaks and groans, they transmitted, *We have been here for centuries. Why should we move?*

"The stream has shifted course, and so must you. The spirit-fruit trees will die otherwise."

Things live, and things die, they replied. *Yet here we have always remained.*

He shook his head in exasperation, then focused on the fire. "Little Flame!"

Out zipped the tiny flame all the way to Koren's feet. Its tip looked up at him expectantly.

"You have restrained yourself well so far," Koren said.

The flame hopped, excited.

"Now, I need you to put a little more heat to the roots of these oaks. Don't burn them, mind you," Koren said sternly.

The flame tilted its tip forward, showing that it understood.

"I simply need you to—" He was cut off by the arrival of a messenger.

"The elder is waiting," the messenger said.

Koren sighed. "Look after Little Flame," he called over his shoulder as he jogged away from the children.

In about the time it would take to drain a cup, he arrived at a cliff draped with vines, flowering in various colors. A waterfall cascaded in their midst, down into a turquoise pond.

Koren circled the left side of the pond to attain the cliff, then mounted steps carved into the rock face, two at a time, until he reached the top of the waterfall.

He straightened his robes and hair, which now hung loose to his waist, then, feeling for the thin stream of golden elixir pooling deep beneath his navel in his stone kernel, Koren listened. Sensing the connection, he cycled the elixir once through his dawn channels, then reached into his kernel again, this time connecting with the water element residing there.

Using the force of his will, he bound the water element to the elixir, then, with a flick of his sleeve, propelled the stream of elixir outward through his palms. No one else would be able to see the stream, but to him it resembled liquid light.

He connected it with the waterfall, then gave a mental command. Most referred to this as "wielding." He saw it as simple communication. The waterfall opened like a curtain, and he stepped through.

Once his eyes had adjusted to the darkness, green crystals glowing on the cave walls revealed a shape the size of a horse lying in one corner. The elder's nine-headed dog, Theliane. Her central head dozed on her front paws, while the other heads drooped in various directions.

The central head tilted and opened an eye. "She's waiting," the dog's deep voice rumbled.

Leaving the crystals to pass through the Hall of Ishairo, Koren finally arrived in the main cavern where the elder sat, bent over a stone table, her back to him, long silver hair shining in the light of the fireplace.

He clasped his hands and bowed to her back. Although the elder was blind, she somehow saw everything, even behind her.

As Koren settled onto the stool across the table from her, the elder sat up, straight and tall. In face and form, she appeared no older than forty—strong and slender, with unwrinkled skin. But her presence emanated the wisdom and authority of one who had lived an age.

She fixed her blind, all-seeing eyes on him. "Have you found it?" Her voice was tough as the roots of a desert willow, smooth as a porcelain mask. Though she had spoken softly, the sound filled the cavern.

He dipped his head. "Yes, Elder."

"Then it is true." She looked down again at the five translucent stones scattered on the tabletop, passing her hands over them. Two were black, two white, and one with both colors, each marked with glyphs on every side. Jewels taken from Ishairo's own breastplate in the previous age.

Koren glanced at the stones, unable to read them. "What do you see?"

"That our time of destiny is at hand."

He frowned. "But not in any immediate sense, surely. Ishairo's heir has yet to make himself known."

"Golden Umbrage has returned, its light unshrouded after three millennia," she said, her voice grave. "And thus the Celestial Seal, likewise, casts its light upon the world once more. The heir walks among us even now."

Koren folded his hands, twirling his thumbs around each other. Why now? Things were good the way they were.

"You must return to where you first beheld Golden Umbrage," the elder said, her gaze heavy. "Look for a sign, be it ever so slight, that may reveal the first clue to the seal's hiding place."

"But the heir himself will know how to find the seal. The writings say it will draw him."

"The ancient writings do proclaim that the seal shall draw him—or her—unto it, yet nowhere is it written that the heir shall find it unaided." She fixed him with a steady white gaze. "Do you deem that the Order of the Ember was established merely to ponder the portents, then to fold our hands and sit idle as fate takes its course?"

Koren unfolded his own hands. "But finding the seal will bring about the Great War. Surely we don't wish to hasten it. If we—"

The elder raised a finger. "The Celestial Seal, though it be the rightful inheritance of Ishairo's heir, shall yet grant ultimate dominion to whomever lays claim to it. And do not think that we alone have heeded the portents—for there are others who have watched and waited, their designs unknown. We dare not suffer the seal to fall into strange hands."

A chill prickled the back of Koren's neck.

"We must be first to uncover the seal," she said. "Therefore return to Ma'yanar Forest and search every shadowed hollow, leaving no stone unturned, till the portent reveals itself and guides us to that which we seek."

A thought occurred to him, but he hesitated to ask. He traced his fingers absently over the little porcelain bird tucked away in his waist pouch.

"Supposing we do find it," he said, resisting the urge to twirl his thumbs. "Might we not simply keep it safe here in Peach Blossom Grove? After all, if there's no seal, there will be no Great War. Things would remain the same."

"Nothing ever remains the same," the elder said, gathering the stones into her hand. Then she tossed them onto the table and bent over them—their meeting was over.

Koren rose and left.

"Why now?" he mumbled to himself as he passed Theliane. The dog opened her eyes, stretched, then rolled away from him onto her side.

He loathed the idea of returning to the old forest. He had work to do. Did it not matter to the elder that more mortals of Peach Blossom Grove would die, possibly this very day, if the spirit-fruit trees weren't healed? Some here were nearly as old as him, an age unsustainable by a mortal; they needed to eat the fruit frequently.

When he parted the waterfall, however, the elder's voice rose behind him. "Threats upon ancient trees will earn you nothing but silence, and the crystal streamlet chooses its own course. Yet, I have weighed the risks. Go to the oaks and speak thus: that a tributary of the streamlet shall be granted to them."

Koren jogged down the steps of the cliff face, returning the way he had come. As he neared the place where he had left the children, however, frantic shouts greeted him. Children were rushing back and forth from the oaks, whose roots were now ablaze.

The trees rustled their leaves while children dashed handfuls of water onto the flames. One girl managed to wield a tiny stream overhead before it crashed, soaking her.

Murderer! Koren heard the oaks say. *It burns!*

Little Flame hopped excitedly from tree to tree, reigniting whatever the children managed to put out.

Koren touched the fire element in his stone kernel and bound it to the elixir, then streamed it outward, connecting with the fire, taking it under his command. He ordered the blaze to shrink. Then he wielded water. Bubbles popped in the river as the water roiled before lifting six handspans high, sending spray onto everyone. It undulated through the air toward the oaks, then fell, dousing the burning ground.

Little Flame stopped mid-hop and shrank, as though trying to blend in among the cinders that flickered in the smoking roots.

Koren pointed at it. "Back to your cave," he said, then repeated the command in the Old Speech.

Little Flame's tip drooped downward, and it burned a slow, reluctant path back to its abode in a nearby outcropping of rocks.

Placing a hand on the trees one by one, Koren wielded wood to regenerate the charred bark. The wounds healed into a crust that fell off like a scab, leaving bark as fresh and green as that of a young shoot.

"Move your roots away from the crystal streamlet. If you do this, I will make you a tributary."

A sulky stillness persisted for several breaths. Eventually, though, grumbling whispers rustled through the leaves.

Roots broke free, small tendrils whipping out of the ground, spraying grass and soil. Dirt churned around them, and little by little, the great trees shifted, propelled by their deeper roots.

In the time of a stone's warming in the sun, the place where the thicket had stood was transformed into a patch of loamy soil.

Koren pulled the earth element from his stone kernel and raised a hand to direct his communication. Stones skittered, and then the ground shook, and children jumped aside as it split into a deep trench that traveled from the crystal streamlet all the way to the spirit-fruit trees. Shimmering water filled the trench.

He repeated the action to form a narrow tributary from the side of the stream to the oaks. They swayed appreciative branches.

Soon, the bark of the spirit-fruit trees brightened by slow degrees until it resembled newly polished silver, and then fine, silvery-green leaves pushed out. Small fruits like blueberries appeared on the branches one by one.

Yet the crystal streamlet, whose bending course flowed far into the land, dried up little by little until only the tributary and the course to the spirit-fruit trees remained. The children watched silently, worry written on their faces. But the streamlet extended itself a few paces beyond the silver trees, and burrowed underground, apparently content to remain.

Koren let out a long exhale. The stream would not disappear. The mortals of Peach Blossom Grove were saved.

The spirit-fruit grew moment by moment, until at last they resembled large, deep blue pears. When they finally started glowing from within, the children cheered.

Koren waited for their excitement to calm before addressing them.

"That's all for today," he said.

They bowed to him, hands covering their fists, before racing away, leaving him to his thoughts.

What kind of world awaited the children, he wondered, now that signs of the Celestial Seal had reappeared?

He removed the small porcelain bird figurine from his waist pouch and traced a fingertip over its faded black wing, thinking of the time he had bought it long ago.

"Nothing ever remains the same," he murmured, returning the bird to his pouch. Then, like Little Flame, he trudged a slow, reluctant path back to Ma'yanar Forest.

Chapter Eight

THE BRIDGE OF HEAVEN ELDER

Koren headed into Ma'yanar Forest and found the marked tree. *Perhaps the elder is wrong*, he thought, scanning the place where he had seen Golden Umbrage. Why would anyone else be studying the portents leading to the Celestial Seal? It had been three thousand years, after all.

Yet there are beings in the world more ancient than that.

If such beings were to find the seal, all of Arizan would be lost.

He determined to focus his mind, and set once again about his task of studying shadows and light, but the sounds of people came to him, just as they had earlier in the day, except this time the crunch of leaves and shuffling feet was unmistakable. Not only were people in the forest, they were very close.

He slid into a shadow and watched. Soon, a man appeared, long, flowing hair on his snow-white head, his bearded face gazing at the ground as he moved briskly in Koren's direction.

His clothes looked similar to Koren's: blue robes with long, wide sleeves in the prevailing Min fashion. Except, whereas Koren's were unadorned, this man's sleeves were elaborately embroidered with bridges and clouds. He lifted his head to reveal a deeply lined face Koren hadn't seen in five years.

"Henzan," Koren said, smiling, and stepped into the light.

"Old friend!" The elder from the Bridge of Heaven Sect strode forward, bright eyes shining. Thirty to forty people followed, their stench assaulting Koren from ten paces away.

As the two friends exchanged greetings, Koren eyed the group. Only two were disciples; the clothing of the others—rough-spun and filthy—gave that away. One of the men wore a tunic that looked to have been woven from some kind of plant fiber. A fisherman, perhaps.

"What luck," Henzan said. "I can never quite remember which trees mark the entrance to your mysterious sect. I was expecting to have to wait days to see you. I told them as much." He indicated the people.

"Who are they?"

"A gift." Henzan gave him a knowing look. "They escaped from Her Majesty's dungeon three days ago."

Koren frowned. "Criminals, then."

"You need to get out more," Henzan replied with a chuckle. "A wielder attacked the empress at the Tailu Festival. Now they're all a target. Though I'm not even sure these ones are all wielders, truth be told. Not enough of the old blood left for it. But you're a better judge of that than me."

"They traveled six hundred fen in three days?"

"By riverboat."

A fifteen-day journey upstream, in three days. "Then it looks like at least a few here know how to wield water." They would have worked together. Untrained wielders could do very little on their own.

Koren used his immortal senses to probe them. Apart from a boy several years shy of manhood, and four or five others, none of them made his senses tingle. Even without further testing, he knew Henzan was right: most of them weren't wielders at all.

"You're sure they weren't followed? Our villagers use this forest to come and go."

A confusion of lomi swooped by, making the people huddle together. The streaks of glittering light circled them, then disappeared through the trees.

Henzan followed the streaks with his eyes. "I can't say. But any search party wandering into this place won't stay long."

Koren bowed. "That a person as important as yourself should risk such a thing proves there is still much good in this world."

"You give me too much credit. I came upon them here earlier today, and quite by chance."

"Who rescued them, then?" Koren asked.

"They won't say." Henzan lowered his voice. "But I overheard some whispers about the Min Daughter."

"It's more likely that she ordered their arrest."

"Not sure. When I was at the Tailu Festival—recruiting for our sect, you know—she spoke out in public to save a wielder from the saw."

"She set a wielder free?"

"Well, no," Henzan said. "She had him beheaded."

Koren made a wry face and raised an eyebrow.

Henzan laughed. "You're probably right. Still, I'm not the one taking them in. It is you who deserve praise."

"First, let me see what I can do," Koren said, and reached for the spirit jade vial hanging from his neck.

The vial was the size of his thumb and engraved with flowers and leaves that glowed faintly. Ignoring the people's stench, he approached them and held it up, then asked who could see it—whoever could see the vial could also drink the golden elixir contained within. Only the elixir itself knew who was worthy to drink, who would ultimately treasure the gift. To Koren's happy surprise, all of them raised their hands.

He removed the stopper and handed it to an old man first, explaining that in order for them to come to his village, they needed to drink from the vial. Obviously too tired and desperate to care, nobody even asked questions.

The old man took a sip, then jerked, as though stung by a bee, before swallowing with a shudder. Light flashed briefly in his eyes. Each person after him reacted in the same manner. From now on, they could all move in and out of the hidden Veil of Ayenashi.

As he returned the vial beneath his collar, Koren could feel it had already refilled itself. "Thank you for bringing them, my friend," he said. "I'll get them to safety immediately."

"Actually, I was hoping we might talk first." Henzan gestured to his disciples, who started handing out bread from sacks. Then, as the people ate, he strolled toward a more private place, asking Koren to follow. "I came to the forest in hopes of persuading you to join me for tea at Greenstalk Village."

Koren tapped a palm to his forehead. "Forgive my rudeness. My mind has been elsewhere. I never asked what brought you here, down from the mountain after all this time. Recruiting new disciples, was it?"

As Henzan's gaze shifted to the tree behind him, Koren realized it was the one he had scored. He placed a hand on his waist, hoping his wide sleeve would hide the line he had made in the bark.

"I just told you what brought me here," Henzan said, eyes glinting. "The prospect of tea with an old friend. The question is, what brought you? It's not often you venture outside your sect, if memory serves me."

The question threw Koren off-balance. "I was...on an errand for our elder."

"Fascinating. What kind of errand?"

"To check on the health of the forest," Koren said, cringing inwardly at the lie.

Henzan's eyes flicked to the marked tree again, his gaze seeming to linger as a breeze lifted his white hair to the side.

Koren risked a glance backward. The mark he had made was larger than he had realized. He shifted himself to stand directly in front of it and leaned back.

"Speaking of forests," Henzan said, "something came to my attention recently when I was playing a favorite game." He scanned the ground, sweeping leaves aside with one foot.

An uneasy feeling crept over Koren. He was tempted to ask what Henzan was looking for, but he feared the answer.

"It's a game long played by the Bridge of Heaven Sect," Henzan continued. "Very old. I'm not sure you know of it. Actually, I'd be surprised if you did."

He was certain Henzan was referring to the game of Umbrage. Koren breathed deeply, calming himself.

"I'm older than my appearance would suggest."

Henzan chuckled. "I believe it. You haven't acquired a single gray hair in fifty years. I guess there are secrets neither of us can share." His smile held the barest hint of bitterness.

Koren reached for the vial. "I've told you before, it's—"

"Yes, yes, the invisible elixir that you'd give me if you could. It shows itself to unskilled travelers," he said, with a glance back at the people ravenously stuffing bread into their mouths, "yet not to those of us who could truly benefit." He waved a hand. "It's no matter. Keep your secrets, my friend. I may not be ageless like you, but I am growing more powerful. The essence-nurturing method of the Bridge of Heaven Sect has its benefits."

Sunlight streamed through the trees, and sparkles danced in the shafts of light. The lomi were apparently growing restless.

A murmur of wonder came from the people, who pointed at the dancing sparkles. Henzan stared. None of them would be able to see the lomi's faces, but in the sunlight, their shimmering forms were still visible to mortals.

"This forest is full of secrets," Henzan murmured. There was something unsettling about his tone.

Henzan's eyes moved away from the lomi and settled on the ground again—right next to the marked tree. He shifted aside more leaves with his foot, and Koren waited with dread for the appearance of Golden Umbrage.

But the only thing underneath was more rotting leaves.

His friend glanced up at him and winked. "But even if you won't share your secrets, I'll still share mine. The game I was talking about is called Umbrage."

Koren fought not to react.

"We play it with spirit stones," Henzan said, studying him. "It was created during the Black Reign, to train wielders secretly. Do you know it?"

"What does the game have to do with forests?" Koren asked, avoiding the question.

"Perhaps nothing. Something in an old scroll just piqued my curiosity."

Henzan's gaze darted to something on the ground and Koren's shoulders tensed.

Only a mouse. It scurried into the underbrush.

"Why were you studying the scroll?" Koren asked.

"Oh, it's purely academic," Henzan said with a shrug. "Few people in our sect know how to read the old scrolls, so it amuses me to try. But lately I've uncovered hints that the game of Umbrage relates somehow to an item of great power. Fascinating, isn't it?" He stroked his long beard. "The scroll also contained clues buried in signs and portents that would lead to this item. One of our disciples thought he would find something in Black Valley, and went searching." He shook his head sadly. "Never came back."

"Nothing ever returns from Black Valley," Koren said.

Henzan sighed. "Still, I've been pondering these writings on my journey, thinking how gratifying it would be to discuss them with a scholarly-minded friend."

Henzan's expression was amicable, his eyes sincere. Koren took in the group of people huddled together, eating the man's bread, and suddenly felt ashamed for his earlier suspicions about his honorable friend. Koren had always known him to be interested in knowledge simply for its own sake.

And perhaps something in Henzan's scroll could help him find the Celestial Seal. Would it be so foolish to discuss the matter, at least in very general terms, with an old friend?

"I'm always available for a chat with you," Koren said, returning Henzan's smile. "I'll meet you at the Greenstalk Teahouse tomorrow."

Chapter Nine

PAPER TETHER

The noose Zinchen held in her hands was not made of rope, but of paper. It was silky and thick, the kind reserved for official purposes. Covered in the flourishes of a scribe's hand, it contained information that, as likely as not, had been calculated to hang her.

This was the second letter she had received from Countess Ellie. Though the first was a simple request for Varanaken warriors on the borders of Hanmar, this one was peppered generously with phrases like *widespread disorder*, *complete disregard for the law*, and *out of control*—totally different from the first, almost as though they had been written by two different people. More troubling, however, was that it painted a picture of a region in chaos—an assertion Zinchen knew firsthand to be false.

Vexation simmered inside her. Her most faithful countess was trying to discredit her, and she couldn't puzzle out why.

She shook one of the silver bells on the table before her, and a eunuch opened the door.

"Send in Countess Ellie's envoy," she said.

He bowed and left.

Since this was a private hearing, the Royal Court Hall was empty, apart from Zinchen. She rolled up the letter and slid it back into the smooth scroll case.

Countess Ellie's support had been one of the crucial elements in her plan to unite Shudon under the Min banner; Zinchen had intended to send her palace negotiator to the countess in person this very week, to present the idea to her and test Ellie's position. Zinchen couldn't afford to reveal her plans to her other nobles until she had gained Ellie's support. Though her countesses might desire expansion in theory, they would not risk draining their own coffers and sacrificing their men without proper persuasion. And since the House of Hanmar was the most influential noble house in Zinchen's realm, if Ellie pledged her support, the rest of the nobility would follow.

And now Ellie's betrayal.

"Envoy Lee of Hanmar!" the eunuch announced.

Zinchen stared ahead, expressionless. She would make a show of conducting a fair audience, all while uncovering the extent of Ellie's disloyalty. With this information, she could discredit the woman publicly. Then no other noble family would be tempted to follow Ellie's example.

A short, gaunt man with a goatee sauntered up the hall toward the dais. His chartreuse outer robe was embellished with a chaos of yellow pigs, covering inner robes of sky blue and orange.

As was expected, he lowered himself to the ground, making the last few paces on his knees, then touched his forehead to the floor. His hair was swept up into a topknot, secured with a bronze hairpiece in the form of—Zinchen squinted—was that a frogworm? It was the first time she had seen such a ridiculous design.

"Rise."

He performed an almost comically extravagant bow.

"Your Imperial Majesty," he began, "under the wings of your wise leadership, the Min Territories has experienced a long period of harmony because of your great enlightenment. Many improvements have come to pass in Min because of your wisdom, Your Supreme and Splendid

Majesty. Hanmar is deeply grateful for this, and offers you sincere and overflowing thanks."

He dipped into another theatrical bow. "So that I won't weary you with a lengthy presentation, I beg you to hear my brief summary with your customary graciousness, for Hanmar has found certain people in our land to be a contemptible scourge."

With an introduction this long, how brief could his summary be? She needed to cut the vine before it strangled the tree.

"Your countess requested Varanaken reinforcements," she said before he could continue. "Then, in a second letter, she painted a vivid picture of distress entirely uncharacteristic of her style, but without requesting reinforcements. Explain."

"There have been numerous wielding incidents, Your Majesty. The countess fears Hanmar will be overrun."

So this was Ellie's game. Reporting that wielders were running rampant in Hanmar would mean Zinchen's law—and therefore her rule—was ineffective. But in order to expose Ellie's treachery, she needed to pin her down.

"Curious," Zinchen said. "Hanmar's problem has always been Ghenz raiders. Where do these wielders come from?"

"They come from everywhere, Your Majesty. That's the problem. They hide in plain sight."

The envoy's vagueness had been deliberate. Zinchen turned the scroll case in her hand, recalculating. It appeared to be made of antler, its soft honey color telling the story of having been frequently handled. The case was intricately carved on its entire surface, mountain ranges and rivers alternated horizontally one on top of the other along the length of the scroll. A depiction of the province of Hanmar. In the middle, a tiny bridge connected two mountains across the river between them, hidden in plain sight—like Ellie's deceit. Keeping information about the wielders' origins vague made pursuit impossible. Clever.

But the game ended now.

"How many have you caught?"

"Your Majesty?"

"Wielders. How many have you caught and eliminated?"

He shifted on his feet. "There are too many to catch, Your Majesty."

"So there are regular wielding incidents, from innumerable wielders, coming from everywhere at once—but none have been detained?"

Envoy Lee cleared his throat. "That's correct, Your Majesty."

She fixed him with her gaze. "I assume you have interrogated their families?"

"I do not think family is a concept half-breeds can understand, Your—"

"Answer plainly."

"Ants, Your Majesty. The wielders are all Ants."

Zinchen raised an eyebrow. "You are asserting that the Ants of Hanmar can wield?"

"Yes, Your Majesty, and since they breed like rats, the threat is multiplying daily."

This man was either a liar, or a fool. She had no patience for either.

"Have you ever seen an Ant wield, Envoy?"

He hesitated, as though carefully constructing his answer. "Not personally, Your Majesty, but I am an expert in deciphering clues, and I am convinced by the signs I have seen. *Decipherer of Riddles and Enigmas* was my official profession before I came into the service of the countess." He drew himself up as he said it, as though he thought Zinchen would be impressed.

"Your profession has served you ill," Zinchen said. "Ants cannot wield." It was an established fact, something to do with the genetics of half-breeds, borne out by history and by Zinchen's own experience. It was the very thing that made them safe slaves.

A hint of pink colored his ears. "I have discovered that the runaway slaves from Ant farms, Your Majesty, are most often wielders. And as you know, Ants mostly give birth to doubles and triples. It's impossible to keep track of them."

"As you said, Envoy, Ants are prolific. If there were any possibility that Ants could wield, the problem would not be limited to Hanmar."

"No," Envoy Lee said, too loudly, and his ears turned red. He checked himself, bowed low. "Your Majesty, the Ants are wielders in disguise." His voice trembled. "They do terrible things, looting, robbing, raping. They burn things, flood rivers, call up tornadoes. They are descended from Antiquitals, as you know—the worst kind of wielders that ever existed. They're vicious, dangerous rats." He was breathing heavily now.

So he was a fool, then. Zinchen studied him calmly. "Ants are a necessary part of society. Without them, who would undertake the professions contaminated by death?"

"But they are also vagrants and strangling smile addicts, roaming around. Their acts are hidden. They should all be rounded up and executed, like the Jeng emperor does—" He stopped himself and cast a nervous glance her way. "Though the Jeng emperor possesses only a dim flicker of the radiant brilliance of Your Majesty's boundless wisdom."

So Ellie was a Jeng sympathizer? Perhaps some of her ancestors were Jeng; it would make sense. Hanmar did sit on the Jeng border.

"The young emperor does not rule Jeng," Zinchen replied. "The regent governs—or his wife, more likely. As for the rest, no Ant in history has ever wielded. I will waste no more talk on this."

The envoy's face grew red, and a shadow of desperation flashed in his eyes. "Then perhaps the wielders aren't Ants, Your Majesty. Please, forgive my ignorance." Another theatrical bow. "But we are still overrun."

Zinchen folded her hands and took a breath for patience. One might have thought the most powerful noble house in Min would have a more competent envoy.

"What does the countess seek? *Specifically*."

"Gold, Your Majesty."

Why resort to veiled threats for such a simple request? Zinchen had been expecting Ellie to request more lands in exchange for her silence about the so-called wielder threat.

The envoy's eyes darted to the side nervously. Was he afraid Ellie would punish him? Zinchen glanced again at the frogworm hairpiece. The animal was most often depicted in children's fables as a personification of opportunism and greed. Fitting.

Her gaze fell on the opposite end of the chamber where the tall lanterns flanked the doors, filling the hall with a faint scent of candle wax, blended with the fragrance of star anise and lemon peel, her personal incense. She considered her next move.

Ellie deserved to be publicly humiliated for this shameless attempt to swindle her, that was clear—but perhaps there was a better way. The woman's treachery could be used for Zinchen's advantage.

Zinchen regarded him coolly. "So, despite this unprecedented infestation of wielders, Countess Ellie has decided after all that she would rather have gold than Varanaken warriors, the very persons honor bound to take care of such a problem."

Sweat beaded on his brow. "The countess didn't think it right to deprive Your Majesty of your soldiers. She is resolved to recruit locally."

"I see. How much gold does she request?"

"Well, she'll need to pay the men and repair significant damage. She was hoping for, say, twenty thousand gold petals." His voice rose at the end of the phrase, like a question, as though Ellie had instructed him to see how much he could get away with.

At least now Zinchen was clear on what had to be done. The woman was obviously desperate. Instead of exposing her publicly, Zinchen would expose the lie in private, then agree to provide the gold she needed in exchange for supporting Zinchen's cause. That, in turn, would influence the other nobles.

It was time to end the audience.

"Very well," Zinchen said. "Hand over the evidence."

He hesitated, the pink creeping back up his ears. "Evidence, Your Majesty?"

"Official documentation of sightings, eyewitness reports, and so on."

"Er..." He searched around himself, as though expecting to find the documents scattered about his feet.

"You did bring evidence, Envoy?"

"Well, not exactly, Your Majesty."

She gave him a hard look. "You request twenty thousand gold petals—enough to pay three hundred soldiers for an entire year—without presenting evidence of the need?"

He dropped to his knees and bowed.

"I cannot send gold in these circumstances," Zinchen said to his frog-worm pin. "But I shall do better. Marne Wessel, my chief investigator, will travel to Hanmar to assess the situation. You may tell your countess that once I have Marne's report, I will send any amount the situation justifies."

She picked up her bell, and a silvery tinkle echoed through the hall. "I shall send Marne directly. Watch out for a green carriage with the tailu-bird."

Envoy Lee looked like he would respond, but the eunuchs arrived. He kowtowed, then backed away several paces on his knees before the eunuchs escorted him out.

She rolled the tension from her shoulders. Ellie would not be expecting an investigation. When she realized Zinchen had uncovered her dishonesty, rather than risk punishment, Ellie would have no choice but to pledge her support for Zinchen's cause.

Zinchen would use the noose intended to hang her to tether one of the most powerful noble houses to her instead.

Lina hastened up the hall, concern written on her face.

Zinchen straightened. "What is it?"

"Lord Yan was poisoned on the road here, Your Majesty. He's at the Houses of Healing now."

Word of Yan's visit had reached her within days of Shelan's death. She feared he might bring news that some in Jeng suspected her plot and would try to preempt it. More likely, her brother was poisoned before he even left.

"How does he fare?"

"Your Majesty...a master healer has been called."

Zinchen hurried down the dais stairs, pulse racing. Her brother was on the brink of death.

Chapter Ten

SUBJECTS AND ALLIES

Zinchen swept past the red lanterns and into the Houses of Healing. Sugi, Midra's assistant, leaned over a counter, labeling a jar. Shiny pots of red, yellow, and orange filled the shelves behind her, herbal decoctions used in the treatment of various ailments.

On the right, Zinchen passed a scroll painting depicting a human figure, covered in lines representing the body's various dawn channels. Sugi noticed her then and rushed forward, bowing low.

"Take me to him," Zinchen said.

"Right away, Your Majesty."

They turned into a hallway where a wooden medicine cabinet covered in small square drawers lined an entire wall. On the opposite side stood a succession of lattice doors.

Sugi opened the last one, a room with vents along the top of the wall and the sweet, pungent smell of mugwort smoke hanging in the air. The vents were supposedly there to allow the smoke to escape, but judging by the thick haze, they weren't terribly effective. Red lanterns hanging from the ceiling, each bearing some healing word scrawled in Midra's hand, cast smoky halos throughout the room.

"Straight ahead, Your Majesty." Sugi indicated a bamboo screen painted with herons and the logograms for longevity written from top to bottom.

Zinchen hoped her brother could still talk. If he died before they spoke, there was no telling how far her plans would be delayed.

But when she rounded the screen, her hopes of conversation vanished. Yan lay on a pallet, eyes closed, face pale and drawn, a sheet pulled over his naked body like a corpse.

Kneeling beside him was a man who took fine, golden needles from a metal tray and, with a quick twist and thrust of the wrist, deftly placed them into various points on Yan's body. A baton of dried mugwort lay extinguished on a table beside him, evidently the cause of the haze in the room. Yan's labored breathing filled the silence.

Frustration clawed at her—everything was conspiring to slow her down. If Yan died, who else could she trust in the Jeng Palace?

He groaned, and guilt pricked her insides. This was her little brother, the one who had chased her around the pond as a child, who had fished with her by the river. She ought to see him as more than a game piece on a board.

He had been better at fishing, she recalled, yet had always willingly shared his catch with her. More importantly, he had worked hard these past few years, establishing himself in the Jeng Palace—for her sake.

Fondness mixed with grief at his current state, and she leaned forward to caress his black hair, now slick with sweat.

"Get well, Brother," she said, pleased at the genuine emotion in her voice.

Midra appeared behind the screen and lowered her white-templed head. "Your Majesty, I didn't realize you had arrived."

The kneeling man, however, continued working.

Midra cleared her throat. "The empress has arrived, Master," she said.

Still, the man made no indication he had heard. Zinchen motioned for Midra to be silent; master healers were always odd.

He took Yan's pulse, tilting his head as though listening, then placed a final needle into Yan's arm before turning to a large wooden chest with shoulder straps for travel—the paraphernalia of a master healer—and opening its metal clasps with a click.

The smell of herbs wafted out, something like grass and ginger. She had never watched a master healer work before, or seen inside his chest, and leaned over to look. A tray of small squares lined the inside, each filled with dried herbs or minerals. He removed the tray to reveal a similar-looking one underneath.

As he took the second tray in his hands, he half turned to Zinchen. "Please excuse my rudeness," he said, making a perfunctory bow. "Your Majesty's brother is not yet out of danger."

When he removed a third tray and set it down, Zinchen's eyes widened: spirit stones filled the squares at the bottom of the box, their vibrant colors glowing, as though filled with fireflies. Many were a blend of two colors—something she had never even known existed—each with veins of the other color running through it, beautifully coherent.

In a quick mental calculation, Zinchen estimated their worth at around two thousand gold petals—ten times the yearly income of a successful merchant house. Did all master healers roam around carrying such treasure? It was a wonder they weren't afraid to travel...especially in Jeng.

A sweet, floral fragrance filled the air as the man placed a green spirit stone on her brother's chest.

"Banfay, master healer, at your service," he said, finally standing. He bowed with the elegance of a courtier.

His light beige robes were embroidered around the collar with blue flowers that somehow looked masculine, and a neat topknot secured the upper portion of his black hair, with the rest falling straight down his back.

By her guess, he was around thirty, yet his eyes held the wisdom of one who had seen many things. Something in them unsettled her.

"Please continue," she said, gesturing to Yan.

He lifted the edge of her brother's sheet to reveal his side. A spot in the flesh darkened, then a wound appeared, growing slowly. When it reached the size of an apple, it started to fester.

Zinchen covered her nose. "What is that? I thought he was poisoned."

"The spirit stones are drawing the poison's effects to the outside, where they can be healed, rather than leaving them on the inside, where they cannot," Master Banfay said. He scraped the wound until it was clean and raw, then packed it with healing herbs.

It seemed like an apt metaphor for what was needed in Shudon.

Then he placed a pink spirit stone on Yan's forehead, its glow intensifying as he muttered to it in a strange language. Color returned to Yan's cheeks, and he blinked.

Zinchen silently thanked the Six.

Midra dipped her head respectfully. "Master Banfay, your skills are truly spectacular."

He returned the sheet to her brother's side, and Zinchen knelt beside him.

"Did something go wrong?" she whispered to Yan.

His eyelids fluttered, and he mumbled something incoherent.

"Damage to the vocal cords is a secondary effect of the poison," Master Banfay said. "He needs more time."

But she didn't know if she could afford that. Hadn't he said her brother was not yet out of danger? He could still die.

She glanced around. Midra and Sugi watched with rapt attention as Master Banfay worked.

"Leave us," she said, dismissing everyone.

But while Midra and Sugi bustled out, Master Banfay simply slid a needle between Yan's eyebrows, underneath the stone. "I'm afraid I'll need to stay. The spirit stones won't work without me."

Zinchen folded her hands to contain her impatience as he muttered over the spirit stones, whose floral fragrance increased as Yan's color grew rosier.

After what seemed like an eternity, Yan licked his cracked lips and spoke in a raspy and barely audible voice, "Water."

After he had drunk, his gaze shifted to Zinchen, as though noticing her for the first time. He attempted to sit up, only to collapse onto his side.

"Forgive me," he croaked.

"Nonsense, Brother. You need to rest."

He looked so weak, she nearly paused, but the moment Master Banfay declared him out of danger and left the room, she spoke. She could wait no longer.

"What brings you back to the palace?" she asked. "Did something go wrong?"

"Just the opposite. The chief document inspector has vowed to name me his replacement upon his retirement."

Zinchen exhaled a soft laugh. "The most powerful position in the Jeng court. And all the more so for how few people realize it."

He blinked his agreement.

"You did well to come in person," she said. If such a message had been intercepted, it could have endangered his entire appointment.

She had more questions, but it felt wrong to continue before she acknowledged his brush with death.

"Who do you think poisoned you? Did you avoid Vice Regent Caliss's people, like I said?"

"I was careful."

"Is there anyone else who would benefit from your silence?"

"There are rivals for the inspector's post. I thought I had outmaneuvered them." He considered it. "But the Min-kezu are divided. There are some I'm not certain are loyal to Min—my servant reported seeing one of them meeting with the Shazori."

The Shazori would, of course, do everything possible to stop Zinchen's plans, if they knew them. A Min-led Shudon would mean dismantling their regency and disempowering their entire faction.

"If anyone suspects you're playing a deeper game, we need to reconsider our secrecy." She let out a quiet breath. Why would the Min-kezu oppose her? They were still of the House of Min after all—*kezu* being an old word for "lesser family," or "little sisters" in the eastern Min dialects.

"The heart of the people is the most difficult thing to obtain," she said, "even that of our relatives. However, the Min-kezu are still family—they must come around. With their help from within the Jeng Palace, Jeng will be mine before my forces even arrive."

"How are you planning to do it?"

Zinchen considered her answer. Lina was the only person she ever shared her strategies with, apart from Tori occasionally, when she needed the girl's help.

"There is your part, for which you have my thanks," she said. "There would be no chance of winning over the Min-kezu without your hard work."

He dropped his eyes in evident pleasure.

Should she tell him more? He had risked his life for her, after all.

"Then there are four other steps to victory," she said, "some of which are already underway. I have located crafters of etched weapons and armor, for instance." She watched his reaction.

As expected, Yan's eyes glittered. "The Arun clan still exists?"

"Very much so. As soon as they have been relocated to a suitable area, their forges can be relit and production can begin."

Yan looked impressed.

"The second step is to ensure the united Varanaken tribes join me." She would be invincible with the power of the tribes joining forces with her military.

"And the third step, of course, is to obtain the consent of the first-tier nobles, since their own armies must join the effort."

"Are they favorable?"

"I have reason to believe Countess Ellie of the House of Hanmar will soon pledge her support. After that, others will follow."

"You are truly gifted, Sister," he said with a look of admiration. "What is the final step?"

"That one is the easiest, but takes time: Tori's alliance with Prince Filo."

"An alliance with the second-in-line," he said, nodding. "Clever. But what's the delay? Is the princess uncooperative?"

"I simply need to ensure the best terms. It's the nature of such things."

"Mother would be proud," Yan said, his eyes shining with emotion. "You'll do everything she would have. Jeng needs your rule—they can't even control their Ghenz allies."

"The Ghenz have always been ruffians and remain so," Zinchen said. "One cannot ally with such as them."

Centuries before, the Ghenzan seafarers had arrived as raiders in Jeng, but when they allied with Jeng two hundred years ago as the land's protectors, instead of reforming, they simply aimed their depravities at Min.

A cloud covered Yan's eyes. He hesitated. "You said you needed the united Varanaken tribes. I wonder whether that will be so simple."

"Meaning?"

"The Varanaken are loyal to their lords, who in turn are loyal to their matriarchs, above everyone else."

"Everyone but me," Zinchen said. "The ten matriarchs and the lords beneath them are sworn to uphold the old vows."

"But if you'll forgive my saying so, Sister, they seem to regard themselves more as your allies than your subjects."

The statement irritated Zinchen, all the more because she suspected it might be true. Every year, the Varanaken lords appeared before her to renew the pact of protection made by their ancestors—the united martial brotherhoods—who had joined forces with Yanai Sumi in order to overthrow Antiquital rule. And at no time during these yearly vow renewals did they ever explicitly refer to themselves as her subjects.

Was it possible they weren't completely loyal to her?

"And I heard a troubling rumor," Yan said. "One of the Varanaken matriarchs has commissioned a new banner for her tribe, different from anything her ancestors used—featuring a rising mountain above the sun."

Zinchen frowned. "The sun represents the sky...where birds fly."

He nodded. "Including the tailu-bird." Symbol of the Royal House of Min.

Some, it appeared, disdained even alliance—they were dreaming of dominion.

"I will think on this," she said, forcing a quick smile. "But now I must go. I will return to check on you tomorrow."

She left him drifting off to sleep, then passed under the red lanterns outside, unsettled by thoughts of the Varanaken.

Chapter Eleven

MUZZLED

A fly walked across the table, hesitated at a green bowl, then hopped onto the translucent white flesh of a dragon eye fruit and let down its tongue.

Tori watched listlessly, cheek propped against her fist as the creature rubbed its hands together. She considered swatting it but couldn't bring herself to. They had too much in common. At any moment, either of them could be squashed without warning.

The memory of the blood dripping into the bowl at the naming ceremony flashed in Tori's mind, and she shuddered.

Be grateful.

She pushed herself to her feet, feeling stiff from so much sitting, then looked around at Anlin and Elnora. Yumay was out on an errand.

"That smells wonderful," she said, strolling to a side table where Anlin worked with unhurried dexterity.

She was mixing an original incense scent—something she had no doubt learned from her parents, master incense creators.

"Cedarwood and cinnamon," Anlin said. "I'll fragrance your clothing trunks as soon as it's finished. I think you could use something to promote joy and warmth right now."

That was an understatement. The past two days had been an eternity of mentally replaying the naming ceremony over and over, including everything that would have gone wrong had it not been for Elnora's quick thinking.

Tori slid open a pair of double windows and sagged onto the windowsill. Dragonflies flew over a zigzag walkway, hovering above the light green pond surrounding it. A koi fish shimmered among the lily pads, carefree.

Her mother could still find out. Might she already know?

Impossible. Wan had cured Tori years ago, almost the moment she had first manifested. Elnora was the only one in the world who had any idea what she had been.

She sat, then stood, then sat again.

"Do you want me to read to you, Princess?" Elnora asked, holding up a book with a brown paper cover, no doubt the latest romance novel she had picked up at the market "to see how bad it was."

But before Tori could respond, a clear voice rang outside the entrance hall. "The empress has arrived!"

Tori tensed. Her mother never visited.

Eunuchs hurried to open the door, and an instant later, her ladies were on their feet, bowing.

"I will speak with the princess alone," the empress said, sweeping past them.

The whole roomful of people bowed to her mother's back, then cleared out.

The empress strolled into the sitting room, mounted a low platform on one side, and sat on a long, stuffed-silk seat beside a window, just before the door to the moon room.

Tori bowed. "Hello, Mother. What brings you here?" she said, keeping her tone light. She refused to give her mother the satisfaction of thinking she could perturb her.

Making a point of keeping her movements casual, Tori sank into the seat across from her, but she felt like she was sitting on pins.

Her mother glanced around the room, gaze resting first on the half-finished game of Disdain sitting on a low table, then on an intricately carved jade incense censer on the shelf.

A nostalgic look crossed her eyes. "That was Granny Nuwang's, wasn't it?"

Maids bustled in carrying a lacquer tray with gold filigree handles, but the empress dismissed them with a flick of her fingers. They halted mid-step, then hastened out backward, nearly spilling the tea.

Her mother held out a hand and casually examined her rings. "An odd thing happened a few nights ago. A group of wielders escaped from the dungeon."

Tori's gut tightened.

"I guess they're more resourceful than you give them credit for," Tori said, matching her mother's casual tone.

Her mother chuckled. "Indeed. They seemed to have wielded the guard's keys right off his belt. Still, that's no excuse for laxness. I had him replaced."

Hair stood up on the back of Tori's neck. The guard had been executed.

"But the strangest thing happened in the end," her mother continued. "The wielder who was left told the new guard that the Min Daughter had freed all the others. Can you imagine? Shameless liar." She shook her head. "He carried on so badly, apparently, that the guard had to execute him." She watched Tori carefully. "Still, it's odd, isn't it? I mean, why would a person release only some of the wielders?"

Tori lifted her chin. "Why are you telling me this?"

Her mother shrugged. "You are the chief equitess-in-waiting now; soon you will see all sorts of odd cases. You would be seeing them already, if grief hadn't made your great-grandmother slow. Still, in three days, after Shelan's funeral, you will be the chief equitess's shadow, no longer free to come and go as you please."

"You seem to forget I'm under house arrest," Tori said dryly. "And while we're on the subject, why *did* you make me chief equitess-in-waiting?"

Her mother folded her hands on her lap. "Because I can."

As the words hung in the air, Tori's scalp prickled, her earlier feelings of powerlessness returning.

"But more importantly," her mother said, "because I need someone who is sympathetic to my cause. Shelan would have hindered me."

"So Shelan's death was no accident," Tori said, feeling sick.

"A ruler must look to the greater good. Something you'll learn in time."

Tori flushed with annoyance. "You think I don't know about the greater good? Who was it that saved the Arun clan from extermination?"

"You can hardly take credit for that. I seem to remember it being the Minister of the Right who swayed the court in the end."

"Then tell me how come they relit their forges three moons ago?"

The empress's face took on a curious expression. "So you were acting in court?"

"I learned from the best."

Her mother's lips curled into a slow half-smile.

"And what cause, exactly, do you suppose Shelan would have opposed that I won't?" Tori continued.

"That is what I came to talk to you about. Did I ever tell you about my recent visit to the Houses of Healing?"

Her mother knew she hadn't, so Tori didn't reply.

"When your uncle Yan was there, I watched the master healer work on a festering wound on his side. The healer scraped it, then packed it with herbs before bandaging it." Her gaze wandered, as though she was thinking. "And it occurred to me, trying to fix the troubles of Min right now is like putting a bandage on a festering wound. As long as Shudon is divided, evil will simply ooze over the border between Min and Jeng. Ghenz will still raid the land, traffickers will still deal in our Min-born slaves. The wound must be scraped and packed with strong herbs before healing can come."

As long as Shudon is divided? Her mother's meaning hit and Tori's composure fell away. "You want to overthrow Jeng?"

"I want to fulfill my destiny—and intend to."

"Mother, think of what you're saying. Ants will get pushed to the front lines, they won't stand a chance. Countless other people will die. It'll be a bloodbath."

Her mother raised an eyebrow. "For Jeng, perhaps. But our army will have etched weapons and armor, remember? Well done getting the forges relit for me so soon, by the way."

Tori's throat tightened.

Her mother picked something off her sleeve and smoothed the spot with her hand. "As for the Ants, why breed them on Ant farms if not to put them to use?"

"That's repugnant," Tori said. "And you'll have a revolt on your hands the moment you take the throne. Do you realize that? The people of Jeng think only Thana rule has heaven's blessing. In their minds, rule by Min would corrupt the 'true' Shudoni way. They'll never accept someone who isn't of Thana blood."

The empress wore a patient expression, as though waiting for Tori to realize she had just said something foolish.

Tori stood, breathing slowly through her nose in an effort to restrain a rising surge of anger. "This has nothing to do with healing the ills of Min. This is all for your own glory."

"A ruler's glory is the people's glory," the empress said. "As is a united land. Actually, my goal is the same as Ishairo's."

"Except you're nothing like Ishairo. He united the land to rid it of evil. You'll destroy your own people for nothing."

Her mother lowered her brow. "Foolish girl. I am not destroying Min, I am saving it—and you are going to help me."

"Think again," Tori said.

"I require cooperation, and intend to have it. Do not mistake me, I will not hesitate to sacrifce anyone necessary to achieve my ends."

She knows.

Tori's legs trembled. She lifted her chin to hide it. "I don't know what you mean."

"Then I suggest you do not find out. It gives me no pleasure to take away those dear to you, but I will do what I must."

A silent breath escaped her; her mother thought Tori was protecting someone else.

Feeling weak from the nearness of her disaster, she sat. One wrong move, and her mother would discover the truth.

"Now, there is a matter you will help me with," the empress said. "Marne Wessel is traveling to Hanmar tomorrow to finalize Countess Ellie's support. You will research the finer points of Hanmar lore for her, and in particular, take note of any references to Ants in their region, and their absence of wielding ability."

Tori furrowed her brow. "Why?"

"Necessary for the negotiations." Her mother waved a dismissive hand. "You know, Hanmar and their odd ways. Anyway, note down all such references and give them to Marne in the morning before she leaves."

Tori tightened her fists. A better person would stand up to the empress. They would do something to save the countless souls who would otherwise die in this senseless war.

But she'll find out.

Two severed heads flashed in her mind, shot through with arrows, and a vein pulsed beneath her temple. She pressed her lips together, muzzled.

"Marne will arrive back from visiting family early in the morning," her mother said. "I have left instructions that she should leave immediately, so be waiting at her residence at dawn."

Tori nodded. "Would you like to see my brief before I give it to her?"

"I trust your judgment." The empress rose, then looked through the window at the setting sun. "Begin soon, so you can still get some sleep tonight," she said, as though she cared anything about Tori's well-being. "Tomorrow will be a long day—the Grain Dedication Ceremony, followed by the feast."

Tori nodded again, then remembered with irritation that her carriage had been confiscated. "Will we be riding together?"

"A carriage will be sent for you. I am dining with Lord Kai tonight, and will go straight from his residence to the ceremony tomorrow."

And with that, she was gone.

Tori kept her composure until she heard the front door close, then pinched the bridge of her nose, blinking away the tears before they could form.

Chapter Twelve

THE WELL OF DISSOLUTION

The main passageway of the Hall of Heavenly Fragrance led into the empress's private library.

Tori entered, then strode between standing candelabras that lit the pillared path to the Lore Room, the gathering place of the oldest writings in Shudon. Darkwood cases lined its walls, each filled with scroll bags in colorful silk, their tassels brushing against small identification plates below.

She sat in her mother's throne-like chair. "Get me scroll numbers sixty-three and sixty-four," she said to Elnora.

References to the Ants' inability to wield would be found in the oldest texts, those written closest to the time when humans and Antiquitals began to intermarry, at the beginning of the Fourth Age. She glanced at the darkening windows. Hopefully she'd find what she needed before midnight.

She shifted aside the ink and brushes that occupied the center of the dark wood desk, along with a brass incense burner in the shape of a badger. As she slid it to the outside edge, the badger released a scent of star anise and lemon peel.

This section of the palace contained her mother's most precious writings and most peculiar treasures. No one was permitted entry without the empress's consent, apart from Tharun, the librarian, and the soldier who guarded the treasure room down the hall.

As Elnora laid out the scrolls, Tharun shuffled in with a lighting pole. The elderly eunuch lit the nine-branched candelabras by the door, then the standing lanterns, slipping the pole under their crescent-moon roofs. Candlelight brightened the room.

Tori unrolled the first scroll on the lore of Hanmar, its embossed ink vivid under the lanterns' glow. Images of *kamen* and *lomi* filled the beginning—the animal guardians and nature guardians who had long vanished out of existence, if they ever existed at all. Such scrolls were written by the loremasters, keepers of ancient lore, long ago.

Images of Ishairo the Sunderer came next, with accounts of how the earliest peoples of Hanmar had fought by his side.

Nothing useful here.

Tharun lit the last of the hanging lanterns, replaced the brass lion-snake latch that secured it, and, with his pole, hung it on the ceiling over Tori's head, lighting up her desk.

Tori ran her finger farther down the scroll. In one account, the people of Hanmar were depicted as peaceable folk who liked their food and drink. In another, they were valiant warriors who engaged in battles against spirit beasts over some kind of sacred artifact called the Well of Dissolution.

The conflicting accounts, however, made no mention of Ants. She moved on to the second scroll. But all she found were stories highlighting the people's reverence for the Old Magic of Tey Zuben, a fact everyone knew and entirely useless for Marne's purposes.

She blew out a frustrated breath. What would her mother do if she found nothing at all? The empress's search for whichever person she thought Tori was protecting would inevitably lead to Tori herself.

If she couldn't produce any information about the Ants, she should at least find something that would help Marne finalize Ellie's support.

She massaged her forehead, trying to recall Countess Ellie from when she'd seen her in a court session, years ago. Perhaps something she had learned then would help her mother's cause.

Ellie was the only one of her mother's twelve provincial managers that ever sent her rations in early. This showed her to be conscientious and her land to be prosperous. But that was no help. Tori's stomach knotted.

By the time evening had darkened to deep black, there were no scrolls left to request, so she had released Elnora to roam around. She knew where she'd be—the empress's late great-aunt, Auntie Chune, had written a series of romance novels, meant to be treasured heirlooms, but Tori brought them home to make her ladies laugh. Elnora claimed to hate romance books, yet somehow she could always be found reading them.

A chaos of scrolls crowded the floor around Tori's feet. The thought of old Tharun tottering at the top of a ladder to put them back made her gather the heap in her arms and head to the shelves.

As she replaced the final scroll, the metal plate of a shelf in one corner caught her eye. The label read *The Lesser Works of the Peoples of Shudon*, the oldest of the ancient lore from around the world. She hadn't thought it would be relevant to Ants in Hanmar, but as there was nothing else to try, she took down the first three scrolls. They had been constructed in the old way, ink writings on connected bamboo strips, and written in ancient logograms.

The first scroll started with an account of the origins of birth charms, and the history of nobles wearing their own charms for good luck, instead of merely as proof of matrilineal parentage.

Tori had never seen her own birth charm, though she knew it was in her mother's treasure room. Her mother had always said that, as Min Daughter, hers was too precious to risk being lost. Refusing to let Tori see it at all, however, was simply another power play.

She tightened her jaw. She was tired of her mother's control.

After the account of birth charms, a tale of a place in Hanmar made her pause—a location so steeped in the Old Magic that it affected their very waters.

She leaned closer. The magic had affected the people's ability to commune with nature, it said—an old way of referring to wielding. Those who drank the waters apparently lost their ability to wield altogether. The scroll named the place where the waters came from—the Well of Dissolution. It was the same sacred artifact she had read of earlier.

The second scroll mentioned the well again, and the third actually gave its location: according to a faded map, it had been located in the foothills right behind the modern-day Hanmar Manor. Knowing how the people of Hanmar both preserved their heritage and revered the Old Magic, it was probably still there. The magical waters weren't lost in some half-forgotten myth, they were still accessible, for those who knew where to look.

Tori's breathing quickened as she pondered this, eyes fixed on the lantern light that danced along a single gilded line framing the desk. If she could somehow get to the Well of Dissolution, all her troubles would be over.

But how could she? She didn't have a carriage. She couldn't even leave her residence without guards. Pain throbbed between her temples; she was nothing but her mother's puppet.

Frustration flared inside her, and she swatted the badger incense burner with the back of her hand, hitting it against the black stone floor with a metallic crash. It bounced several times before rolling round and round in circles.

The patter of footsteps sounded and Elnora rushed through the door. "Princess?"

"It's nothing," Tori said, rising to pick up the badger. "The censer fell."

Elnora placed a hand over her heart and slouched with relief. "While I was browsing the books, the treasure room guard left the library, to relieve himself, I guess. Then I heard a crash. I thought someone had broken in, trying to reach the treasure room."

"That would be pointless. The treasure room's protected with Tey Zuben wards."

Tori's gaze fell on the scrolls and a feeling of inner smothering took her. Her research had been fruitless.

But that thought gave rise to another, subtle at first, like a whisper in her belly. Then the thought took shape, growing in urgency, until she was sure that if she didn't act now, she might not have another chance.

And for her plan, she needed luck.

She looked at Elnora. "When did the guard step out?"

"Only moments ago."

"Do you have your Tey Zuben lockpick?" She did. "How much skill does it take to use it?"

"None," Elnora said. "It's magic."

Tori asked to borrow it, then glanced toward the place where Dan and Bokoon were stationed. "Keep the three guards talking outside the library until I come."

Then, tucking the scroll with the map into her robe, she clutched the lockpick and hurried away.

Chapter Thirteen

FACE AT THE WINDOW

A short time later, Tori left the empress's private library, heart pounding. What she was about to do was riskier than anything she had ever done before.

Stepping outside into the night, she and Elnora headed to her residence, but no matter how fast she walked, her guards were always two steps behind. She didn't have room to breathe, much less think.

When they finally reached her front door, she faced them. "I'm ill. I'm not to be disturbed till tomorrow."

Bokoon made a wry face, as though he didn't believe a word and meant for her to know it.

She didn't care. What mattered was that he stayed put.

Inside, everything was dark and silent, with the fragrance of cinnamon from Anlin's incense still permeating the air. Tori went straight to the sitting room, where Elnora lit a lantern, then gave her a questioning look.

She felt like a wound-up spring, ready to make her move, but she had to be patient; Dan and Bokoon needed time to settle into complacency at their post.

She reached into her robe and drew out a smooth bone tube. "The lockpick worked. I got this from the treasure room," she said, opening the tube and tipping out its contents.

Elnora's eyes widened. A birth charm, translucent blue, glowed faintly in Tori's hand. The inside had the fathomless quality of a deep pool, even though she could look through and see her fingers on the other side.

"I don't know how your lockpick bypassed the wards; they're sealed with my mother's blood."

"It's imbued with the Old Magic," Elnora said, slipping the lockpick into her waist pouch. "Granny said it's ancient. You told me the empress spent a long time in Tey Zuben—maybe the Old Magic somehow seeped into her blood, and the pick linked up with that somehow."

Tori examined the smooth, cool stone, mesmerized. In the center, swirls of dark blue and seafoam flowed around each other, in constant motion.

As she turned it over, something caught her eye and she squinted, holding it up to the light, tilting it to get a better angle. Strange logograms had been carved into the very center of the stone.

Her eyebrows lifted sharply as the logograms detached themselves and flowed along with the swirls, changing shape again and again, so that it was impossible to discern their form.

She slid the charm back into the tube. Knowing she held something her mother had never intended for her gave her a sense of satisfaction, and control.

"Why did you take it?" Elnora asked.

"Because I need all the luck I can get. Go wake Yumay. I'll tell you everything in a moment."

"And Anlin?"

Tori shook her head. "I'm not sure how well Anlin would hold up under my mother's questioning. The less she knows, the better."

Moments later, Yumay emerged, rumpled from sleep.

Tori faced her ladies, every bone buzzing. Dan and Bokoon should be settled by now, which meant she had to work fast. "I'm leaving the palace tonight," she said.

Elnora's eyes widened. "What? Why?"

"To take control of my life," she said, unable to reveal the full reason in front of Yumay, who now looked fully alert.

"What's your plan for getting past them?" Yumay asked, indicating the front door, where Dan and Bokoon would be.

"I told them I'm sick. And even if they don't believe it, they'll never expect me to leave through the moon room," she said, tilting her head in its direction. "There's no gate in the back garden after all—only walls."

Her gentlewomen exchanged looks.

"Do I have enough money to get to Hanmar?" Tori asked, looking at Elnora.

Elnora thought for a moment. "You have three gold petals, around two hundred silver drams, and a few skades. Hanmar is a six-day journey by carriage. You have enough for eight moons, if you live simply."

"Farmers could live two years on that," Yumay said.

Tori furrowed her brow. It always disturbed her how little the common people had to get by on.

"The real question is, how are you going to get there?" Yumay said. "I don't think my people can break your carriage out."

Tori gave a half-smile. "My carriage may be locked up, but Marne's isn't. Since she's visiting family, she would have taken her personal carriage, which means the official one will still be parked at her residence. I just need you to make sure my driver is at Marne's with the horses hitched in the time it takes to eat a meal."

Yumay nodded.

"And I need you to get your people to intercept Marne tonight," Tori said. "She's supposed to be here by dawn, but she can't be allowed to return for at least another two days."

Yumay looked uncertain. "I'll do my best. What should I tell Dan and Bokoon?"

"That you're going to get me medicine." She coughed loudly for effect.

Yumay smirked, and left.

But Elnora knit her brow. “Couldn’t you ask the empress to send you, instead of sneaking out?”

“The Grain Dedication Ceremony is tomorrow. I’m expected to attend,” Tori said. “Don’t worry, I’m about to fix everything. Just get our things and meet me in the moon room. Pack light, we need to be able to move fast.”

A short while later, Tori and Elnora snuck through the back garden, shouldering their packs. Though Elnora’s pack was twice as big as hers, Tori still shifted uncomfortably, trying to get the right position. Carrying her own pack was rare, and the servant’s cloak she wore bunched under the straps. Thankfully, the cloak had been laundered since her visit to the dungeon.

She gave a pat to her waist pouch, which held her three most precious possessions—the stones for Wan’s game of Umbrage, the broken shell, and now, the bone tube with her birth charm.

They slipped past the drooping willows, half hidden in shadow, and as they neared the back wall, the faint noise of partygoers met them from several houses down.

Tori mentally prepared herself to climb, but before they could reach the wall, her guards’ voices came to her, getting louder moment by moment.

“Quick!” Elnora pulled Tori behind a willow just in time as Dan and Bokoon rounded the corner.

She pressed herself against the tree as the guards strolled into the back garden.

“Why in the name of the Six aren’t they out front?” Tori whispered.

Elnora pressed a finger to her lips—Dan was headed to a stone table only two paces away from where they hid. Tori tried not to breathe. If he sat down, they would be in his direct line of sight.

“Let’s stay out front,” Bokoon said.

Dan stopped walking. "She's probably already sleeping. She's sick."

"So she says. But better not take any chances."

The two circled around to the front again, and Tori sagged with relief. Then, with a nod to Elnora, she jogged to the wall.

Jamming her foot into a groove between the stones, she gripped with all her might, then hauled herself up, the way she had seen Elnora do on the outer wall of the dungeon. Thankfully, this wall was much shorter, and she quickly reached the top, though her hands smarted.

After a quick look around to ensure the path was clear, she climbed down the other side and landed on the dirt, feet planted, knees bent. She'd learned her lesson about bad landings. Elnora landed beside her.

They slunk past the backs of several residences, homes of senior courtiers and ministers. Though it was well past midnight, lantern light and conversation still brightened many of them.

Just before the main path joined the one to Marne's residence, laughter drifted from the home of the Minister of the Right, as though from a small party. Tori pulled her hood forward on her face as she began slipping past, but the moment she and Elnora cleared the back gate, a guard stuck his head over the top of the wall.

Tori swiveled away from him.

"Evening," the guard said.

Elnora, her neck tilted downward to keep her face in shadow, dipped her chin. "Evening," she answered, in a calm voice.

Seemingly satisfied, the man continued his patrol in the other direction.

Tori wiped sweat from her palms, walking as quickly as she could without drawing suspicion.

At the end of the path, they turned left onto a wide lane. Marne's house was at the end. The lane was mercifully dark and quiet.

When they reached Marne's wall, Elnora peeked over the top. "All clear."

They crept through the gates into a dark outer courtyard, keeping to the shadows. Marne's servants might still come to use the outhouse.

A square-shaped structure stood in a dark corner up ahead. Although Tori's carriage looked much the same, she had never fully appreciated just how much it resembled a miniature house, complete with crescent-moon eaves. The horse hitch in the front of the carriage rested on the gravel.

She tiptoed toward it, cringing with every crunch beneath her feet. The muted turquoise green of an official palace carriage looked gray in the dark, but the giant tailu-bird painted alongside the petal-shaped window was unmistakable, as were the words *Palace Investigator*. People would recognize this thing anywhere.

Tori squared her shoulders, hoping she wasn't making a mistake.

She passed the window, then mounted the step at the front. Unlit lanterns hung on either side of the door, above rectangular latticework panes flanking the doorframe.

She stepped in, sliding herself along a low, square table that occupied the center, then sat on a padded bench, twisting to roll down a bamboo curtain behind her to cover the window's transparent pane.

Before Elnora could step in after her, footsteps crunched on the gravel. Elnora scrambled in just as lantern light shone straight into the carriage door, onto Tori's face. Her heart lurched.

But Elnora visibly relaxed. "Thank the Six," she whispered, motioning for the person to hurry.

It was Ingan, her driver, leading two horses. Relief washed over Tori.

Ingan made quick business of hitching the horses, then sat in the driver's seat and looked behind him through the doorway. "Where to, Your Highness?"

"I'll tell you later. For now, just get me out of the palace complex, fast. Take the south gate." It was the only gate open at this hour, used by palace suppliers.

He hooked his lantern on a pole extending past the horses, then lit the two lanterns on either side of the door.

"Must you light them both?" Tori asked.

"A carriage without lanterns will be noticed, if you'll forgive my saying so, Princess." He dipped his head respectfully. "As will going fast."

Tori gritted her teeth. "Getting caught will get me noticed, too." But he had a point. "Fine," she said. "Go as fast as you can without drawing attention."

Ingan's leisurely pace turned her stomach in knots through the eternity that was the upper circle of the palace complex. But when the carriage finally sloped downward, indicating their descent into the middle circle, Tori let herself breathe.

Through the gap in the bamboo curtain, she saw that they were now passing the scholars' houses. The court scholars, at least, would already be in bed.

They soon arrived at the guest residences, the last houses before the lower circle. Tori's shoulders released their tension. Her mother had no guests visiting at the moment.

Suddenly, a man stepped into the road.

"Whoa," Ingan said, rolling the carriage to a stop. Tori's heart thumped in her ears.

Ingan whispered through the closed door, just loud enough for her to hear. "Should I take the road to the right, Princess?"

The road to the right would get them away from the man, but they would have to ride all the way back up to the upper circle again in order to turn around. One of the ministers would be bound to spot the carriage.

"Keep going," Tori said.

"I can't, Princess. He's blocking the way."

"Marne Wessel, palace investigator?" a nasally, self-important voice called out.

"Er, that's right," Ingan said.

"Splendid. Envoy Lee of Hanmar. Let Lady Marne know I'm here."

"The countess's envoy," Tori whispered to Elnora. "I thought he had already left. Tell him Marne's asleep."

Elnora covered her face with her hood, then cracked the door. "The investigator's sleeping," she said, her voice faltering. "Please make way."

“Sleeping? The bumps on this road would wake the dead.” The man chuckled heartily at his own joke. “Tell her I’ll be brief. I just need to—”

Elnora shut the door before he could finish, and the envoy made some exclamation, evidently offended, but the sound of receding footfalls signaled his departure.

Tori waited for the carriage to move again, but it stayed put.

“Ingan?” she whispered. No response. She cracked the door, but her driver wasn’t there. She closed it, then shifted the bamboo curtain slightly, to peek out.

Eyes outside stared back through the window, looking surprised. For half a beat Tori froze, then jerked the curtain closed. Her pulse skipped.

Footsteps approached again and the carriage rolled on—Ingan had been the one she had heard walking away.

“I think that was Envoy Lee,” Tori said. “He seemed to recognize me.” She scrubbed her face with a hand. “What if he says something to my mother?”

“He looked like he was leaving,” Elnora said. “And if he’s headed to Hanmar, you’ll see him there anyway.”

Tori tapped on the door. “Ingan, where did you go?”

“The envoy’s carriage was too far out in the road. I went to tell his driver to move.”

In less than the time it would take to eat a meal, they arrived in the center of Silver Fox Springs. Scattered lanterns lit up empty streets, and the only movement in the town square came from an Ant crew kneeling on the ground, scrubbing bloodstains from the white stone.

The smell of blood drifted into the carriage, making Tori heartsick.

It took five more days to clear the scent from her mind.

Chapter Fourteen

SONS OF ELITHIA

The chants of the Scholars of Fyeng filled the air as a line of yellow robes, embroidered with gold and silver, trickled through the towering arched entrance of Silver Fox Springs. The archway's deep blue tiles and golden tailu-birds dazzled in the sunlight alongside a dedication to Zinchen, engraved in gold.

"They certainly do drag on," Zinchen murmured, as the women moved at a snail's pace along the white limestone of the Grand Processional Way.

Her grandmother looked at her from across the altar but said nothing. She had been like this ever since Shelan's death. Zinchen was surprised at how hard she had taken it.

She felt a stab of regret; she had never meant to cause her grandmother pain. If only Shelan hadn't been so bullheaded and cantankerous.

The fact that Shelan's place by the altar stood empty didn't help matters. Tori should have been there beside her great-grandmother as chief equitess-in-waiting, but once again, the girl had shirked her duty. Her maids had reported her sick in bed—no doubt a case of simple exhaustion from staying at the library too late, despite Zinchen's warnings. Still, she had instructed Midra to check on Tori later, just in case.

Or perhaps she was simply worried about her lover. Lina had so far been unable to discover any information on him. At first, Zinchen had wondered whether he had been one of the wielders released from the dungeon, but Tori had seemed so shaken yesterday by the threat of Zinchen exposing him, she had concluded he must still be operating as part of society.

The High Scholar of Fyeng finally came into view, leading a tame ox and a wild horse, and the people dipped their heads to the guardian of the ancient practices of Shudon, devotee of Suro, the Sovereign Spirit.

Out of nowhere, a Varanaken on horseback casually crossed the procession, forcing the scholars behind him to stop.

Zinchen's lips tightened. She had brought in the Varanaken to help manage the crowd, not to disrespect her scholars. Disrespecting the Scholars of Fyeng was akin to disrespecting her. She scanned the crowd, noting the places where Varanaken sat on horseback, and Yan's warnings came back to her.

As the High Scholar led the animals to the bottom of the altar platform, one Varanaken used his horse to push a small group of people backward, even though they were standing behind the lines Zinchen's soldiers had set. The soldiers nearby noticed, but instead of standing their ground, they made the deferential gesture of beating one fist to their chests.

Zinchen narrowed her eyes. She hadn't put the Varanaken over them, yet her men cowed to them.

The canopy above her fluttered noisily in the breeze as the scholars slaughtered the ox below, while the crowd waited in reverential silence. The scholars were unique in the world in that they could not be contaminated by death, and so they required no Ant servants to kill the animals for them.

A short while later, the High Scholar ascended the platform, holding a bowl of ox blood in one hand and a closed lantern in the other, containing the ever-burning flame of Fyeng. The woman tilted her head, allowing the light of heaven into the open top of her tall, rectangular hat. Though the fabric of the hat was black, like her robes, it had been embroidered with so many gold circles that it shone.

A clear bell rang out, signaling the beginning of the blessing.

The High Scholar opened a panel on her lamp, and a small tongue of ever-burning flame leaped into the bowl-shaped depression on the altar, lighting the incense and wood that lay there. The scent of woodsmoke and cloves filled the air.

"Of old in the beginning, there was the great chaos, without form, and void," she said. The bell rang again. It would ring at the end of every sentence the High Scholar spoke.

"The six planets had not begun to revolve, nor the two lights to shine. In the midst of it, there existed neither form nor sound. Suro came forth in her sovereignty and first did hover above the darkness and brood upon the realm of the impossible."

As the scholar slowly poured the blood into the flame, Zinchen tried to keep her gaze from wandering, but she couldn't help scanning discreetly for the Varanaken. One of the Varanaken's horses shifted, backing into a soldier. The Varanaken turned to look, and the soldier beat one fist to his chest in that same gesture of respect.

Zinchen became aware she was frowning and looked up into the sky, pretending to be bothered by the angle of the sun.

The High Scholar continued. "You, O Suro, made heaven; you made Arizan; you made Ketuan, the Great Mother. All things became alive with reproducing power, and Ketuan birthed the Six."

Zinchen's grandmother then reached over to the narrow table beside the altar and grabbed a golden cup filled with osmanthus wine, the preferred drink of Suro. Beside it sat a golden plate of winter wheat.

The chief equitess swirled the wine, then poured it into the fire. At the sound of another bell, Zinchen sprinkled in a fistful of wheat, releasing the smell of roasted grain. Their unified actions were a tribute to their ancestor, Yanai Sumi, who was both empress and chief equitess.

Zinchen's eyes drifted back to the Varanaken. Yan had said they were loyal to their matriarchs above all—a fact that had already unsettled her.

But now, it appeared that her own soldiers regarded the Varanaken as superiors, meaning that, practically speaking, they also ranked beneath the Varanaken matriarchs in the chain of command. So who really controlled her military—she, or the Varanaken matriarchs?

She ran a finger lightly along the cool, fine edge of the empty gold plate. She had been so enamored with the idea of etched weapons and armor that she had never considered someone other than herself might command them.

One of the scholars scooped ash from the fire and descended the steps, then poured it onto the back of the wild horse that had been led in the procession and swatted its rump. The people cheered as the horse raced back to the wilderness, bearing away from them the ashy stain of their sins, allowing the blessing of harvest to flow from heaven.

"Now, O Suro, look down from heaven and once again bless this land with reproducing power, this great land that you have placed into the hands of your faithful servant, the serene and majestic Empress Zinchen."

A gong sounded, and Zinchen bowed her head, the vibrations shaking her bones. When she lifted it again, music began, and, as befitted an empress's generosity, her servants handed loaves of bread to everyone in the crowd and also gave each a silver dram.

One of Zinchen's soldiers caught her eye from among the crowd—Joktan, son of Elithia the Widow. He and his brother Javin were the two she had personally chosen for her troops. Although Joktan was in no way blocking the road, a Varanaken appeared to be demanding that he move aside to let him pass. Joktan stood his ground, staring at the Varanaken defiantly. The Varanaken finally sniffed and maneuvered around him.

Curious, she scanned the crowd for Javin.

Dancers twirled through the streets, elegant women in long, flowing robes, their colorful ribbons simulating the essences of wind and water, a tribute to Yanek, god of weather. She found Javin beyond the dancers.

To her delight, he was directing a group of Varanaken around the lines he had apparently set. They looked down on him from their mounts with characteristic Varanaken haughtiness, but nonetheless complied.

As they passed, one of them spat not far from Javin's feet. Javin casually glanced at the ejection, then turned his attention elsewhere, utterly unperturbed. Zinchen smiled.

"What do you think of the sons of Elithia?" she asked her grandmother later as they made their way to the carriage. The fragrance of roasting ox meat overtook them, along with the beat of a drum.

But her grandmother stared glumly at nothing, apparently lost in her grief.

Zinchen would talk with her later. Inwardly, though, she knew her instincts had been right in appointing the sons of Elithia. Perhaps with these two, she could turn her army around.

Chapter Fifteen

THE IVORY SWAN

Zinchen took her seat on the dais in the Hall of Nine Flavors, signaling the beginning of the feast. Her grandmother sat beside her.

Behind them, a decorative screen shielded from view the table of the senior palace attendants, where Lina presided. Although Lina's status as Imperial Speaker more than qualified her to sit in the hall itself, her habit was to stay as close to Zinchen as possible.

The vantage point from the dais allowed Zinchen an overview of the entire feasting hall, with her ministers and senior intimates seated closest, each of them at their own low table, and after them, the guests of honor. Not only did these places provide the best view of the entertainment, but their seats had been placed in front of the bronze pillars supporting the Hall of Nine Flavors, a symbolism that would not escape them—Zinchen was acknowledging their importance to her reign.

Her eyes fell on Lord Akiren among her honored guests, who, even without his chest guard and sword, was unmistakable as a Varanaken lord.

The hall rose and bowed, then spoke in one voice. "We greet you, Empress, incarnation of Min. May you live forever and ever!"

Zinchen responded with a sweep of the hand. "Rise and be merry. Eat and drink your fill."

As the Jo dancers started the grain dance, subtle and elegant, guests at adjacent tables began toasting one another, while servants moved around with platters of food and drink.

She turned to her grandmother and lifted her goblet. "To your health. I am pleased you look so well."

Hopefully the festive atmosphere would pull the elderly woman out of her joyless state of mind; the sooner Zinchen could get her advice on the Varanaken, the better.

But her grandmother's face remained grief-ridden. "Yes, I look well. Winds uproot the green reed, yet pass over the cracked stone."

Zinchen considered her response, looking first at her goblet of osmanthus wine, then at the thimble beside it, a small cup roughly one-fourth the size of a normal one, with an allover braided design. It was half filled with *ackhee*, a bitter, burning perversion of grain wine.

The words came to her, and Zinchen evoked what she hoped was an expression of grief. "May Shelan's journey through the labyrinths be brief," she said.

This seemed to appease her grandmother, who nodded and finally took a sip of wine. Then she set her goblet aside and downed the contents of the thimble.

Zinchen suppressed a grimace. Ackhee was how she imagined dishwater must taste—if it were mixed with poison and set on fire. She would have liked to ban it from the palace altogether, but her foremothers had established it as one of the traditional drinks of the Grain Feast, osmanthus wine being the other. She was required to drink one of each tonight, for good luck.

Perhaps the drinks would numb her grandmother's grief enough to make her reasonable. She studied the guests as she waited for the ackhee to take its effect.

The gaunt-faced Minister of the Left was seated directly across the hall from Lord Varu, the minister's son. Varu noticed Zinchen looking and raised his cup, eyes smoldering with something like desire.

She dipped her chin and moved on, noting the illustrious personages in attendance from all over Min as she searched for her real object of interest at the other end of the hall. There, behind the pillars, were long tables for her junior intimates, allowing them a view of the entertainment without making them the focus of attention.

At last she found a young man leaning to one side. Lord Kai's eyes crinkled at the edge of a laugh, evidently either telling a joke or responding to one. Quiet warmth filled her chest.

"How is Yan?" her grandmother asked.

"Better. He returned to Jeng yesterday to take a prestigious new appointment. I have put precautions in place to prevent a repeat."

Her grandmother nodded. "It was close for a while."

"It was. The poison was beyond Midra's skill. Thank the Six that a master healer was traveling through at just the right time."

"Poor Shelan. The master healer could have helped her, too." She gave Zinchen a strange look. "Such an odd thing, her horses spooking so close to the palace. Her people were taking every precaution." She sighed wearily. "But Tori is the new chief equitess-in-waiting. What a comfort to me, to still have someone from among my children's lines to succeed me."

The statement stung. Was she purposely dredging up Zinchen's past failure of the equitess examinations?

"It is the first time since Yanai Sumi," her grandmother continued, her eyes taking on a disturbing glint, "that the titles of chief equitess-in-waiting and Min Daughter will be joined. Though I suppose that fact didn't escape you, my dear."

Zinchen stilled. If her grandmother really suspected her of causing Shelan's death, things would never be the same between them.

Sometimes the best defense was to offer none. She would feign ignorance, and hope it worked.

She turned her gaze to the Jo dancers and ate and drank in silence. When they finished, a group of entertainers arrived, holding bamboo cages filled with little birds.

When they opened the cages, the birds flew once around the hall, then twirled and dove to the sound of flutes. Whenever the flutes stopped playing, birdsong echoed the last line of the melody. Laughter and applause filled the place.

Zinchen's mother had always maintained that animals were useful only as food or transportation, but she had to admit, this was entertaining.

She chanced a look at her grandmother, who, thankfully, appeared amused. She decided to try again.

"Grandmother, there is something I would like your advice on."

The old woman nodded.

"As you know," Zinchen said in a low voice, "the Varanaken are crucial to my plans. But I have begun to doubt their loyalty. What measures can be taken to ensure they do not rebel?"

Without giving the matter any thought, her grandmother replied, "I urge you to carefully consider your motives, my child. I also desire unity, but we must always question our own intentions, for one's reasons are just as important as one's actions. If the reasons for our goals are misguided, the actions we take to achieve them will also be improper. This will ensure you never do anything contrary to the soul of equity."

The statement nettled her. Her grandmother was pressing a point—Zinchen had never been equitess material.

"At the end of my life," Zinchen said, "I will stand unashamed before my foremothers when we meet in the labyrinths. That is reason enough."

Though she looked unconvinced, her grandmother gave a nod. "Then the Varanaken should not be your chief concern. Your priority must be Tori's alliance with Prince Filo. This should take place within the next twelve moons, to give his people time to accept her."

The response was perfectly reasonable, yet it, too, irritated her. If she had needed advice on the alliance, she would have asked.

"There will be adequate time for that," Zinchen said.

"Has the girl agreed, then?"

"From now on, Tori will do as she's told."

Her grandmother raised an eyebrow, but she merely said, "Then you're lucky Rozalia has waited so long."

"Why should she not? She would never succeed in placing Prince Filo on the Jeng throne. As Tori's primary intimate, Filo will have more power and privilege than he could ever hope for in Jeng."

"It's true that Rozalia has everything to gain, but she might still have given up hope, and allied her son to someone else. It has been eight years since the proposal, after all."

Zinchen gave a half-smile, amused by the absurdity. "The longer the bait is placed, the more ravenous and trusting the fish becomes. The more influence one wishes to have over a family, the longer one must wait to ally with them. But we digress. It is the Varanaken that concern me. I need someone I trust to oversee them. What do you think of Joktan and Javin, the sons of Elithia?"

"Elithia the Widow?"

"I was observing them at the ceremony earlier," Zinchen said. "They seem to possess a rare strength of character. I am considering promoting them to commander."

"Both of them?"

Zinchen dipped her chin.

"To what end?"

"To be generals, in time. I believe they have what it takes."

"You don't need more generals," her grandmother said, eating a morsel of food.

"What I need is loyal people to lead my soldiers," Zinchen said, starting to suspect her grandmother was being purposely contrary. Although she couldn't prove Zinchen had anything to do with Shelan's death, it was clear she still harbored suspicions.

The old woman tsked. "A man's propensity for conflict always leads to instability and suffering. Women are the only suitable generals for a prosperous military."

"It is true that military strategy has always been the domain of queens," Zinchen said. She herself had studied it most of her life. "But generals follow the empress's command, so what difference does it make if they are men?"

"How often is an empress in the field of battle? In times of crisis, soldiers must make decisions on the spot. They cannot send to you for everything. A wise and discerning woman is therefore needed. Properly guided, a man's strength becomes profitable, but this guidance cannot come from another man, any more than the blind can lead the blind. One only needs to look at Jeng to see that," she said with a quiet scoff, and took a sip of wine

"I am talking about the military, Grandmother, not ruling a nation. And truthfully, Jeng was no more prosperous when its regents were women. They were still Shazori, after all."

Her grandmother shook her head. "It wasn't the Shazori that ruined Jeng. Things began to decline thirty-six years ago, something you are too young to truly remember. It was when the young Jeng empress died without a daughter, followed by the regent, and the weak decision was made to let the regent's son take over on her death, instead of one of the regent's capable daughters—just because the child emperor was a boy and supposedly needed a man to guide him. The new regent then became power hungry, as men tend to do. The Jeng Palace has never recovered, and probably never will, since the Thana line seems cursed now to produce only male heirs." She lowered her eyes for a beat, no doubt reflecting on her own failure to produce a daughter in her time.

Zinchen waved a dismissive hand. "By my guess, the one running things behind the scenes is the regent's wife—Vice Regent Caliss. My sources say she's cunning."

A hush fell over the hall as a woman in rich, dark robes approached the dais. She was a distinguished poet known by all of Min, and when she opened her mouth to speak, the entire Hall of Nine Flavors seemed to hold its breath. Her latest poem had been composed especially for tonight's feast.

The woman began in a weighty voice, dripping with conviction:

"Under the veil of evening's fading light,

An ivory swan, lovely as the moon,
With wings spread wide, rose into the night,
Leaving behind the glow of the lagoon.
She ascended to where mortals only dream,
Where instead of jewels, stars did crown her head,
Girding herself with dignity supreme,
So that under her gracious reign abundance spread.
No shadow beneath her radiant rule did loom,
For treasures fell with every flap of wings,
And from these jewels a milky pathway bloomed,
The White River, of which every mortal sings.
Knowledge prospers wherever she may tread,
And the black-crowned night heron lifts its head."

The guests exulted over this obvious allegory for Zinchen, with the black-crowned night heron being a well-known representation of wisdom and insight.

A renowned bonden player came next, a man who had traveled a great distance. He was tall and lean, with sleek black hair that fell past his hips. His instrument was carried ahead of him and placed on a low table.

He flicked his wide sleeves aside as he sat, then began to strum and pluck the strings. An almost otherworldly sound filled the hall as his hands glided across the instrument's elongated surface.

The song was deliciously long, like a summer's day spent in the raptures of youth's first love.

Zinchen's eyes found Lord Kai again.

Her grandmother nodded, smiling, as the man played.

"Beautiful, isn't it?" Zinchen said, hoping to turn the conversation back to the Varanaken. She lifted the thimble of ackhee to her lips and tipped its filthy contents back. A shudder racked her body, followed by beads of perspiration, then a momentary blur to her vision as she tried to return her focus to the bonden player. He was now taking his bow. She clapped, then fanned herself. A swallow of the peachy osmanthus wine cleared the bitter taste. "So you have no advice for me, then, about the Varanaken?"

"My advice is to promote capable women generals among your ranks and to let the Varanaken deal with the Varanaken," her grandmother said.

"Such as Lord Akiren?" Zinchen said, making a subtle sign toward the Varanaken lord.

Her grandmother nodded. "He rules his men with a firm hand. Just recently, one of them dishonored himself by taking his clothes off in public when drunk. He was sentenced to soul-cutting."

"That seems excessive," Zinchen said. She had witnessed this ritual of self-disembowelment once before, a bloody punishment for a criminal.

"The Varanaken are dangerous warriors, my child. Such people need harsh discipline to keep them under control. But their own matriarchs and lords can see to that."

The answer may have been intended to put Zinchen off, but she nonetheless found the nuggets of wisdom she had been searching for: she needed to make use of the Varanaken matriarchs and lords.

When the entertainment ended at last, the time of personal conversations and individual toasts between tables began.

Zinchen seized her moment.

"Call Lord Akiren," she said to a nearby servant.

In about twice the time it would take a candlewick to catch, the Varanaken lord stood before her.

"Lord Akiren, what a pleasure to have you among us. Bring some vrath," she said to the servant. "The special reserve."

After a round of toasts, the Varanaken's straight-backed composure loosened.

"I trust Your Majesty is satisfied with the service of Dan and Bokoon?" he said.

Zinchen maintained her pleasant expression. If she told him they were incompetent fools, he might sentence them to soul-cutting, and she'd have to start over.

"They have the potential to be on par with their fathers, given enough time," she replied. A *great* deal of time.

This appeared to please him.

She signaled the servant to pour him another cup of vrath. "Lord Akiren," she said, "I would be particularly grateful if you could train two young soldiers in my service."

Distress shadowed his face, and he jumped to his feet, bowing low. "My deepest apologies, Your Majesty," he said, eyes on the floor. "Varanaken ways are for Varanaken alone."

So that was how it worked. She had no idea their ways were so ingrained that they could refuse the particular request of their empress.

"Oh, but their father was Varanaken," Zinchen said smoothly, indicating for him to take his seat. "Sadly, he died before ever meeting the lads."

No one knew who their father was, of course—so he might well have been Varanaken.

Lord Akiren looked at her questioningly. "Who are these soldiers?"

"The sons of Elithia the Widow."

"I've heard of her. It is said that she had five husbands who died in the space of five years. I never realized one was a Varanaken. Do you know which tribe?"

"I'm afraid not. It was a walking marriage." She motioned discreetly for the servant to pour him another cup. He accepted it gratefully and drank. The servant poured again. Varanaken drank vrath like it was water.

He nodded thoughtfully. "Then it appears that training in the Varanaken ways is their birthright. I will do our people's duty." He dipped his head, then drained his cup.

Zinchen toasted him again, smiling. Once Joktan and Javin were trained, they, in turn, could train Zinchen's other soldiers—men who were truly loyal to her. She sincerely hoped Elithia's sons weren't in the habit of removing their clothing when drunk.

A woman in a simple white tunic slipped past Zinchen's side vision and disappeared behind the servant's screen. Sugi, Midra's assistant. A moment later, she reappeared and exited.

Lina came to Zinchen's side, whispering so only she could hear. "Your Majesty, Marne is at the Houses of Healing. She was waylaid and robbed on her way."

Zinchen forced her face to remain placid as she whispered back. "On the road to Hanmar?"

Lina hesitated. "No, Your Majesty, on her way back to the palace. She never went to Hanmar."

"But the night watch saw her carriage leave just before daybreak."

"That was the information I received. However..." She paused. "Midra has just returned from Princess Tori's residence. She isn't sick at home. It appears"—discomfort grew on her face—"she was the one who took Marne's carriage."

Chapter Sixteen

THE COPPER CHAIN

Sometime after dark, Lee arrived at the "Gray District" of Waterwheel—an unsavory corner of Min known to him by reputation only—thumping around on his seat as the hired driver took pains to hit every pothole.

He had been riding nearly one full day, having purposely left the Min Palace long before dawn. As he had only stopped along the way for essential purchases—and, of course, to arrange a hired carriage, completing his disguise—his muscles felt tired and sore.

The carriage pulled into an alleyway the likes of which Lee had never seen. It was a thing of cautionary tales, complete with broken garbage barrels, rats, and a drunkard slumped against the wall, sitting in what Lee could only guess was a puddle of his own vomit. Beyond the drunk, a tattered paper lantern illuminated a door with a well-worn step, and above it, a weather-beaten sign embedded with a chain covered in peeling orange paint, and scrawled with the words *The Copper Chain*.

Lee leaned toward his carriage driver—whose body odor he could smell perfectly, given the lack of a door between them—pulling his tunic up over his nose. "Are you quite sure this is the only Copper Chain in Waterwheel?"

"The one and only." The middle-aged man had an expression that said he had seen it all, with skin so coarse and leathery, Lee could almost imagine him being made into a saddlebag when he died.

Peering into the darkness beyond the tavern, Lee found himself wishing he hadn't left the palace so soon; his contact's message had only reached him once he was outside palace grounds. Truthfully, he had lingered there one full day after his audience with the empress, expecting an invitation to the Grain Feast—which would have been only proper for a man of his station. But when none had come by midnight of the next day, he thought to save himself the indignity of being seen on palace grounds during a feast he was not invited to.

The feast might still be going on right now. He regretted not waiting longer for his invitation.

The nippy spring night felt like rain, and the clouds covering the moon looked like they had no intention of budging. He pulled his cloak over his shoulders and coughed. The knobby brown fabric smelled like it had never been exposed to fresh air, or a washboard. The woman who had sold it to him swore it was new, and he realized now she had merely meant unworn. Though another odor told him that interpretation might be questionable as well.

As he stepped outside, a surprising chill penetrated his flimsy tunic, sending a shiver up his legs.

"That'll be two drams," the driver said.

Lee took one silver coin from his pouch. "Here's a dram for the wait. You'll get the second dram, plus one more, when I return."

A cloud shifted overhead, revealing the driver's mirthless face. "I'll be needing those two drams now, or you can find your own way home."

Two rats crept cautiously out of a hole in the wall, looked at Lee, then scurried up to the drunk. They sniffed around him for a few moments before setting in to nibble at the discarded contents of his stomach. Lee shuddered and gave another silver coin to the driver.

"The wait'll cost you two more," the man said, pocketing the coins and holding out a calloused hand again.

"Four silver? For a ride to Waterwheel?" Lee pointed to the rickety carriage. "In *this*?"

"That'll buy you as long as it takes to eat a meal," the man said. "And if you get back in time, I'll be needing the final two drams before we set off. Some folks get confused as to what they owe once they get to where they're going."

"You must take me for a fool, man. I'll give you one dram for the wait, not a half-skade more."

The driver picked at his teeth with a fingernail, then flicked whatever it was he had fished out, forcing Lee to jump aside.

He lifted the reins. "Good night to you. This ain't no place for loitering."

Lee frowned. How dare he, the insolent rube. Even in Lee's preposterous disguise, the driver should be able to recognize his betters—Lee had forgone his usual dignified topknot and frogworm pin, opting instead to let his hair hang limp on his shoulders in what he hoped was more of a ruffian look.

He attempted to stare the man down, but now found that he could no longer make out his face at all. He could, however, distinguish the clicking sound the man had used to rouse his horse on the journey here. The carriage moved.

"Wait!" Lee pulled out two more coins and shoved them at the driver. "Do not budge, mind you. I'm a powerful man. You'll be sorry if you cross me."

Though Lee couldn't see the driver's expression, he could feel his eyes on his cheap cotton cloak. "Whatever you say, m'lord." The man picked his teeth again. "Just be quick. Like I said, this ain't no place for loitering."

"Insufferable," Lee muttered as he stepped into the alley. "If he were my driver, I'd have him whipped." He considered having his own driver whipped anyway, just to prevent any such behavior.

Though he pulled the cloak over his nose, not even the dank fabric could compete with the stench that assailed him as he tiptoed past the drunk and his rats.

He rushed into the tavern, closing the door behind him. Smells of roast pork and garlic mixed with odors of sour wine and sweat to form a fetid olfactory cocktail. Still, anything was better than the alley.

Boisterous conversation filled the place, accompanied by what Lee felt were unnecessarily loud eating noises. People held wooden bowls to their lips, slurping as they shoveled food into their mouths with their chopsticks, or else scraped metal tankards or thudded clay cups on the tables. A monstrous burp won out over the clamor and was immediately rewarded by a round of raucous laughter. Lee grimaced.

He scanned the place until he found what he believed must be the dark corner where his contact had told him to wait. Hanging oil lanterns gave the place a tawdry glow, and he held to the edges of the room, hoping to make his way across unobserved.

A serving girl dressed in a tunic with a splotch of grease down the front passed him on the way, balancing a tray full of tankards. "Be with you in a bit, sweetheart," she called to him over her shoulder in a loud, throaty voice.

Lee hunched and walked more quickly, then sat at a heavy table made of blackwood, the same material that had apparently been used to build the beams supporting the ceiling.

It wasn't until he had settled in that he noticed he was not quite alone. In an even darker corner was a man twice his size, with one half-closed eyelid and a misshapen nose that appeared to have been broken in several places. He sat cleaning his fingernails with a large knife.

Catching Lee staring at him, the man snarled. Lee quickly looked away, squeezing himself as far into his corner as space would allow.

Moments later, the serving girl reappeared, a rough bamboo tray tucked under one arm. "I'm Lim. What can I get you?"

His eyes darted briefly to the unsavory character in the shadows. "Is there any place more...private?" he whispered.

Lim glanced over at the man and laughed. "Don't you worry about Druce. He don't never attack nobody first. Unless..." Her eyes wandered to a dark stain on the floor, which had the unmistakable look of something—or someone—that had been dragged.

She pursed her lips thoughtfully. "Just don't say nothing to him. Don't look at him neither, and you'll be fine. Now, if you're hungry there's roast pork, but you'd better order fast because it's nearly gone. Comes with a bowl of rice and baked bread—baked in a real oven," she said proudly. "We've got rice wine, of course, and jinju from the region's own distillery, but that costs a bit more." She took in Lee's cloak with a glance. "The beer's cheap, though, just two skades, and not half bad. Brewed right here by our beloved innkeeper himself." She emphasized "beloved" with a note of sarcasm.

Lee looked over to the bar where a portly man with a greasy ponytail and a heavily stained apron that looked like it might have once been white barked orders at serving girls. Behind the innkeeper, plates and bowls sat on the ledge of a square in the wall that evidently sectioned off the kitchen. He turned to the window and hollered something. A female voice shrieked back.

Lim grinned. "His wife. She's our cook."

A brief shouting match ensued between the couple, which ended when a loaf of bread came hurtling through the window and whacked the innkeeper in the head.

For a moment he stood there rubbing the spot where the bread had hit, picking crumbs from his hair. Then he grabbed the loaf from the floor, dusted it off and blew on it with two quick breaths, and plunked it on a nearby table where two men sat eating.

Lee had once heard of a man in the region who was known to ferment his beer with saliva. He suspected he had found him.

"So what'll it be?" Lim asked, moving the tray to her hip and resting her arm on it.

"I'll have the wine."

As Lee waited for his drink to arrive, he discreetly searched the place for his contact. There were mostly groups of men seated at the tables, with a few rough-looking women thrown in.

At one table, a man with hair bursting out of the neckline of his robe played cards. Beside him was an old smaller man with a gray beard and tattoos all up his arm. He sat nursing a cup of something. Across the table was a young woman who might have been attractive if she hadn't been so unkempt. She slammed a card down and took a swig from her tankard.

A man who was visibly drunk stumbled over to her and spoke in her ear. He reached out to touch her shoulder but she grabbed his little finger and twisted it, forcing him to his knees. Lee winced.

The hairy man at the table threw his head back and laughed, until finally, the old man at the table gave her a stern look and spoke a word. She let the drunk man go, spat on the floor beside him, then spun back around in her chair and folded her arms in a temper.

The man on the floor looked at her resentfully, then staggered off toward a staircase in the far corner.

The narrow, blackwood staircase tilted ten degrees to the left, causing the already stumbling man to have to hold on with both hands to keep from sliding off it all together.

When he was safely at the top, he disappeared down a dark hall just as another man emerged. This second man was dressed in robes of plain, but fine quality linen and, unlike the drunk, looked to be every bit in possession of his wits. He ran his eyes once over the room, searching.

Relief washed over Lee at the sight of him, followed by anger. It was his contact, Hong.

"How dare he keep me waiting in this hovel," Lee grumbled.

Hong laced his fingers and stretched, then turned and disappeared down the hall.

"He must not have noticed me. He wouldn't recognize me dressed like this."

As Lee considered whether to wait or climb the stairs, the warmth of someone sliding up next to him made him start. Then terror flooded him—it was Druce.

The man fixed Lee with one savage eye, then flicked his gaze pointedly to something under the table. Lee followed the movement and gasped: Druce's knife was pointed at Lee's side.

His heart beat wildly, but he tried to keep his head clear. Lim would be back any moment with his wine. She seemed to know this man; surely she could talk him out of whatever insanity he was planning.

Before he could formulate a plan, however, hot breath hit him in the face, rank with beer and stale garlic.

"Time to go for a walk," Druce growled. He grabbed Lee's arm and hoisted him to his feet.

"Now, just a moment," Lee croaked. "I didn't talk to you. Or look at you. And Lim will be here with my drink any time now."

In response, Druce lifted Lee clear off his feet and sailed him over the stain on the floor toward the staircase.

"I—I'll pay you," Lee choked. "Anything you want, Countess Ellie will pay—" His words cut off with a squeak as the knife pressed so hard against him, he could almost hear it slice through his flimsy tunic.

"Quit your blubbering."

Lee searched frantically for Lim. She was on the other side of the room, back turned. He considered screaming, but the press of the knife made him think the better of it.

As Druce sailed him through the room he sent silent pleas for help to anyone who would look at him. But either no one understood or no one cared, because anyone who met his eye looked away again just as quickly.

Druce pulled him effortlessly up the tilting stairs and into the narrow hallway, where blackwood doors dotted plain, whitewashed walls at intervals too close together to belong to rooms of any decent size.

Though light from the tavern filtered up the stairs a certain distance, by the time they arrived at the end of the hall, Lee could only make out the barest of shapes.

Druce removed his hand from Lee's arm, leaving a throbbing handprint in its place.

"Stay put," he growled, and fumbled with the door latch.

Lee couldn't have moved if he tried. He was so terrified he was sure he would wet his trousers. He wanted to devise a clever plan to escape, but found he couldn't think. This was the end, and he would die in a hovel.

The door creaked open and light blinded him as Druce's meaty hand shoved him into the room, making him stumble forward and land on his knees.

When he looked up, he was face-to-face with Hong.

"Nice to see you again, my lord," Hong said, wearing a genial smile. "I see you've met my associate." He jerked his head at Druce, who reached down and hoisted Lee to his feet.

"Y-your associate?" Lee's brush with death had taken away his ability to speak coherently.

"Hope he didn't give you too much of a fright. He can be a bit...intense. Now then, let's get down to business, shall we?"

He led the way to a table with three stools around it, and in the center, a white clay pitcher with three tiny matching cups.

Sitting back against the wall, Hong poured himself a cup of clear liquid, and downed it. Then he filled the other two cups before refilling his own.

Still trembling, Lee obediently slumped onto the stool Hong indicated. He needed something to calm his nerves and suspected whatever had been poured would do the trick.

He picked up the cup in front of him and sniffed. Sharp fumes made his eyes water, but otherwise the drink smelled pleasant, delicious even, like strawberries. He took a generous swallow, then spluttered and coughed. His lips went numb, and his throat and chest burned terribly.

"Nice, isn't it?" Hong said. "It's called Volcano Flower. High-class stuff. What was it, Druce, five drams a bottle?" He chugged it back and nodded approvingly.

Druce pulled his stool so close to Lee their arms touched, then set his knife carefully on the table and picked up his cup, which looked like a toy in his massive hands.

To Lee's surprise, the savage closed his eyes, brought the drink to his nose and inhaled deeply before taking a long, appreciative sip, like a connoisseur.

"So, you'll be happy to know we're all set to clean up those half-breeds for you," came Hong's good-natured voice.

Lee looked into his cup again, his head spinning. "What do you do with the half-breeds that you, er, clean up?"

"Our sponsor has need of them," Hong said. "That's all I know. Now, on to the matter of payment. I assume you brought the gold?"

The question irked him. He felt humiliated by his ineffectiveness in getting what he wanted from the empress, and he resented being questioned by his inferiors even more.

"Things didn't quite go as planned."

Hong leaned forward, resting his arms on the table so that his biceps bulged. "How's that, then?"

Druce rested a hand on his knife, stroking the blade with his thumb.

"Well, the empress didn't exactly go for it. I even tried to get her to give us twenty thousand gold petals instead, but she—"

Hong pounded a fist on the table, jolting the cups—and Lee. "We agreed on a hundred thousand!"

"Yes, about that." Lee cleared his throat. "You see, unbeknownst to me, the countess had sent a letter ahead of me—tying my hands, as it were. It made the letter I had fabricated come off a little awkward. But it makes no difference. The empress was in no mind to give money."

"So you got nothing at all?" Hong looked at Druce, incredulous, then back at Lee. Druce growled.

Lee opened his mouth to say something, but no words came.

"Then we got no further business together," Hong said. "Druce, escort him out the back way."

Druce picked up his knife and scowled, evidently irritated to be called away from his drink. The image of the dark stain on the floor flashed through Lee's mind.

"No, wait!" he said, ducking through Druce's grasp. "Wait, please. Just give me a chance to talk."

Fumbling in his pouch, he grabbed a translucent stone, light pink with dark rose veins. Its gentle glow showed it to be a spirit stone.

"I got this from the empress. You can have it." He held it out with shaking hands.

Hong took it and looked it over. "Nice. What's it do, then?"

"It's a red-violet headache stone. I had the worst headache on my arrival to the Min Palace, and the healer let me use it. Completely cured me in the time it takes to drain a cup. Naturally, I kept it. But it's yours now. Could be useful after a night of indulging. Would also fetch a handsome price with the right merchant. At least one gold petal, I'd say."

Hong showed it to Druce. "What do you think?"

Druce studied it with his good eye. "Upward of a petal."

Hong slipped the stone into his pouch. "All right," he said. "Talk." He poured another round of Volcano Flower for himself and Druce, who appeared placated.

Lee cleared his throat. He needed to regain control of the situation. Thus far, he had been treated shamefully, and furthermore by men so far beneath him they should feel honored to even be sitting in his presence. He would carefully but firmly remind them of their place.

"Now remember that we're in this together," he said, his voice quavering more than he liked. "You're not the only one who lost from this. I was to get a share, too. Not only that, but a man of my position has a reputation to protect."

"I just don't like wasting my time," Hong said, leaning against the wall. "You're the one with the half-breed problem. Our sponsor is happy to leave them to you."

Images of his sister all those years ago, crying on the ground, clothes torn, flashed in Lee's mind. "Let's not be hasty. I've thought of a way we can work together. The empress is sending a delegation to Hanmar to investigate the claims I made, you see. They'll stop at the countess's estate in Westrill first, before moving on to the hamlets, and since both the palace investigator and her daughter will be coming, I thought we could—"

Hong held up a hand and exchanged a look with Druce. "The Min Daughter's traveling to Westrill?"

"Yes," Lee said, nodding vigorously. "And as we all know, an equitess's word on such matters holds all the weight of the empress herself. So I was thinking, if your men can continue the, er, theatrics and such, it will convince her that Ant wielders are real."

Lee stood straighter, more confident, contrasting his body language with Hong's undignified sprawl to highlight his own superior station and lend his words more weight. "She'll take word back, and the empress will have no choice but to send gold. Any amount necessary, I'd wager. We'll hire your men and"—he cleared his throat—"and of course I'll take my small fee for arranging things. Then you can clean up the Ants, as agreed."

Hong looked at Druce. "You think the empress would really send the Min Daughter for something like this?"

Druce looked doubtful.

"I saw her myself," Lee said. "She's traveling with the palace investigator, in the investigator's carriage."

For a long moment, Hong stroked his chin, looking at the ceiling as though calculating. Lee congratulated himself for reigning in the situation. In a few mere moments he had demonstrated his superior planning abilities, and in a few moments more, these hooligans would be falling all over themselves to serve him.

"Change of plans," Hong said. "The delegation never makes it to Westrill."

Lee started. "What?"

"What do you think, Druce? Will they take the Processional route?"

Druce nodded.

Hong considered this, then turned to Lee. "They'll have to ride through Puddletown, in any case. You said you had contacts in the area, men who are willing to work 'in the dark,' as it were?"

Lee frowned. "Yes, but I don't see—"

"Druce, have the boys make sure there's no room at the Round Cello, or any of those other fancy inns in the villages before Puddletown. The princess's delegation can only take rooms at the Laughing Skunk."

"The Laughing Skunk Tavern?" Lee scoffed. "There's no way the palace investigator, much less the Min Daughter, could ever be induced to take such lodgings." The very thought was outrageous. "Anyway, what difference does it make where they sleep?"

"You want your half-breeds taken care of, don't you?"

Lee looked around the room for the first time, noticing the bare walls and lack of windows. He tried to imagine the heir to the throne spending the night in accommodation like this and couldn't.

"They'll simply keep traveling if no suitable lodging is found," he said.

"Not if they arrive late enough. A problem with the carriage wheel, perhaps?" Hong looked at Druce, who nodded. "Our boys can't be seen out in the open, so your contacts will need to see to the wheel," he said, turning to Lee.

Lee stared at one man, then the other. "What in the name of the Six are you planning?"

"Taking down the Min Daughter would weaken the House of Min beyond repair," Hong said easily as he poured another round of drinks. He took a sip and followed it with a long, contented "Ahh."

The casualness of his manner made Lee shiver. Betraying the House of Min had never been his intention, and the thought made him feel sick.

"I can't be involved in anything that would endanger the life of someone from the imperial family. I would be sentenced to death by a thousand cuts! *We* would," Lee said. "Have you thought of that?"

Hong laughed. "Just see to the wheel, we'll take care of the rest. And if they decide to keep traveling through the night"—he shrugged—"even better. I'll have men waiting along the road after dark in both directions. Working on a deserted road at night is even easier than at the Skunk."

He pulled at the seam of his crotch and leaned back on the wall. "And actually, taking down the Min Daughter is exactly what needs to happen. Tell him, Druce."

Druce was busy inhaling deeply from his cup, eyes closed. "Our sponsor supports the weakening of the House of Min."

"The gold we'll get from our sponsor for this job would give our boys the breathing room they need to take care of the Ant problem," Hong said. "That's what you want isn't it?"

Lee's humiliating audience with Empress Zinchen came back to him. The empress had refused to get rid of the Ants, had even dismissed the very idea of them being a threat. The image of his sister returned, and his blood boiled. Those loathsome half-breeds were everywhere, like rats. And like rats, they needed to be exterminated before they contaminated decent society.

On top of that, the Min empress clearly didn't value his talents. She had all but mocked him when he had mentioned his skills as a decipherer of enigmas.

"Who exactly is your sponsor?" Lee asked shakily.

Hong smiled. "Someone high up in the Jeng court."

The Jeng emperor? No, it was ridiculous to think that the sheltered young emperor would have ties with people like these. His regent, then?

He remembered what Empress Zinchen had said about the vice regent being responsible for the Ant regulations in Jeng. So Vice Regent Caliss was their sponsor, Lee thought, feeling satisfied at how easily he had puzzled it out.

"All right, I'll do it." Lee picked up his cup and chugged back the remainder of its contents. Once again, his whole torso was on fire. The room spun around him. When his eyes refocused, he found he was sitting on the floor.

“Good,” Hong said cheerily, lifting Lee to his feet. “With the investigation stopped and the House of Min weakened, our sponsor will have no problem taking care of your Ant problem.”

Hong shook his hand, making Lee lurch forward, then refilled their cups and held his in the air.

“A toast to our new, and improved, arrangement.”

Chapter Seventeen

LIKE CLEAN SNOW

"Bleed him again," Caliss said, holding out a cup.

A young man—her lover of the past three moons—slept on the pallet beside her, bathed in the glow of firelight flickering behind crimson curtains.

She brushed away the dark hair falling into his eyes, then traced his face with the back of her hand. "Darling," she whispered. "So beautiful and brave." She shivered with anticipation, waiting for another taste of his essence.

While the others stood by with bandages, Strond, her chief guard, knelt and sliced the young man's wrist. Thanks to Caliss's concoction, he remained sleeping as rich red filled the chalice in rhythmic spurts.

It had taken persuasion the first time, but the promise of wild pleasures and fine food had finally won him over. Now, he treated the bandages on his wrists like any other aftereffect of their intoxicating nights together.

"Are you sure it's not too much?" Strond asked, fiddling with one of the braids in his beard. "This is the third time tonight."

"The faster I accumulate dawn-essence, the faster I can unite the clans," Caliss said.

She pulled the chalice from his hands and poured her essence into it, a stream of inky shadow no one but her could see. The etchings on the chalice danced frenetically in the firelight, strange creatures swaying in some mysterious ritual.

As they did, the blood yielded its own essence, separating into a clear, iridescent layer that sat on top, like oil on water.

Caliss brought it to her lips and sipped. She had chosen just the right frequency to bleed him. If she did it too many times each moon, it would affect the quality.

But this was perfect. The dawn-essence was deliciously pure, with a subtle, earthy taste, like clean snow, and evaporated off her tongue like strong liquor if not sipped in a quick, steady pull.

I need so much more.

The thought rose up from somewhere within her, and an uncontrollable thirst made her tip back the chalice, gulping.

The taste of blood jolted her. If too much blood mixed in, the essence would dissipate and vanish.

She sipped the rest, carefully avoiding the blood, then cycled the essence through her dawn channels using the breathing techniques prescribed in the *Dawn-Essence Manual*.

Warmth filled her. But then, instead of power trickling into her stone kernel, the warmth simply vanished.

She thrust out the chalice and snapped, "Give me more."

Strond sliced her lover's other wrist.

This time, Caliss sucked in carefully, siphoning the essence off the top.

The pure essence expanded in her dawn channels as she cycled it, and deep in her abdomen, her stone kernel pulsed with anticipation.

With every cycle she completed, more new dawn-essence trickled into her stone kernel. According to the *Dawn-Essence Manual*, reaching the second level of kernel expansion would require far more essence than the first level did.

She was a long way from the second level, but everything counted.

"Poor sod's on his way out," a faraway voice said.

Her stone kernel pulled the essence in greedily. "I need more," she heard herself say.

"Regent, you want me to do something?"

Strond's voice disturbed her, but she tried to focus. If she stopped cycling now, the essence that remained in her dawn channels would be lost.

"Regent?"

She snapped out of her trance. "What?"

Strond jerked his thumb toward her lover.

Her eyes took in the blood-soaked sheets, then the bright red bandages covering his wrists.

"Put pressure on it!" she said, leaping to her feet.

She darted to a table at the end of the room, opened a small chest, and pulled out a black porcelain ointment box.

"Smear this on the wound," she said, throwing it to Strond. "I can't afford to lose him."

Grabbing tree bark shavings from another drawer and shoving them into her mouth, she chewed, then pushed the shavings past the young man's lips.

He made a weak groan.

Caliss massaged his chest, trying to keep the blood flowing into his heart instead of out, but the bandages appeared to get redder.

"Can't you press any harder?"

"It's too late, Regent."

"Shut up and press!"

She clapped her hands over Strond's, pushing as hard as she could.

A long, slow breath streamed from her lover's lips. Then nothing.

Caliss kept the pressure on.

"He's gone," Strond said, pulling his hand away.

She stared at her lover's beautiful face, unable to do anything else.

But when his face turned pale and his lips grayed with death, loathing filled her. She had been sure this one would bring her to the next stone kernel level. She had been cheated.

"How could you do this to me!" she screamed, flinging aside the drapes, and then she was throwing silk cushions, kicking over goblets.

When exhaustion calmed her at last, she glared at her guards. Five towering, muscular men avoided her gaze.

Vindur, the youngest, scratched his head through tousled blond hair. Others played with their beards or stared at the floor.

"I'm terribly vexed, Strond," she said, trying to regain control of herself. "A source of blood this rich is hard to find."

"Don't worry, Regent. You'll find another by next new moon. Men his age are always looking for a good time."

She sniffed in irritation. "If it were that easy, don't you think I'd have ten of them? I have to choose carefully."

She grabbed her outer robe from the floor and shrugged it on. The smell of it disgusted her, an unsavory blend of lamb grease and body musk on top of her usual incense.

The taste of tree bark made her mouth pucker and she wiped her lips.

It just didn't make sense. Bark from the dragon-blood tree was supposed to stop bleeding, but it had made him bleed more.

"Didn't the old herbalist say it did both?" Strond asked.

Caliss looked up sharply, annoyed to have spoken aloud.

"This is your fault," she said, tying her sash. "You should have been monitoring him." She looked around at her guards. "All of you."

Her sixth guard, Krigo, still snored by the wall, a testament to his unchecked consumption of liquor the night before. Several jugs littered the floor around him.

Next to Caliss, a low table with scrollwork legs held the remnants of a joint of roast lamb and a bowl of fruit. She grabbed an apple and threw it at him.

The apple hit his chest. Krigo awoke with a lunge but stopped when his gaze landed on the chalice, and instead, he went to stand with the others.

"Look at this," she said, motioning to her dead lover.

Vindur stared at the body for several breaths, then grinned, gold tooth flashing, and nudged the body with a foot. A limp arm slid off the pallet and onto the fur-covered floor. "Look, Regent. He's all floppy."

"Stop it, you oaf." Caliss grabbed the ointment box before any blood touched it, then closed its gold filigree latch and returned it to the drawer.

"And it's Vice Regent, not Regent," she said. "Be careful how you throw that title around."

She picked up the chalice and ran a finger over its etchings, scowling. They sat motionless now that the chalice had absorbed all the blood, the inside of the bowl once again pristine.

"And just how long should we be careful?" Krigo said, crossing his arms over his chest. "While you satisfy your lusts, the Ghenz are still without a land."

"I'm not here to satisfy my lust. I need to pull extra dawn-essence from somewhere, and man's blood just happens to be the richest source. These things take time."

"You dishonor us with this wait. You dishonor your mother." He spat. It landed partly on the stone floor, partly on one of the furs.

"Krigo is a fool," Strond said, and slapped the side of the other man's head.

Krigo ducked away from a second slap. "Am I? What's stopping her from taking the title right now?"

"I've told you before. The Shazori Council has to elect me." Or rather, she would force an election. Once the Shazori Council realized the united Ghenz clans were backing her, they'd be too scared not to vote her in. But it had to be all the clans—a threat from her band of guards would not have the same effect. "I can't simply stroll in and take my husband's place. House Shazori would throw me out. All the people would."

Of course, becoming imperial regent of Jeng was merely a stepping stone. Once she came into her true power under the Watani, nothing and no one would be able to oust her.

Krigo shrugged. "So then we'll wipe out House Shazori."

"No one is wiping out my house," Caliss said.

Krigo glared. "Your mother was Ghenz. You are Ghenz."

"I am both. And I have to wait till the right time."

"Or maybe you already know the wise women won't acknowledge you as Mattah. Maybe you just can't work the relic," Krigo said, feet planted, legs apart.

Quick as a flash, Strond struck him in the mouth, drawing blood.

Krigo's massive knife was out at once, with Strond's following almost as fast.

The other guards moved, two men to a side, pulling the opponents apart.

"You dare insult a Mattah?" Strond growled.

"There hasn't been a Mattah in centuries." Krigo spat on the floor again.

"Enough!" Caliss forced a stream of dawn-essence into the chalice, lighting up the room with a blinding flash.

The men shielded their eyes. Thankfully, the chalice only required a first stone kernel level to activate.

Strond sheathed his blade, holding Krigo's gaze.

Krigo shot Strond a black look as he sheathed his own, then wiped his bleeding mouth with the back of his arm. "If she's the Mattah, why not go to the wise women right now? She'd have the might of the Ghenz clans behind her today. They'd elect her as regent tomorrow."

"I *can* operate the relic," she lied, "but to do it right, I need more essence."

He would never know the difference. The only thing certain was that if she asked the wise women to test her with the relic right now, she would fail. Then the Ghenz would kill her for impersonating a sacred Mattah.

A knock sounded at the door, and a maid entered.

With downcast eyes, the girl knelt, then bowed till her forehead touched the floor, light brown braids splaying out on either side of her.

"The regent is waking, my lady," she said softly without looking up. "He's asking for you."

Caliss walked to a red settee and sat calmly, running her hand over the soft brocade. A carved bronze looking glass hung from the stone wall opposite, and she stared at her own reflection.

"Do you see anything unusual here, Skada?" she asked.

"No, my lady."

"What, then, do you see?"

The maid answered without hesitation. "I see my lady preparing for the day."

Caliss leaned toward the looking glass and rubbed smudges of kohl liner from beneath her eyes, vestiges of a long night. Her pupils were large in the dim light, making her blue eyes seem almost black.

"You may go."

The girl rose and backed out, eyes never leaving the floor.

"You're all dismissed," Caliss said. "Get to your posts. Strond, attend my rooms at once."

"Yes, Regent."

She made an irritated gesture at the body on the floor. "And somebody...clean that up."

They all bowed, but not as low as they ought.

Chapter Eighteen

A WOMAN'S TENDER HEART

The regent gripped his trousers to drag shriveled legs over the side of the bed where sunlight fell on the canopied bed frame, making its mythical carvings glow.

Caliss fixed a smile onto her face and glided into the room. "You're up early, dearest," she said, kissing her husband's bristly cheek.

Loreshi glanced in the direction of her chamber. "Dressed already?" He closed his eyes and pressed fingertips to his temples, sighing. "I've been dreaming of the mermaids again."

"You must resist those dreams, Loreshi, darling. Promise me you will."

A maid bustled toward the door, leaving with a chamber pot and a pile of dirty linens.

Caliss grabbed her arm. "Get the healer's apprentice. We need the lord regent's medicine right away."

The girl hurried out.

They had to keep this illness from progressing for as long as possible.

"There's something I need to discuss with you," Loreshi said.

She perched on the yellow velvet couch beside the bed. "Yes, dearest?"

But before he could answer, a coughing fit took him. His face contorted, veins bulging, eyes wide and desperate.

The sight repulsed her.

She focused on the bed frame instead, where a goat-like creature with a woman's head and a wicked expression played the flute for a group of mesmerized shepherds.

Every splutter and choke made her wince; Loreshi needed to stay alive long enough for her to secure her position.

The maid bustled in, followed by the healer's apprentice, pushing a cart laden with porcelain bowls and boxes of herbs. The boy tapped two fingers on the pressure points of Loreshi's chest, and the fit ended.

Caliss let out a relieved breath. Her sources had been right: the apprentice was gifted in the nurturing of medicinal essence. He was half-Ghenz like herself, though he didn't look it. Both points were an advantage. She had secured his apprenticeship personally, a fact unknown to anyone but the boy.

The boy removed a handful of herbs from a wooden box and crushed them into a tureen of steaming water. The smell of licorice root drifted out, along with something that reminded Caliss of fresh hay. He blew on the tureen and stirred.

Loreshi watched him, leaning against the bed frame, looking exhausted.

"You have a council meeting this morning, don't you?" he said to Caliss. "There's something we need to discuss."

You already said that.

"Yes, dearest?"

"How are my heirs getting on?"

She prickled at the term—not that she had ever wanted to bear him an heir, but still. What passed for his heirs now were cousins so distant they might as well have been Min.

"What did you want to know about them?"

"Their maturity. Their readiness to lead. Fen, for instance."

"Fen?" She chuckled softly. "Mulish as ever."

He frowned. "Jiro, then."

"Dough-faced and self-important."

A patient half-smile. "An unbridled tongue is unbecoming in one so pretty. Now, no more jesting. I need a serious answer."

She hadn't been jesting, but returned his smile anyway. "If you want the truth, the council is like a pack of dogs, constantly competing for bones among themselves, everyone wanting to be on top. No one works toward higher goals." Like herself.

Loreshi's face grew perplexed.

The apprentice placed a bowl and spoon on the table next to Caliss's couch, shifting the items on his cart to reveal a golden herb box—the longevity herbs for the Jeng emperor, whom the apprentice would visit next.

The boy turned as though to leave, but as he did, Caliss slipped a small red vial from her sleeve, shifting so none but the boy could see—a precaution in case of the unexpected arrival of servants.

He opened the box just long enough for her to tip in three drops from her vial. A puff of red smoke appeared, and he closed the box on it. The whole operation was finished in the space of a breath.

As the apprentice left, Caliss filled the spoon with Loreshi's medicine, the clink of porcelain waking him from a light sleep.

"I feel my life ebbing," he mumbled.

"Then you must take better care of your health," she said, bringing the spoon to his lips.

He turned his head away. "It's bitter. Makes me cough."

"You're coughing because of excess internal humidity. This medicine will help."

"Medicine can't help me, Caliss. Not anymore. I have to choose a successor, before it's too late."

Caliss stiffened. "So soon?"

If Loreshi named a successor, the council would never elect her, even with the Ghenz clans' intimidation. The Shazori wouldn't risk flouting the law by rejecting a named heir; it would give any dissenters fuel to incite a revolt among the people. It was the same reason Caliss couldn't use the Ghenz clans to simply take over; she needed a formal vote.

And if she didn't secure this position, everything would be lost. When the Watani returned to rule Shudon, they would only grant power to those cunning enough to have already claimed it; the messenger had made that point clear.

"Your health is improving, Loreshi, darling. You mustn't think of such things." She smiled and held out the spoon again.

He swallowed, then started coughing uncontrollably. Caliss motioned for the maid to hold him upright, but the hacking continued.

As he coughed, his eyes grew wide and strangely focused, as though seeing into a realm beyond sight.

"They grasp for me," he wheezed. "They stare at me with their milk-white eyes, seaweed hair fanning out around them. They pull me deeper...deeper. The labyrinths are never-ending."

Caliss's hand trembled, and the medicine spilled. Without thinking, she reached out and shook him. "You have to stay alive!"

He flinched, and the coughing ceased, his eyes refocusing on her.

Fearing the outburst had revealed her true intent, she dropped her gaze to the spoon, and brought it to his mouth.

Loreshi swallowed, grimacing. "You have a woman's tender heart, Caliss," he said, giving her hand a squeeze. He brought it to his lips and kissed it.

It was a sincere, close-eyed kiss, the kind she had scoffed at whenever she had seen men do it in the past.

He had never kissed her hand before.

Tears flooded her vision, and she stroked his cheek. Once she was voted in as regent, she would have to end his life, of course. But whenever she imagined it, the thought pained her.

She fed him another spoonful. "Do you remember the day you saved me?" she said, voice hoarse with emotion. In her mind's eye, the long yellow rug and the polished wood floor transformed into black dirt with team lines drawn into it.

He nodded, eyes sympathetic. "I remember. Nobo had pinned you."

Nobo had laughed as she thrashed and screamed. Feelings of shame and fury from that day came flooding back. She would never be held down again.

Loreshi traced his thumb across her hand, and she took a breath, mastering herself.

"You walked in like a hero and pulled him off," she said. "When Mama told me of our betrothal years later, I was so happy."

Maybe she didn't have to kill him after all. Maybe he could simply step down from the regency.

She looked at him earnestly. "Why don't you make me your successor?"

She had been sitting at the head of the council table for twenty years, after all—when Loreshi could no longer hide his illness. She had more than proved herself.

He gave an indulgent smile. "A woman wants to lead the council."

Caliss stared at him, incredulous. "Every regent in history has been a woman—your mother held power for thirty years."

"And her soft heart almost took the Shazori down. If I hadn't seen to the empress in time, the regency would have been dissolved." He shook his head. "Women simply don't have the strength to make the hard choices."

"Have you forgotten who's taken charge of the poisonings since your illness?" she said.

Loreshi had taken ill only five years after seizing the regency from his sisters, and though he had successfully eliminated the empress, it had fallen to Caliss to ensure the empress's son never reached twenty—the age of majority—all while leaving him healthy enough to produce an heir. Now she was doing the same with the son's son—the current emperor—who, at nineteen, was weakening daily. And all these years, Loreshi had never once acknowledged her impeccable work.

Irritated, she paced the yellow rug, stepping through the stream of sunlight illuminating the red logograms for wisdom and integrity.

"There's no use pouting," Loreshi said. "The council tolerates you in my absence, but they'll never again see a woman at their head."

Red framed the edges of her vision, and she gripped the blanket. Her nostrils flared with the effort of resisting the urge to smother him, but she mastered herself again. She always did.

Releasing the blanket, she sat on the edge of the bed and propped a bolster behind his head. "If Empress Bethari had birthed a daughter all those years ago, the council would still be comprised of women. Surely you see that, darling. You could never have changed it. And do you know something else? I'm the reason people think the Thana imperial bloodline has a genetic disorder. I was the one who developed a poison subtle enough to mimic the progression of a natural illness. Before me, people were getting suspicious."

He sighed wearily and patted her hand. "Yes, my flower. You have good ideas. That is why I need you to help me choose between Fen and Jiro."

Something on her hand caught his attention. He drew it in and studied her fingernails, face steeped in disapproval.

"What was it this time? A rabbit? A dog?"

She balled her hands behind her back, inwardly cursing herself for having washed them so hastily. "A rabbit," she said.

"When are you going to stop? Real longevitists don't drink blood."

"Well, I had to work with what I could get."

"That technique was never meant to be used, or even found. Those texts were hidden for a reason."

"Never meant to be used? The most powerful people in history used it."

He puffed disdainfully. "The Watani are a fable. Those texts were written by blood longevitists, rebels banned by their sects long ago."

Her eyebrows twitched. The *Dawn-Essence Manual* had been meant to be found—by *her*. Twenty years before, she had discovered the Watani writings in a hidden place, but recently, a letter appeared there, claiming to know who she was. She had been shaken—she had supposed the

Watani to be long extinct—but when she replied, she had received instructions to deliver her response in person.

Loreshi was a fool. The Watani were no fable—they were frighteningly real.

Her mind raced back to the alleyway the night she had first seen the messenger. The hooded figure had been leaning against the wall, arms folded, far less tall and broad than Caliss had imagined. When it spoke, she realized it was female.

A tilt of the head had revealed a scaly face beneath her cowl, with slit-pupiled eyes and nostrils flaring where a nose should have been. The messenger had bared rows of jagged teeth, and in one lightning-fast strike, killed an unseen intruder, then kicked his body aside and licked her knife.

Caliss had frozen as the messenger's clawed hand settled on her shoulder—the soft, scaly cheek brushing hers as she whispered in hissing tones, releasing the smell of old fish from her breath—then she'd spun away, cloak flaring out behind her as she leaped atop a wall.

But Loreshi was always dismissing her. She wished she could leave him alive just so she could watch him grovel in the dirt when he saw how wrong he was.

"If they are a fable," Caliss said, rising, "then a fable has served me well. I'm fifty-three years old, and most people mistake me for thirty." Her lovers usually thought she was younger.

He squeezed his eyes shut, pressing fingertips between them. "We still need to speak of my heir, and now I have a headache. Give me a moment."

She reached into her stone kernel, looking for reassurance that she was on the right track, but all she found was regret at how empty her kernel still felt. It might take many moons before she reached the second stone kernel level. And more than one lover at a time was out of the question; the kind of blood she needed was simply too hard to find.

Wasn't there anything that would help her progress faster? The Ghenz wise women could no doubt offer wisdom, but she feared them. Though she wouldn't have to go claiming to be the long-awaited Mattah—at least not yet. Perhaps she could simply talk with them. She had heard they helped those they favored.

Would they favor her?

Another violent cough contorted Loreshi's face, and she shuddered with disgust.

She raised her voice above the noise. "If you have a headache, my dear, you should rest. I need to go prepare for the council."

Then she walked out, leaving the repulsive hacking behind.

Chapter Nineteen

BROKEN JOURNEY

"Hanmar Province!" Ingan announced on the sixth day.

Tori looked through the carriage door, which he had left open to let in the fresh air. Rice terraces, lit up by the noonday sun, swept down around them in deepening shades of green, then in the distance, transformed into mounds with what looked like wavy lines drawn on them by an artist to represent rippling water.

"Are you sure we'll reach House Capel before nightfall?" Tori asked. By her estimate, they were around fifty fen away from the noblewoman's house where they would spend the night.

"As long as we—begging your pardon, Princess—don't stop too long for the meal."

"That won't be a problem," Tori said. "I'm so hungry I could eat a whole teahouse in half a candle-burn."

Though they had left at dawn as planned, a faulty horseshoe had forced them to make an unexpected stop at a smithy. The repair had taken forever, and though it was now long past midday, they had not yet stopped for a meal.

"There's one nice village coming, if you don't mind holding on," Ingan said. "Though it'll be a bit rougher for a while."

"Rougher? My backside already feels like a horse trampled it."

Her only respites since they had left the smooth paving stones of the Grand Processional Way four days earlier were her nights spent at inns, sleeping in impossibly hard beds.

"Rougher villages, Princess. This here region is known as the outhouse of Hanmar, if you'll pardon my using the term. At least that's what they called it when I lived in the province a while back."

Elnora snickered on the opposite side of the table.

"Named for Puddletown," he said. "The village smells like a puddle of..." He stopped himself. "Anyways, the province transforms after that; north and south Hanmar are like night and day. But we'll pass through Puddletown real quick, late afternoon, if all goes well, and just before that, there's a nice village where you can buy food."

"Are you sure staying at House Capel is wise?" Elnora asked, plucking a white stone from the board in front of her and holding it between two fingers. Elnora had had the presence of mind to bring along a game of Disdain to break up the monotony. "Why not just stay at the nice village?"

Tori pushed a black stone forward. "No more inns. I need at least one good night's sleep before talking to Countess Ellie. I have to be able to think straight."

Elnora didn't look convinced. "But what if the empress contacted Lady Capel?"

"She's more likely to contact Countess Ellie. But any messenger will be two days behind us."

At least, she hoped so. Now that she thought of it, Yumay hadn't seemed confident she could delay Marne for that long. And a messenger on horseback would be faster than Tori's carriage.

"Thank the Six I made it out," she breathed.

Elnora studied the board. "Believe me, Princess, there are worse places than the palace." She placed her stone with a soft click.

"Not for me," Tori said. "Not anymore."

They pulled onto a dirt lane that stretched ahead of them for many fen, crossing several villages consisting mainly of tall wood buildings jammed together and decorated on every floor with a succession of windows draped with laundry.

As they rode past one village, a family of Ants on the roadside drew Tori's attention. Five little children between the ages of three and six—twins and triplets, by Tori's guess—dug in the dirt, shoving whatever they found into their mouths, while a young, weary-faced mother sat leaning against a tree, nursing a baby on each breast. Silver hair glinted on every head.

Tori rapped on the carriage wall, and they rolled to a stop.

"They look hungry," she said, and jerked her chin at a bag on the bench beside Elnora.

"I'm sorry, Princess. We finished last night's buns this morning."

Of course. And if they had had anything left, she would have eaten it herself by now. "Give me a dram, then," she said.

Elnora reached into the pouch very slowly. "I know it's sad, Princess, but if we're going to reach House Capel before nightfall, we can't feed every Ant we see. This is the fifth family today."

"I didn't know there were so many."

Elnora handed her the silver coin. "You've only got three drams left."

"That can't be right. I thought I had two hundred."

"That was six days ago."

Tori's mind went to Veyli, from her childhood. "There was a time when an Ant was my only friend. When I help them, I feel somehow like I'm helping her."

"Where is she now?"

Tori turned away. "That was a long time ago. Anyway, when the drams are finished, I'll still have three gold petals left for the journey."

Her gaze found the family again. The children's wide eyes were studying the carriage with curiosity, while the mother's showed concern.

"Come to think of it, give me a gold petal," Tori said.

Elnora pressed her lips together and took out a string with three small golden flowers hanging from it by their square-cut centers. She untied it and slid off a flower.

Tori nodded toward the family. "Let them have it."

"That's very generous of you, Princess," Elnora said, unable to hide the apprehension on her face. "This will feed them well for at least two moons."

As the ride continued, the road sloped upward, and the stones on the Disdain board slid so much Elnora had to pack it away. She took out a small book with a brown paper cover and started reading silently, scoffing out loud now and then, while Tori stared out the door, thinking of the Well of Dissolution.

She opened the bamboo scroll she had taken from the Lore Room and ran her gaze over the map. Its exact location was unclear; Tori could only see that it was located in the lands behind Hanmar Manor. Which made her position tricky.

Once again, she considered how to get Countess Ellie to reveal its location. Though the countess would never refuse a direct request from the Min Daughter, Tori needed to find out without asking directly; she couldn't risk her mother, or anyone else, thinking Tori needed it for herself.

She had already talked through some possible approaches with Elnora, but since Ingan could hear much of what they said unless they whispered, she hadn't said a lot; she didn't want to spend the journey whispering. Not that she doubted Ingan's loyalty, but the less he knew, the better for him.

The carriage rolled to a halt, and soon, Ingan was yelling for someone to move. A crowd of people blocked the street—none of them paying him or the carriage any mind; their attention was on a man in a circular thatch hat.

The man smacked together two bamboo stalks with a loud *clack-clack*—a roadside storyteller. Tori leaned forward, peering through the carriage door. She had never seen one in person before.

"Should I clear a path, Princess?" Ingan asked, placing a hand on his horsewhip.

She shook her head. "They won't be here all day."

The storyteller put down his sticks and started beating a small drum. "Listen, one and all, to a story of long ago! This is a tale of the Third Age, a tale of Ishairo the Sunderer."

He beat the drum in time as he spoke, the soft, steady rhythm giving his words an entrancing quality.

"During the Black Reign, when Shekahai's twisted creatures roamed freely on the face of Arizan, a swarm of mogs multiplied in the shadows, emerging every moon to devour peaceful villagers.

"One day, they entered the village of Ji. They swelled themselves to unnatural heights and vomited molten fire onto the people's houses. When the villagers fled, the mogs shot their spiky fur at them, like poisoned darts."

The people's wide eyes were fixed on the storyteller.

"Ishairo was only a youth in those days, a lad of fourteen or so. He was on his way home from a long voyage in the mountains with his father, Banguan. Banguan, a great martial hero, had been training his son in the way of the bow.

"They sat down just outside the walls of Ji to eat a meal of bread and water. But before they could take their first bite, screams rose from inside the village.

"Ishairo sprang to his feet and, against his father's warnings, rushed through the gate. Several villagers already lay dead on the ground, the black marks of mog darts creeping across their skin like a poisoned net. Others ran as the mogs pursued them, the entire village on fire."

The storyteller's drumbeats picked up their pace.

"Banguan, intent on saving his son, sought Ishairo everywhere, but he was unable to find him in the chaos. For the fact was, the lad had already disappeared behind a house. He had noticed a mog following a little girl there, and went after them.

"The house blazed as a towering mog stalked toward the girl—she was only six—licking its ravenous lips. For although mogs will eat anyone, they prefer those with tender, untainted flesh."

The children in the crowd stared at the storyteller with horrified fascination.

"The little girl stood frozen in fear," he said, "tears streaming down her rosy cheeks. But Ishairo would not have it so."

The drumbeats intensified.

"He drew his blade and ran to meet the fearsome beast, sword glowing with righteous fury, then leaped into the air, bringing the sword down toward the mog with the intention of cleaving it in two.

"But the monster rounded on him and shot out its spikes—*fwit, fwit, fwit*—into Ishairo's flesh. The lad dropped to the ground, dying, sword sliding from his hand."

The drumbeats slowed, and the storyteller's listeners gaped. Some of the children covered their eyes.

"The mog, having dealt with his adversary, turned again to the little girl and bared its razor-sharp teeth. It had only now to make one leap, to tear into her tender flesh.

"Ishairo, though barely able to move, grabbed one of the burning spikes buried in his body and yanked it out. Then, with the last of his strength, he scraped the spike across his sword—which, as all of you know," the storyteller said, eyes bright, "held Ishairo's stone kernel. Blood and poison dripped from the spike onto the sword. Then suddenly, the sword flashed blue, absorbing both spike and poison."

The drumbeats rolled.

"Ishairo leaped to his feet, totally cured. His sword had given him immunity against mog darts!"

The listeners cheered.

"And so, while the mog's attention was turned toward the girl, Ishairo, using the force of his dawn-essence, jumped high in the air, sailing above the mog. He plunged the point of the sword down into the monster's back and straight through its heart in a gush of black blood.

"Then, having saved the girl, Ishairo shot through the village, his sword aglow, slaying every mog in sight.

"Now, the mother of mogs had been watching it all from a rooftop, and intended to make the lad pay for killing her children. At that moment Banguan, unaware of her up on the roof, ran to the house where she stood, looking around frantically for his son. She made the connection between them. He and Ishairo were clearly outsiders, being the only ones not trying desperately to escape. For though mogs are evil, they are clever, you know," the storyteller said, tapping his head. "She turned her sinister eyes on Banguan and expanded her chest, intent on consuming him with her fiery vomit.

"At that very moment, Ishairo ran into the square and spotted his father beneath the mog's gaze. But alas, he also knew he was too far away to help.

"So, grabbing his bow, he aimed it the way his father had taught him, and drew back the string. Just as the mother of mogs opened her mouth and leaped toward his father, Ishairo let his arrow fly.

"The mother of mogs plummeted to the ground and landed at his father's feet, shot through the heart. Black blood spurted into the square.

"Banguan, seeing the bravery of his son and also that he had learned the lessons of archery, did not discipline him for his disobedience of running into the village, but instead, as always, gave him a nod of approval.

"And this, friends, is how Ishairo saved the village of Ji!"

The listeners erupted into a round of applause.

"Thank you for listening to my true story," the storyteller said, holding out a metal plate. "My name is Old Man Fung. That's right, just like the song, but without the talking donkey."

At this, people dropped skades into the plate and left.

"I don't think I've heard that one before," Elnora said, as the carriage rolled forward again.

"It almost sounded like something from *The Lesser Works of the Peoples of Shudon*," Tori said, her gaze falling on the bamboo scroll in her lap.

"Have you figured out what you're going to say to Countess Ellie?"

Tori ignored her tingling nerves. "I'll think of something."

They drove in silence for a time before reaching the village Ingan had told them of. It was far nicer than Tori had expected, given what she had seen of Hanmar so far. Tori and Elnora walked past its mud walls, leaving Ingan to guard the carriage.

A pretty building with a wood-and-stone exterior greeted them the moment they cleared the gate. Potted flowers stood on either side of its doorstep, and octagonal paper lanterns graced the eaves, blowing back and forth across a brightly painted sign that read *The Round Cello*.

Tori raised an eyebrow. "Not bad for the outhouse of Hanmar."

Several paces away, food stalls lined the dirt road, with crowds of people gathered around them.

"It's hard to believe so many people live here," Tori said, moving toward the stalls.

But as she came closer, the tired faces and ragged clothes seemed out of place. Filthy hands stretched eagerly toward a stall handing out bowls of soup.

"Find out what's going on," she said to Elnora.

Elnora disappeared into the crowd, then returned a short while later. "Refugees," she said. "A nearby village was attacked by Ghenz raiders."

A disproportionate number of Ant families stood by, each with numerous children. Tori's mother was right: the Ghenz were a lawless, merciless bunch, a plague oozing over from Jeng.

"No Ants!" the soup man shouted, twisting to avoid one of the families reaching toward him with outstretched hands, then giving a bowl to someone else.

"How dare he?" Tori said, striding forward, but Elnora stood in her way.

"Let me go, Princess. You never know, you might be recognized."

A small commotion ensued as Elnora argued with the seller. He continued serving soup to the humans, shaking his head and waving his free hand whenever Elnora spoke. She was getting nowhere.

Tori pushed through the crowd, frustrated to not be able to reveal who she really was.

She held up a gold petal. “How much soup will this buy?”

The man looked at her, astonished.

“How much?” she repeated.

“About two thousand.”

“Good.” She slapped the petal onto the wooden counter. “Feed the Ants.”

But instead of taking the money, the man’s face reddened angrily. “The mayor gave instructions to feed *people*. She won’t take kindly to wasting the village resources on half-breeds.”

“Ants *are* people,” Tori said, her neck growing hot.

Families pushed past her, reaching for soup.

With a grunt of disgust, she snatched up the gold petal and walked to the bun merchant across the road.

“You have anything against feeding Ants?” she said, with a nod at his stacks of bamboo steamers.

He grinned, revealing several missing teeth. “I got nothing against gold.” Apparently he had been watching her exchange with the soup man.

“Good,” Tori said. “See to it that you feed *only* Ants until this runs out.”

He dipped his head, then slipped the petal into his robe and started hailing over Ants and passing out buns. Droves of women, men, and children with feathers or bark on their skin, shoved cloud buns into their mouths with teary-eyed gratitude.

Suddenly, Ingan ran through the gate, panting and looking around. His eyes landed on Tori, and he rushed over.

“Begging your pardon, Princess, but we’d best leave. As it is, it’s not certain we’ll make it before nightfall.” He rushed out again.

Tori glanced at the sky, taking in the angle of the sun. “I had no idea we’d been here so long.”

“And you still haven’t eaten,” Elnora said. She motioned to the pretty inn near the village gate. “The Round Cello looks like a nice place. Why don’t we stay here for the night?”

"No more inns," Tori said.

They arrived back at the carriage to find Ingan brandishing his whip at two greasy-haired men. After shooting Tori an evil look, they fled.

Ingan scowled. "That lot's been slinking around here the whole time you were gone, but when I got back just now, they were actually touching the carriage. No chance to steal, though, I think. They didn't seem to be carrying anything."

They rolled on again, but by the time Ingan announced Puddletown, the sky had darkened with night and rain clouds.

They arrived at a gray village whose gate was more of an idea than an actual barrier. A large frame had been cobbled together using battered wood, without even a symbolic wall to hold it up. Tori was surprised to see that the main road, instead of going past the village, as usual, actually veered down a dirt path leading straight through it.

When they had ridden for about the time it would take a candlewick to catch, long wooden buildings flanked them on either side. The quality of the road forced them to roll very slowly, and Tori bounced in her seat as the carriage jerked through potholes and what seemed like randomly placed cobblestones.

Open doors dotted the length of the long buildings, which Tori at first thought were the rooms of a single house. But a brief glance inside the rooms as they passed revealed different families, each sharing the small space.

The smell of urine and excrement grew so strong that Tori had to shut the carriage door and cover her nose. She peered at the road through the windowpane, expecting to find raw sewage, but all she saw was how uncomfortably close the buildings were on either side of them. Anyone standing outside their house could reach out and touch the carriage without leaving their front step.

Thankfully, only a few people stood outside in the growing gloom, lighting the lanterns by their doors and gaping unapologetically at the carriage as it passed.

When Ingan stopped to light the carriage lanterns, the sky finally broke in a heavy shower, and people began closing their doors. On one side of them, though, the door remained open despite the rain, and through her streaming window, Tori saw a group of people walking from the back of the room to surround a firepit, where an old woman leaned over an enormous pot nestled among coals.

The people kissed their fingertips and tapped them once on their hearts—she was evidently the family matriarch—then everyone squatted around the pot and reached in with their chopsticks.

"What are they doing?" Tori asked.

Elnora gave her a questioning look. "They're eating dinner."

"I can see that, but why are they squatting?"

"Because they have nothing to sit on."

As the carriage started rolling again, Tori spotted another family doing the same. The sight sat heavy on her chest. How did people live like this?

One long house row came to an end, and a few paces later, another began. This one, however, had no light streaming out of doors, no hanging lanterns to illuminate the darkened street. People lurked in the shadows under dripping eaves, arms folded across their chests. The potholes had turned into muddy puddles that splashed with every bump, and the carriage lanterns reflected off the wet ground in pools of liquid light.

The feeling of being watched grew on Tori, and she rolled down her curtain.

"How much farther to House Capel?" Tori asked Ingan, cracking the door.

"Another twenty fen," he said.

"Can't you go any faster?"

As though in response, a massive jolt rocked the carriage, throwing her and Elnora sideways. The carriage stopped, leaning heavily.

A moment later, Ingan stuck his head in.

"There's a problem with the wheel," he said.

"Well, hurry up and fix it. I want to be out of here as soon as possible."

"Yes, Princess."

But by the time he opened the door again, the road was pitch-black.

"I've never seen such a thing," he said, wiping his face on one sleeve. "Three of the spokes broke clean through, like they were sawed. The wheel caved in."

A few paces away, the red glow of pipes lit up the faces of two men, who then vanished beneath the dripping eaves.

Elnora cast an uncomfortable look in their direction. "We need to leave, Princess."

"There used to be an inn in these parts," Ingan said. "It was called the Laughing Skunk, if memory serves me, though I never visited myself. Want me to take a look around and see if it still exists?"

Tori nodded.

The moment the door closed behind him, Elnora drew a small knife from her pack, gripping it like she expected to thrust it into someone at any moment.

Tori raised an eyebrow.

Elnora shrugged. "You never know."

Thankfully, she didn't need it. After an uncomfortably long stretch of time, Ingan stuck his head in again.

"It's still around," he said, and glanced down the road ahead, now invisible beyond the light cast by the carriage lanterns. "I guess it's better than walking twenty fen in the dark."

He pulled his hood forward to keep off the rain. "I'm no fighting man, Princess, and the roads outside Puddletown are far away from help. Sometimes robbers wait there to try their chances, sometimes not. But even if there aren't robbers..." He tilted his head at the pipe-smoking men. "Someone else will take the horses if we leave them to go to House Capel. And if we take them along, we'll have to lead them, seeing as you ladies don't ride, so I expect we'd be tempting thieves either way on a dark road." He shrugged. "Still, it's not for me to decide. You give the order, Princess. I'll follow."

"Seems to me we're risking the horses even at the Laughing Skunk," Elnora said. "I wouldn't trust the stabling anywhere in this village."

"And you'd be right not to," Ingan said. "No, if you stay at the inn, I'll sleep in the carriage, make sure no one troubles it. People don't usually trouble a man in a carriage right outside someone's front door. And if they did"—he patted his horsewhip—"they'd have a sore time of it. In the morning, I'll find some honest soul to help us get the wheel fixed. There are still a few such people about."

"Or we could go back to the Round Cello," Elnora said. "It's closer than House Capel."

"That's a popular inn in these parts," Ingan said, "and I guess you can see why now. This time of night, they'd only have sleeping space under the tables—and that's if you're lucky."

Elnora frowned. "Under the tables?"

Tori shook her head. "Either way, we'd be walking in the dark. I'd rather not be going backward."

"It would be better to walk backward a hundred fen than to spend the night in this place," Elnora said.

If they went to House Capel, there was a risk of meeting robbers. But that wasn't certain, and when they arrived, there would be comfort and good food.

As she looked at the broken-down buildings around her, guilt pricked her insides. People were squatting to eat, too poor to afford seats, yet she was willing to face robbers rather than live among them for one night.

Tori squared her shoulders and stood. "Take us to the Laughing Skunk."

Chapter Twenty

THE LAUGHING SKUNK

The rain had slowed to a drizzle, but Tori still stepped carefully behind Ingan to avoid the dirty puddles, which now seemed to make up more of the road than the road itself. Though the air now smelled slightly fresher, the outhouse odors lingered.

At the end of the deserted lane sat a tired two-story building made of wood, its dingy thatched roof dripping with rain. Windows cast out dim light over the two cobblestone stairs leading to a door with a skunk painted on it. The creature held its belly, face contorted with laughter, mouth open and eyes closed.

Ingan showed them in, then promised to return in the morning.

Fiddle music and pipe smoke filled a large common room, along with the smells of stew and spilled beer, a welcome change from the odors outside. At the far right, a fire blazed in a freestanding fireplace, lighting much of the room. At the opposite end, a woman lounged on a raised stage floor, one leg dangling off the edge as she played the fiddle for couples dancing in a small clearing.

Tori and Elnora walked through, squeezing behind chairs, but the tables had been jammed into every corner, leaving barely enough room to move.

A skinny woman with disheveled hair appeared from behind the fireplace, shouldering a tray of food.

Elnora raised a finger to get her attention, but she bustled past and called over her shoulder, "Find a seat anywhere; I'll be right there."

As they searched for somewhere relatively clean, the bottoms of Tori's shoes stuck to the floor with every step, then peeled away unpleasantly. But at least no one seemed to notice her. With her plain cloak, she fit in perfectly.

Somehow, the skinny woman found them in the crowd the moment they sat down. She wiped her hands first on her apron, then over her hair, before finally looking at them with a distracted air.

"What'll it be?"

"Dinner and a room for the night," Elnora said.

"You're in luck. We've got plenty of both."

She hailed a serving boy to bring them dinner, then led them up a creaky wooden staircase to a door in the middle of a hallway, handed them a key, and hurried off again.

The tiny bedroom consisted of two thin beds and had a rank smell.

"The sheets must have dried badly," Tori said, wrinkling her nose.

"Then at least something here has been washed," Elnora said, eyeing the floor.

Tori understood at last how the Round Cello could offer sleeping space under the tables. She suspected it would have been just as comfortable. It certainly would have been cleaner. They locked the door and went back down to the common room.

While they waited for dinner, Elnora wiped the sticky table with the edge of her cloak. "Disgusting."

"This is how common people live," Tori said, proud of her equanimity.

"Apologies, Princess, but we were all commoners in Tenisha-ko, and we still knew how to keep things clean." She looked at the floor, wrinkled her nose, and used her foot to fling something aside. "A dirty place has nothing to do with being common, or even poor. It has to do with being lazy and nasty."

A few paces to their right, a serving boy holding a tray bustled through a door beyond the fireplace, took a long spoon from the tray, and reached into a pot hanging over the fire to fill several bowls. Tori's stomach growled as the boy turned away from her, squeezing through the tables to serve the other side of the room.

She studied the faces of the people around her. Two unkempt youths threw their heads back in laughter and slammed their hands down, making their cups rattle. A woman a few tables down slurped stew with a wooden spoon, stopping now and then to run her tongue over rotting front teeth. Three scrawny men in threadbare tunics nursed large mugs.

Tori tried to relax but couldn't ignore the feeling she was in the wrong place.

The fiddler stopped playing and hopped off the stage, and the dancing couples found their seats. Soon, the stage filled with people setting up what looked like some kind of theater performance. They dragged out crudely painted cutouts of mulberry trees and a few chairs, and just like that, the play began.

Tori had a hard time following the performance, but parts of it made her suspect this was a poor rendition of *Among the Mulberries,* a classic normally only shown in the Brazepool Theater. Evidently, none of the performers here had seen the play—which was understandable; the Brazepool Theater was reserved for nobles.

She eyed the players curiously; unlike their drably clad audience, they were dressed in bright robes and too much face paint. One man cradled a pipa, holding the pear-shaped instrument like it was a lover and strumming its four strings with such ferocity it sounded like fighting cats.

He croaked the first verse of the play's signature ballad, also called "Among the Mulberries"—a song well-known by everyone, not just nobles. As he sang, the other players pretended to be deeply moved.

Then a female player wearing plain servant's clothing crept out with exaggerated stealth to stand behind those who were watching the man sing. Though she looked to be upward of fifty years old, she wore her hair in pigtails, with bright circles of rouge on her cheeks.

"This isn't at all how it goes," Tori whispered to Elnora, beginning to feel annoyed. *Among the Mulberries* was one of the most beautiful plays in antiquity, and these people were ruining it.

Then she chided herself. The players were doing their best with their fragmented knowledge. They would have no doubt gone to see the play in the Brazepool Theater had they been allowed.

"This is 'The Merry, Merry Berry Girl,'" Elnora whispered back. "That one there is the young berry picker, sneaking in to watch *Among the Mulberries* behind her noble mistress and guests."

Tori leaned in, interested now. That made much more sense. She had never actually seen this play—it wasn't the kind of production the Brazepool Theater would perform—but she vaguely knew the story.

"Wait, *that*'s the berry picker?" Tori pointed at the woman in pigtails. "She's ancient!"

Just then, the fiddler from earlier emerged from a dark corner and began playing "The Merry, Merry Berry Girl," which, of course, everyone in the world knew. The woman with pigtails grinned widely, then hopped and twirled in a sprightly little dance.

To Tori's surprise, the entire tavern started keeping time, clapping and stamping their feet. Tables were pushed aside, the dance area filled, and fiddle music, claps, and singing overwhelmed the tavern.

A circle of women formed, just like for the summer dances in village squares all over Min, and every few measures, one of the women entered the circle and danced while the other women clapped. When that woman skipped out again, another would take her place.

A circle of men surrounded the women's circle, and every time a woman finished dancing in the center, a man would step forward and offer his hand, and the couple would continue dancing outside the two rings.

Tori had seen the dance before in Silver Fox Springs. Many romance novels were based on the stories of couples who had met at the berry dance, including those written by Auntie Chune.

The two ill-kempt young men from before approached Tori's table and extended their hands, one to her, one to Elnora. But Elnora put a protective arm around Tori and shook her head. The men looked dejected, but then they shrugged and went to stand outside the women's circle with the other men.

"This sort of thing is all right for the likes of me, Princess, but not you," Elnora said, talking loudly over the noise.

"The likes of you? You're a noble."

Her gentlewoman's expression softened. "I'll always be grateful for what you did for me. With all my heart. But deep down, I'll always be a Tenisha-ko village woman."

The door opened and a large man with light red hair peered in. Bearded and gruff, he had the look of a Ghenz raider, and for one awful moment Tori feared there might be a raid. But she quickly dismissed the thought—no one in their right mind would raid Puddletown.

This was confirmed when his two companions followed him inside, shaking the rain from their heads and sitting at a table. All were broad, with braided beards and greasy, light-colored hair. Their fitted trousers had been shoved into heavy boots in the Ghenz fashion, and knives hung from the leather belts around their waists.

As they ordered mugs of beer, Tori noticed one of them held a knife under the table.

"I don't like the look of them," Tori said.

Elnora followed her gaze and frowned.

The one with the red hair chugged back his beer, then wiped his mouth with the back of his arm, scanning the room. He gestured to the others, who did the same. They were looking for someone. They appeared to scrutinize each dancer intently.

The first man's eyes left the dancers and moved methodically over the empty tables, starting near the fireplace and coming closer and closer to Tori. Then his pale gaze locked on hers. An uneasy feeling gripped her.

Elnora must have sensed it. "Let's go to our room," she said, glancing at the stairs to their left.

Tori shook her head. "They're closer to the stairs than we are, and it will be deserted up there. The kitchen is safer."

They tried squeezing between the chairs to get to the kitchen, but the dance had packed them too tightly.

Elnora pulled her to the floor. "I'll clear the way," she said, then shuffled on hands and knees through the crawlspace beneath the row of tables, pushing aside any encroaching table legs to make an orderly tunnel as she made her way toward the fireplace; the kitchen was just behind it.

Tori followed, hands and knees sticking to the dirty floor. On an impulse she threw a glance over her shoulder to see if she could spot the men's feet, but when she turned back an instant later, Elnora was already far ahead.

Suddenly, a hand grabbed Tori's ankle. She screamed, but the music and singing swallowed up her voice as she slid backward on her belly, the wood floor burning her skin.

As tables and chairs flew by, Tori seized a passing table leg with both hands just in time to see Elnora disappear around the fireplace. Tori kicked furiously, keeping her grip locked on the table, but her palms were starting to sweat.

Hands grabbed both of her feet now and yanked savagely, and her sweating palms lost their grip. The hands dragged her out and thick arms gripped her waist, impervious to her bucking and twisting. When the man set her on the ground to get a better grip, she spun and kicked him in the shin, screaming again into the cacophony.

Quick as a flash, a second man twisted her arm behind her, fingers digging into her flesh. The point of a knife in her back made her stiffen.

Hot, rancid breath filled her ear. "That's enough of that," he said. "We're going to take a walk."

Fingers digging into her arm and the point of a knife in her back, Tori was pushed between two other massive men, who shielded her from view as the three marched her out the door and into the jarring cool of the night.

Her pulse thumped in her ears as they forced her to the left, dragging her through the puddles beside the tavern, its walls forming one side of a dark alleyway. Music and merrymaking drifted out of the window they passed, and soon Tori found herself standing in a dark yard behind the building.

A cat's eyes flashed in the dim light. It hissed, then darted into the shadows. Foul odors hung in the air from garbage that had been left to bake, and as Tori's eyes adjusted to the darkness, the silhouette of tree branches took shape, curling down like claws.

A rectangle of light appeared several paces ahead as the back door of the tavern opened. Tori made to shout for help, but when a drunk stumbled out and, though barely able to stand, started relieving himself off the back step, she gave up hope.

Though she could no longer feel the knife point in her back, the thug's grip tightened on her arm, warning her to stay quiet.

The smell of urine wafted toward her, momentarily overpowering the reek of the garbage. Then the drunk stumbled back inside, and the rectangle of light disappeared.

The thug who had been holding her swung her around to look at him. He had pale blond hair, and his eyebrows bristled in the faint light.

"You have the wrong person," Tori said, lifting her chin, struggling to keep her voice level.

"Is that so, Min Daughter?"

Her heart hammered against her ribs. "What is it you want? Gold?" She thought with regret of how she only had one gold petal left. She hoped it was enough. "Name your price."

The man licked his lips and looked her over. "What do you say, boys? Should we have some fun first?"

Fear and anger sliced through her. "Harm me, and you'll face the saw."

The man laughed.

"Quit your fooling, Skrem, and get the job done," a gravelly voice said. It was the man with the red hair. Beside him, a man with a scar that split apart his top lip turned murderous eyes on her.

Icy clarity doused her. *They mean to kill me.*

Suddenly all fear vanished, and only one thought remained: *I have to live.*

Tori spat, hitting Skrem in the face. In an instant of surprise, he loosened his grip, and she kicked him in the groin as hard as she could.

Skrem doubled over, and she wrenched free, dashing past the other men toward the mouth of the alley, screaming. But an arm caught her around the ribs, and a massive hand planted itself over her mouth and nose.

Tori bucked backward, hitting what felt like the man's chin. The hand on her mouth slipped just enough for her to grab it with her teeth.

She bit down hard, tasting the dirty tang of sweat, then a spurt of salty, coppery blood.

The man screamed and cursed, shaking his hand, rattling her head. But Tori held on—injuring him was her only chance to survive. Punches rained down on her side and back; she only bit down harder.

The man shook his hand hard then, and her front tooth tore loose with a crack. He threw her off and she thumped on the wet ground, the man's scarred lip growing fainter in her vision as she scrambled backward like a crab until she hit the cold alley wall. She huddled in the corner as cursing and the thud of heavy footsteps pounded after her.

Searching frantically in the darkness, her hands groped everywhere for something she could use to defend herself. But all she found was decomposing food.

"Please release the princess," a calm voice said. "Otherwise, you'll have to excuse my aggression."

The thug with the scarred lip stopped in his tracks and looked back. A silhouette of a man with a topknot and flowing robes stood beneath the hanging branches.

Skrem and the redhead rushed the man, while the one with the scarred lip watched, knees bent as though ready to spring. But as his accomplices surrounded the new man, the thug with the scar spun on Tori again.

In a flutter of robes and swinging black hair, the new man floored his attackers, then landed in front of the scarred thug and dealt him two sharp blows to the neck. The thug collapsed at Tori's feet.

The dim light revealed that her savior wore the robes of a master healer. Hands clasped calmly behind his back, he looked down at the crumpled body and moved it aside with his foot.

Skrem and the redhead, who had been lying on the ground a few paces away, rubbed their heads and stood, then rushed the healer, brandishing knives. Both attacked at once, but the man ducked easily, casually stepping around their blades as though they had been moving in slow motion.

As she watched, a faint ringing rose in Tori's ears, increasing in volume until it dampened every other sound. Uncontrollable shivers hit her, coming in bursts that made her teeth chatter, sending blood from the torn one dribbling down her chin.

As Skrem slashed out, the master healer swept his foot around in an elegant motion, tripping him. Skrem thudded to the ground. Before he could get up again, the healer dealt him two sharp jabs and he collapsed like a sack of rice.

The redhead, though, had moved behind the master healer and raised his knife. Tori whimpered, pressing herself into the wall, hands covering her mouth as he plunged his blade into the healer's back.

But instead of crumpling, the healer spun, grabbed the redhead's wrist, and giving a slight twitch, forced his blade to release. It hit the ground. The redhead swore furiously as the healer pinned the thug's arm behind him, moving him in a circle, as though leading a disobedient donkey. No blood stained the master healer's back. She must have imagined the knife strike.

Once again, he dealt two sharp jabs, then released the thug, who dropped like a stone.

A moment later, the master healer was kneeling in front of her. She realized then that her back and ribs were aching terribly from the scarred man's punches, and the bursts of shivers made her jaw clench over and over on her torn tooth. She moaned.

The man looked at her with solemn, profound eyes. "Come inside," he said, "and I'll tend to your injuries." Then he took her arm and lifted her to her feet.

Tori glanced back nervously as they left.

"No need to worry," he said. "They'll be out cold till tomorrow night."

"What about after?" she asked, her teeth chattering. "Won't they come for me?"

"Not unless someone with greater skill than mine releases their pressure points."

He gave her a flat look. "No such person exists."

Chapter Twenty-One

DRUNKEN DREAMS

Shivering and dazed, Tori walked through the door and stumbled on something: the innkeeper, kneeling on the floor, sweeping shattered crockery.

The master healer caught Tori by the arm before she fell, and he led her over the shards, then headed to an area she hadn't noticed behind the stage: an alcove with a few empty tables.

Though the dancers had all cleared the center of the tavern, the alcove was still the only place in the room that looked quiet.

Out of nowhere, Elnora appeared and threw her arms around her. Tori gasped in pain.

Elnora pulled back, alarmed. "You're bleeding, and shivering!" She threw her own cloak over Tori's. "What happened?"

Tori couldn't meet her eye. She felt, somehow, that she had caused it all, though she didn't quite know how. She took a breath to steady herself, then flinched at a stabbing pain in her side.

"I'm fine," she said, but her voice trembled.

"You're cold as ice," Elnora said, grasping her shaking hands. She called out to a passing servant, "Bring us warm wine!"

"That is the very thing she needs," the master healer said.

Elnora blinked, apparently just noticing him. She looked him up and down, her eyes halting on the embroidered flowers on his lapel that marked his profession.

"I'm Master Banfay," he said. "Do you have a room?"

Elnora nodded.

"Take her there and wait. My trunk is upstairs; I'll bring it in a moment, along with the wine."

She gave him directions to their room, then accompanied Tori up the stairs. Tori held her sides, sucking in painful breaths with every step, her torn tooth making her entire head throb.

Needing to know how bad it was, she probed the tip of her tongue over it. Sharp, jagged pieces poked her, and she shuddered.

Elnora, unhooking the door lantern and shining it into the room, frowned as a cockroach scurried away, burrowing into a crack in the wood floor.

Tori had only just sat on the hard, thin bed when the door creaked open, making her jump in fright, setting off another shooting pain.

Master Banfay entered and handed Elnora a cup of wine. As he closed the door, however, panic hit her. What if he wasn't a master healer at all? He might be here to kill her.

"Where's your trunk?" she demanded, her breath coming in short bursts as she leaned away from him, pain exploding through her.

He held up his hands slowly, like a trainer calming a spooked animal, then hooked his thumbs under shoulder straps she hadn't noticed. He lifted a trunk made of smooth, pale wood off his back.

"Right here," he said, setting it gently on the floor, watching her all the while.

Tori lowered her head. "I don't know what's wrong with me."

As she drank the wine, Elnora watched her, looking like she would cry.

"I'm so sorry, Princess," she said, when Tori had finished half. "I thought you were behind me."

Tori stared into her cup, her throat tight.

"Where did you go?" Elnora asked. "What happened?"

Tears filled Tori's eyes and threatened to spill over. She quickly wiped them, shamed by her weakness of mind.

"Someone tried to kill your princess," Master Banfay said, setting gold needles in a neat row along the edge of the bed. "And they seemed to have been looking for her specifically."

Elnora paled.

Master Banfay turned to Tori. "Show me your tooth."

Tori lifted her upper lip. Elnora gasped, but Master Banfay merely gave a nod and continued his preparations. He lit a stick of dried mugwort and placed it in a small metal tray, then turned to Elnora. "Let her finish the wine, then have her lie down. By the way she's holding her side, I'd surmise she has a few broken ribs."

As the wine took effect, the edge of Tori's nerves softened, along with the shudders and stabbing pains.

Master Banfay motioned to the cylindrical bolster at the head of the bed, directing her to lie down. "I need to take your pulse," he said.

He slid a small silk cushion under her wrist and pressed two fingers to her skin for the space of several breaths, tilting his head now and then, as though listening. After, he picked up a golden needle and inserted it between her brows with a quick flick.

Another faint prick told her a needle had been inserted at the top of her head as well, and though neither of them hurt, tears streamed down her temples, onto the pillow beneath her.

With every prick, more tears flowed, as though the golden needles were drawing out her pain. He held the smoking stick of mugwort close to her side then, and razor-edged warmth seeped into the cracks of her ribs.

Tori closed her eyes and drifted along a river of drunken dreams.

In one dream, tangy, dirty sweat mixed with blood in her mouth, and she heard a crunch as her teeth ripped out. In another dream, needles bored into her gums, making her twitch, and bloody white roots forced themselves painfully back in place, gums knitting together in a puddle of warmth. A final dream consisted only of a flat stone, white, and cold as ice, burning into her forehead. The stone grew until it consumed her, chattering in the voice of a child.

When she woke again, she didn't know how long she had slept, only that she no longer felt like crying, and all her pain was gone. She ran her tongue across a smooth, perfect tooth.

As Master Banfay put away his golden needles, regret filled her for her earlier suspicions.

"You saved my life," she said. "Thank you."

He gave a nod.

"How did you discover me?" she said.

"I was coming down from my room to have a meal," he said, "then had the sudden urge to go out for a breath of air." He raised his brows. "Puddletown air. I've learned not to ignore such impulses." For an instant, his eyes shone with a mysterious light. "I had barely stepped outside when pieces of a conversation drifted in from the alley. Then I heard you scream."

Tori lifted her chin. "I'll see to it that you're handsomely rewarded."

"No need." He turned to pack his trunk. "I was well paid at the palace."

So this was the master healer her mother had mentioned, the one who had helped her uncle Yan.

"You must have left the palace the same time as us," Tori said. "How did you end up here?"

"Same as you, I expect. The Round Cello was full, even under the tables."

"I'll reward you all the same," Tori said. Then, remembering her dwindling funds, added, "As soon as I return home."

He closed his trunk with a click. "You need to eat," he replied, then looked at Elnora. "Take her to the alcove behind the stage. She needs quiet—she'll remain easily startled for a while. I'll join you in a moment." He picked up his trunk and left.

A short while later, Tori and Elnora sat at a quiet table, the walls of the alcove shielding them from the clamor of the rest of the tavern. Master

Banfay joined them and waved over a serving girl. Soon, three portions of stew steamed in front of them, alongside three bowls of rice.

The aroma of pork and rosemary made Tori's mouth water, and she remembered she hadn't eaten since morning. She was about to ask Elnora to pay, when Master Banfay slipped two drams into the serving girl's hand.

"And a jug of warm wine," he said. "Keep whatever's left."

The girl looked at the silver with bright eyes, then bowed gratefully and hurried away.

"I appreciate the gesture," Tori said, "but the least I could do was pay for the meal."

He waved away the comment, then made a well in the middle of his rice bowl and carefully scooped stew into the center. "I'll be traveling to Westrill tomorrow," he said, "so I can only accompany you that far. After, I recommend you hire guards to escort you to your final destination."

Warm relief flooded her. "That's exactly where we're headed. We're going to see the countess."

Master Banfay's hand slowed as he lifted a spoonful of stew to his mouth, like someone trying to solve a puzzle. He sat for a while, chewing thoughtfully.

"Westrill is one of Hanmar Province's most fascinating places," he said at last, and took a sip of wine. "But be prepared; nowhere remains the same forever."

Chapter Twenty-Two

THE SEEING STONE

Flags of cream and gold lined the wide gravel driveway into Hanmar Manor, leading Tori's carriage to a circular forecourt where two rows of guards stood at attention, spears pointed upward, creating an aisle from the gravel to the manor steps.

A woman clad in the rich black-and-gray silk robes of a manor administrator walked through the entrance of the massive stone building and stood at the top step, while maids and eunuchs rushed toward the carriage.

Would any of these know where the Well of Dissolution was? It wasn't a secret, but few people were interested in old lore. How would she tell who was? And could she bribe them, if she couldn't find an opening to ask the countess to reveal it?

She pondered this while Elnora put the last pin in Tori's hair. Her gentlewoman had somehow squeezed one palace robe for each of them into her pack, along with the jeweled hair ornaments that designated the Min Daughter, and they had dressed along the way.

As Tori stepped out of the carriage—now in perfect condition, thanks to Ingan's efforts—the maids and eunuchs waiting nearby exchanged confused glances, then bowed low, apart from one maid, who took off running so suddenly toward the manor it made Tori flinch. Master

Banfay, who had ridden up front with Ingan, had said the jumpiness could last many moons.

The maids and eunuchs parted to let Tori through, and a moment later, the administrator was rushing down the steps to meet her.

The woman arrived at the carriage, cheeks flushed. "Your Imperial Highness," she said, bowing low. "My deepest apologies for not greeting you sooner. We were expecting Marne Wessel."

Tori kept her expression neutral. "Marne Wessel was detained."

"Of course," the woman said breathlessly. "What an honor. Please, come in." She made a sweeping gesture toward the steps.

As Master Banfay descended the carriage and turned toward the path leading back into town, the administrator flashed a horrified look at one of the eunuchs, who ran after him, assuring him that suitable lodgings could be found on the manor grounds for the Min Daughter's master healer.

Two golden lion sculptures with fishes' tails guarded the doors of the Great Hall. Tori looked down at the marble floor as she walked, fascinated by the crystalline veins running through the stone, like tiny rivulets, while sculptures and even the enormous bronze candelabras lining the walls had been carved with drips or references to rivers and seas. Everything seemed to suggest water, as though hinting at the nearness of the Well of Dissolution.

Above all, the place exuded a faint vibration that Tori could only guess came from the Old Magic, which, according to the lore, infused not only the Well of Dissolution but also permeated Hanmar Province itself since many ages past. Her birth charm hummed in its tube through the waist pouch. She pressed a hand to it. It had come from Tey Zuben, the only place on the face of Arizan where the Old Magic still thrived, and it was reacting to the atmosphere in the manor.

At the beginning of her mother's reign twenty years earlier, around the time of Tori's birth, her mother had forged an unprecedented trade agreement with Tey Zuben, in honor of Tori's late grandmother, Empress Nuwang. In the agreement, Tori's mother had exchanged Hanmar's unique shipbuilding strategy for access to exotic Tey Zuben spices. But spices weren't all that came over on the new river-and-sea worthy ships. Tey Zuben stonemasons and artisans soon formed a subpopulation in Hanmar, bringing with them items humming with the Old Magic, so that not only was the land itself infused with the Old Magic from ages past but, thanks to the skill and tools of Tey Zuben artisans, the very stones of the great houses were as well.

Quick footfalls approached, growing louder, until two tall, slender people with golden hair came into view. A woman and a man, each in flowing cream-colored robes, swept toward her. Tori recognized Countess Ellie from the annual court sessions, when it had been Ellie's turn to provide one moon's worth of provisions for the Min Palace.

The most powerful of her mother's twelve provincial managers stopped before her, bowing low. Two steps behind, the man whom Tori assumed to be Ellie's primary intimate did the same.

"Your Imperial Highness," Ellie said in a smooth contralto. "My deepest apologies that I wasn't here to greet you. They told us Marne Wessel would be coming."

"There was a change of plans," Tori said. "Please, rise."

"Prepare rooms suitable for the Min Daughter," Ellie said, addressing one of her eunuchs. Her eye then fell on Elnora, visibly taking in her clothing. "But keep Marne Wessel's rooms for the princess's gentlewoman."

This gesture solidified Tori's hopes. By giving her gentlewoman the quarters reserved for people of elevated rank, such as Marne Wessel, Countess Ellie was indicating that receiving Tori was like receiving the empress herself. This boded well for Tori's mission; she shouldn't find it too difficult to direct the conversation.

As Elnora was taken to her quarters, Ellie led the way to a room with arched windows set in walls of inlaid marble. Sculptures, paintings, and silver vases served as decoration, while gilded moldings framed a ceiling painted with bright mythical scenes.

"We're so grateful for the empress's concerns over our problems in Hanmar," Ellie said when they were seated in silk chairs beside a small table laden with tea and many-colored cakes. "Sending the Min Daughter was beyond all expectation."

Her intimate nodded. He was handsome, with a wide, ready smile and clear blue eyes, like Ellie's.

As they talked and ate, Tori noticed Ellie exchange quick, loving glances with him, and she wondered how many other intimates Ellie had. A woman in the upper nobility might have two or three, but Ellie's position as matriarch of the House of Hanmar could have afforded her more.

In any event, he was evidently her favorite. At one point, they both reached for a cake at the same time and, though subtle, their hands remained touching an instant too long to be anything other than a hidden caress.

A eunuch dressed in the cream and gold of Hanmar Manor entered, interrupting them.

"What is it?" Ellie asked.

His eyes flickered to Tori's hair ornaments and robes, and a look of recognition crossed his face. He bowed low to her, then returned his gaze to the countess.

"My lady, it's the barrier."

Ellie stiffened slightly, her eyes showing concern. "Breached?"

"They're checking it now, my lady."

She nodded her dismissal.

Her intimate flashed her a look of concern, but Ellie answered with a subtle shake of the head. He looked relieved, and reached for his cup of tea with long, graceful fingers.

Though she had been hoping the subject would arise naturally when Tori had asked of the old landmarks in the area, Ellie still hadn't mentioned the well. Tori would need to bring around the conversation now, before any more concerning messages came. She didn't know what the barrier was, but if the eunuch returned with bad news, it would complicate Tori's mission. And she still had to address her supposed reason for being here.

She mentally reviewed the facts: her mother wanted to work out the details of Hanmar's support for—how should she say it? Perhaps her mother's "unification initiative." Tori's first step, then, would be to get Ellie to reveal what exactly had been discussed. After, she could find a way to relate that discussion to the Well of Dissolution.

"The empress would like to finalize some particulars," Tori began.

Ellie placed a hand on her intimate's arm. "My dear, you no doubt have more interesting things to do than listen to women's conversation."

He smiled and put down his tea. "I must admit, matters of state are a little beyond me." He rose and bowed. "If you'll excuse me, my hunting party is waiting."

As he left the room, Ellie watched him fondly. "He so enjoys his hunting."

Not knowing what else to say, Tori nodded. "It's a healthful activity."

After the door had shut, however, the earlier concern returned to Ellie's eyes.

"Before we continue, Princess, there's something I must tell you." Ellie lowered her head, as though confessing a fault. "Things are not exactly as I communicated through my envoy. Envoy Lee is reliable enough, and skilled in many things. But..." She hesitated. "Well, sometimes, one had better trust too little than too much, if you see what I mean."

Tori tried to mask her confusion. "That is sometimes the wisest course of action."

"The thing is," Ellie continued, "I didn't request Varanaken just to deal with wielders." She looked up at Tori through her lashes. "Not entirely."

Tori kept her face placid. Her mother had told her Ellie had agreed to support her war. What did that have to do with requesting Varanaken?

Unless Ellie hadn't agreed to any unification efforts at all. She had probably requested Varanaken, and the empress meant to use the opportunity to manipulate Ellie's support. Typical.

"Why did you request them?" Tori asked.

"We've been having trouble with Ghenz raiders on our borders. Their whole mission is to weaken Min with raids so they can take over, just as their ancestors did with parts of Jeng." A look of disgust flashed on her face. "Ghenz believe every place they set foot on should be theirs, did you know that? And Jeng, of course, can't control them, or won't, as long as they don't raid Jeng lands. But lately the raids have increased to the point where my soldiers find it difficult to handle them, even with my magical wards."

"Magical wards—is that the barrier your eunuch was referring to?"

Ellie gave a nod. "My people are investigating a possible breach as we speak."

"I saw the effects of a raid on my way into Hanmar," Tori said, recalling the Ants lining up for soup. She hoped the bun seller kept his word about feeding them. Then the Ghenz thugs at the Laughing Skunk appeared in her mind's eye. She forced them out.

"I may need to travel to the border personally to repair it," Ellie said. "It takes a great deal of time and effort, so I must beg your indulgence if I need to leave our audience early."

"So your envoy mentioned wielders to entice the Varanaken here, but your real purpose is to use them to repel the Ghenz."

Ellie looked embarrassed. "There have been rumors of some wielding incidents, though I'm not entirely convinced they were real. I suspect some troublemakers are trying to spread fear. That's why in my letter I merely requested Varanaken warriors on the borders of Hanmar, then instructed Envoy Lee to mention the rumors in case the empress felt she needed something to motivate the Varanaken. The fact is, they're far more motivated by hunting wielders than Ghenz, yet they're the only ones with the skill to fight them." The countess's eyes took on a troubled light. "Yet there's more than that. Far more. But perhaps it's better if I show you."

She walked to a small table where an item sat covered in a multicolored cloth, then removed the cloth to reveal a box, two handspans square, and brought it to the table. It looked to be made of walnut, ornately carved and embellished with gold leaf.

She lifted the top off with both hands. Inside, an iridescent orb the size of a small melon was nestled in dark velvet. She pulled it out and set it in front of Tori. Glowing colors swirled deep inside the otherwise colorless stone.

Ellie's eyes were flecked with something that looked like fear. "An ancient seeing stone from Tey Zuben," she said, then spoke something into the orb in the Tey Zuben tongue. Tori recognized its sounds from her mother's occasional conversations with Tey Zuben emissaries.

"Place your hands on the stone and look inside," Ellie whispered.

Tori did, but the swirling orb only reflected her eyes.

"I don't see anything."

Then her breath caught as the colors cleared, and a dark room appeared, distant, as though she were looking through a window at something far away. People surrounded a throne, palms open, with fire and water and small tornadoes swirling in their hands—wielders. Around them were beings of fire or vines or molten steel. It came to her suddenly that she was looking at Antiquitals, though they were too far away for her to see them clearly.

At their command, starving peasants knelt before the dais. She couldn't see the ruler's face, only the black granite throne, carved with the symbols for the elements. This was Antiquital Emperor Zanith, the one who had starved Shudon, and whom Yanai Sumi had defeated with the help of the Great Tailu-bird.

The scene vanished, and instead, a book appeared, flying off the shelf of an ancient library. It opened to a page with colored ink drawings rendered in an ancient style, while beneath them, logograms appeared line by line:

The children were fair, lithe of limb and hard as iron, with hearts as black as their father's—Rebdu, one of the sons of the Six.

And like their Antiquital mother, Renna, they were drawn to the dark powers of Arizan and sought to commune with them.

An old fable, then. A story of the Children of the Six, and their children after them.

The children of Rebdu and Renna became a great clan, worshippers of the Fox Dragons.

But they sacrificed their mother, Renna, and were corrupted, scaled of skin and lizard-like in form. They were called Watani—"lizard" in the Old Speech—and were cruel and skilled in war.

Tori couldn't recall any such story, but before she could think of it further, the book vanished, and in its place she seemed to see the back of a cloaked person walking past a village on a sunny day. She could tell by the villagers' clothing that this was a scene of ancient times.

As though on a whim, the cloaked figure set the village ablaze, killed the people, and drank their blood. When it turned, Tori saw its face was scaled and lizard-like.

The scene shifted like an awful dream. Now an army of gruesome scaled warriors marched, brandishing spiked weapons in a vicious battle. Was this from Ishairo's time? Except Ishairo had conquered them, banishing them to the islands of Hoto Watani, formed from the landmass that broke off when he split Shudon with his sword. Here, though, the Watani were winning.

Blood splattered inside the stone, and Tori jerked her hands away.

The scene vanished, and the orb glowed softly again. Ellie returned it to its box.

"What was that?" Tori asked, feeling unsettled.

"An oracle," Ellie said. "I was searching for knowledge about my border, and saw those stories instead."

"Old fables?"

Ellie shook her head. "The oracle only shows what really was, what is, or what is perhaps to come." She looked at Tori with urgent eyes. "If the scenes you saw haven't already happened, they could. Everything must be done to stop this."

Tori kept her face neutral, despite the ridiculousness of the statement. She had known the people of Hanmar were deeply superstitious, but until now, she hadn't fully appreciated how much.

The thought sparked an idea.

"Perhaps there's something in the ancient lore that can help," Tori said. "In fact, I think there might be something right here in Hanmar. There's a story of an ancient well whose waters could remove wielding."

"The Well of Dissolution," Ellie said.

Tori squinted, as though trying to recall the name. "Yes, that's it. If the Watani ever did appear, the waters of this well could be introduced into their own water supply. If it's as powerful as the lore says, it might take away their powers."

Ellie opened her mouth to say something, but the same eunuch from before rushed in and bowed low.

"Apologies, Your Highness," he said to Tori, then turned to Ellie. "My lady, it's confirmed. There's been a breach."

Ellie straightened. "Has the area been searched?"

"Yes, my lady. It's clear of Ghenz for now. But there's word of small raiding parties roaming close by. You shouldn't delay."

Ellie stared at the door as he left, a thoughtful look on her face. "Unity is the only defense against things to come," she muttered to herself, then turned her gaze to Tori. "There was a time when Shudon was united, long ago. That was a time of Shudon's strength."

She dropped her voice to a low whisper. "Tell the empress that if such a path ever opens before her, she can count on the House of Hanmar." She rose and walked with Tori toward the door.

So the House of Hanmar would be in support of her mother's war after all. Tori shivered at her mother's uncanny instinct. Well, that was one message she would not be delivering.

But her time was running out. If Ellie left before she got the information about the well, she might never get it.

Ellie spoke before Tori could. "May I speak freely?" she said, stopping at the door. "My hope is to persuade the empress to station Varanaken permanently at our borders. This will secure against the Ghenz threat for now, and against any...greater threats later."

"I'll do my best," Tori said. "But I still think the well could be useful. Tell me where it is, and I'll investigate to see if it's suitable for your purposes. Then you can repair your breach in peace, knowing the matter is being looked into."

"Apologies, Princess, I wasn't clear." Ellie shook her head. "There is no well. The Well of Dissolution was destroyed by raiders centuries ago."

Chapter Twenty-Three

INTO THE DARK

Waves crashed over Tori's head, plunging her into cold depths just beyond the feverish pull of an underwater maelstrom. She wanted desperately to undo the thing she had done, but couldn't remember what it was.

She cried out—a little girl was stuck at the bottom of the whirlpool, thrashing about like a rag doll. Hands broke the surface of the water, grabbing at the girl, but the maelstrom's grip was too strong.

Then, like a monster spitting out bones, the maelstrom spewed the girl's limp body into the open air.

Tori sat up in a cold sweat, blinking to clear the guilty vision of dark water, until fragments of cream-and-gold brocade curtains broke in. She was on her bed in Countess Ellie's guest suite.

Footsteps pattered into the room, and the bed curtains slid aside.

"You'll be all right, Princess, you hear?" Elnora said in her musical accent, placing a gentle hand on Tori's back, pulling her into the present.

Her gentlewoman stood in her night robe, her head dotted with small buns tied with strips of cloth. Elnora had insisted on spending the night on the couch rather than in Marne's suite.

Guilt gave way to hopelessness as the last of the dark water vanished and her conversation with Countess Ellie returned. Sleeping or awake, Tori would never escape what she was.

"You didn't happen to bring your herbs, did you?" Tori asked, rubbing her temples.

"I'm sorry, Princess. The mortar and pestle were too heavy to run with."

Tori waved the apology away, then dropped her face in her hands.

"Master Banfay is staying on the manor grounds," Elnora said. "Should I call him?"

While she hated to bother the master healer in the middle of the night, especially after all he had done for her, at this moment, she feared if she didn't see him she might never sleep again.

In about twice the time it would take to drain a cup, Master Banfay arrived.

"I apologize for calling you out so late," Tori said pleasantly, to mask her dark mood.

Surprisingly, he looked as fresh as someone who had awoken from a restful night and was already about their tasks.

"I understand you're having trouble sleeping," he said, opening his trunk and selecting herbs from two of its square compartments.

"I'm used to nightmares," Tori said, "but tonight they're more vivid than usual."

"An aftereffect of your recent trauma," he said, matter-of-factly.

As he crushed herbs in a white mortar and pestle, an aroma like cinnamon bark wafted out, mixed with something mildly musty—dried mushrooms, perhaps. Elnora watched intently, her hair now free from its ties and hanging in perfect curls around her shoulders.

"Black-eyed pokeweed and creeping bloom," she said. "I didn't know they could be used together."

He looked up. "You have some skill in herb lore. Few people can identify these."

He mixed the herbs into boiling water and handed it to Tori. Their bitterness made her shudder. Then he lifted out two trays from his trunk to reveal a layer of twinkling spirit stones, many of them a blend of two colors. Their floral fragrance filled the air.

He chose a white one and, when she had lain down, placed it on her forehead. A faint smell of jasmine filled her nose.

As he whispered to the stone in a language she didn't understand, a cool radiance pulsed from the stone into her head, sucking away the darkness that had plagued her mind only moments before. The coolness turned colder, till it was so cold it burned.

Tori plucked it off. Master Banfay studied her from the bedside chair, his gaze keen and unsettling, as though he could read her mind.

A thought seized her then: *He knows I'm a wielder.*

She stood. "I'm much better now. Thank you for coming."

But Master Banfay remained seated, face expressionless, apart from the glow in his eyes.

"Why are you really here?" he said.

The question alarmed her. She walked to the door, intending to show him out.

"I don't think that's any of your business," she said, reaching for the handle. But the memory of his rescue returned, and she lowered her hand. "What I mean is, I'm not permitted to discuss matters of state."

"Except you're not here on matters of state, are you?"

"Meaning?" She tried to sound unconcerned.

"The empress puts wielders to the saw," he said, eyes fixed on her. "But you don't agree."

Elnora watched the exchange with anxious eyes.

"People here say Ellie's been having trouble with wielders," he said, then started packing his trunk. "I'm guessing you came to investigate that claim—without the empress's approval."

She turned her back to him, folding her arms around her. "I'll thank you to leave now, Master Banfay. Your services are no longer required."

"The wielders you released are safe," he said. "Hidden."

She spun to face him. "I have no idea what you mean."

But there was a look of complicity in his eyes. "I know the things you do are out of love for your people."

Tori studied him a long moment, until her ability to read people reassured her he was sincere.

"So," he said, "why are you really here?"

A small table stood nearby, laid out with stationery marked with the crest of Hanmar Manor. She sat there and neatened the papers as she considered how to respond, shifting the brush and the ink stone, one in front of the other, then sliding the stick of red wax and the seal parallel to everything.

"Tell me first what you meant about the wielders."

"My village has hidden them," he said simply.

Tori glanced up at him in surprise.

"I received news by hawk that they arrived nine days ago," he said.

She let out a silent breath. She hadn't realized until now how worried she had been about them.

"I'm here to stop a war," she said, finally responding to his question. It was the safest response. "The empress is determined to unite Shudon under the Min banner."

The statement rankled her, not only because of the half-truth it contained but also because it emphasized her hopelessness. After everything she had risked, she still had nothing.

"And was Countess Ellie persuaded by your arguments?" Master Banfay asked.

Tori sighed wearily. "The countess supports a unified Shudon. She believes this is the way to stave off an imminent invasion by..." She hesitated; talking of a mythical species like they were real sounded foolish. "By the Watani."

Master Banfay's expression betrayed nothing. "What makes her fear this?"

"Images in a Tey Zuben seeing stone."

He seemed to consider this for several breaths.

"I can't comment on the visions in a seeing stone," he said at last. "But if stopping a war is what you desire, there might be another way." He peered at her intently. "If the empress could summon a nonhuman army to help achieve her ends, would she?"

Irritation prickled Tori's neck. "Ants have less of a chance in battle than humans."

"No one fears the Ants," he said. "I'm talking about an army so fearsome, the sight of them will rob the other side of the will to fight."

Tori raised an eyebrow. What was he talking about? Elnora sent her a questioning glance.

"Long ago, there was a jewel," he said, "known as the Septad. It belonged to the first queen of the Royal Tribe, the ancient foremother of Ishairo. She used it to control the Antiquitals and so brought peace to all of Shudon."

The story sounded familiar. "What does that have to do with the army?"

"Everything. Antiquitals *are* the army. They are like nature: powerful and destructive, yet useful if harnessed properly. Whoever controls the Antiquitals controls Arizan. The Septad can ensure this. The other advantage," he said, "is that its power is so great that every other magical item is rendered useless in its presence, permanently." He held Tori's gaze. "Items used to detect wielders, for instance."

First the Watani, now Antiquitals? The first were a myth, the second exterminated centuries ago.

Yet everyone had thought the Arun clan had died off, too. Tori had discovered them by chance, through one of the secret aid missions Yumay's people had been conducting on her behalf. Her mind went to the etched bow and arrow the governor of Kiir had presented to her mother's court, and she studied the master healer. His eyes lacked the wild-eyed naivety so often present in the gaze of the superstitious; instead, they were steady and keen, betraying a sharp mind and deep wisdom.

Master healers traveled more lands than Tori even had knowledge of. What had he seen?

"You speak as though Antiquitals still exist," Elnora said.

A knowing look was his only response, but it was enough to stir an irrational hope. If she had the Septad, she wouldn't need the magical water of Hanmar. She could present the jewel to her mother as a gift, while disabling everything that could ever implicate her again.

It was a future she might never reach, and that thought made her ache. Yet the tantalizing image remained, and her fragile hope transformed into a burning desire.

"Do you know where to find this jewel?" she asked.

"I know someone who would. The elder of my village. But if you want to go there, we must leave tonight."

"I can't do that. I need to say a proper goodbye to Countess Ellie, or..." *Or she'll figure out my mother didn't send me.*

Elnora leaned in and whispered, "Princess, didn't you say the countess left for the border? Not that you should go with him, mind you." She eyed Master Banfay dubiously.

"Regardless," he said, "the empress will have sent people for you. If you don't leave tonight, you won't have another chance."

With everything that had happened in the past two days, Tori had been too distracted to think things through. But he was right. Her mother was no doubt furious; she wouldn't have merely sent a messenger, she would have sent Tori's guards to bring her back. Traveling on horseback, they could be here any moment. Yet if Tori went home now, she didn't know what would happen.

If she left a message with Ingan however, promising her mother the Septad, and adding a hint of what it could do, it would assuage the empress's anger. The Septad would further her objectives of uniting Shudon, after all.

"Where can my mother reach me? I'll need to give her an address."

"Tell her Greenstalk Village," he said. "There's a reliable hawking post there."

Tori brought to mind the maps of Min lands. "Greenstalk is three days away from this part of Hanmar. I'll send a hawk to my mother when we arrive, letting her know where I am. That way, she'll get it before my driver, Ingan, reaches the palace with my letter."

"Your calculations are based on travel in a carriage," Master Banfay said. "On good roads. We'll have neither. Count six days."

"Fine. I'll instruct Ingan to leave Hanmar in two days' time, then." It was safer to arrive at her destination before telling her mother the address. Less chance of being intercepted on the road.

Tori scribbled a note on the manor stationery and sealed it, then said, "Ingan is housed near the stables. I'll slip this note under his door on our way out. Just give us a few moments to get ready."

Master Banfay's gaze flicked to Elnora. "Someone should stay behind to meet whomever your mother sends."

"My gentlewoman goes with me," Tori said.

He seemed to consider this, then gave a nod and pulled out a silken thread that hung from his neck. Its pendant appeared to be a tiny jade vial, except that it emitted a faint light.

Looking at Elnora, he held it up. "Can you see this?"

Her mouth quirked. "Do I look blind?"

"Drink it," he said, slipping off the thread and opening the vial's stopper.

Elnora paused. "Why? What is it?"

"Elixir. You can't enter my village without it."

Her brow creased into a questioning look, but he shook his head. "No time. I'll explain later."

After a glance at his master-healer's trunk, then at Tori, she took the vial.

"The princess should drink first."

"No need," Master Banfay said, turning his keen eyes on Tori. "The princess already drank it—many years ago."

Chapter Twenty-Four

POETIC ENIGMAS

Koren leaned over the old scroll at Greenstalk Teahouse, tracing a finger down the vertical lines of glyphs while Henzan looked on thoughtfully, sipping tea. In the two weeks since they had begun meeting here, neither of them had been able to puzzle out anything from the scroll that would help Koren find the Celestial Seal.

From their quiet corner beside a second-story window, the teahouse smells of steeped jasmine and roasted barley mingled with the fragrance of meat skewers from the outside marketplace below. Since most of the teahouse customers tended to congregate on the bottom floor to socialize, the top floor afforded them much-needed privacy.

Koren read through the enigmatic poem again, brow furrowed in concentration.

Cling to paths shown by lovers of green,
Cloaked in shadow and shifting light.
Heed the voiceless, see the unseen,
And they shall order your footsteps aright.

He drummed his fingers on the polished wood table. Though he sensed that this scroll held the key to recognizing the signs and portents that would lead him to the first clue, he couldn't openly discuss all the possible interpretations without admitting to Henzan that he was looking for the Celestial Seal. He had to keep his questions vague, which, in turn, produced vague interpretations.

At least they had both agreed that the scroll referred to something in Ma'yanar Forest. If only they could agree on what.

"Heed the voiceless..." Koren said. "Deer have no voice, and they are lovers of green. Perhaps this speaks of something found along the paths of woodland creatures?"

"That doesn't fit with the scroll's artistic tone," Henzan said. "The glyphs used all have some feature in their shape that points to intelligence, indicating that who or whatever this voiceless thing is, it will have an intelligent mind, capable of providing guidance in finding whatever item the scroll refers to." He squinted at it, turning his teacup in his hand. "Maybe it's referring to hunters. Hunters of the forest could be guardians of some ancient secret."

Koren shook his head. "There are no hunters in Ma'yanar."

"Can you be sure? The forest is immense."

"I know the forest well," Koren said.

"Hermits, then? There have to be others living there apart from your sect."

Koren didn't try to explain that his *sect*, as Henzan called it, didn't actually live in the forest itself; Henzan would never believe in the Veils. Those portals would be dismissed by him as nonsense, since they were something which the rival Silver Cloud Mountain Sect believed in strongly, and worse, they were something for which no evidence existed.

Either way, they were getting nowhere. Koren was beginning to wonder if he shouldn't just tell his friend the truth.

He peered at Henzan, who was stroking his long, white beard, staring intently at the scroll. They had known each other for half a century, certainly enough time to know someone well. And though they didn't see each other often, Koren believed his friend to be sincere. The old sect elder came down from the mountain only twice per year to recruit new members, but otherwise he was a scholar at heart, devoting his life to cycling dawn-essence and studying old writings. Surely someone like him could be trusted. And without Henzan's help, Koren feared he would never find the seal.

An image came to him of the prisoners Henzan had saved, hungrily eating the man's bread.

He turned to his friend. "I'm afraid I haven't been entirely honest."

Henzan gave him a puzzled look.

"Unlike you," Koren said, "my interest in this scroll isn't purely academic. I'm looking for the thing I believe this scroll refers to."

"And what is that?"

"The Celestial Seal."

Henzan set his cup down. "Surely that can't be it. I thought the Celestial Seal was lost to time." He looked down at the scroll.

"I hope not," Koren said. "I've been commissioned to find it. My sect has a duty to keep the seal safe." He fixed an earnest gaze on Henzan. "Please, I need your help interpreting this."

His friend's eyes shone. "Of course. Why didn't you say so before, old friend?" He chuckled. "This changes everything. I've studied this scroll for years, but now that I know what I'm looking for, interpreting it will be easy."

Henzan slid the scroll close and peered down at it for a long while as he sipped his tea.

"I have it," he said at last. "Those lights in the forest, the laughing ones that dart past people—you said they were ancient spirits, forest lomi. Like in the old tales."

Koren nodded.

Henzan tapped the scroll. "An ancient writing pointing to the Celestial Seal would never reference transient beings, like hunters or hermits. It could only be talking about spirits. Look here at the glyph for voiceless. This puzzled me for some time. The usual glyph used in scrolls refers to something abstract, a voiceless concept, for instance, an unarticulated belief. But this glyph is unusual; it refers to something concrete that can't speak." He frowned and looked up. "Lomi can't speak, right?"

Koren shook his head. They could understand him when he spoke, but they themselves used no words. He sat back, letting the idea settle. "And there can be no greater lovers of green than the nature guardians themselves," he said.

Henzan nodded. "And look at this: 'Cling to paths shown by lovers of green, cloaked in shadow and shifting light.' Lomi leave paths of light when they move. Since the Celestial City of Jade was said to be the realm of pure fire, surrounded by flaming trees, it makes sense that these forest spirits would be the first sign leading to the seal forged in that city. And where the scroll says 'they will order your footsteps,' it means you must follow them."

Koren's pulse quickened. The first clue was within reach.

He bowed. "Thank you, old friend. You've done me a greater service than you could ever know. The paths of the lomi will certainly lead me to the clue I'm looking for."

Henzan smiled his usual friendly smile. "Then let us follow and see where they lead."

Chapter Twenty-Five

BLIND TRUST

After dark on the sixth night, Tori awoke to the croaking of frogs. Master Banfay had recommended they use their nights to travel and their days to rest, so they spent today dozing alongside a stream. Once they had eaten a meal of bread and dried meat, they set off again.

Master Banfay led them through the shadowy landscape with the familiarity of someone strolling in his back garden.

"Are we getting close?" Tori asked after they had walked a while.

"This is our last night. Tomorrow, we'll travel to my village by day."

Ever since they had left Countess Ellie's manor, Tori's mind had been occupied with staying out of sight. Now that they were close to their destination, however, a new worry set in.

"You seem confident I can get the Septad," Tori said. "What makes you think so?"

He adjusted the trunk on his back. "Because you have need of it, to do a noble thing. Those who have tasted the elixir are guided by it toward their destinies, and the things they need are provided."

Tori looked away, rankled again by the half-truth she had told. What if the "noble thing" wasn't the real thing?

"Master Banfay," Elnora said, misinterpreting Tori's discomfort, "the princess doesn't remember taking the elixir. Do you think you could let her try it again? If your gatekeepers ask when she's had it, she won't be able to say."

"It's not a matter of saying," he replied. "A person cannot physically enter my village unless the elixir runs through them. The village is hidden in one of the Veils of Arizan."

Tori furrowed her brow, trying to work out his meaning.

"What are Veils?" Elnora asked.

"Myths," Tori said.

Master Banfay nodded. "But not *merely* myths. The Veils were created by the Six before they left this world to live in the Celestial City of Jade. When the Six still walked the face of Arizan, each of them created a special place as a gift to their children, something to remember them by when they were gone."

"Greenstalk Village isn't hidden," Tori said. "I've seen it on maps."

"Veils exist within other places. My village is hidden in the Veil of Ayenashi."

Twigs snapped loudly, making Tori flinch. She stopped, pressing a hand to her racing heart.

"Just a fox," Master Banfay said over his shoulder.

Elnora wrapped an arm around her. "Don't worry, you hear? Master Banfay said the jumpiness won't last."

Tori rubbed a faint burning in her wrists. In the dim light, the veins under her skin seemed darker than before. Somehow she felt that this, too, had been caused by the attack.

"Couldn't you let her just try the elixir again, to put her mind at ease?" Elnora said. "You said you have the obligation to give it to anyone who can see the vial."

To Tori's surprise, he lifted the silken thread from his neck and handed it to her, then watched blandly as she pulled the stopper from the little glowing vial and tipped it to her mouth.

Nothing, not even the touch of liquid on her lips. She tipped the vial back farther, then peered inside.

"It's empty."

"As I said, you've already had it. You can't drink the elixir twice." Master Banfay reached for it then and slipped the thread back on.

Tori turned to Elnora. "You tasted something when you drank it?"

"Yes, Princess. It was like fine liquor—sweet in the mouth, burns a little in the chest. It gave me a jolt, too, like that sting you get when you rub a fur collar with your hands."

Tori pondered this, the rustle of leaves under their feet filling the silence.

"How do you make it?" Elnora asked Master Banfay. "I've never tasted anything like it. You must use special alcohol and herbs. Dried fruit?"

He shook his head. "No one can make the elixir. You know the story of Ishairo and the purple lightning?"

Elnora nodded. "Suro sent purple lightning on Ishairo's sword, making him immortal, and he climbed Mount Ketwanen to offer rice and osmanthus wine on her altar. Fire struck the mountaintop, and he was taken up to the Celestial City of Jade. The next new moon, the constellation of Ishairo appeared in the sky."

"What does that have to do with the elixir?" Tori said.

Master Banfay looked at her over his shoulder. "Everything. His offering created the elixir. But you'll learn more of that at my village."

Tori remembered the warring Watani she had seen in Countess Ellie's seeing stone. "Why didn't Ishairo use the Septad, instead of his sword?" If anyone had need of it for noble purposes, it was him.

He thought about it. "You'll need to ask the elder."

"And you're sure your elder will help me?"

"I can't see why not."

Another image of Countess Ellie's seeing stone flashed in her mind, this time of the Antiquitals. If the Septad could control powerful creatures like them, it could kill her.

"Why hasn't anyone else used the jewel in all these years?"

He looked up at the crescent moon. "The elder can answer your questions."

Tori's pulse skipped nervously. She might be about to find an artifact from the legends. Was she ready to face whatever this might mean? What if it knew her motives weren't pure?

She pushed down a spike of nerves. She had to take everything on blind trust: first, that she had taken the elixir and would get into the village, then—and more importantly—that the trip wouldn't be in vain.

Master Banfay had told her nothing solid. The lack of certainty was unbearable, and yet she continued to foolishly hope.

Could she stand it if she didn't get the Septad after all? Could she bear the disappointment? The hopelessness?

But blind trust was all she had.

"We'll camp here," he said, arriving at a copse of trees. "Try to rest; we wake at dawn. The last part is best traveled by day."

Tori took a deep breath, settling her nerves just a little. The prospect of seeing the Septad, of handling it, terrified her. Yet if this item of myth actually existed after all this time, then maybe the world wasn't as broken as she thought.

"Where are we?" she asked, putting down her pack.

He pointed through the trees toward the horizon. "Look and see. Recognize it?"

But everything ahead of her was shadow. There was only the far-off howl of wolves, calling to some distant thing, hoping it would hear.

Chapter Twenty-Six

PEACH BLOSSOM GROVE

The next morning, Master Banfay led them over gently sloping hills until they came at last to a road. On the other side of it, a menacing forest dominated the horizon. From memory, the maps put Greenstalk Village around five fen to the east, which meant that this forest must be Ma'yanar—the haunted forest.

Master Banfay headed straight for it.

"I thought we were going to Greenstalk," Tori said, trying to keep her voice casual. "Isn't that where the Veil of Ayenashi is?"

He shook his head. "The Veil of Ayenashi is in Ma'yanar Forest."

"But you gave Greenstalk as the address to send letters."

"Because it's the nearest hawking post. Now quickly, follow me. It's still not safe for you to be on the open road."

As the dark forest entrance loomed closer, she thought guiltily of how she had sent the prisoners there. But they had survived—Master Banfay said they had all made it to his village and were safely hidden. Then again, if some of them had died in the forest, would he know the difference? She pushed the uncomfortable thought aside.

The dense vegetation gave way, and suddenly she was surrounded by birdsong and the fresh smell of spring. Shafts of sunlight filtered through the branches, filled with fountains of sparkles that spilled to the ground. She squinted at them, trying to figure out what they were.

Elnora stretched out a hand. "These dust motes are beautiful." The instant she touched the light, however, it disappeared. She jerked back her hand, eyes searching the branches above.

A beam of light darted past, making Tori jump. "What was that?" she asked, heart racing.

"Forest lomi," Master Banfay said.

Another beam swerved around her, and ethereal giggles echoed through the air, sending chills up her spine. Elnora clasped Tori's hand and placed each foot in Master Banfay's exact footsteps.

"What are forest lomi?" Elnora asked.

Master Banfay turned and looked at her in surprise. "Have you never read the histories? They're nature guardians, lesser spirits created at the beginning of the world."

Elnora looked around nervously, then hurried to keep up. "Back home we call them Rootfolk. I thought they were myths."

"Lomi won't hurt you," he said. "Kamen, on the other hand..." He walked through a stream of pulsing sparkles.

Instead of following in his footsteps, Elnora pulled Tori around the sparkles and whispered, "You can trust the boat, but still watch the sky." She raised her eyebrows significantly. "What are kamen?"

"Animal guardians, but you won't see any of those." He looked at Elnora uncertainly. "You don't hunt, do you?"

She shook her head.

He nodded. "Then you'll be fine."

Giggles and swooping lights followed them a long while, until Master Banfay finally stopped at what seemed like a random spot. "We're here."

Tori looked around—nothing was different. She and Elnora exchanged glances.

"Follow me exactly," he said, walking away slowly. Suddenly, he vanished.

Tori's breath caught, and she realized she hadn't watched his exact footsteps. Elnora's wide eyes showed that she hadn't, either.

Using her best guess, Tori walked forward. A cool, fluid resistance hit her head, flowed down her spine, and clung to her clothes, as though she were walking through a curtain of water. Sounds muffled, apart from the tinkle of trickling droplets, and the earth felt slick beneath her feet.

A moment later, the sensation ended, and she checked her body, finding it dry. All that remained was a feeling of pleasant freshness. Master Banfay stood a few steps ahead, poking idly at the ground, and at the sight of him, relief flooded her—she was in!

She looked around and gaped—the forest burst with color. It was as though she had been viewing the world until now through a dull, gray-tinted pane, and had finally stepped into the open. The air, too, had a purity she had never imagined possible, and everything felt alive in a way that didn't seem rational.

Elnora popped into sight, looking pale, and Master Banfay finally looked up from the ground.

"Welcome to the Veil of Ayenashi," he said. "Be happy. Very few mortals ever set foot here."

From then on, swaying trees bordered their path, along with bubbling fountains where birds bathed, splashing merrily. Lomi filled the place, shimmering and dancing, flashing and swooping, spinning feverishly inside shafts of sunlight.

Every now and then, Master Banfay would pat one of the trees and whisper to it, and its leaves would rustle, as though in response.

"It's like they can understand him," Elnora said, with a nervous laugh.

"Of course they can," he said. "All the trees here in the Veiled Forest are sentient."

Elnora, who was walking close to the line of trees, stepped away, looking uneasy.

Beautiful birdsong rang out overhead, and Tori peered upward, spotting the source of the song: pale yellow feathers stood out against a dark branch, and delicate shades of green, blue, purple, and orange painted the curved beaks of two tiny birds. They lifted off the branch and flew around each other in a circle, as though playing a game.

Tori smiled. "Adorable."

The birds suddenly alighted on the branch again, fixing their shining black eyes on her. Then one of them flew straight down, landing with little curved feet on her shoulder. She let out a short, surprised laugh.

The bird flapped its wings to stay on as she walked, its tiny claws tickling her.

"This is incredible," Tori said, her head fixed straight ahead to keep from disturbing it.

Elnora smiled. "It's a shame you were never allowed a pet."

"My mother follows precedent. Her mother was bitten by a dog as a child, so when she came into power, she banned all animals from the palace, except those kept for food. After she died, my mother continued the practice."

"Maybe this one will stay with you," Elnora said.

But as soon as the words were out, the bird took flight and returned to its mate, who welcomed it with singing.

After a while, the forest ended and a path covered in pink petals greeted them. A grove of blossoming peach trees bordered the sides.

Soon, a beautiful village came into view, with little arched bridges that passed over a watercourse dotted with flowering lily pads. Conical hills shrouded in mist rose in the background, behind the village's soft colors.

People carried baskets or guided little children along paths of crystalline pebbles. Lines of trees laden with fruit stretched out on the right like a well-tended orchard; much of the fruit should have been out of season in the spring—pears, apples, cherries—and all of it was bigger than any Tori had ever seen.

At the head of each line of trees sat fruit sellers, their stalls surrounded by customers chatting and picking up fruit. No money was exchanged; instead, people traded items. One woman held up a necklace of simple beads, and several fruits were counted into her hands in exchange.

At first, it struck Tori as odd—the trees were clearly public property: from time to time, a passing child would pick a fruit and eat it openly. But the joy on the people's faces told her they weren't trading because they had to. They were doing it for the sheer pleasure.

A jarring voice shattered the scene's tranquility. "Fresh fruit! Get your fresh fruit here!" A man with a basket hanging from his neck paced back and forth among the customers. One or two people spared a glance in his direction, but most ignored him.

"Get your fresh fruits here! Just two skades apiece!"

"Why is nobody buying from him?" Elnora asked.

Tori's mouth twisted. "Apart from his obnoxious voice?"

"That's Old Griff," Master Banfay said. "He sells his fruits for skades instead of trading, so there aren't many takers."

"Maybe he needs the money," Elnora said. "Could I go see what he has?"

Tori shrugged, and with that, Elnora walked away. The man extolled the virtues of his fruits loudly, the same free fruits hanging from every tree.

Tori shook her head. "I guess nowhere is safe from charlatans."

As they strolled on, vibrations shook her belly, and she looked around to see who was causing it. But it seemed to be coming from everywhere—Master Banfay had said his village harbored wielders, after all. She resolved to ignore it and focus on her surroundings.

Every building was flawlessly maintained, from polished wood porches, to the shining tiles of crescent-moon eaves. But one building in particular made her stare: a stately three-story structure crafted entirely of jade. Its pillars were so light they were nearly white, while its roof tiles were made of something she had never seen: jade the color of sea-foam, glistening in the morning sun.

"What is this place?" she asked, keeping her eyes on it as they passed.

"The Pavilion of Honorable Logograms," Master Banfay said. He shot her a wry look. "Otherwise known as the library."

Elnora returned, an apple in each hand. "These are amazing," she said, eating one of them. She held the other out to Tori.

"Charlatan fruit? No thanks."

With an indulgent smile, Elnora slid the uneaten apple into her pack before taking another bite of the one in her hand.

The village surprised Tori. She hadn't imagined it would be so bustling, that this many people had tasted the elixir.

"How many people live here?" Tori asked.

"About seven thousand," he said. "Although the master healers and peacekeepers—" Something caught his attention. "Look," he said, jerking his chin, "there are your prisoners."

About a hundred paces away, a group followed a woman who was talking and pointing, clearly giving a tour. But these people were well-dressed and walked with an air of confidence, nothing like those she remembered from the dungeon.

"Are you sure?"

He nodded. "They're the only new group big enough to need a guide. As I was saying, we're about seven thousand, but master healers and peacekeepers spend most of their time outside the village."

"What are peacekeepers?" Elnora asked.

"Look." He pointed to an immense, open-air arena beside the watercourse, comprised of three levels that rose one behind the other like giant steps and surrounded by a wall of rough-hewn stone.

On the top level, children moved slowly through some kind of martial form. The level below held a group of adults training with long staves.

Master Banfay led them up the stairs through a tall wooden gateway that connected the walls, stopping just inside the lowest level, where a crowd watched two men spar in a dirt circle.

The master healer unshouldered his trunk and set it next to his feet, then folded his arms on his chest, watching. One of the men was clearly from Hanmar, with hair the color of ripe wheat that flowed to his shoulders. He stood a head taller than his opponent and fought with a sword.

The other man was slim, with short, dark hair, and although he held two long knives, a bow hung on his back.

The man from Hanmar stalked the ring with controlled, predatory ease while the slender man watched, alert and coiled, as though ready to spring. The first man's face came into view, and Tori raised a slow eyebrow—he stood broad and golden, like a sunlit pillar, with a face that made sense of the many women packing the front, watching him.

Weapons rang and steel flashed in a flurry, but before Tori could follow what was happening, the crowd cheered, and the men separated, bowed to each other, and sheathed their weapons.

"Who won?" she asked, but as the golden-haired man slipped through the crowd, so many people clapped him on the back that it left no doubt in her mind as to the victor. He acknowledged each of his well-wishers with a humble dip of the head. Then he strode to some weapons racks lining the wall and stood for a few moments, polishing his blade.

He had only just sheathed it when a group of children ran to him from behind, brandishing wooden swords. One boy lunged, striking the man on the hip. The man turned, but instead of scolding the boy, or ignoring him, he snatched a wooden sword from the rack beside him, and held it out in challenge. The boy grinned and lunged again, striking over and over as the man blocked him so effortlessly that the long sleeves of his robe didn't even swing.

It ended soon after: the boy's sword slipped from his hand and skittered across the grass. He hung his head, evidently shamed, but the man picked up the sword and held it out—hilt first, like a real weapon—then bowed to the boy, like a real opponent. The other children looked on, astonished, and when the man had walked away, they cheered and clapped their friend on the shoulder, like a real champion. The man's lips twitched with the hint of a smile.

Warmth spread through Tori's chest at this act of kindness, so small, yet so rare and precious. She studied the man's broad back as he mounted the steps to the second level, sword strapped to his hip, golden hair shining like that of the ancient warriors painted on Countess Ellie's ceiling.

He seemed so different from the dullards who courted her at the palace. Would it be too much to hope he was a noble?

"We'd better move on," Master Banfay said, hoisting his trunk.

Outside the arena they passed a white stone building.

"The weapons house," Master Banfay said as they walked by. "Everything in there is made of sentient metal."

The demonstration at court of the bow and arrow came back to her, and she stared at the building, trying to imagine an entire storeroom filled with such things.

"So, what did you say peacekeepers are?" Elnora asked.

"There are three traveling professions in Peach Blossom Grove," he replied, "master healers, alchemists, and peacekeepers. Those"—he pointed a thumb back toward the arena—"are the peacekeepers. You already know what master healers are, and alchemists are the money makers." He turned to nod at the jade structure shining in the distance behind them. "Everything you see here is paid for by them."

The old writings had sometimes referenced alchemy in vague terms, but Tori couldn't picture how it worked.

"Being a master healer pays well," Tori said. "Surely it's not just the alchemists who bring in money."

"Master healers rarely make a profit," he said. "Anyone who's ever bought a top-grade spirit stone understands that."

They soon came to an arched bridge with flowering peach trees at the end, followed by several white cottages. Bamboo porches gave the cottages a cozy charm, and slate gray roof tiles shone in the sun, with pink lanterns swinging from their crescent-moon corners.

Master Banfay stopped at a cottage, turning right and left as though looking for someone. "I had expected to see my father at the training grounds," he said. "I need to check which one of these you can stay at."

A few more paces took them to a stone path surrounded by neatly trimmed hedges.

"Ah, good," he said, as a young man in light blue robes came into view from the direction Tori hadn't yet discovered.

The man was tall and trim and strode toward them with courtly elegance. He was stunningly handsome: the very image of masculine beauty, the way Tori had always imagined the male members of the Six—dark, brooding eyebrows, full lips, dimpled chin. Yet his beauty, oddly, didn't stir her to anything but respectful admiration; she might have been gazing at the youthful portrait of one of her grandfathers.

Like Master Banfay, a topknot secured half the man's black hair, leaving a masculine fringe to frame his face, while the rest hung straight down his back. A tiny white gem shone on his forehead like a little star.

When he was close, he gazed straight past them toward the village.

Master Banfay clasped his hands and bowed. "Father."

Elnora's eyes bulged, reflecting Tori's sentiments. They looked the same age.

"I've brought—"

"I am sorry, Banfay. Can it wait?" the man said, looking as though he would pass them.

"I just need to know which cottage to put them in."

The man stopped, first taking in Elnora, then Tori. His face was kind, but like Master Banfay, he held her gaze intently, as if he could read her thoughts, and his eyes sparkled with a strange light. She looked away.

"These three cottages are empty—any of them will do," he said, and strode away.

Master Banfay shrugged, then opened the closest front gate.

"Your father certainly has aged well!" Elnora said, eyes still wide. "I'd like to know which herbs he takes!"

As they made their way to the door of the cottage, several more people passed, wearing the same shining gems. Every one of them somehow looked both ancient and young, even those whose hair was snow white. One of them met Tori's stare as she passed, and that same disturbing light flashed out of their eyes.

Master Banfay opened the door. “Drop off your bags. I’ll take you to the elder now.”

“Just one question,” Tori said, as soon as the people were out of sight. “Who are all those wearing the white gems?”

Master Banfay reached into his sleeve, then tied something around his forehead. When he looked up again, a little white gem hung in the middle of his brow, and his eyes shone with the same strange light.

“Those,” he said, “are the immortals.”

Chapter Twenty-Seven

THE ELDER

Tori followed Master Banfay in silence, trying to decide whether she should address him differently now that he was immortal.

I don't even know what an immortal is.

Longevitists sometimes referred to their sect elders as immortals, but Master Banfay looked far too young to be an elder. And although she wasn't intimidated—she refused to be—it seemed sensible to keep any questions to herself until she could figure out the protocol. She hoped this happened before she met the elder—the elder's impression of Tori could make the difference between finding the Septad or not; she had to impress her.

Elnora, on the other hand, was evidently awestruck: she walked beside Tori with hands folded, lips pressed shut, stepping as softly as possible.

They soon came to a stone wall covered in patches of purple moss, which turned out to be bunches of tiny flowers. She pointed them out to Elnora.

"*Warm clover*," Master Banfay said when he noticed Elnora studying them. "Good for warming the interior, when a patient suffers chills."

Elnora glanced at his star-jewel and nodded.

"They bloom only on the fifth day of the fifth moon each year, to signal the coming of warmer weather," he said.

At the end of the wall, a copse of oak trees greeted them, their grandeur speaking of centuries, yet their bark green as a young shoot's. Tori ran her fingertips over one of the smooth trunks and could have sworn she felt it shiver.

On the ground, a crystal-clear streamlet trickled past, twinkling. She followed it. It wound through the copse and into the sunlight, where it flashed like a gem, blinding her. When her eyes refocused, the sight ahead of her made her halt: an arc of silver trees, shiny as a new dram. Fruits like blue pears hung from their branches, except that, like spirit stones, they glowed from within.

Master Banfay didn't spare them a glance as they passed, whereas Tori couldn't stop staring. A few paces later, the streamlet tunneled underground and disappeared.

"That's where we're going," he said, his gaze on the cliffs and conical hills lining the horizon. He indicated a cliff shaped like a cresting wave, with a waterfall flowing off the tip. Tori's stomach tensed. She might leave that cliff knowing where to find the Septad...or, like in Hanmar, be sent away with nothing.

Since Master Banfay's tone was as conversational as ever as he pointed out several other places of interest while they walked, Tori deduced that no particular protocol was necessary when speaking to immortals.

"Is this a longevitist sect, then?" she asked.

He shook his head. "Longevitists are united by the desire to expand their stone kernels and increase their power. In Peach Blossom Grove, we are more like family. Our goal is simply to live in peace, and do good in the outside world. Having said that, to achieve our ends, we do employ many of the same practices and forms as longevitists. Essence cycling, for instance; except that, where longevitists cycle their essence, we cycle—and are guided by—the elixir."

Everyone understood dawn-essence. It had existed since the dawn of the world, created when Ketuan released her first breath. Elixir cycling was another matter, but before she could ask him to explain, they arrived at their destination.

The wave-shaped cliff towered more than two hundred handspans high, its rugged face softened by draping vines of pink, blue, and yellow flowers. At its center, a shimmering waterfall tumbled into a pool of a deep turquoise color, scattering mist, which caught the light and unfurled rainbows.

Master Banfay led them around the left side of the pool till they came to a crude staircase hewn into the cliff face. He started walking up and motioned for them to follow, but Tori stood rooted to the ground. The stairs had no rail, and were barely three handspans wide—at least to her nervous gaze. He was halfway up before he looked back again, spinning on the narrow steps so carelessly it made her stomach lurch.

"Come. This is the elder's home," he said, then turned and continued up.

Tori considered making the climb on her hands and knees, but her dignity wouldn't allow it.

"Lean on the side of the cliff, Princess," Elnora said. "I'm right here behind you."

"That's no comfort. If I fall, I'll take us both to our deaths."

But she followed Elnora's advice and squeezed herself against the cold, damp cliff, forcing her rigid legs upward, one step at a time, willing her eyes away from the neck-breaking drop.

At the top of the stairs, mist hit her face, and the waterfall roared in front of her. The stairs ended in a ledge that, while not as wide as she would have liked, was at least wide enough to allow her to breathe again.

"Well, this is it," Master Banfay said.

Tori looked around. "Where?"

"The elder's cave is on the other side of the waterfall. A word of advice: run in, or the force of it could push you backward into the pool."

She stared at him in disbelief. "Tell me you're jesting."

"I'd open it for you, but alas, I'm not a wielder," he said, stepping aside.

Tori let out a breath. "Come on, Elnora. Let's go."

"I'm afraid you'll need to go alone," Master Banfay said. "The elder will be expecting only you."

Bracing herself, Tori filled her lungs and plunged into the falls. The icy force of it knocked out her breath, and she stumbled into darkness, gasping.

Spots of green light appeared, one by one, until her eyes finally adjusted: she was standing in a cave no larger than her cottage's sitting room, with walls covered in green crystals.

To her left, a faint light shone through a wide arch cut into the stone—an entranceway.

She passed under the arch, shivering at the top of four steps that overlooked a hall. Its smooth stone walls were covered in carvings of mythical creatures, and intricate designs had been engraved into the stone blocks that made up the floor. Lining both sides of the hall were six porticoes with pillars and crescent-moon roofs, each apparently hewn from a single block of stone, and a statue more than twice her height stood guarding the entrance of each.

All of the figures held a sword, though each displayed a different heroic pose, and as she crept through the hall, she recognized them as depictions of Ishairo from various old tales.

At the end of the hall, an opening in the rock above let down a stream of light onto the head of a seventh figure, larger than the rest. Tori stared up at it, teeth chattering from cold, trying to puzzle out which story it came from. This time Ishairo leaned on his sword, which he held point down with two clasped hands, his head bowed, eyes closed serenely.

His posture spoke of sadness, and a heaviness settled on her. She took a breath and straightened herself, trying to focus on the reason she had come.

Suddenly, a great shadow loomed over her, and Tori cried out in fear. She turned to run, but a rumbling voice rooted her in place. "Don't be afraid."

Out from the darkness behind Ishairo stepped a nine-headed dog the size of a horse.

"The elder is expecting you," the dog's central head said, while the other heads sniffed at the air around her. "Follow me."

Tori went, legs trembling from fear as well as cold, leaving the final statue of Ishairo behind. When they had reached another cavern, the dog moved aside, letting her through.

Unlike the little entranceway, this cave was enormous, comprised of various levels, and though parts of it lay in shadow, it was, on the whole, well lit. Thin shafts of light streamed down from above, while a fire roared in a fireplace carved to look like a tiger's mouth. Beside it, a figure with long silver hair and light-colored eyes sat straight-backed at a table of stone. Her robes were white, tied with a silver sash. The elder.

"Welcome, Tori, Min Daughter," she said, her smooth voice resonating throughout the cavern.

Tori stepped onto a wide stone bridgeway that led to the elder. The closer she came to the woman, however, the closer she came to a presence that emanated such majesty, Tori had to fight the urge to kneel.

When she was close enough to see the elder's face, she struggled to contain her surprise: the eyes she had thought were merely light-colored showed themselves to be completely white. She was blind.

"Come, sit," the elder said, indicating the stool across from her. Then she lifted her hand and flicked it, as though swatting away an insect, and a warm gust of wind blew out of nowhere, drying Tori's hair and clothes. Tori looked around, wondering where it had come from.

"I had not realized the Min Daughter was counted among the Royal Tribe," the elder said, "nor had my eyes discerned her noble lineage before this moment."

Thrown off-balance by the elder's reference to her sight, Tori said, "Min Daughter is the title of the heir to the Imperial House of Min." She immediately felt foolish—of course the elder knew this!

"I speak of Ishairo's Royal Tribe," the elder said.

Tori knit her brow, trying to work out the puzzle—Ishairo had been the sole heir of a family who, at the time, was known as the Royal Tribe, but he had no offspring. How could she answer in a way that seemed respectful? She wanted to make the right impression.

"I don't believe my ancestry can be traced back to Ishairo's near kin," she said at last. "My ancestor, Yanai Sumi, was known to have other origins."

"All belong to the Royal Tribe who have partaken of the sacred elixir," the elder replied. "For its essence flows ever through your dawn channels. Did you not know it?"

A soul-deep tremor shook her, churning up questions of when she had first taken the elixir, and why.

"Elder," she said, "what is the elixir?"

"To understand this truth, you must first understand that which came before," she said. "As all know, at the end of the Third Age, Ishairo defeated the Watani and their fell gods, the Fox Dragons. With a mighty hand he did plunge his sword into the ground, and the ground quaked and rent asunder, and from the depths a great geyser of water gushed forth. It surged with such terrible force that the very land upon which the enemy stood was borne away across the waters, to the farthest reaches where the sea dragons make their dwelling.

"Then there was great rejoicing in the land, so great that the sound of triumph rose unto the high heavens, even to the Celestial City of Jade, the abode of Suro herself. And Suro, on hearing the exultation, inquired as to its cause, and learned of the fall of the Fox Dragons, and of the sundering of Shudon that had borne the enemy away, and she was well pleased. And so, as the ancient songs declare, she sent forth a light, both dreadful and wondrous, upon the blade of Ishairo—a radiance like unto purple lightning, wherein she did bestow upon him the gift of immortality.

"Never before or since was such a boon granted to any mortal, and so she named him Emperor of the Nine Directions, and bestowed upon him the Celestial Seal, that sigil of authority forged in the Celestial City itself, where flames burn undimmed and ever pure. Do you know how the story ends?"

Tori knew it well, and she was glad to have an opportunity to impress the elder. "Yes. This granted him the authority to rule Shudon from the Celestial City of Jade."

"Indeed. Thus did Ishairo depart from the people, that he might ascend the hallowed heights of Mount Ketwanen and stand before the great altar of Suro, to make his sacrifice of rice and osmanthus wine, as was ordained of old. In so doing, he would fulfill the final rite required for him to take his place in the celestial abode.

"And so, at the appointed time, upon the eve of the new moon, he set forth on the sacred path with his sister-in-law—Anaiah, the ever faithful." She turned her white gaze on Tori. "Do you know of her?"

Tori nodded. "She was the wife of Jilo, Ishairo's sworn brother who had fallen in battle."

The elder looked pleased. "And there was another who went with them, one the stories do not tell of—one of ancient days—a nine-headed hound, a High Spirit of ages past who had guarded Ishairo from his birth, watching over him in trial and triumph."

Tori had never heard this part. She glanced uncomfortably to the corridor where she had last seen the frightening beast. Was this one an ancient High Spirit as well?

The elder continued, "And at the end of their journey, Anaiah perceived that Ishairo's thoughts were troubled, and she urged him to unburden himself to her. And so he did, and she understood that he had made a plan as they were ascending the sacred heights. She shuddered within herself, for this plan was one only an immortal could have contrived, for Ishairo had been granted immortality and thus had gained the knowledge of an immortal. In the depths of his soul he perceived what the sacrifice of an immortal could accomplish, and his heart was glad. Thus, he laid bare his purpose to Anaiah and prayed her to do his will.

"And he gave her a small vial made of spirit jade, that rare and wondrous stone as is only found in the hidden places of Shudon. This was the same vial that had been bestowed upon him in his youth by the nine-headed hound. You may not know this," she said, looking at

Tori, "but spirit jade, when filled, never runs out, and Ishairo's guardian hound had gifted it to him that he might never want for medicine in his time of need.

"This same vial then he entrusted to Anaiah when at last they reached the summit, where sat the great altar of Suro. Then did Ishairo set forth his offerings—rice and osmanthus wine—upon the altar, and lifted his eyes to heaven, preparing to fulfill his fate."

A faraway look crossed the elder's face, as though she watched the scene in her mind's eye, and a shadow of pain crossed her face. "And from the vast heavens a great sphere of white fire descended with terrible majesty. But before it struck the altar, Ishairo, swift as lightning, smote the stone with his sword, crying aloud, 'If I offer nothing but rice and wine, my blessings shall be mine alone. But if I offer my sword upon the altar, many shall share in my happy fate.'

"And his sword pierced the altar of Suro, and its sacred stone shuddered and cracked. But it did not rend asunder as the land of Shudon had—for this was the altar of Suro. So the fire of Suro descended upon the altar, consuming the rice and the wine, along with the vessels that bore them. The sword, though, remained unscathed, for it held Ishairo's stone kernel, and he was already bound in immortality.

"Yet nothing, neither mortal nor immortal, can wholly withstand the fire of Suro for long. The blade melted from hilt to tip, becoming a lake of molten gold, clear as crystal. Vast it was, for it was wrought of an immortal's kernel. Then Ishairo, his strength spent, collapsed upon the ground, and his form shimmered like gold. His body became like a mist, until nothing remained of him but a cloud of golden dust. The golden dust whirled in the air, as though reluctant to leave, then at last drifted to the lake and descended upon it, till it was gathered in and lost to mortal sight."

The elder paused, face heavy with emotion. "And the lake was named Kenjing, which in the Old Speech means 'Lake of the Sword.' And Ishairo had bidden Anaiah that when his sword was unmade, she should fill her vial with the waters from the lake." Her white gaze met Tori's. "This water is the elixir."

Silence filled the cave, broken only by the crackling of the fire as Tori tried to absorb what she had heard.

"Now Tori, Min Daughter," the elder said, "what is it you seek? Though I can see many things, I cannot see all."

Tori's stomach tensed. Her moment had come.

The command in the elder's voice, the majesty of her presence, the gravity of Ishairo's tale—it all made her request feel so trivial. How could she, after all she had just heard of sacrifice, admit that the one thing she wanted was to be free from her mother's threats?

As she studied the elder's ageless face, somehow aware that the woman was older than anyone she had ever seen, Tori considered how to proceed. The very old usually looked kindly on the young, didn't they? If Tori said the right thing, surely she could convince the elder to help her. Only, she wasn't sure what the right thing was. What would someone who had seen everything value most?

Tori squared her shoulders. "I'm here to stop a war," she said. It had worked with Master Banfay, after all. "My mother wishes to unite Shudon under the Min banner by conquering Jeng. I came to ask you to help me find the Septad."

The elder fixed her with grave white eyes. "And how would the Septad help you?"

"I was told Antiquitals still exist," Tori said. "My mother could use it to summon them."

A shadow of displeasure darkened the elder's face.

"Not to fight," Tori said quickly. "One look at them would bring Jeng to its knees. The war would be over before it began, saving countless lives. If you could tell me where it is, or even give me an indication of where I might begin to look..."

The elder shook her head. "The last Septad was wrought thousands of years ago, before the time of Ishairo. It has since returned to Ketuan's Veins, unmade by its maker."

Tori's arms dropped to her sides, fingers slack.

"Could someone make a new one?"

"You ask a hard thing. The very first maker of a Septad was Ailin—firstborn of Ayenashi, the Water Matron; her power shaped it in the earliest days. But among mortals, such a feat could only be performed by a sixfold wielder."

Tori's face prickled.

Working with a wielder won't contaminate me. I'm cured.

"In the annals of time," the elder continued, "only three such people have walked the face of Arizan: Ishairo, foremost among them; his ancestor, the first queen of the Royal Tribe; and finally, one from among my own council—Master Koren. I am certain, however, that he will not help you."

Her disastrous search for the Well of Dissolution overshadowed her, and a knot twisted in her stomach. *I'm not destined to fail*, she told herself. *I can't be.*

"Please, just let me speak with him," Tori said. "I'm certain I could convince him if given the chance."

"The Septad is a jewel beyond all others, and forging it requires rare skill. Master Koren has neither the time nor the will to bend his mind to such a craft."

"I've come all this way," Tori said. "And isn't the cause a good one?"

The elder considered this, the crackle of the fire again filling the silence.

Finally, she nodded. "Then I grant you my approval to try. Ask Master Banfay to make the introduction—but temper your expectations, lest disappointment find you."

Tori launched herself back through the waterfall to where Banfay and Elnora waited; her mind was so preoccupied with arguments she could make to convince Master Koren, that she barely heard Elnora's whispering questions, and they reached the bottom step before she could register fear.

As they neared the residences, however, the approach of male voices brought her back to the present. The two men she had seen sparring earlier were headed in her direction.

Tori's hands darted instinctively to the hair plastered to her forehead from her exit through the waterfall. She nudged Elnora. "Quick! Fix me."

Elnora glanced at the men, then responded with a burst of fluffing and smoothing that stopped when the men were a few paces away.

As he approached, Tori fixed her eyes on the golden-haired man, her lips curved into a bare smile. To her mortification, he walked straight past without looking at her, nodded at something his friend said, then turned into one of the cottages and shut the door.

Embarrassment burned her skin.

"It's probably for the best," Elnora whispered, with a meaningful glance at Tori's hair.

She was right—this was the worst possible time to make a first impression. Tori pushed the incident from her mind.

"Master Banfay," she said, "I would very much appreciate if you would introduce me to Master Koren. The elder said the Septad has to be made, and he's the only one who can make it."

He turned a questioning eye on her. "I already introduced you. Outside the cottages."

The image of the courtly man with the disturbing eyes came to her, and Tori's fingers stilled halfway through adjusting her wet sash. "Your father is Master Koren?"

Master Banfay nodded. "I'll see what I can do."

Chapter Twenty-Eight

GLADE OF CELESTIAL VIRTUE

Lavish residences sprawled outside Zinchen's carriage window as the Glade of Celestial Virtue came into view. Entering the walled quarter where her intimates lived always provided both satisfaction and regret: satisfaction at having made seventy-seven advantageous alliances—an auspicious number in the eyes of the people; regret at the scarcity of intimates worth her time. Their mothers were worse, silk-robed vultures salivating for wealth and power behind simpering masks.

She let out a quiet breath, longing for a few moments of peace.

The carriage rolled to a stop beside a bamboo-spout fountain that trickled water into a stone basin, a reflection of the simple elegance of Lord Kai, her seventy-seventh intimate. Of all her intimates, he was the least complicated, and the one with whom she felt she could be almost completely herself. Perhaps that would be enough to make her forget her frustrations—for a little while, at least. Tonight, that was all she desired.

As her driver opened the carriage door, Zinchen reached for a small wooden box on the seat beside her, tucking it into her robes. Servants rushed out to greet her, followed by a handsome young man who took the stairs two by two.

Lord Kai smiled down on her and bowed. The moment they were in the house, however, he wrapped her in a warm embrace—something none of her other intimates would dare. But his simplicity of taste reflected his simplicity in all things, including simple, honest affection, and she let herself melt into him, breathing him in. He smelled like the first bloom of spring.

Here, in the presence of someone so fresh and full of promise, she could pretend for a while that she was no longer the incarnation of Min, but simply a woman, safe and loved.

She led the way to a window overlooking the gardens, where they took their seats at a table laden with elegant dishes. Male servants—no females were allowed to attend her intimates—came and poured the wine.

"Is something the matter?" he said, taking a sip from his cup. "You look burdened."

Of course he saw it. She masked her emotions flawlessly—no one else would have noticed. But he did. Always.

"When is an empress not burdened?" she said.

"What can I do to help? Give me a task to ease you." He reached over to touch her hand.

She took a bite of chicken to signal the beginning of the meal. "The burdens of the crown are mine alone to bear. But you ease me with the ease of your conversation. Here, I will forget my hassles for a while."

She meant the words, yet her mind churned as they ate. It had been fourteen days since Tori's defiance, and still nothing was resolved.

Irritation sparked faintly inside her. If Tori had compromised Zinchen's plans with Countess Ellie, that wielder lover of hers would pay with his life. The problem was, Lina still hadn't found him.

Then, of course, there was the matter of Dan and Bokoon—an escalating parade of incompetence. The moment Zinchen had discovered Marne's carriage was gone, she knew Tori's destination, and had dispatched the girl's guards on horseback to intercept her before she could reach Hanmar.

Four days later a note arrived by hawk—which Zinchen had naturally received the same day—reporting that they had seen no sign of the princess on the road and were headed to Hanmar Manor.

Two more days, and Countess Ellie's own hawk arrived, saying she had met with Tori that very day, and would write more via messenger.

After a further three days, Dan and Bokoon had shown up again at the palace, empty-handed.

It had become farcical, a comedy of errors, only stripped of amusement. Zinchen had sent them straight back to Hanmar, four days ago now; at a suitable pace, they should have reached Hanmar Manor yesterday—and yet, no message.

Her lips tightened. They deserved severe punishment, that was clear. If it weren't for her need for their lord...

Lord Akiren's face came to her then, his slow progress with Joktan and Javin compounding her irritations. As though two already trained soldiers required another lifetime to learn the Varanaken's ways. Delay bred weakness, and she couldn't afford either.

Kai was staring at her in that quiet way he had. Determined once again to forget her frustrations, Zinchen turned her mind to the official reason for her visit.

"Now tell me," she said, "what does your mother request?"

"There are four courses planned. If I tell you now, you'll have no reason to stay for the next one."

"When have I ever needed a reason to dine with you? Our last dinner was five days ago."

His eyes shone playfully. "In that case, my mother says she hopes you're well, and also hopes you'll consider giving her niece a title, spare a few gold petals for the grain stores, and send her a more competent court scribe—preferably before the next moon."

"She will have my decision in three days."

He dipped his head. "Now remember, you gave your word—you have to stay till the end."

She smiled. Her other intimates fawned over her, as men of position might be expected to. Flattery, after all, was their mother tongue. But Kai...he gave his heart without calculation, a quality so rare. Rarer still was the fact that she wanted it.

In her forty-five years she had only ever felt this way once: with Lord Tam, Tori's late father. But though she had been much younger then, her love for Tam had been a mature love: all respect, stripped of passion. With Kai, she felt like a girl. And like a girl, she sometimes wondered if it was too good to be true.

In the silences that peppered their dinner conversation, she simply watched him. He took a sip of wine now and paused, cup in hand, a shaft of sunlight bathing his jaw in a warm glow, transforming him into an artist's sculpture, painfully unreal.

"Well, then," she said, when dinner ended, "the only question that remains is whether you can persuade me to stay *past* dinner." She raised an eyebrow.

He hid a smile. "I'll do my best."

They moved to a gazebo overlooking a koi pond, and Zinchen patted the little box she had managed to keep hidden throughout the meal. Now seemed like the right time.

"How is your archery coming along?" she asked, sitting on the gazebo bench.

"Improving. But I still have a long way to go. Here." He took a pink silk bag from his sleeve. "I know how you love feeding the fish."

The bag was filled with oats, which she sprinkled into the pond. A mob of koi fish materialized, splashing over each other feverishly, like men competing for a prize.

"Is Lord Varu still in the lead, then?" In spite of his insufferable mother, the son of the Minister of the Left was her next favorite after Kai, and a skilled archer.

"He is. Last week he shot a hundred and forty-nine birds in a single day."

"Impressive." She made a mental note to have Lina send him a reward.

Kai nodded good-naturedly. "No one can beat him, especially poor Lord Janek. He has given the forfeit feast for six weeks running."

"If he is always last, why does he insist on competing?"

Kai shrugged. "Only the Six know. He constantly complains he's running out of wine. Personally, though, I think he simply enjoys playing host."

"And where did you place last week?" She sprinkled the last of the oats and dusted off her fingertips.

"Third."

Zinchen exhaled a soft laugh. "In no time, you will be first."

He smiled, eyes lowered. There was a disarming innocence about him that brought a tender ache to her chest. He was young, of course—twenty years her junior—but still far too old for innocence. And yet, it was there. It was nothing like simplemindedness, either; Kai was sharper than the brushstroke of a court scribe, and knowledgeable about many things. Yet he was just... She searched for the right word, her eyes drifting past the pond and into an unspoiled garden. Yes, that was it. He was just wholly unspoiled.

Not for the first time, she wondered how he had ever grown undisturbed among the thorny, grasping nobility.

"I have something for you," she said, slipping the box from her sleeve.

He opened it. His face registered first curiosity, then surprise, then delight. "Etched metal," he said, gaze locked on to the gift.

"The same etchings I saw in court—do you remember I told you? I had them replicated by the clan who made the originals. Now you will win all of the archery competitions."

Kai's face fell. "I'd rather do it on my own skill," he said with note of apology. "The master archer you sent to teach me says I'm coming along well." He held the box reverently in two hands. "But I'll use this for my hunting. I've always wanted to hit an eight-point stag, but I was afraid to miss the mark and make it suffer."

Something like pity filled her. Kai was a person of rare purity. Purity couldn't survive in the palace. The palace only respected power.

Still, perhaps there was one way, something she had been pondering lately.

"Use the gift as you wish," she said. "You must have already earned the admiration of the others, coming in third out of—how many compete?"

"Usually around fifty," he said, looking modest.

"Fifty. Which means two-thirds of the men see you as capable. This will be useful when you are head of the intimates."

She waited for her words to register.

His eyes widened, and a flush spread over his cheeks, the twist of his lips displaying a mix of embarrassment and pleasure.

"You will need to mask your emotions better than that," she said, smiling. "Governing people, even if it is only seventy-six, requires a show of neutrality."

"My mother is only a regional governor," he said. "I'm not worthy to be royal consort."

"You are worthy if I say you are."

A shadow crossed his face then, and he said, "Some might not accept it. Some are jealous."

Her eyes narrowed. She needed the loyalty of all the houses she had allied with, and jealousy threatened loyalty. More than that, though, it bothered her that anyone might be looking unfavorably on Kai.

"Why should they be jealous? I more than fulfill my duty to them. Every one of them lives like a king, and no one is denied their biannual meetings—where, I might add, most of their houses' requests are granted."

But she knew their jealousy's true source. Outside the requisite biannual meals, few were chosen for anything more. Her small group of favorites therefore were inevitably observed with jealous eyes by the others. As a favorite, an intimate provided his mother with more opportunities to make requests of Zinchen, as well as inspiring in each of those women the hope that their son might further elevate his standing by siring a royal child—ridiculous, at Zinchen's age, but there it was. And among her favorites, most of her free nights were spent with Lord Kai. It made sense that he would evoke the greatest jealousy of all.

How dare they. As though her intimates had any right to judge her private choices.

"My intimates will accept any decision I make. As for their mothers, they have already done well in allying their sons to me; they can hardly expect more. There can be only one royal consort, after all."

"It's more than that," he said, discomfort growing on his face. "Recently I received"—he looked down at the etched arrowhead, brushing a thumb over it—"a mysterious gift. Sweets. At first I thought it was from you, but then there was no note..."

"And?"

"Since I wasn't sure what to think, I gave it to one of my servants and forgot about it—until he ate some."

"What do you mean?"

"Well, first his cheeks turned pale, then his fingernails turned blue. After that, he fell unconscious."

Her spine straightened.

"Midra cured him, thankfully," he said.

"Did she say what it was?"

He looked at her hesitantly. "Moonshade essence."

Poison.

She went completely still. She would not permit this; someone would be made to pay with their life.

"Why didn't you tell me sooner?"

Kai took her hand and kissed it, then drew her into an embrace. "I didn't want to you to worry. It's just...when you mentioned promoting me to royal consort, I thought you should know that things among the intimates aren't as simple as they may seem. We might hunt together, have tournaments, laugh together at dinners. But at the heart of it, we're all still rivals, and my rank is the lowest among them." He met her eye. "Please don't worry. I won't be eating any mystery food."

The protectiveness of his manner softened something inside her. She commanded more power in her little finger than he could ever dream of, yet his only desire was to keep her safe.

She nestled against him and breathed in his purity, determined to preserve it.

"Shall I play for you?" he asked, clearly trying to lift her mood. He gave a signal, and a servant brought in a cushion with a priceless jade flute on it, a gift from Zinchen.

She reclined on her side to show she was at ease, and a soft, dreamlike melody flooded the atmosphere, drawing in even the fish. But her mind remained restless: promoting Kai to royal consort might be his only protection. She needed to put the pieces in place fast.

The arrival of a messenger in black-and-gold livery disturbed her thoughts.

"Your Majesty," he said, out of breath. "Dan and Bokoon are waiting in your private audience chamber. They said they have news of the princess."

Chapter Twenty-Nine

TIMELY LETTERS

Zinchen narrowed her eyes at the men standing before the dais. Dan and Bokoon, who stood with straight-backed Varanaken confidence, nonetheless began shifting from foot to foot as the silence pressed on.

"You were instructed to return with the Min Daughter," Zinchen said at last. "How is it you are standing before me empty-handed?"

Dan dipped his head, eyes shifting nervously. "We had ridden two days when we intercepted the princess's carriage driver, as well as Countess Ellie's messenger..." His voice trailed off as though he had lost his train of thought.

Bokoon, evidently more confident from having addressed Zinchen in the past, came to his rescue. "Your Majesty, the driver confirmed the princess was no longer at Hanmar Manor, and since he didn't know where she was, and since the messenger was on foot carrying a letter from the countess, we thought we had better bring it to you without delay." He held out a rolled paper, sealed with yellow wax.

Zinchen steepled her fingers. "You saw fit to intercept royal correspondence," she said, frost in her voice. "Without my leave."

The men flinched.

Her brother Yan had been right. The Varanaken were not aware, it seemed, that they were her subjects: they had no regard whatsoever for discerning her will—a defect she would be able to remedy once Lord Akiren finished training Joktan and Javin.

She made a subtle gesture, and Lina took the letter. As Zinchen read it, however, her displeasure cooled.

Countess Ellie spoke at length of the great honor, etcetera, of receiving the Min Daughter in her court, of the princess's poise and wisdom and beauty, and so on. Zinchen, scanning through the fluff, landed at last on a phrase that piqued her interest:

May Your Majesty's reign prosper, like the golden era of your august ancestor Yanai Sumi, like the victory of Ishairo in the establishment of a united Shudon. And be assured that in all things, the House of Hanmar is in every way forever at your service.

She dissected the countess's meaning. Ishairo and Yanai Sumi had one thing in common: each, under their own banner, had unified a broken land—Ishairo first, joining disparate clans into one united Shudon; then, much later, when Shudon had split into north and south, Yanai Sumi had consolidated the fragmented southern queendoms into one empire—the Min Territories. Countess Ellie was hinting that she not only understood but also unequivocally supported Zinchen's cause.

A smile glowed faintly within her. Tori had succeeded, and, judging by the tone of Ellie's letter, far better than Marne Wessel would have. Zinchen had never even told Tori the true nature of Envoy Lee's request.

The girl's insight is impeccable. Something like pride expanded Zinchen's chest.

She also understood now why Tori had gone to such extremes: stealing an official carriage in the middle of the night, with all its accompanying risks. This, above all, confirmed that Tori indeed had a secret lover and wanted to prove her worth in order to protect him. Love made young people foolish. Although Lina's people had been unable to discover who he was—her labors had merely uncovered a handful of noblewomen's sons who had been trying to court the princess—Zinchen had no doubt the mystery of the wielder lover would soon be solved.

Dan and Bokoon shifted nervous eyes between her and the letter in her hand.

She took a measured breath. Their incompetence was noted; she must move on.

"What did the princess's driver say? I assume you interrogated him."

"Nothing helpful, Your Majesty," Bokoon said. "Just that the Min Daughter spent the night in Puddletown due to a faulty carriage wheel, and arrived safely the next day at Hanmar Manor."

She tilted her head to Lina, speaking under her breath. "What do you know of Puddletown?"

"Not a place for the Min Daughter," Lina said.

Zinchen exhaled. *Predictable.*

"Anything else?" she asked the men.

"The driver also said a master healer rode with the princess to Hanmar and took lodgings within the manor grounds."

"A master healer?"

"Yes, Your Majesty. Apparently the same one who attended Your Majesty's brother here at the palace. The driver lost track of them after that. He said both the princess and the master healer left in the night, without his knowledge. He assumed they went together."

How odd. Even though it was prudent for Tori to travel with someone other than her gentlewoman, the question still remained: Where did she go?

"And yet you still failed to find her, as instructed. She was on foot; you, on horseback. It would have been an easy thing." She looked at them coldly. "Explain."

The Varanaken lowered their eyes.

"There are many directions she could have gone in, Your Majesty," Bokoon said. "But we did get this."

He produced a paper from his leather chest guard, bowing as he offered it. "A letter from the Min Daughter."

Zinchen remained silent until she had mastered her incredulity. "And you have chosen to wait until now to deliver it."

They deserved to be flogged. But good relations with Lord Akiren was a currency that was still worth keeping; she could little afford to throw it away for a pair of fools.

Lina handed her the letter. A note written in Tori's hand confirmed she was indeed with the master healer in question, and furthermore was apparently taking her to find some kind of relic that would apparently ensure Zinchen's victory. The girl really was working to prove her worth.

She barely had time to consider the letter when a messenger wearing black-and-gold palace livery arrived and knelt, holding out another. "This just arrived by hawk from the Min Daughter, for Her Majesty."

Zinchen scanned the note. "She's at Greenstalk Village," she said to the Varanaken. "Head there immediately."

"Yes, Your Majesty. We'll bring her back right away."

"Did I tell you to bring her back?" she said, her voice sharp now with impatience.

They stared at their feet.

"Until I send word, you are to remain there, and this time, do not leave her side, even for a moment—she must not so much as sneeze without you stepping in to block the draft."

She dismissed them with a flick of the hand.

When Tori returned, she would have guards posted on every corner of her house. First, though, she must determine if this relic, this Septad, was worth having.

"What do you make of this, Lina?" she said, unrolling Tori's first letter again.

Lina leaned in to read it, then nodded. "Master healers are a rare breed, Your Majesty. They have access to a great number of strange things."

Yan's dramatic recovery replayed in her mind's eye.

"And the Septad? Can it do what she says?"

"I've never heard of this item," Lina continued, "but from what the princess implies, it appears to be an item of power—possibly derived from the Old Magic. But the loremasters would need to confirm whether it will work the way the princess claims."

"Yes," Zinchen said slowly. "The loremasters." It had been decades since she had walked through their mysterious cavern as a child, so long ago that the memory of them had dissipated into a colorless haze.

"We will visit them now. I presume you know the way?"

Lina dipped her head. "Yes, Your Majesty."

Chapter Thirty

LOREMASTER JIN

As Zinchen passed between the standing candelabras that flanked the Lore Room, and followed Lina through the labyrinth of darkwood shelves filled with scroll bags in imperial colors, the memory reconstituted itself bit by bit, like pieces of a puzzle. She had followed her mother through the same path once before.

At the backmost wall, Lina stopped. She dragged her fingertips over it, then pressed, and the stone under her hand sank backward into the wall. A long crack appeared from ceiling to floor, and the wall slid aside with a grinding sound to reveal a stone staircase that disappeared downward into darkness.

Lina grabbed a torch off the wall, and they descended into a dimly lit cavern with arches hewn from stone.

More memories returned. Her mother had spoken to her kindly that day, and had told her of the great sway the loremasters had once held among the Min people due to their incomparable knowledge—which Zinchen needed today. Her mother had then revealed her hopes that Zinchen would someday use the loremasters to advantage, expressing her confidence in Zinchen's strength, confidence that Zinchen would be the one to finally fulfill the dreams of their foremothers by uniting

Shudon under the Min banner. The memory inspired her—and stung. That confidence had died long before her mother did.

After some time, they turned left at a fork in the corridor.

"Where does the right side lead?" Zinchen asked.

"Your Majesty's spy tunnels. My network uses them to access all areas of the palace complex."

Zinchen glanced toward the dark passageway, eyebrow raised. "All areas? From here?"

Lina smiled. "Right down to the lower circle."

She relied on Lina for information, of course, but had given little thought to how it was obtained.

The passageway ended in a room where a fire roared behind an iron grate. Beside it sat a ring of silk armchairs that had once aspired to opulence, bringing to mind a place Zinchen had visited in her youth—a noblewomen's tavern, a place where blossom wine flowed and secrets were traded between sips.

Would the loremasters' secrets prove as useful?

Lina knocked three times at a door on the far end of the room, then opened it and stood aside.

A heavy, time-worn table dominated the space inside, and surrounding scrollshelves glinted under the light of a massive candelabra overhead. Leaning over one end of the table, reading, was a man in the flowing black robes of a scholar.

He looked up from his scroll with a face that seemed to be lined by at least a hundred years, which meant he was much older. Although their lives were dedicated to the preservation of knowledge, loremasters were still a branch of longevitists, and so practiced essence cycling—which meant they always looked younger than their age. Lina, who was herself a longevitist, was forty-five—Zinchen's age—yet she looked fifteen years younger.

The man gave Lina a slight nod of recognition, then turned his eyes to Zinchen. A moment later, surprised realization lit his face, and he pushed himself to his feet, bowing.

"Loremaster Jin," Lina said, "Her Majesty has need of your knowledge."

Zinchen ran a hand over the ridges formed by the table's wood grain, exactly as she had done all those years ago. She sat, taking in her surroundings, the room of lore too secret even for her personal library. So little had changed—and yet so much. Her eyes found, partly concealed behind one of the shelves, a half-open door with the edge of a simple bed peeking through, a detail she hadn't remembered.

"You may sit," she said to him.

He lowered himself laboriously into his chair.

"Is that your bed?" she asked, glancing at it. He no doubt used it for nights he wished to dedicate to reading.

The old man smiled. "Yes, Your Majesty?"

She studied him. "Do you remain here always?"

He indicated the bookshelves with a sweep of the hand. "Why would I ever leave? Within these scrolls are many lands and times. I may go anywhere I wish, right from this room."

She dipped her chin. "Yet you are evidently the only one of your group who feels this way. There are six loremasters, are there not?"

"Five, Your Majesty. One of our sisters sadly departed to the labyrinths not many moons ago."

"My condolences," she replied in a measured tone. "You all descend from the same lineage, I believe."

He dipped his head. "We all come from the same clan. Thousands of years ago, our ancestors ascended the Black Mountains to receive instruction in lore from the Children of the Six themselves."

Such knowledge had never fallen under the purview of an empress. There were always more pressing matters to attend to—military strategy, resource allocation, court governance. Yet it was strangely comforting to know that some people lived outside the demands of court, that some were still dedicated to preserving the ancient lore, quietly and without acclaim.

"Does your knowledge extend to an item known as the Septad?" she asked.

"The Septad is an ancient thing." Loremaster Jin shuffled to a shelf and grazed his hand over it, searching, before finally settling on something. "Unfortunately, very little lore has been written on the subject," he said, offering Zinchen a book in his open palms whose every page was constructed from several bamboo strips, bound together. "This here is all that ever was."

Zinchen opened it. Glyphs had been carved in columns down each strip and painted with ink. These signs and figures belonged to the Old Speech, a language long dead, the ancestors of ancient logograms. Very few people could read glyphs—among them Zinchen. She had been made to study them as a child.

Ancient logograms, on the other hand, were marks she had never mastered, and they now only existed in the Arun clan's etched metal and a few obscure works of history. Once, they had drifted into common use as language shifted away from the Old Speech, while glyphs had remained the preserve of queens. Later, modern logograms replaced them both, and the two ancient writing systems had for centuries now been all but forgotten.

She focused on the glyphs.

Ailin, eldest of Ayenashi the Water Matron, shaped the Septad in the Age before Ages, the first line read. *She forged it to gather the strength of the elements, that her kin might bend the knee, and she alone would bear the crown.*

Zinchen studied the glyph for *Ailin*—it curved like a crescent cradling flame, her name carved between three strokes: one for water, one for crown, and one for will unbending. The lower mark spiraled outward, as if even ink could not contain her ambition.

Though she had never before seen the glyph for *Septad*, she was able to guess: seven strokes, sharp and clean, drawn in a circle bound like law. Six bore the marks of the elements—air, earth, fire, metal, water, and wood. The seventh, set in the center, held no element at all. Just a line split down the middle, unfinished. To Zinchen, it was not a flaw but a promise: What was broken could unite the whole. The many could be made one.

She continued reading.

Yet though she wrought it, her sisters and brothers—offspring too of the Six—held the power to break what she had made.

And break it they did, in the burning veins of Ketuan. But not before they beheld its workings and set down what they learned in a secret place, hidden deep upon Mount Ketwanen.

Though Zinchen had already finished half the book, reading glyphs was a laborious task, and she couldn't spare the time.

She slid the book to the loremaster, pointing to the last place she had read. "Summarize the rest for me, if you would."

He ran his finger down the columns of figures. "At the beginning of the Third Age, five generations before Ishairo's birth, Antiquitals ruled mercilessly over humans. Ketuan, though she was already a mountain, in her compassion summoned a group of humans to her. This group ascended Mount Ketwanen, and there heard her voice echo forth from the trembling rock. She gave them wisdom, and understanding, and insight, and set them as princesses and princes upon Arizan to rule it, and appointed from among them a queen and her king. And to the queen, she passed on the knowledge to make the Septad."

Loremaster Jin's finger stopped. The book had ended.

"But what is the Septad?" Zinchen asked.

"It is a powerful jewel, so say the legends, an amalgamation of spirit stones drawn from Ketuan's own veins."

"A jewel," Zinchen said, trying to picture it. "How big? And how does it work?"

He shook his head. "No one knows. The last one was made over four thousand years ago, before the time of Ishairo. All that was known of its workings was that it gave power over the elements, and with that, power over the ruling Antiquitals."

Zinchen pondered this. How could such an item ensure her victory?

"Is it possible that Antiquitals still exist?"

"There have been stories, Your Majesty. But no one knows for sure."

She held his gaze. "What do *you* believe?"

He hesitated. "That such beings would have no difficulty remaining unseen, if they wished it."

So that was how Tori meant to ensure Zinchen's victory.

Zinchen tapped a finger to her lips. But how would the people receive such news? Would their loyalty wane if it were known that she employed such terrifying creatures as Antiquitals to fight for her? Would they fear her? Hate her? Simply be in awe? Awe was healthy. Fear was manageable. But hatred? That was unpredictable.

Yet victory was the surest path to loyalty—people didn't pledge their hearts to the cautious, they pledged them to the victorious.

She addressed the old man again. "If one were to obtain the Septad and all its associated powers, what would be the practical effect?" She paused. "Would it—hypothetically—guarantee victory in war?"

Loremaster Jin nodded. "Whoever controls the Antiquitals, controls nature. Whoever controls nature, controls the outcome of any war. If the Septad exists somewhere still, the person who finds it would be invincible."

The logic settled into place with satisfying precision. As long as victory was assured, the Antiquitals' power could be reframed—not as a monstrosity, but as a sign that nature itself had bent to her will.

Very well. Tori had asked for one moon to bring back the item, a mere twenty-eight days; she would grant it. And if the Septad worked as promised, she might even spare that wielder lover of hers.

"Send a hawk to Greenstalk Village," she said to Lina quietly. "I want Princess Tori to have my answer today." She inclined her head to Loremaster Jin. "You have been helpful. If you ever have need of anything, Lina will see to it. You have only to ask."

"Thank you, Your Majesty," he said, polishing the bamboo strips. "But I have everything I need right here."

Chapter Thirty-One

ECHO OF THE BELL

The morning after meeting the elder, a knock sounded at Tori's cottage door.

"That must be Master Koren," Elnora said, rushing to open it. Tori drew herself up taller, preparing to make her request.

But instead of the elegant man Tori had seen the day before, a young girl, somewhere around twelve or thirteen years old, peered in curiously, eyes shining beneath a straight black fringe of hair.

"Yes?" Elnora said.

"Are you Tori?" the girl asked, looking Elnora up and down.

Elnora's mouth flattened in wry disapproval. "*Princess* Tori, I think you mean. Or, if you like, the Min Daughter, future incarnation of Min itself—and no, I'm not her."

The girl rolled her eyes. "It was just a question. And outside titles mean nothing here, you know." She craned her neck to look inside, then spotted Tori and pointed. "Is that her?"

Before Elnora could respond, the girl shouted over her shoulder, "Quick, it's her!"

Two more girls of around the same age peered over the first girl's shoulder, whispering, "That's the princess who saved the prisoners."

One of them smiled and waved. "Hi, Tori!"

Tori tensed at the casual use of her name. Merely speaking to commoners was an honor to them, one she often deliberately bestowed. But she had never been addressed so flippantly before—at least, not by anyone who knew who she was.

"You dare to call the Min Daughter by her first name?" Elnora said, shooing the girls. "Out you go!"

Before she could close the door however, the first girl called out, "But Master Banfay said to meet him at the training grounds. We're supposed to take you there."

"No thank you," Elnora said. "We'll find our own way." She shut the door with a sharp clap, her face tight with indignance.

"It's fine," Tori said, shrugging off the incident. "Look at this place: it's completely cut off from the world—literally. How can they know any better?"

Admiration shone in Elnora's eyes. "Your humility is truly amazing, Princess. You'll be the best ruler Min has ever known."

They left the cottage by the same path they had taken with Master Banfay the day before and soon arrived in the heart of the village. More murmurs of "princess" and "released wielders" floated past her as she walked, but nobody so much as dipped their head, much less bowed. She forced a blank expression to hide her discomfort.

As they neared the arena—or training grounds, as it was known here—three immortal women approached from the opposite direction. Each had long, white hair, flowing robes, and a star-jewel that flashed on her forehead. One turned keen, unsettling eyes on Tori, making her feel suddenly naked. Tori turned her head away and scanned the training grounds.

In contrast with the day before, the grounds were empty apart from the top level, where a group of children sat listening to an instructor who stood half hidden behind a tree. As Tori watched them, a voice called out from behind her.

"Good, you're here." Master Banfay strode closer. "Follow me," he said. "I'll take you to my father."

Tori told herself that success was inevitable. After all, hadn't she persuaded an entire court countless times? Still, her stomach clenched.

Master Banfay led them up the stairs and inside the walls where, without yesterday's crowd filling the square-shaped space, the layout of the level was now unobstructed. Four grassy triangles surrounded the dirt circle where the two men had sparred the day before, each triangle containing items for martial training: wooden dummies, targets for bow practice, and weapons racks holding, among other things, wooden swords.

Opposite the entrance gate, more stairs took them to the second level, where a carpet of grass covered the ground, and a small red hut stood in one corner.

They came at last to the top level. A platform stood near the back wall, holding an old stone well with a wooden roof. The group of children were seated in front of it, listening to an elegant figure of a man standing with his back to Tori—Master Koren.

He stamped his foot. Tori's breath caught as the earth rippled in a long line, twisting and turning around the children like a mole burrowing just beneath the surface. The children squealed as it zigzagged between them, making them jump to their feet to move out of the way. They chased it. When it stopped, the children stood still like statues, but with eyes alert, watching for the next trick.

Master Koren stamped again, and a shallow hole opened in the ground. He snapped his fingers, and fire flashed into the center of it.

He was wielding—brazenly—as though he were a performer shuffling cards at someone's private party.

She furrowed her brow, studying him. Why would a man of such refinement openly shame himself?

"Father, this is Tori," Master Banfay said, interrupting. "She's here to speak with you."

Master Koren turned, looking first at his son, then at Tori and Elnora, his gaze penetrating right through her, just as it had the day before. Tori couldn't meet his eye, but she lifted her chin anyway, preparing to speak.

Before she could however, he turned to his son. "I'm in the middle of a lesson, Banfay. She'll have to wait."

Irritation prickled her.

Elnora's face flushed angrily, and she looked like she might speak, but her eyes shifted to his star-jewel, and she pressed her lips together.

"The elder sent her," Master Banfay replied.

His father's shoulders drooped slightly, and he returned his gaze to Tori. "What can I do for you?"

Tori took a fortifying breath. "I've come on an errand of the greatest importance," she said, launching into a prepared speech. "The empress of the Min Territories has plans to attack Jeng. In order to prevent war, I need a Septad, which I understand you can make. With it, I can secure the help of the Antiquitals. Not to make them fight, you understand. Just to—"

Master Koren held up a hand. "The answer is no. I have no interest in the wars of mortals." He turned away.

"But you're the only one who can do it," she said to his back. "I'm not asking you to take part in the war, I'm merely asking you to make the Septad. You can name your price; I'll pay any amount."

He turned slowly to face her, subtle amusement on his face. "Do you imagine it's the matter of payment that concerns me? And supposing you do stop this war, what makes you think there won't be another? And another one after that?"

He shook his head and walked back to the children. "That's all for today. Remember to practice." They bowed and raced away.

Tori stepped quickly to his side. "Please," she said, keeping her voice steady. "The elder sent me to you for this very purpose." Which wasn't entirely true..."And I've traveled for days."

Master Koren appeared unmoved.

"People will die," she said. "Many people." That much was true, at least. After all, she wasn't the only one who would benefit from the Septad, even if she was the one who needed it most at this moment.

He shook his head. "Mortals must have their wars. They seek them out like fire seeking dry leaves. Peace doesn't come from winning, it comes from waiting."

"But if we wait—"

"I won't be making the Septad," he said, his voice kind but firm.

At that moment, a messenger arrived and handed him a note. He read it, then slipped it into his sleeve. "Excuse me," he said to her, then rushed away.

Just today, her mother had sent a hawk, granting Tori's request for time. How could she admit defeat so soon?

Elnora came to her side as Tori stared at Master Koren's retreating form, the hopelessness of her situation nearing the farther off he went. She couldn't go back like this. Her mother would find out what she was; it was only a matter of time.

An itchy burning made her scratch at her wrists, and the veins on them seemed to have darkened.

Master Banfay appeared to notice. "May I see?"

She held out an arm. He examined her wrist intently, then shifted his gaze to her hairline and her eyes.

"But these things are hereditary," he muttered to himself, looking puzzled. A moment later, a look of realization crossed his face, and he met her eye. "Do you have any idea who your parents are?"

"You met my mother—or did you mean my late father? His name was Lord Tam of House Thana, the lesser branch, in Jeng."

"Your *birth* parents," he said.

She tilted her head. "I just told you."

He gave her a strange look, then reached into his waist pouch and pulled out a box. "Take this," he said, handing her a black pill the size of a cherry. "It will settle your wrists."

The pill was soft and chewy, with an earthy, mildly sweet taste. The pearls that had been vibrating in Tori's stomach ever since she had arrived in Peach Blossom Grove suddenly stopped.

"Come with me," he said.

"Where?"

"To the well." He nodded at her wrists. "There's something I need to know before I can treat that."

As she followed with Elnora, her mind remained on Master Koren, his refusal twisting like a knife. She cast a glance behind her at the gate where she had seen him leave. People trickled through it now steadily, and all around, the ring of weapons rose above the clackety-clack of users planting blocks and strikes onto wooden dummies.

They stepped up the platform to the well, and Master Banfay lowered the rope. When he pulled it up, Tori stepped back in surprise—instead of a wooden one, a shimmering crystal bucket flashed at the end, filled to the brim with clear water.

The water receded slowly, yet without dripping through the bottom. It simply disappeared, leaving the bucket completely empty.

"Give me your finger," Master Banfay said.

Alarm coursed through her suddenly, the memory of the naming ceremony playing in her mind. "Why?"

Elnora stepped beside her protectively, but then, with a glance at the stone on his forehead, lowered her head. "Do you think maybe you could tell her why first, Master?"

"Diagnosis. I need to know if that is what I believe it to be," he said, with another nod at her wrists.

This isn't the palace, Tori reminded herself. *This is a different test.*

She held out her finger, and with a fine golden needle, Master Banfay pricked it. Two drops of blood landed in the crystal bucket, and he lowered it back into the well.

As Tori sucked her fingertip, a bell she hadn't noticed before rang suddenly inside the roof of the well, startling her. Master Banfay nodded as though his suspicions had been confirmed. Then the bell rang again, and a look of mild surprise crossed his face.

When it rang a third time, people from all levels of the grounds stopped and looked up toward the well. On the fourth ring, they poured up the steps, crowding in and filling the air with excited murmurs.

It rang a fifth time, and finally, a sixth. Astonishment covered Master Banfay's face.

The people's murmurs ceased, replaced by perfect silence. Only the haunting echo of the bell remained.

The wide eyes of the onlookers told her something wasn't right.

"What was that bell?"

"This well is a tester of ketua," Master Banfay said. "The number of rings reveals the type of ketua a person has. Most often, it rings once, indicating a unique ketua. Rarely, it will ring twice, for a dyadic ketua. You have a hexatic ketua."

"Could you be clearer?"

"It means," he said, holding her gaze, "that you are a sixfold wielder."

Tori went utterly still. She wasn't cured. She was still a wielder. No, not merely a wielder—she was six times worse.

The underwater maelstrom from her nightmares swirled in her mind's eye. She blinked, clearing it, only to find the witnesses to her disgrace still staring at her. To her dismay, among them stood the golden-haired man whose sparring she had admired the day before.

She lifted her chin and stepped off the platform, but she couldn't lift her eyes.

As the crowd parted reverently before her, people reached out, brushing fingertips across her sleeves.

She arrived at the gate with as much haste as dignity would allow and slipped through it, but she was still unable to outpace her nightmares' watery scenes.

Chapter Thirty-Two

VOICE OF THE VOICELESS

Koren rushed into Ma'yanar Forest where Henzan was pacing back and forth. He looked disheveled—how long had he been waiting?

At the sound of Koren's footsteps, Henzan looked up, eyes brightening, "Ah, you're here!"

"Your note said it was urgent."

"I've found something; come quickly," Henzan said.

Koren followed him to an enclosure of trees where a globe of lomi hovered in the air, shimmering like sunlight on a rippling pond. He stared at it, stroking the edge of his jaw. The lomi were active by nature, even when they tended to plants and trees. He had never seen them so still before.

"I'm an outsider, I can't interpret their meaning. But I knew they sensed we've been trying to find something," Henzan said, excited. "Didn't I tell you?"

"You could be right. Perhaps they understand we are looking for something, and also that we have been trying to follow them to it. In coming together, they eliminate the possibility of causing confusion, since we can now follow one large group." Koren spoke to the sparkling cloud. "We understand you. Now show me where you wish to lead."

The lomi simply hovered in place, pulsing.

"Perhaps they are leading us right here," Koren said, scanning the gnarled roots and underbrush around them. Yet he and Henzan had already searched this hollow, days before.

Determined to incite the lomi to act, Koren waved a hand through the cloud, scattering them. "Go. Show me what you want me to see."

But the lomi simply re-formed into the same shimmering mass. What was he missing?

The message from Henzan's scroll came back to him:

Cling to paths shown by lovers of green,
cloaked in shadow and shifting light.
Heed the voiceless, see the unseen,
and they shall order your footsteps aright.

Over and over, he read the words in his mind. *Heed the voiceless. See the unseen.*

Finally, he smiled softly. "We have it all wrong. The scroll was not telling us to follow the lomi. It was telling us to listen to them."

"But you said they couldn't speak," Henzan said.

"The truth is, I have never asked them." Koren looked at the lomi. "I am listening. Tell me what I must know."

The lomi ignored him.

But then, had they ever obeyed when he had addressed them in the common tongue?

"Chui zeingto zhu mein nau lao!" he said in the Old Speech. *I command you to speak; reveal your secrets.*

The lomi's facial expressions sharpened; every one of them was looking at Henzan. Some of the tiny faces displayed apprehension, others disapproval—evidently they did not wish to reveal their secrets in front of a newcomer.

Koren hesitated, embarrassed. If not for Henzan's help, he would have no chance of finding the Celestial Seal. Yet the lomi's faces expressed a steely determination; no command of his would sway them.

"I am sorry," Koren said. "But they will not speak in your presence."

Disappointed surprise covered Henzan's face. "Are you sure?"

Koren nodded. "I am."

Henzan made a visible effort to brighten his face, then spoke good-naturedly. "That's no problem. But you will tell me what they say, won't you? I'm greatly interested in anything that pertains to my scrolls."

"Of course I will, I swear it. Thank you for understanding."

The instant the sound of Henzan's footsteps receded, the lomi trembled in the air. Tiny sparkles, one by one, shifted out from the rest, and Koren looked on with marvel and disbelief as the sparkles formed an intricate pattern of glyphs made of pure light.

He read the words.

When six fingers shall grasp the wind,

the veil shall part, and the path be revealed.

A riddle. His first instinct was to consult Henzan again, but something told him the interpretation would require a deeper wisdom than mere academic study. Besides, he was obligated to report his findings to the elder anyway.

He returned to the village and entered the elder's cave.

"I have seen the portent, Elder," he said, standing before her. She was seated by the fire, where there were no other chairs. "I need your wisdom to decipher it."

He described what the lomi had done and detailed the glyphs. The only part he left out was Henzan's involvement, so as not to disturb her peace—the elder didn't know him as Koren did and might be overly concerned.

She considered his words for a long moment before finally speaking.

"Six fingers signify the six elements," she said, "yet elements themselves may grasp nothing. Thus, the riddle speaks of a sixfold wielder, and grasping the wind is to connect with the element of air."

"But I have connected with air thousands of times, yet the way is not open."

"And thus, this riddle does not pertain to you," she said. "For this very day another sixfold wielder was revealed."

Koren's voice pitched upward. "In Peach Blossom Grove?"

The elder gave a nod. “It is none other than Tori, the Min princess who but recently arrived. My heart tells me that, be it in triumph or in failure, Tori’s fate is intertwined with our own. Such is the path that has been set before her.” Her face grew pensive. “It would be well for us if she would devote herself to the study of wielding, for when she at last lays hold of the air element, the way to the Celestial Seal shall be made known.”

Koren closed his eyes, the solemnity of the matter sinking in. For the first time in his 225 years, he would be training another sixfold wielder—he could finally pass on all he knew.

“Gather the council,” the elder said, “and summon Tori at once. We must consult her without delay.”

Chapter Thirty-Three

THE WISDOM OF FORGETTING

Stones skittered beneath Tori's feet as she hurried away from the humiliation of her public exposure. After spending her life trying to forget how defective she was, she had discovered she was far worse—and far more vulnerable. The training grounds' bell had reminded her it would only take a moment of inattention on her part, and a quick test on her mother's, for a true disaster to occur.

Halfway to her cottage, a gazebo came into view—tranquil, untainted, free—floating alone among pink lotus blossoms. It called to the longings in her mind.

The small arched bridge that led to it ended abruptly at the water, the gazebo floating about one pace away. She judged the distance and hopped on, rocking it.

The motion steadied, and Tori leaned over the rail, the peacefulness of the place working on her like a soothing balm, numbing the sting of her test at the well, setting her mind to rights.

Trees—their arms stretched upward luxuriantly, as though taking their first breath of the morning—lined the banks on the other side of the pond. Nestled among them, a spacious pavilion sat open to the breeze. The scene spoke of tranquility and ease, concepts she simply couldn't reconcile with what had just occurred...with what she was.

The confusing reverence of the onlookers at the well came back to her, and she pinched the bridge of her nose, squeezing her eyes shut. She didn't know what to think. All she knew was that she needed the Septad more than ever.

"It must be anchored in place," came Elnora's mumbled voice. She was leaning forward, head tilted, evidently searching the water beneath the gazebo. A moment later, she hopped on and looked at Tori with guilty concern.

"I should have stopped him. I'm sorry, Princess."

Tori focused on the floating blossoms, determined to keep hold of her tranquility. "I'm fine. Let's just forget about it."

Elnora leaned on the rail beside her. "Actually...I'm not sure the people will. I heard them talking. You're kind of, well, a hero."

Tori stared at her. "You're jesting."

But before Elnora could reply, the sound of male voices swelled in the air, drawing their attention. The golden-haired man from Hanmar was walking with the slim, dark-haired friend she had seen him with before. They turned to cross the bridge.

Tori's jaw tightened and her gaze flitted foolishly around the gazebo, searching for an exit, but in no time the two men had crossed the bridge and stepped easily over the water, making the gazebo sway.

The dark-haired man smiled. "Usually Senrik and I are the only ones watching the plays from here," he said in a tone of familiarity, as though they had been friends for years. He spoke with a hint of an accent Tori couldn't quite place. "Looks like word is getting out." He bowed, his hands clasped. "Ruvien, son of Sapeen. This here is Senrik, son of Helza."

Senrik looked at her, the quiet generosity in his eyes flooding her with a disproportionate sense of relief. Clearly, he didn't judge her.

He bowed and clasped his hands—they were powerful and scarred, speaking of battle, skill, and certainty.

Remembering the behavior of the young girls that morning, it occurred to her belatedly that she should probably return the gesture, but before she could, the men walked to the gazebo rail. Senrik slipped the sword from his waist and eased it against the gazebo wall, patting the top of the hilt with the gentleness of a father patting his baby. Then he leaned over and looked out onto the water.

Tori and Elnora exchanged glances; the place they had been standing now had men on either side of it. But since there was nowhere else with a view of the open water, they returned.

Senrik was on Tori's right, and when a breeze blew in, a hint of masculine agarwood fragrance from his clothes swept over her like a caress, making her breath quicken. She steadied it.

He must be a noble. Who else could afford to fragrance their clothes with agarwood?

A large, flat sailboat drifted into view. The pavilion across the water filled with people, many of whom pointed at the boat, or clapped.

"You said this was a play?" Tori asked.

Ruvien nodded. "One of the tales of Ishairo. Same time every week."

"Why does nobody else come here?" she asked, glancing at the overcrowded pavilion. Her answer came when the boat wheeled around, leaving them with only a side view.

Elnora studied the boat appraisingly, nodding. "Impressive tacking."

Senrik leaned over to look at her. "You know something of boats?" he asked in a smooth tenor.

"My people live on the sea," Elnora said.

"Seafarers, then, like my ancestors. Do your people revere Yarin, too?" As he spoke the name, he touched the back of his knuckles to lips, then to his forehead.

Elnora gave a short laugh. "My people revere their nets and their fishing spears."

"So, Senrik," Ruvien said, throwing Tori a smile. "Ever think a sixfold wielder would be sharing our perch?"

Tori tensed, but Senrik's expression reminded her she was among friends. He dipped his chin. "It was an honor to have met you before I go."

"You're leaving?" She looked into his eyes, noticing their color for the first time: the same candid blue as a summer sky.

"Later today," he said. "With the peacekeepers. We were going to leave this morning, but one of the men turned an ankle. The healers are working on him."

Tori tried not to study his mouth as he talked. His teeth were nearly perfect, but a slight misalignment beside the front ones gave him a dangerously irresistible charm. She realized then how close they were standing, and her pulse quickened.

He seemed to notice, too: his eyes flicked to the space between them, and he gallantly eased himself a half step backward.

"Can somebody please explain what peacekeepers are," Elnora said. "I asked Master Banfay, but never really got an answer."

"Traveling fighters," Senrik said. "We travel around Shudon, protecting people living in dangerous places—bandits and such."

So not a noble, then, Tori thought, deflating. No nobleman, no matter how honorable, would join a band of traveling fighters.

Could she get away with taking a Hanmar commoner as lawful intimate? She wasn't empress, after all, merely the Min Daughter. And hadn't they already called her "the princess with the common touch"? Besides, anyone she allied with could be elevated; titles could be granted.

A flush rose to her cheeks; this was the first man who had ever provoked such thoughts.

"How does someone become a peacekeeper?" Elnora asked.

"Train with the weapons masters for a year," Ruvien said. "A year at the least—all depends on your skill level. Senrik could have skipped it, though. He mastered weapons as a baby."

Senrik gave a faint smile. "They still put me through my paces here. Ruvien, now—he shoots like nothing you've seen."

"I'm a fair shot," Ruvien said, and shrugged. "Couldn't escape that really, with parents like mine—father's a bowyer; mother was a fletcher. Got my first bow when I was five. But"—he waggled his eyebrows—"Peach Blossom Grove's where I learned to play with blades."

He shifted his outer robe aside. Hanging from his belt were two gleaming knives with decorative handles.

For a long while, they watched the performance in silence. The narrator's voice was barely audible from where they stood, but Tori managed to follow it.

A deep gong sounded, and the play actor portraying Ishairo climbed a green hill in the middle of the boat and stood at the top. Someone wielded fire. Tori's eyes widened—but the crowd clapped.

The fire flashed above Ishairo's head, then disappeared, and he crumpled onto the hilltop, grasping his sword. Someone threw a sheet of golden silk over him.

"Is that the elixir?" Elnora whispered to Tori.

"I think so."

A young girl stood over the silk cloth, hands raised above her head, holding a little pot that shone in the sunlight. She made a scooping motion, as though filling it with water, then walked slowly down the hill. She sat and hung her head, then whipped a cape around in a dramatic flourish, covering herself entirely.

Applause drifted from the pavilion, signaling the end of the performance.

Elnora pursed her lips to one side. "Well I have no idea what that was about."

"That girl's Ishairo's sister-in-law, Anaiah," Ruvien said. "After she filled the spirit jade vial with elixir, she stayed on Mount Ketwanen till she faded from memory."

"How did Master Banfay get it, then?" Elnora asked.

"The elder found it a long time ago," he said. "So how'd you like the play? They do a different one each week—though sometimes they'll take a break and do music instead. Senrik's been known to play the kinara and sing when forced—voice like a bard."

"I'd like to hear that," Tori said, holding Senrik's gaze, a smile on the edge of her lips.

He hesitated, as though trying to interpret her tone, then gave a small smile in return. "When the peacekeepers come back for a break, I'll play for you."

"Did you learn to play here, or back home?" she asked. The kinara wasn't normally associated with Hanmar, but then again, Hanmar had access to everything.

"Back home people prefer the varglinn, but either is easy enough, once you know the other."

She knit her brow, picturing the crude instrument made of wood and horsehair. The varglinn was a Ghenz instrument—no one in Hanmar would touch it.

Her composure faltered: the varglinn; Yarin, goddess of the sea—they both pointed to one thing. Her luminous picture of him disintegrated. Senrik was a Ghenz.

She turned from him and made idle conversation with Elnora, needing to regain her equilibrium. His kindness toward the boy with the wooden sword came back to her, and she felt she had been lied to. Yet he had never been dishonest. In fact, he had been entirely open about who he was from the start. She had just been too blinded by admiration to see it.

As she mentally sifted through their conversation, his placid willingness to be associated with such people almost repelled her more. Wasn't he ashamed, considering how dishonorable, how utterly depraved the Ghenz were? They were a scourge on every land they set foot in, and a danger to Min. If it had been her, she would have done everything in her power to forget her demeritorious past.

The thought dropped on her, heavy as stone. *Such great wisdom, burying your own darkness in forgetfulness. Yet, how well has that wisdom served you?*

The bridge creaked behind her, and the gazebo swayed with the weight of someone stepping on. Master Banfay. Tori looked away, the sting of his test returning.

Senrik and Ruvien bowed. Elnora, after a glance at Master Banfay's star-jewel, did the same.

"My father wishes to speak to you," Master Banfay said to Tori. He looked at the others. "All of you. You are summoned to the elder's council." He turned and left.

"The council of immortals who oversee Peach Blossom Grove," Ruvien explained to them cheerfully. "It pays to rub shoulders with a sixfold wielder."

Tori hid her grimace.

"Let's go," Senrik said. He pointed to the cliff shaped like a cresting wave, indicating the opposite side from the elder's waterfall. "It'll take time to reach Council's Rise."

Chapter Thirty-Four

THE ELDER'S COUNCIL

Just as Tori's legs despaired of climbing another step, the cliff known as Council's Rise leveled, and a small pond twinkled into view. From somewhere out of sight, a stream fed it from higher ground—no doubt near the seat of the elder's council.

Hope and dread wrestled in her chest. Had Master Koren changed his mind? Would the council mention her test at the well? Surely that news couldn't have spread so fast.

A wooden barge floated on the pond, straining against its rope, then drifted in again, thumping the dock where two men played a game of cards. Behind a desk some paces away, a woman sat writing on a long paper.

One of the men spoke without looking up. "Name?"

Elnora stepped forward. "Princess Tori, Min Daughter."

"Who?"

"Let her through." The woman gave Tori a nod, dipped her brush, and continued writing. "It's the sixfold wielder." She said it like it was a compliment. Tori forced her expression to remain smooth.

"My apologies," the man said, opening the barge door. "Right this way."

The men grabbed the ropes to activate a pulley, and in no time, the barge was across the pond and floating uphill on the stream.

The ground leveled again, and they floated into another pond where another two men pulled them in. They stepped onto a second small dock, this time facing a wide pavilion.

Facing them was a trellis canopy woven with sunlight and lacy vines that glistened with dewdrops. Tori stepped beneath the pale blossoms adorning the canopy; they filled the air with a scent so fresh and so fine it seemed to have wafted in from the dawn of the world, when everything was perfect and new.

To their left, trees arched over a grassy path that led to a table. Five women and four men with white gems on their foreheads sat on either side of the elder like a row of solemn judges, every one of them with snow-white hair, apart from Master Koren. Tori inhaled slowly, bracing herself. She had addressed august councils before; why should this be different? Ancient, luminous eyes met her gaze, scrutinizing her. She looked away.

"Be seated," the elder said, motioning to four empty chairs across the table. Then, without warning, "Why did you not reveal you were a sixfold wielder?"

Tori paused long enough to master her humiliation. "Because I didn't know. I thought—I hoped—I was cured."

Senrik and Ruvien exchanged puzzled glances.

The immortals stared with disapproval or incredulity. But the fatherly warmth in Master Koren's eyes was even more unsettling.

"She speaks the truth," he said. "Banfay informed me her stone kernel was sealed."

Tori furrowed her brow. How did Master Banfay know?

"What offense did you commit to merit this punishment?" The woman on the elder's right—who wore her star-jewel on a purple ribbon around her forehead, adorning a face of chiseled stone—peered at Tori accusingly.

"I don't know what you mean."

"Perhaps you will tell us, then, how did your stone kernel come to be sealed?" The woman on the elder's left side looked at Tori kindly, hands folded under her chin, wide sleeves falling away from braceleted arms.

"It happened when I was twelve, at a place called the Door of Golden Ash. My teacher took me there."

The immortals whispered to each other in a language Tori had never heard.

"Go on," the elder said.

"That's it. It was a portal of some kind—one that removes wielding."

"We know very well what it is," the hard-faced woman said. "We want to know what happened there."

It was a memory Tori had forced herself to forget. Now, as she tried to revisit it, she struggled to recall the details. Images of lightning and rain flashed in her mind. "It was nighttime, in a forest. I stepped into a golden mist, and my teacher came with me. When I stepped out again, the wielding was gone."

"He lived?" the woman with the bracelets asked, brows raised.

Tori nodded.

"A mortal supplied the strength to seal the kernel of someone with a hexatic ketua—how extraordinary."

"Yes. He was extraordinary."

"How long did he last?" the hard-faced woman asked.

A lump formed in Tori's throat, and her voice came out tremulous. "Five years. He was twenty-nine when he...died."

Wan had known it could kill him, but he had done it anyway. When he had stepped out of the portal, his black hair was streaked with white. He walked with a cane for the rest of his life.

"He no doubt meant well," Master Koren said, "but it was foolish. A wielder's kernel should never be sealed."

A sudden, angry defensiveness sprang up inside her. How dare he criticize Wan? "He didn't have much choice. In case you were unaware, the outside world isn't exactly friendly to wielders."

"Sealing was meant for longevitists," Master Koren said calmly. "It was used by the ancient longevitists as a punishment, to keep evildoers from expanding their stone kernels and becoming more powerful. But longevitists, unlike wielders, deal only in dawn-essence; they do not have the concern of ketua—the residual elements in their kernel that produce wielder's venom. When your kernel was sealed, your ketua was also bound—a dangerous choice."

Elnora opened her mouth to speak, but her gaze flitted over the immortals, and her voice came out small. "The princess has never had any venom." She gave Tori's hand a supportive squeeze.

"Incorrect," Master Koren said, and Elnora shrank slightly. "All wielders have venom, though a wielder is normally immune to her own. Sealing the stone kernel, and thus binding the ketua, upsets this immunity. Although there is always a small chance that a wielder's venom will turn against her when her kernel expands, a bound ketua increases this chance a hundredfold."

Tori sat up straighter, a chill gathering inside her.

"Expands?" Elnora asked meekly.

"To the next kernel level." He looked at Tori. "Master Banfay mentioned you have dark veins on your wrists. May I see them?"

She hesitated, concerned about what he might find, but reluctantly lifted the edge of one sleeve and held out her wrist. The immortals leaned in.

"Does it often itch or burn?" Master Koren asked, clearly still on a campaign to criticize Wan.

"No," she lied, covering her wrist again. "Why?"

"To ensure your venom has not turned on you, of course. Since you have not yet had your first stone kernel expansion, it would still be curable, but we would need to take care of it now. For someone with a hexatic ketua, it could be fatal if it is not tended to early enough."

"Sealing my kernel was the best thing that ever happened to me. Now," she said, meeting the immortals' penetrating gazes, "why was I summoned here?"

"To be granted a choice," the elder said. "You seek to stop a war, do you not?"

"Yes. But when I asked Master Koren to make the Septad, I was denied." She looked at him pointedly.

"Even had I wished to make it—which I do not—I could not have done so," Master Koren replied. "A Septad will only bind itself to a single wielder, its maker; no one else can claim dominion over it."

Tori tilted her head, recalculating. If that was the case, her mother would also be unable to use it. Yet that wouldn't stop it from saving Tori—she could figure the rest out later.

"In any case," Master Koren said, "a further complication is that one of the stones required to make the Septad, I do not have the skill to obtain: the Ghost Stone."

"An item of great worth," the elder said, "and of particular connection to the Veil of Ayenashi: it was said that Ayenashi herself hid one in this very Veil. Long have I desired to look upon it, but though Master Koren can sense its presence, never has he uncovered its resting place."

"If Master Koren can't find it, what chance does this pup have?" the hard-faced woman said.

"If heaven so decrees, she shall find it." The elder fixed her gaze on Tori. "The choice is yours: let your mother's war run its course, or remain here and bend your mind to acquiring the knowledge needed to forge the Septad."

Tori furrowed her brow. "Are you saying *I* would make it?"

"If you were to master the ancient art of alchemy. You would require training in the ways of weaponry as well."

"Weapons training? Whatever for?" The thought of plunging herself into men's activities was ridiculous, almost to the point of insult.

"To fashion the Septad, you must seek out spirit stones of a rare and potent nature. Save for the Ghost Stone and one other, all the rest lie hidden upon the heights of Mount Ketwanen. You would thus be bound to journey there, yet you could not do so unprepared: before you embarked, you would first need to master the skills that would serve you."

The idea of traveling to Mount Ketwanen daunted her—before coming here, she had been certain the place was a myth. But she pushed the thought aside; she would not sabotage herself with weak-mindedness.

The elder looked at Senrik and Ruvien. "You two were set to depart with the last company of peacekeepers. Though Master Maeli has already gone," she said, indicating an empty seat opposite Master Koren, "she awaits word by messenger hawk, that she might know whether she and her company should tarry for you at the outer camp. If it is still your will to depart, you may do so. Or, you may remain here, that you might be on hand when Tori's training is complete. Master Maeli can give you nearby assignments whenever the need arises, and when the time comes, you will journey with Tori to Mount Ketwanen as her sworn protectors."

Ruvien's face lit up. "Would a mythical mountain happen to have magical beasts?"

"Ketuan, in her time, was master of all," the elder said. "The lesser spirits, caretakers of Arizan—High Animals, High Water-creatures, and High Birds, Fire Dancers and Metal Friends, the kamen and the lomi—all these were bound to her service, sworn to be her companions and servants. Yet in the ancient past, some were beguiled by the treacherous whispers of that rebel spirit, Shekahai, and followed her into shadow. When Ketuan became a mountain and slumbered, her companions remained, but her deep rest also called forth those spirits who had long concealed themselves in the hidden places, and those foul and twisted magical creatures wrought by Shekahai's own fell magic."

Ruvien raised an eyebrow. "Is that a yes?"

The elder smiled. "It is. But you would do well to understand the nature of magical beasts, lest you be caught unawares. I do also possess a map that will be of service, upon which is marked the main gathering places of such fell creatures, so you can steer your paths wisely."

"If we have your map to guide us, why should I learn weapons training?" Tori asked.

"First, because evil things are not bound to one place," the elder replied. "They may roam where they will. Second, because not all peril is born of evil. There are creatures that, though not wicked, are no less deadly."

Unlike in their first meeting, her voice now carried the tone of a trusted adviser—sincere, grave, and laced with solicitude.

"When I first came to see you, you seemed..." Tori paused, choosing her words, "less than concerned about my request. Why the sudden interest?"

"That relates to matters beyond your reckoning," a condescending male voice said. It came from a man in a red cape and golden breastplate, sitting at the far end of the table.

"You clearly underestimate my reckoning," Tori said, in a flash of irritation.

A small smile tugged at the edges of the elder's mouth. "My eyes beheld the founding of the Min Territories at the hand of your ancestor, Yanai Sumi," she said, "and I recall the sorrow that made the peasants wail during the reign of the Emperor Zanith. I was there before that even, when the Min Territories was nothing but a dream unborn, and the queendoms of the north united in force under Empress Li, birthing the Jeng Territories. With my own eyes I witnessed the Unification War," she said, her face taking on a wistful expression, "when Ishairo did tie together the lands of Shudon, driving back the Watani and their fell gods, the Fox Dragons. And Uzo here"—she indicated a rugged, broad-shouldered man—"was a warrior in Ishairo's host. Chan," she said, indicating the man in the breastplate and cape, "was one of his generals." She motioned to the women on either side of her. "Su-Mei, Yeibe, Linari, and Zanda were his trusted military strategists, minds that shaped the tides of war. Thus, when General Chan says that our reasons lie beyond your reckoning, he speaks truthfully."

As the words sank in, Tori felt utterly small—not the object of reproach, just infinitesimally young, an acorn amid ancient trees. The memories at this table spanned millennia; hers barely reached beyond her mother's inequity. What weight could her voice carry here? What did her plans matter, in the scheme of the vast world?

She remained silent, and for several breaths the only sound was the trickle of the distant stream.

"Nonetheless," the elder continued, "it appears your purpose aligns with ours, and for this reason I would lend you my aid. Should you choose to remain, you will be taught all you must know. Your time would be given foremost to alchemy, however, for it is through that ancient craft that the Septad may be wrought."

"I thank you for your generosity," Tori said, bowing.

The elder dipped her chin. "You will present yourself before me after the second moon, that I might judge your progress. If I am satisfied, you will remain four moons more to complete your training."

Six moons total. Which left a mere two moons to travel to Mount Ketwanen and back again. As Min Daughter, she couldn't be absent for more than eight moons at a time without jeopardizing her succession rights.

"And I look forward to beginning your wielding training in the morning," Master Koren said pleasantly.

Tori stilled, hoping she had misunderstood.

"Take this to the Pavilion of Honorable Logograms," he said, drawing a thin jade slip from his sleeve, "and exchange it for the locked scrolls. Though we will need to begin with the basics, I suspect we will move on to much more interesting things before too long. To start, though, the main thing you must remember is never to wield in public outside of Peach Blossom Grove. This is forbidden, on pain of banishment."

"I won't be wielding at all," Tori said. She looked at the elder for support. "You said I'd be studying alchemy and weapons."

"Upon the revelation of your hexatic ketua, you were summoned here forthwith. Could you truly not discern the connection? And did I not speak plainly before when I said that only one of your kind may forge the Septad?"

One of your kind. Tori's cheeks heated. "I thought it was enough for me to *be* a sixfold wielder. I didn't think I'd actually have to wield."

"My child," the elder said, "Antiquitals will not be bound by a Septad that is not wrought by a wielder of great power. Yet the lack of such knowledge is no fault of your own; Antiquital lore is a most obscure branch of knowledge; few writings endure on it, even in the Pavilion of Honorable Logograms."

Elnora cast Ruvien a questioning look. "The library," he whispered.

"But," the elder continued, "it may be understood thus: just as the elements are bound by immutable laws, so too are Antiquitals bound by laws of their own. Consider the wind—it will turn the sails of a mill, grinding flour to feed a village, or, in the wrath of a storm, it will uproot trees and lay waste to that same village's homes. A fire, likewise, will cook a meal to stave off hunger, or warm a winter traveler, preserving her life. Yet in its unbridled fury, fire will consume a forest, turning every living thing to ash until quelled by a stronger degree of water or stone. So it is with Antiquitals. They are beings of vast might, but they are not unbound; they are both all-powerful and utterly vulnerable, for they either follow the order of their nature, or be overcome by the will of a wielder with the power to command them."

"I'm not that person," Tori said.

"Nobody is. This is the very reason you have need of the Septad, for it is only through this jewel that your will can bind them. But mark this: only a powerful wielder may make a Septad powerful enough to bind."

The Septad didn't need to be powerful—its existence alone would save her from tests at the palace. Did she dare tell them the truth?

"A lesser Septad would serve my purposes well enough," Tori said carefully. "Surely, great power is not required in every case. Fire is sometimes a small flame; wind a gentle breeze. I don't need a vast army—even a few Antiquitals would suffice."

"No Septad can be made without wielding," Master Koren said, his face now stern. "To make one, you must use the wielding forms to unbind your ketua and expand your stone kernel. Then you must embrace wielding fully."

Her fingers went to her waist pouch and found the broken shell, its dulled edge preserving sharp memories. She couldn't render Wan's sacrifice worthless.

"I'm not that person," she said again, voice strained, shoulders flaccid with defeat. Without the Septad, everything collapsed; yet how could she look her past in the eye and simply embrace it?

Master Koren frowned and returned the jade slip to his sleeve, an action that struck her like a reprimand.

"Are you certain?" the elder asked.

Tori dropped her eyes.

Chairs slid on the grass with a quiet *she-shush*, and when Tori looked up again, the council was gone.

"Come on," Senrik said, rising. "The barge will be more difficult after dark."

Chapter Thirty-Five

A HEAVY GARMENT

The last light faded from the sky. By the time they reached the bottom of the hill, the air was filled with tiny floating lights, and grapefruit-sized lanterns along the ground marked their path, glowing gently, like little moons.

Tori could acknowledge the beauty of it all, but she couldn't feel it; her past weighed on her too heavily, like a suffocating garment.

"Can somebody explain what just happened in there?" Ruvien said, scooping his hand through the floating lights, then opening it to find it empty. "Why didn't you want to train with Master Koren?"

"It's complicated," Tori said, picking up her pace.

"But he's incredible—isn't he, Senrik? No one could train a sixfold wielder better."

Images of waves and lights glowing at the ends of long poles flashed in her mind, and she walked faster still.

Ruvien jogged to catch up. "But we're still going to Mount Ketwanen, right?"

Tori didn't respond. He looked back at the others. "Right?"

"The princess needs time to think things over," Elnora said.

He halted. "Ketwanen is *the* legendary mountain. Traveling with the peacekeepers would be nothing compared to this. I'd finally be able to finish my family's beast lore."

Senrik glanced at Tori. "I don't know all your reasons for hesitating, but you could do a lot of good with a Septad."

If you only knew, she thought bitterly.

The spirit-fruit trees soon greeted them, silver branches lit up with blue lights, while the rivulet that had flashed blindingly in the daytime now glimmered quietly beneath the stars. Just before reaching the cottages, it twisted and veered out of sight.

"This is ours," Ruvien said, stopping at the first cottage. "Where are you?"

"Last one on the row," Elnora said.

He craned his neck to find it. "Good. I'll stop by in the morning. If you're my only way to Ketwanen," he said to Tori with a wink, "then I'll just have to persuade you." He and Senrik went inside.

Tori practically ran. But no sooner had she touched the front gate of her cottage, than Old Griff, the obnoxious fruit seller from the day before, called out to them in his jarring voice.

"Halloo! Elnora, isn't it? You ladies look like you could use a nighttime snack. I'm selling five apples for three skades, tonight only. Practically giving them away."

"Nobody wants your overpriced apples," Tori snapped. "You will leave this instant, or I'll throw you out myself. Come on, Elnora."

The man paled, but she slammed the door before he could do more.

She sank onto a chair beside a small square table by a window where soft light filtered through the latticework, casting geometric patterns across the wood. Elnora lit a lantern, scattering them.

Tori stared at an empty teapot on the table in front of her, mulling over the elder's council. It had been like arriving at a picnic concerned about not liking the food, only to be attacked by a colony of hornets. She should have been decisive, one way or the other; she should have known her path, and taken it. Still here she was, wavering.

She slumped.

A swath of yellow silk hanging from ceiling to floor a half-dozen paces away, swept apart in the middle and draped onto brass wall hooks, revealing a space with two canopied beds sitting on a low platform. It beckoned to her. But though she longed for sleep, she knew only nightmares awaited.

She looked away from the platform and slid a teacup from among the two sitting on the table in front of her.

"I think I'll have some tea," she said, letting her head fall into her hands.

Elnora put water to boil. "Are you thinking of not going through with it?"

"I don't know what to do."

Elnora looked thoughtful as she measured leaves from a wooden box and tapped them into the pot. "If you don't mind my saying so, Princess, this might be your only chance." She poured.

Elnora had been at the Door of Golden Ash; it was she who had saved both Tori and Wan from the life-threatening effects of the portal that night in the forest. Her quick-witted faithfulness in Tori's time of need had been the reason Tori had insisted her mother reward Elnora—though Tori had fabricated the reason for it—elevating someone without bloodline, wealth or connections from a common maid to a titled lady, foremost among Tori's gentlewomen. Since that time, Elnora had only grown dearer. But she didn't understand everything; she didn't know.

Tori pivoted the teacup in slow circles, filling the silence with the whispering of porcelain on wood, then gazed at the liquid trembling inside.

"It's time you know something," Tori said, fingers tracing the rim of the cup. "It's a long story—one I'm not sure I can tell." She took a slow breath, steadying herself. "But I'll try."

Chapter Thirty-Six

VEYLI

I met Veyli when I was eleven. My nurse at the time had a secret lover, and every night when she thought I was sleeping, she'd sneak off to meet him. I never told. Her absence was just what I needed.

The fishmonger always left the lower circle well after dark, so, one day per week, I'd dress in my maids' clothes and hide under a blanket at the back of his cart. The odor was unspeakable. But he lived by the river, and to me, any price was worth paying to get there.

I told myself the maids wouldn't notice that their clothes smelled like fish, though I never really knew. One of them gave me odd looks sometimes when she thought I didn't notice.

I'd slip under the blanket again before he left at dawn. Somehow, his fish crates always ended up around me instead of on top, and they never covered all sides—there was always an edge open that let air in, and let me out. Still, I spent every ride in fearful silence, dreading the moment when he would need the blanket for something. He never did. Perhaps he knew I was there, and understood. Perhaps he didn't care. My nurse, thankfully, slept like a hibernating bear, so I could always slip back through my window in the morning undetected.

I adored the river back then, especially on nights when the cormorant fisher boats scoured the water. The lanterns that hung from the ends of their boat-poles covered the river in ripples of enchanted gold, drawing in fish like a spell. And the cormorant birds fascinated me, so willing as they were to catch fish over and over only to cough them up for their masters. The display of loyalty was both touching and disturbing.

What fascinated me most, though, was the loving behavior of fisher-folk toward their children. Veyli was one of them.

We met one night by the riverbank when she was washing a net. When I realized she didn't know who I was, I felt light as a leaf. With her, I could just be a girl, instead of the empress's daughter. I treasured the freedom, and the only thing that marred my enjoyment of her friendship was my fear of losing it.

"My mother thinks you're an Ant," Veyli said one night as she washed a net. It was a job that kept her usefully employed whenever her parents' boat got too full.

"That's ironic," I said, breathing in the river's earthy smell. I skipped a stone on the water.

"What does ironic mean?"

I tried to think. Veyli's people used simple language, and while I tried to do the same with her, it wasn't always possible. And since she was a quick learner, I enjoyed teaching her.

"Ironic means that it's funny, since you're the Ant, and your adopted family doesn't know."

"Oh, yeah, that is ironic," she said, with a cute chipmunk grin. It always made me laugh.

The only thing that distinguished Veyli as an Ant was a patch of metallic gold on the back of her head, just above her hairline. She was lucky.

"I'm glad you look human," I said.

Like most Ants, her real family had been slaves. They escaped briefly, but were recaptured, apart from Veyli. She didn't remember why—she had only been six at the time. Soon after, cormorant fishers had found her wandering, and since fisher families loved children and never seemed to have enough of them to help, they adopted her. It was a beautiful story. I wished I could tell her who I really was, too.

As we played beside a bridge that overarched the river, water lapped languidly beside me, revealing a shell half buried in mud. I dug it out. It was the type of pretty thing Veyli loved—soft white, with a pearly pink underside.

I rinsed it and held it out. Veyli's eyes lit up.

"It looks just like a jewel!" she said. "My ma told me about jewels—they're all beautiful and sparkling and such. I've always wanted to see one." She took the shell and bowed with mock formality. "Thank you, Your Most Regal Queenliness, for this here precious jewel. It will be a sign of our friendship, and I'll hold on to it for all my days."

Then she clutched it in her fist and didn't let go, no matter which games we played.

"I wonder how the birds do it," I said to her, watching a distant fisherman as he pulled a cormorant from the water. A fishtail flopped in its bill.

"Like this." Veyli stretched out her neck, opened her mouth, and made comical gulping motions, loosening her grip on the net.

I mimicked her, and soon we were two laughing cormorants, gorging on fish.

Veyli's net slipped from her hand and drifted into the river, out of reach. She noticed and waded in. Since I myself couldn't swim, this frightened me, and an odd shiver rippled in my belly.

A moment later, a wave swept the net outward, though there were never any waves on the river. Veyli followed.

"No, Veyli, come back."

"If I lose this net, my parents will kill me," she said, wading out deeper.

She lost her footing and started to swim, one hand still balled into a fist.

"Forget the net. I'll buy you another one. I'll buy you ten nets."

Veyli giggled. I was starting to feel frantic.

I sprinted up the bridge, hoping the added height would give me more authority. As I begged her to return, an odd churning in the water caught my eye. It was pulling the net toward it.

"Veyli, go back! There's something there!"

Unthinkingly, I leaned over the bridge and grabbed at her, though I was many handspans too high. The net shot into the churning water, and Veyli swam after it. A moment later, she went under.

My heart stopped. I didn't think about my next move, I didn't calculate the risk; I simply dove.

I surfaced, gasping and paddling desperately, my thoughts buried under my instinct to survive.

My stomach pulsed, and waves rolled in, lifting me for long enough to see Veyli pop up, flailing.

"Veyli!"

The wave dropped me, and I struggled forward, straining to keep my head above water. Another wave, another sight of Veyli. She went under and didn't come up.

Terror flooded me. I couldn't see her, I couldn't help. My one thought was to get to the churning water, and to my surprise, another wave bore me there. It dumped me at the place I had last seen Veyli, plunging me underwater.

Then I saw her. A swirling vortex thrashed her around like a rag doll, the spinning force of it pushing me away, keeping me from grabbing her.

My lungs burned, and I struggled to break the surface.

"Help!" I screamed, coughing and spluttering.

The lights of the fishing boats neared, and a man dove in from the riverbank. It was Wan, though I didn't know him at the time. He swam straight to the maelstrom and dove in.

Lanterns lit up the water, and a fisherman reached out his hand to me. But then Wan came up without Veyli, and anxiety pulsed through me, and a wave swept me from the fisherman's reach. This happened again and again.

I was crying by now, yet not swallowing water; paddling, yet not struggling. Somehow, the waves were holding me up.

Two fishermen shoved their poles into the maelstrom. A moment later, they dragged something out: Wan, with Veyli in his arms.

I splashed and paddled then, trying to get to her, and before I knew it, I was in a boat, coughing, searching for Veyli.

When I found her, I froze. She was in the boat beside me, blue-lipped and unmoving as her mother pounded her back.

It took an eternity to reach the shore. When we arrived, they laid Veyli on the ground and put their fire pots around her. Everyone tried what they could, but still she didn't move. Then her mother was wailing.

I sat outside the fire pots, shivering, feeling I had somehow caused this.

An icy wind gusted past, putting out the fires. The people relit their pots, but Veyli could not be revived. Her mother clutched her to her breast, rocking back and forth, wailing. They had given up.

Anger erupted inside me, making my stomach jump, and the fires went out again. That's when the realization hit: I had put out the fires. I had called the icy wind.

And I had brought on the maelstrom that killed Veyli.

A tiny crab scuttled in, paused, then started digging a hole by my feet. It seemed to go on forever, digging, digging, against the muffled river sounds. I watched it, legs squeezed to my chest, shivering.

Finally, they draped Veyli with a blanket, covering her face, and took her away. I followed them with my gaze till the last lantern flickered out of sight. Then, in a sickened rush, I rolled onto my knees and vomited.

Chapter Thirty-Seven

SCATTERED CONVERSATIONS

Early the next day, Tori sat cradling a cold cup of tea.

"It wasn't your fault," Elnora said with a kind, pitying look.

But no matter how many times she said it, it still remained fiction.

"Dan and Bokoon serve me because their fathers did. These past eight years, they've seen it as a point of honor, serving the one their fathers died to save from fire." Tori stared unblinking at her cup. "They have no idea where the fire came from."

"That wasn't your fault, either."

A sharp knock at the door startled Tori, making her spill her tea—even though she knew it was Ruvien.

"Let's get this over with," she said, with a slow exhale.

The sooner she ended this, the better—for both their sakes. He and Senrik could still join the peacekeepers if they left today, and she didn't want to be responsible for making them miss their chance.

Ruvien greeted them on the doorstep with a wide smile and a wicker basket that radiated delicious aromas.

Senrik dipped his head. He wore dark blue robes that, while not exactly tight, were fitted well to his physique. Tori looked away, irritated with herself for noticing.

"Newcomers always miss their meat," Ruvien said, "so I took the liberty of getting you some. Spring rolls and crispy curd puffs from Greenstalk Village." He gave the basket a quick lift, then turned from the house and motioned them to follow.

"It's barely past dawn," Elnora said, glancing at the sky. "What time did you go to Greenstalk?"

"The heron that plunges first, gets the minnow," Ruvien said. He led them to an area of soft grass between the residences, and sat. "Let's eat."

Tori hesitated. "Actually, we should probably talk about—"

"No serious talks before breakfast," Ruvien said, waving his hands. "I forgot, we also have nettleberry juice." He opened the basket and pulled out four bottle-gourds. "As well as something stronger, for those who like that sort of thing." He winked at Elnora and slipped a sleek silver flask from his belt.

Senrik removed his outer robe and spread it between himself and Tori, then laid his sword on it with the care of a nursing mother. He rubbed a smudge off the hilt before reaching for a spring roll.

"This is good," Elnora said, sipping from her gourd. "I've never had nettleberry before. It's kind of like celery and cherry mixed together."

"More like lemongrass and raspberry," Ruvien said, tipping the flask into his gourd. He leaned back casually onto one elbow and offered the flask to Elnora. "Want some?"

Her mouth twitched in mild amusement. "I'll stick with the juice."

He shrugged.

As they ate, their conversations scattered in every direction: to the peach trees flowering around them, the food stalls at Greenstalk Village, Ruvien's new shoes—in short, everywhere except where they should. Unease grew in the pit of Tori's stomach. The longer she put off breaking the news, the harder Ruvien would take it.

"Listen, Ruvien," she said, "I need to be frank."

" No, no, no. That's not what this is about. This is about *me* convincing *you*. Don't you like the food?" He finished chewing and swallowed.

"Now, the elder said you needed two things: weapons training and alchemy."

And wielding. She actually had to embrace wielding in order to be safe from it. The irony was maddening.

"For weapons training, you won't find better than Master Maeli," he said.

Tori dragged a hand over her face, then stopped. "The weapons master is a woman?"

"There are several weapons masters, but yes, Master Maeli's the chief; she's in charge of training the peacekeepers, and giving us our postings. No one comes close to her in skill. She put Senrik here over her knee and gave him a good paddling. Remember that, Senrik?" Ruvien grinned.

Senrik continued eating.

"Admit it, Senrik. Master Maeli outmatches you."

"I never said she didn't."

What kind of woman could outmatch *him*? Tori's eyes slid involuntarily over Senrik's close-fitting robe. She jerked them away, focusing on Ruvien.

"And if it's the alchemy you're worried about," Ruvien said, "then don't. Master Kwai'le's the only one in the world who really understands ancient alchemy, so he's used to training total beginners."

"Is he the one who supports the village?" Elnora asked. "Master Banfay said alchemy paid for everything here."

"Most things," Senrik replied.

"You know that big auction the longevitists hold each year, where they auction off magical pills?" Ruvien asked.

Tori didn't, but he continued as though she did.

"Well, Master Kwai'le is like a king over there. Whose pills do you think sell for the most?"

"I'm guessing Master Kwai'le's," Tori said flatly, wondering how to get the conversation back on track.

"They go crazy over his work. His pills sometimes sell for two thousand spirit stones—each."

"Spirit stones?" Elnora asked, putting the empty gourds back into the basket.

Ruvien nodded. "Sect currency. And they pay him thousands—for one pill! Which is why, even though he's not a wielder, Master Kwai'le is one of the most highly respected masters in Peach Blossom Grove. You know how they paid for the entire Pavilion of Honorable Logograms? With one of his pills."

Tori straightened, leaning in. "What did you say?"

"That's an exaggeration," Senrik said, shaking his head. "Three stories of jade cost a whole lot more than two thousand spirit stones."

Ruvien shrugged. "Fine—two pills."

"No, not that," Tori said. "The other thing. Did you just say he's not a wielder?"

"None of the alchemists are, far as I know," Ruvien said. He looked at Senrik for confirmation.

"Then why did the council insist I had to learn wielding?"

Ruvien wrinkled his brow, as though trying to recall. "Who knows why the council says things. Either way, with these two masters, you're in excellent hands."

Tori crossed her arms slowly, thinking it through. The council said only a sixfold wielder could make a Septad. Could they have been wrong? Lying?

No. That part was backed by recorded history.

Yet it seemed her former understanding made sense: she simply needed to *be* a sixfold wielder—the Septad's spirit stones reacted differently to sixfold wielders, perhaps. But she certainly didn't need wielding for the craft itself, not if the master alchemist didn't.

Then why push her to wield? She was beginning to suspect the council's insistence had been motivated by some hidden agenda. Maybe they weren't so different from her mother's court after all.

Well, she had plenty of experience playing that game.

Warm relief washed over her, and she dropped her head backward, gazing up at the sky.

"I think I convinced her, Senrik." Ruvien watched her with a half-smile. "So what do you say?"

She nodded. "All right."

Ruvien gave a laugh and a clap of his hands, then held an open palm out to Senrik. Senrik flipped a silver dram in the air.

Ruvien snatched it mid-fall, then looked at Tori. "If you want, I'll take you to meet Master Maeli when she's back."

"She's already back," a low, feminine voice announced.

Two people strolled up the path to the residences, a tall woman in blue-gray robes with fitted sleeves in the Jeng fashion, and a man built like a stone fortress. He walked a few steps behind—her bodyguard, apparently.

Ruvien stood to greet them, followed by Senrik. As he did, a breeze blew through his robes, carrying the dangerously appealing scent of agarwood.

"Hi, Senrik," the woman purred. Her gaze oozed from Senrik's face down to his feet, then slowly back up again, before landing briefly on Ruvien. She gave a nod. "Ruvien."

"Ah, Keya. Nice to see you," Ruvien said.

Senrik dipped his chin, which she took as an invitation to slither up next to him and rest a hand on his arm. Her bodyguard frowned.

"I was surprised to hear you didn't leave with the peacekeepers," she said, brows knit with exaggerated concern. "What happened?" She rubbed his bicep.

Tori prickled. Something about the woman irked her.

Senrik eased away from her touch. "The council gave us a new job."

"Speaking of which," Ruvien said, "we haven't introduced Tori and Elnora."

Keya looked up, apparently surprised that others were present. Her gaze found Tori's and stopped, then darted to the space beside her, landing on Senrik's cloak. Her face darkened. For a breath she looked as though she was considering something, then, instead of offering a greeting, she pointedly turned her back.

"You boys out for a stroll?"

"Breakfast," Ruvien said. "Now we're off to the training grounds. So Master Maeli's back?"

"She arrived last night. Anyway," she said, turning to leave, "I need some spirit-fruit; I injured myself training."

Ruvien waved. "See you later. Ready, Tori? Better catch Master Maeli before her day begins."

Keya swiveled to look Tori over, a slow smile spreading on her face, as though enjoying some private joke. "You're training with Master Maeli?"

Tori stood, meeting her eye. "How is that your concern?"

Keya's smile faded, and she left, her bodyguard following, after a final resentful look at Senrik.

"She's an odd one," Ruvien said with a chuckle, and packed up their things.

As they walked to the training grounds, Elnora whispered, "What was her problem?"

"Besides her glowing personality?"

"She was nice enough to Senrik," she said, and raised an eyebrow.

Tori sniffed. "Well, that's her business."

She pushed the insufferable Keya from her mind and strode forward, ready to meet the weapons master.

CHAPTER THIRTY-EIGHT

THE NIGHT TWINS

The training grounds were empty, apart from Master Banfay. Tori met him on the second level where he stood loading porcelain medicine jars onto the shelves of the red hut. Elnora's eyes brightened when she saw what he was doing.

"Where's Master Maeli?" Ruvien asked.

When Master Banfay replied that she was spending the day at home, Ruvien offered to take Tori there.

As they walked, he briefed her on protocol, and in half the time of a candle's burn, bamboo walls came into view, half hidden by trees.

When they were still several paces from the gate, Ruvien stopped. "Well, let us know how it goes."

"You're not coming?"

He shook his head. "You can get away with disturbing her at home—you don't know any better. Senrik and I, though..."

The men emphasized the point by feigning terrified looks.

"Sending me in alone," Tori said wryly. "How brave."

In that case, she thought, reading into Ruvien's precaution, bringing Elnora might also not be advisable—for either of them.

"You should go back," Tori said to her. "You were interested in Master Banfay's herbs, why don't you see if he needs help?"

Elnora nodded.

"Just remember the protocol, and you'll be fine," Ruvien said, holding up an encouraging thumb as the three of them left.

Tori paused at the gate. She straightened her spine, then pushed into the front garden.

Though the garden looked wild, it was too flawless to be natural: every tree, shrub, and flower was in perfect visual harmony with the others. Birds flitted back and forth feeding their squawking young, completing the image of an ideal springtime. Nothing suggested the fierceness of a woman who trained elite fighters.

Tori ignored the prickle at the base of her skull and stepped onto a stone pathway. At the end stood an austere wooden house surrounded by a covered porch, like Kazani. Unlike at Kazani, however, no servants greeted her.

Tori weighed the risks of knocking; it might be seen as presumptuous—and she certainly wouldn't enter without permission. She continued through the garden, searching for a servant to announce her.

The garden eventually led to a wide-open space. Here, a woman sat on the grass, leaning back on her hands, ankle crossed over her knee. She was staring at a tree where two birds busily built their nest, and although she sat as still as a stone, her gaze was intent, as though seeing far more than twigs and feathers.

On her head, a bronze clasp swept up snow-white hair, and a long, straight horsetail pooled on the ground behind her like a puddle of milk. The sleeves of her light purple robes fluttered in the breeze, rich and gauzy. This was no servant. The next moment confirmed it: when she turned her head, a star-jewel flashed on her brow.

Tori positioned herself in a place where, she hoped, she was neither too close to be judged overconfident, nor too far away to be thought insincere. Ruvien had warned of this. She bowed, hand over fist, the way he had shown her, hesitating a moment to master her tone.

"Master Maeli."

A subtle shift of the woman's head gave Tori the feeling she had been noticed, and dismissed.

"This is my private residence," the woman said in a voice so soft it was evident she expected nothing less than silence when she spoke. "I will be at the training grounds tomorrow. Come find me at sunrise." Still watching the birds, she added, "If you have come about joining the peacekeepers, you are too late. You must wait for the next posting."

Tori took a breath for confidence, squared her shoulders, and approached a half step. "Master Maeli, I am Princess Tori of the House of Min."

The woman seemed to consider this. Then she slowly turned her head. Though the color of her hair seemed out of place on her ageless face, her eyes spoke of long, hard years.

"So, you have decided to remain in Peach Blossom Grove," Master Maeli said. "And now you have a request."

On cue, Tori knelt on the ground the way Ruvien had instructed, the strangeness of the action stiffening her limbs. In all her life, she had only knelt twice: once before her mother, when receiving a rebuke, and once before her great-grandmother, the chief equitess, when receiving an official appointment—neither time with so little certainty.

"Please accept me as your apprentice," Tori said, then touched her forehead to the grass once, twice, three times. She sat on her heels then, waiting, face studiously placid, trying to ignore the whispering dread of rejection.

Ruvien had mentioned three possible outcomes: apprentice, daughter, or nothing at all, and though there hadn't been time to explain, the last one was clear enough.

She set her jaw, steeling herself. If Master Maeli turned her face away, Tori would know it was over.

"In the days of your ancestor, Yanai Sumi," Master Maeli said, her expression grave, "many noble houses thrived. Yet only the House of Min had the courage to put an end to the depravity of Emperor Zanith's treasure voyages. This was a great and noble deed. Your ancestor, Yanai Sumi, was a valiant woman."

Ruvien hadn't mentioned how she should respond if the master referenced two-hundred-year-old events.

Tori feigned understanding, nodding her head sagely. "Yes, she was."

Apparently this was the right response: Master Maeli seemed satisfied. "In memory of your house's honor, and of the difference it made in so many lives, I will teach you," she said. "Rise. Today I have become your mother."

Tori's breath rushed out in relief, and she kowtowed three more times. "And I, your loyal daughter," she said, repeating the words Ruvien had told her. She waited silently, glowing with gratitude.

Master Maeli gestured, inviting her to sit closer. "Someone taught you the protocol—did they explain the meaning?"

"We didn't have much time."

"Then I will tell you. It amounts to this: When someone is accepted as apprentice, their master is bound to teach the fundamentals, after which the apprentice is no longer obligated to learn, nor their master to teach. But I have accepted you as daughter, which means we will forever be bound to one another. This is where the saying comes from: 'A master for a day, a mother for life.' A lifelong bond now exists—on my part, to guide and pass on knowledge; on yours, to honor and obey."

A lifelong bond. In her mind's eye, her mother's face appeared, and wariness prickled her scalp. Could another such bond be desirable?

"Come," Master Maeli said, rising. "I have some time today to teach you the basics; we will go to the training grounds."

When she had stood to full height, Master Maeli's build surprised her: she had the same small, delicate frame as Tori. How could this woman be the chief weapons master?

Tori followed her back to the village, but instead of mounting the steps to the training grounds, they passed them.

"Since the weapon determines the form," Master Maeli said, "before we begin, we will need to find you a weapon. Unlike some masters"—she gave a small smile and jerked her head toward Master Koren, who was making children laugh and squeal on the upper level—"I believe in beginning as we intend to continue."

In time it would take a candlewick to catch, they were standing in front of the weapons house, the white stone building Master Banfay had pointed out the day before, the storehouse of etched weapons. Master Maeli inserted a key into the tall double doors, but before she could open them, Keya came running.

She clasped her hand over her fist and bowed deeply. "Master Maeli."

Master Maeli patted her shoulder and turned to Tori. "Have you met Keya? She is my top student."

Keya smiled modestly.

"Keya, this is Tori; I have taken her as daughter."

Keya's smile faltered, but she quickly recovered.

"Tori, show your senior sister respect," Master Maeli said, pointing out the six stripes on Keya's lapel.

It took Tori a moment to register her meaning. Her jaw tensed. She forced herself to lean forward in a bow, every muscle rebelling against the act as Keya looked down on her smugly.

"We have come to find Tori a weapon," Master Maeli explained. "Once she has learned the basics, I will expect your help in training her."

"I'll do my best, Master," Keya said, but a sly look shone in her eyes.

"Now, what news do you bring?"

"There's another group of bandits in Jeng, out on Emperor's Highway. Also, Ghenz raiders have increased on the border of Min."

Master Maeli looked thoughtful. "Two from the new group can deal with the problem in Jeng, but someone more seasoned must deal with the Ghenz. Tell Muyang's group to leave at once. The rest can secure the villages, as planned."

Keya bowed and jogged away.

"It's a constant challenge," Master Maeli said, "spreading the peacekeepers between Jeng and Min. In the days of Yanai Sumi, the Ghenz warriors kept order in Jeng, if you can believe it. And it was the martial brotherhoods—forefathers of the Varanaken—who kept the peace in Min."

"They're still under treaty to do so," Tori said wryly, her mind straying to the fabricated charges she had read against the prisoners she had released from her mother's dungeons.

As though reading her thoughts, Master Maeli gave a sad shake of the head, then pushed on the doors, making them groan open.

They stepped into a wide hall. Shafts of light streamed through high, narrow windows, landing here and there on three long tables in the center of the room filled with small weapons. Larger weapons—maces, axes, spears—covered the walls.

Tori swept her gaze around the room, stirred with quiet awe. "Is everything here an etched weapon?"

Master Maeli nodded. "Go take a look."

The center table drew Tori's gaze. Lying along the perimeter were knives and daggers, fashioned from varied materials. Some were bright, like polished silver, others gray, like sleek new steel. Still others appeared to have been made of gold, or stone. Their hilts sported complex designs, or were studded with colorful jewels. Ancient logograms adorned them all.

The golden daggers were beautiful, more decoration than weapon. Tori slid her finger along one of the blades, then drew back, sucking a line of blood. She should have known better—of course etched gold would keep its edge.

"Every weapon here has a lineage," Master Maeli said, eyeing the weapons on the wall. "Each belonged to a member of the Royal Tribe in times past, many of them before Ishairo." She looked at Tori. "And they cannot be chosen. The weapon does the choosing."

"Meaning?"

"I will show you," Master Maeli said, coming to her side. "Glide your fingertips over the hilts. When you find one that draws you, pause, see if you notice anything. If not, move on."

Tori tilted her head. "I'm not sure I follow."

"It will soon be clear. Just be patient; the weapons need time to choose."

Tori did as instructed, pausing after each dagger, trying to notice anything at all. By the tenth, though, the only thing she had noticed was a mounting unease.

"What if one doesn't choose me?"

"Do not worry. Give the weapons time."

Tori carried on. Some of the daggers felt cold as ice. Others were warm, like a copper hairpin that had lain all day in the sun. When she had run her hand across them all—more than a hundred—Master Maeli told her to start again.

"Should I perhaps try a different table?" Tori asked.

"You were drawn to that one; give it another pass."

Tori closed her eyes this time, hoping it would make a difference, then walked slowly, letting her fingers trace the points and ridges of carvings and jewels, trying to understand their unknown language.

Suddenly, her fingers buzzed.

"I felt something," she said, opening her eyes.

"What?"

"Something like a low buzzing."

Master Maeli shook her head. "Keep going."

"What should I be looking for, then?"

"Do not worry; when you feel it, you will know."

How could she be certain? If the weapons really were the ones doing the choosing, they had no obligation to choose her.

Tori continued anyway. Although more weapons buzzed now, at no point could she say she *knew*. But when she reached a pair of black double daggers at the end of the table, the buzzing was so intense, it shook her joints. Very quickly, the weapons turned hot, stinging her.

She made to draw back, but couldn't, and when she forcibly jerked her hand, her fist somehow clenched around them. Alarm coursed through her.

"I could use some help," she said, keeping her voice steady.

Master Maeli strolled away from the wall she had been studying and looked at Tori's hand.

"The Night Twins. Interesting." She lifted one side of her outer robe, and a pair of white daggers peeked out. "This is its sister set. Only six sets have ever existed in the history of the world, each embodying a different element. Even though the ones in your hand are the color of the metal element, they actually embody air," she said, pointing out an ancient logogram on the hilt in the shape of interconnecting spirals.

Tori didn't care. The bones in her hand would soon be shaken to flour. "I can't let go."

"Send them a mental command. Think 'release.' But when they do, do not sheathe them; instead, you must hold one in each hand. They will need to fully connect with you in order to work properly."

Tori directed an urgent thought toward the daggers. *Release!*

Instantly, her fist sprang open and the daggers dropped on the table. Her fingers trembled. But as instructed, she gripped one dagger in each hand. Although both hands buzzed now, the intensity was less, making it bearable.

Once her alarm had worn off, the enormity of her good fortune hit her: she was holding an actual etched weapon, and it was hers to use!

As they walked back to the training grounds, Tori stared at the daggers in quiet wonder. They were stunningly black, like obsidian rock, and shone like polished steel. Interestingly, they felt weightless, and neither warm nor cold—apart from the buzzing, it was like holding air.

The lower level of the training grounds had filled in their absence, and as she passed through a group of talking people, several of them reached out to shake her hand. Upon seeing her hands occupied, they settled for brushing their fingertips over her robes instead, like people had done at the well the day before. Tori took a slow, deliberate breath and tried to ignore them.

The second level was mercifully empty, and that was where Master Maeli stopped.

"Just a little while longer," she said, glancing at Tori's daggers.

Tori let her eyes wander across the training grounds' three massive levels. Although there was no sign of Elnora, Senrik, and Ruvien, whom she had missed as she was slipping through the crowd of unmannerly hands and were training on the first level. Senrik slashed and spun through sword forms, while Ruvien amused himself with his bow, nocking several arrows to shoot various targets at once.

"You mentioned the daggers embody the air element," Tori said after a while. "What does this mean?"

"Although it takes much time and dedication, once a person truly unifies with an etched weapon, that weapon will rise to its potential. For the Night Twins, their potential is to form an air blade, extending their reach."

"How far?" Tori asked, admiring the sleek weapons in her hands.

"Ultimately, to the length of a short sword. But that would take years. This is, however, perfect for someone of your size, since you will usually face much larger opponents."

Tori tried to imagine how far a short sword would reach. She hadn't spent much time around weapons.

"Now, we had better discuss your training. The elder will question you two moons from now, which means we must begin immediately. Tell me all you know of fighting."

What should she know about fighting? She was a princess, she had only ever studied military strategy—and that, she had never mastered.

She thought hard for something that might impress Master Maeli. Nothing came. *Better to be honest*, she thought. *I'll look a bigger fool if I'm caught in a lie.*

"The heirs of the royal house are sadly deficient in this area," Tori said.

"They consider it beneath them, you mean?" Master Maeli replied, a smile in her eyes. "'Women to govern, men to fight,' one of the Seven Sages wrote."

"It's what each was built for," Tori said automatically, then inwardly cringed—she had just implied her master wasn't built for her job.

But Master Maeli didn't seem offended, or even to notice. She simply produced her white daggers seemingly out of nowhere, spinning them in her palms with practiced ease. "And there is wisdom in that. A woman's head for strategy is her greatest strength, both in battle, and in life. That is why we are, generally speaking, better able to govern than men. A house of bamboo is stronger than a house of steel, is it not?"

She twirled the daggers between her fingers, letting them roll over her knuckles before flicking them back into her grip. "But while it is true that steel cannot endure the elements as bamboo can, bamboo makes a poor battle sword. In the same way, though a woman's cunning is sharper—and her endurance of life's hardships greater—when it comes to fighting, the one with less physical power is seldom at an advantage. And so, more often than not, the advantage belongs to the man."

The memory of the Laughing Skunk alley forced its way in, along with the pain, the fury, the utter humiliation of her helplessness.

"I was told you bested Senrik," Tori said, pushing the memories down.

"I've had a great deal more time to master my technique," Master Maeli replied, without any hint of satisfaction or pride. "Which brings me to my point: for the smaller person to win, she must be faster and possess the better technique. Speed and technique will therefore be our focus. For your first-level grading, known as the 'one-bar,' we will focus on basic forms." She slapped her daggers into one hand and stepped forward. "I will show you the first three moves now, slowly, so you can repeat them, and prepare yourself for the days to come. This will also finish connecting the Night Twins to your movements."

Holding the daggers in one fist, Master Maeli thrust them downward, then spun and slapped her hands together, taking one dagger in each hand. "Splitting lightning and thunder." She whirled them over her head, then spun with the grace of a dancer, whipping the daggers in a circle around her body. "Circling wolves." With a final sweep, she pulled herself onto one leg, stabbing in two directions, high and low. "Pick the star and exchange it for the moon." She stepped down softly, feet together, brought the daggers together again, and bowed. Then, with an easy flip, the daggers disappeared.

Apart from a lingering admiration of her new master, nothing of the sequence remained in Tori's mind. It must have shown, because Master Maeli said, "Just do what you can. The important thing is to finish training the daggers to your movements."

Tori did her best to visualize the forms. She tried mimicking Master Maeli's fluid, lethal grace, but instead found herself tiptoeing in a circle, arms pointed in the air like a perfect fool. She thrust one dagger up and the other one down, nearly slicing the side of her leg.

Tori's cheeks heated. "That was less than ideal."

Master Maeli peered at her, lips pursed to one side. "Perhaps we should start with something simpler. Just try to attack me."

Tori glanced at her daggers, noticing for the first time their cruel, deadly points. "You're sure you want me to attack you?"

A faint smile. "I said I want you to *try*."

"But what if I cut you?"

Master Maeli strode toward Tori without a word, wrapped her hand around Tori's, then drove the black dagger straight into her own palm.

A cry escaped Tori's mouth as she yanked the blade free. But Master Maeli calmly lifted her hand, wiggling her fingers. Not so much as a scratch.

Tori stared, heart pounding. This wasn't possible.

Then the memory returned of Master Banfay in the alley. Tori hadn't imagined it—the thug *had* plunged his knife into Master Banfay's back!

"Now, attack as fast and hard as you can," Master Maeli said.

Tori took a breath, then charged, slashing. At the last possible moment, Master Maeli casually stepped aside, letting Tori stumble past.

Her master's cool-headed self-assurance impressed Tori more than she ever thought possible, and Tori felt determined to win her approval.

They repeated the exercise five more times.

"That will do," Master Maeli said at last. "Your weapons should be fully connected."

Without looking at them, Tori tried to sense the Night Twins in her hands. She couldn't. They felt like an extension of herself, with only the sensation of loosely clenched fists informing her that they were there at all.

"We can now begin your training," Master Maeli said.

Tori stood straighter to hide her exhaustion. She spent most of her days at the palace in exertion of an intellectual sort, her only exercise coming from long, leisurely walks through palace gardens.

"Today, you will focus on horse stance, which is useful for building stamina." Master Maeli spoke as though "horse stance" were a common term.

Tori knit her brow, trying to interpret it.

"Just sit the way you would on a horse," Master Maeli clarified, "except do it in the air."

"I've only ever ridden in carriages," Tori said, keeping embarrassment from her voice. Not for the first time, palace life seemed to her more like life in a cage.

But Master Maeli's face was serene. "Of course, I had forgotten. Highborn women do not ride horses. Very well, to do horse stance, spread your feet as wide as you can without wavering—like this. Now, bend your legs as though sitting in a chair. Yes. Hold that."

A few breaths later, Tori's legs were burning and visibly trembling from effort.

Master Maeli gave a nod. "Rest. In a moment, you will try holding the pose for longer."

By the time they finished, sweat drenched Tori's robes, and her legs felt like wet noodles.

"You will see," Master Maeli said. "Not many weeks from now, you will be able to remain in horse stance all day."

Tori hoped this was a figure of speech.

She eyed the stairs with dread—two full flights—and considered scooting down on her backside.

"From what I understand," Master Maeli was saying, "you must study alchemy four days per week. We will therefore alternate between alchemy and weapons. Twice per week you will train alone with me, then once more with a group of other students. On top of that, you must practice on your own every day; this is the only way to obtain Unity with the Sword."

"What's that?"

"A subject for another time," Master Maeli said, starting down the steps. Tori followed, resisting the urge to scoot.

"Tomorrow you might be a little sore," Master Maeli said, "so it will be the perfect time to present yourself to Master Kwai'le. It will do you good to spend a day strolling through nature."

Tori exhaled with relief. That sounded perfect to her.

Chapter Thirty-Nine

MASTER ALCHEMIST

It took all of Tori's effort to keep from walking with a limp the next morning. Horse stance had left her legs feeling like they had been crushed by a boulder.

After avoiding people as best she could, or slipping as quickly as possible past the ones she did encounter—shaking their hands briskly just to be free of them—she arrived at last at the master alchemist's cave. It was hidden among the cliffs that surrounded the elder's waterfall, just as Master Maeli had described.

The door at the entrance surprised her—since when did caves have doors? She hesitated; doors implied boundaries, possessiveness. She made to knock, but the wind eased the door open, revealing an empty room. Oddly, the cave was bright inside. Though as in the elder's cave the walls were covered with green crystals, morning sunlight overpowered their glow.

The place looked like a workshop, yet something about it felt too organized, as though arranged to make visitors feel like intruders. A faint medicinal smell of processed herbs hung in the air, the source of which she assumed was a shining pill furnace sitting on a counter. A table and chairs occupied the middle of the room, and a scrollshelf lined the left wall, its cubicles filled with scroll bags of various colors. One of the cubicles was empty and padded with red silk, as though designed to hold something precious.

She moved in the direction of the sunlight. Stone shelves carved into the rock above the counter held black porcelain pill bottles about twice the size of her thumb. Were these the famed magical pills Ruvien had spoken of?

Overcome by curiosity, Tori walked over and picked up a bottle. To her disappointment, the top was sealed with wax and she was unable to look inside. She set it down carefully.

Ruvien had said Master Kwai'le's pills were worth thousands of spirit stones each. As spirit stones were one of her mother's favorite things, Tori had picked up some passing knowledge over the years. A spirit stone—even just the medicinal-grade ones like they had at the palace—cost a minimum of one hundred twenty skades, or four silver drams. And Master Kwai'le was paid two thousand spirit stones!

She did the math. Each of these ordinary bottles contained something worth eight thousand silver drams—three hundred twenty gold petals. That was more than the yearly income of most successful merchant houses.

Was this what mastery meant? Bottling cures into prices no common person could afford?

A shelf of ointment jars followed the pill bottles, then a shelf where spirit stones sat glowing. Many of the stones were an amalgamation of two or more colors, like the ones she had seen in Master Banfay's medicine chest. Perhaps this was the longevitist sect currency Ruvien had spoken of.

She picked up a pink-and-orange stone. Though the outside was perfectly smooth, the inside fascinated her: two different colors seemed pressed together like clay, then, at the point of their union, delicate veins from each side fanned out into the other—pink into orange, orange into pink. This was no medicinal-grade palace stone. No one with a grain of sense would part with two thousand of these for a single pill.

Could Master Kwai'le have made these? But stones—even spirit stones—were found in nature. She tilted it, letting the orange side catch the light. Yet the elder had told her she needed alchemy for the Septad. Alchemy must have something to do with these stones, then—it had enhanced them, perhaps—or the elder's statement would make no sense.

A thrill rose inside her. She was a quick study; if she picked up the technique fast enough, she'd have the rest of her time here to perfect it. She might not even need to stay the full six moons.

But if she failed to learn quickly enough, what would become of her plans? She tried not to think of it.

Beneath the spirit stones, the pill furnace she had noticed earlier shone up at her from the counter. It gave her a wary feeling, like an animal pretending to sleep. How had she even recognized it? The only other pill furnace she had seen was Midra's, and hers was nothing like this. The palace healer's furnace was a tarnished, deformed ball with handles, whereas this one was sleek.

It was the size of a small melon made of what appeared to be black granite, apart from its iridescent hue. It stood on tarnished silver feet carved to look like animal paws, and one end of it had been sliced off to form a hungry mouth. Silver carvings—clouds and mythical creatures—encircled the mouth, etched with ancient logograms. A dark blue spirit stone embedded on top glowed faintly, like a half-seeing eye.

As Tori continued to follow the sunlight, the cave brightened, and, instead of a back wall, it opened onto an enormous plant nursery, with tables of seedlings beneath a latticework trellis.

A stone wall shielded the nursery from the road on the left, and on the right, larger plants a few handspans tall stretched out in rows, forming a small field. The vine spilled white flowers down the trellis pillars, spread across the ground, and crept over the stone wall.

A man wearing a wide bamboo hat and long gray robes emerged from among the seedlings and leaned over a box. Tori's eyes widened. The plants doubled in height, following the motion of his hand. He leaned over another box, then stopped suddenly and straightened.

"Are you coming out?" he said, eyes still on the plants. "Or did you think learning alchemy was like a theater performance you could watch from afar?"

Tori blinked, surprised by his unfriendly tone.

She stepped onto the grass and covered her fist with her hand, the way she had with the weapons master. "Master Kwai'le, I am Princess Tori of the House of—"

"Your titles mean nothing here," he snapped. "If I decide to take you on, you will simply be 'apprentice,' and you will address me as 'Master.'"

Tori kept her face neutral. "Understood."

He made one more plant grow, then came and stood in front of her. He was a man of about sixty, sour-faced, with long, narrow eyes that, for some unknown reason, had laugh lines around them.

"Let's get this over with," he said, waving an impatient hand.

She paused, trying to decipher his meaning.

"Well, go on," he said. "Kneel."

Though she was embarrassed to have forgotten protocol, it was the idea of bowing to this insufferable man that flushed her face. Still, she eased her aching muscles to the ground. Then she made her request, performed her kowtows, and waited. And waited.

He made a show of mulling it over, grimacing as though tasting something bitter. At some point it occurred to her that he might actually reject her, and far from dreading it, she found herself hoping he would, just so she could give him a good tongue lashing and leave.

But who would teach her then? The elder hadn't mentioned any other alchemy masters: if this one refused, it was far more likely that Tori would end up begging him. She shifted uneasily under the image.

"Rise, Apprentice," he said finally. "And to be clear, taking you as my apprentice means that if at any point I see that you're not fit to be an alchemist, I can—and will—terminate the training."

He spun on his heel and returned to the plants he had been tending.

Tori watched him, eyes narrowed. Master Maeli had said an apprentice was bound to be taught the basics. This man wanted to cheat her.

"Well, come on," he said, "or were you waiting for me to serve you tea?" He smirked as though he had just told a clever joke.

Tori took a deep breath. *I am the Min Daughter. I will not be rankled by a grouchy old man.*

He made another plant grow, then brushed off his hands and looked her over with an expression clearly calculated to show how unimpressed he was. "They say you have a legendary hexatic ketua." His mouth quirked wryly. "We shall see how well that serves you. Now, tell me what you know about alchemy."

"Nothing...the elder said you would teach me."

"A *total* beginner? At your age?" He gave a long, exaggerated sigh, then walked past her and back into the cave. This time she followed without being told.

He took a green bag from the scrollshelf, and slipped out a fat scroll made of bamboo slips.

"Read and memorize these," he said, handing it to her.

"Thank you."

"Thank you, *Master*."

Several more fitting appellations rushed into her mind just then, but she pressed her lips together.

She headed to the chairs, trying to decide between one of hardwood and one made of stuffed purple silk. The silk one would be more comfortable, but straight-backed chairs were more conducive to studying.

"One does not sit in the presence of one's master unless directed to do so."

She stared. "Are you serious?"

His expression told her he was.

"But the scroll is long. If I don't sit, it will trail on the floor."

"Then I suggest you make better use of your arms. Standing with the arms raised improves blood flow to the brain," he said, sinking into the stuffed chair. "Three days from now, there will be a test. You cannot move on until you have passed with ninety-eight percent accuracy." He poured himself a cup of tea, then regarded her from under his brows. "Alchemy is no theater performance."

By the time she had plodded through 120 plants, her arms burned with fatigue, and her head spun from thirst. Master Kwai'le had sipped tea the entire time, not once even offering her water.

Well, she wouldn't ask. She'd die of thirst before giving him the satisfaction.

She moved on to another plant, struggling to keep the bottom of the scroll from dragging along the floor. Wan had taught her the basics of botany, so a handful of plants looked familiar—but here there were just so many, each accompanied by a flood of details.

Beside each name was an ink drawing, followed by characteristics, planting times, harvest cycles—besides other things she had never even heard of: associated dawn-essence, preparation techniques, contraindications with alchemical pills. Little notes mentioned side details about the plant's root, flower, and fruit.

She tried her best to commit it all to memory, but it was hard to concentrate. If she had been able to sit, it would have gone more quickly, but between aching legs, tired arms, and a throbbing head, it felt endless.

Why am I even studying this? she thought. She was three-quarters of the way down, and still hadn't seen any spirit stones. She was starting to think there had been a mistake.

She scanned the rest of the scroll, rolling it up as she went. Nothing but plants. Master Kwai'le had gotten it wrong.

Smug satisfaction stretched inside her as she watched him tinkering with the pill furnace at the counter. *Let's see how easily a great alchemist admits his mistakes.*

She cleared her throat, newly aware of how dry it was. "I'm afraid there's been a misunderstanding," she said, trying not to glance at his teacup. "There's no description of spirit stones here. I think you may have given me the wrong scroll." She paused. "*Master.*"

At first, he continued working as though he hadn't heard her. Finally, he pushed the pill furnace aside, dusted his hands, and came to stand beside her.

"There are no spirit stones here," he said, pointing to the top of the scroll with a helpful look on his face, "because, as you can see, this is a scroll for p-l-a-n-t-s." He carefully traced each line of the logograms, as though teaching a child to read.

Indignation surged through her. "I'm here to learn how to make a Septad. Were you not informed I was to study spirit stones?"

"That's the idea, yes."

"Then why am I memorizing plants?"

His expression somehow managed to convey both long-suffering and disdain. "The fact that you ask such a question shows how truly ignorant you are. If you want to make progress in alchemy, you'll need to actually do some work for once—you're not in the palace anymore." He paused. "*Princess.*"

She stared at him, incredulous. "I know very well how to work. And for your information, I've memorized far more than this in the past."

He gave her a wry smile, evidently not believing a word of it.

"To use spirit stones," he said, returning to his tinkering at the counter, "you first need to find them."

"Then teach me that."

"Do you have see-through vision?" he said, using a brush to clean inside the pill furnace.

"I beg your pardon?"

"If you look at the ground, can you see through it? Roots, insects tunneling, and so on?"

"Of course not. And I suspect neither can you."

"Obviously. Which is why," he said slowly, as though explaining to an imbecile, "we need...to learn about...the things...that grow...*above*...the ground."

She furrowed her brow, irritation flickering beneath her confusion.

He continued. “Put another way: if we want to know which dawn-essence exists in a place, and therefore which spirit stones might be found there, we need to observe which species of plants are growing. Hmm?”

She had had enough. “I haven’t the faintest idea what you’re talking about,” she said, locking eyes with him. “That’s why I’m here. To learn. And my understanding was that you were here to teach, not insult.”

He set down his furnace brush a little too hard. Apparently, standing her ground didn’t sit well with him. “Well, let’s start with the *very* basics, then,” he said in a singsong voice. “Certain plants need certain types of dawn-essence to grow. You follow?”

“Yes, Master,” she said through clenched teeth.

He continued in the same voice. “If the plant is there, the requisite dawn-essence is also there. Still following? And that requisite essence comes from the spirit stones far beneath the ground.” He gave a wide smile. “Better?”

“Yes. You might have said that from the beginning.” What in the name of the Six did he have against her?

“Superb,” he said, clapping his hands. “Now that we’ve covered what every five-year-old knows, perhaps you can start chipping away at your vast ignorance by actually studying the materials I gave you.”

That evening, Tori glared at the teapot on her cottage table as though it were Master Kwai’le himself. The things she would have said to him—if she didn’t need him to teach her.

She downed cup after cup of jasmine tea, the warm liquid filling her with deep gratitude while simultaneously reminding her of his selfish tea-drinking. Eventually, though, her anger diminished along with her thirst.

Elnora was busy setting out a meal from the communal dining hall, as everyone called it. She served Tori pan-seared greens, and cloud buns.

"Rough day?" she said, eyes gentle.

Tori dropped her head into her palms and let out a breath.

"How long before you can make the Septad?" Elnora asked.

"I honestly wonder if he has any intention of teaching me at all."

It would have been easy to unload it all—to let Elnora become righteously furious on her behalf. But what good would it do to stoke the fire simmering in her chest? She didn't need more anger. She needed this to work.

She bit into a cloud bun, chewed once, and frowned. "There's no pork in this pork cloud."

"Sorry, Princess. They don't eat meat here."

Tori's eyebrow lifted.

"There's no death in the Veils," Elnora said. "They're not allowed to kill animals here, and even if they did, the carcass would disappear before they could dress it."

So that's what Ruvien had meant when he talked about newcomers missing their meat. It wasn't a terrible thing, she supposed, letting animals just live their innocent lives.

"But I got three kinds of vegetables I think you would like," Elnora said. "They're different from the ones we had last night."

Tori swallowed her flavorless bun and sampled the vegetables. At least they had the decency to taste like something.

"Tell me about your day with Master Banfay. Did you learn anything?"

"Master Banfay says I have potential," Elnora said, looking guilty. "He wants me to assist him. I told him no, of course."

"Why did you say that?"

"You still need waiting on, Princess. They haven't so much as given you a maid. And it's my job to provide you with company—a job and an *honor.*"

"I can dress myself now," Tori said, and offered a smile. "And I'll be busy most days for the next few moons. You might as well learn what you can."

Elnora hesitated, then finally nodded. "All right, I'll tell him I'll learn what I can in my spare time. But serving you comes first."

After their meal, Tori collapsed into bed, eyes on the ceiling. She was too tired to think, but the question whirled in her mind: Would she ever reach her goal?

Chapter Forty

PAVILION OF HONORABLE LOGOGRAMS

After another day of horse stance with Master Maeli, Tori returned to the alchemy cave sore again—but this time carrying a bottle-gourd of water. If she was going to spend the day with her arms raised like an imbecile, she would at least do so hydrated.

The sky was still pink with dawn, and the birds' jubilant wake-up songs filled air: Master Kwai'le had told her to come early. He had no doubt thought a princess too lazy to rise before the sun. She smiled wryly. She had probably worked harder at the palace than he had in his whole miserable life.

A quick search revealed both the cave and the plant nursery to be empty—he was still at home.

So much the better. She could study properly this time—she glanced at the padded chair—and most likely finish before he arrived.

A smile played on her lips as she searched the green bags for the fat bamboo scroll she had studied two days before. But the scroll was nowhere to be found.

Tori touched her fingertips to her temple. Hadn't she seen him return it to the shelf?

She peered inside the nook with the red silk lining, just to be sure, then scanned the shelves above the counter. She scanned the floor, then lowered herself onto her knees to pass a hand underneath the cabinet. All she recovered was a layer of dust.

As she sipped water from her gourd, her eyes roamed, scrutinizing every crevice. Nothing.

She searched the scrollshelf again, this time checking every color, not just green. Though none of the scrolls were either fat or made of bamboo, her growing agitation made her unroll them anyway.

Hidden behind a blue bag was a green one she had missed. She grabbed it, blowing out a relieved breath as the ridges of bamboo slips met her fingers through the silk. This was it. But when she unrolled it, her heart sank: instead of plants, a series of stick figures covered the page.

Each figure had been drawn in a different pose, with descriptions of associated breathing techniques. The first was in a seated position with nothing below it. The notation read: *Horse Stance.* Tori groaned inwardly—her legs ached at the mere sight of it. The second figure was identical apart from the notation, which had changed to *Circulate Essence*. The third figure was, apparently, *Streaming Essence.* Its arms were extended outward, and it looked like it was—she held the scroll closer—about to embrace to a plant.

What in the world?

"I'm glad you've found some wider reading to amuse yourself."

Tori jumped, nearly dropping the scroll. She fumbled to roll it up and shoved it back in place.

Master Kwai'le hung his wide bamboo hat on a peg by the door, watching her with visible annoyance.

"It's customary to greet one's master with a bow," he said. "But I suppose they don't teach basic manners at the palace."

Heat climbed up her neck. She wanted to snap back—something cutting—but instead, she said tightly, "Apologies. You startled me."

He glanced at the padded chair. "Another thing they probably don't teach is that one never sits in one's master's chair, even in his absence."

"I have no interest in your chair." What in the world were chairs for, if not to sit on?

He walked past her, heading outside. "Well, don't just stand there. We've got a lot to cover. Today, you will watch and learn." Then, under his breath, "Hopefully."

She inhaled through her nose, slow and controlled. And he accused *her* of having no manners.

They stopped at a box of seedlings near the back entrance. "Today we will begin phytolyzing plants. Or rather, I will be phytolyzing plants while you watch," he said, but a voice calling from inside the cave interrupted them.

A man stepped outside, holding a hawk on one arm and a slip of paper in his other hand.

Master Kwai'le gave an exasperated exhale and threw up his hands. "Again?"

The man chuckled, then dipped his head at Tori and introduced himself as the miller.

"This is the fourth time," Master Kwai'le said, taking the hawk. "How can a bird clever enough to transfer a letter capsule from another bird's leg onto his own muddle something as simple as flying home?"

He examined an amber-colored jewel hanging from the hawk's neck. The faint glow of the pendant showed it to be a spirit stone, except cut and intricately faceted. "I don't understand. These homing stones are the finest I've ever made."

"Well, you know your business best," the miller replied. "All spirit stones look the same to me. The only things I can tell apart are strains of wheat." He gestured to the paper. "And speaking of business, sorry for reading that. I thought it was meant for me."

Master Kwai'le waved the apology away and slipped the paper into his robe. "I don't know what's wrong with these confounded hawks."

After he had walked the miller to the cave door, he tied the hawk's foot to a perch beside the scrollshelf, examining its pendant once more. Then he shook his head and came back outside, muttering.

"Where was I? Oh yes, plant phytolyzation."

"Shouldn't I be memorizing plant names? Tori said. "Isn't there a test tomorrow?"

"If you had paid attention, you wouldn't be asking," he said, scooping up a seedling rooted in dirt. "But yes, there will be a test. You will be shown drawings of the three hundred and fifty plant varieties you studied, and for each, you must detail the names, characteristics, planting and harvest requirements, associated dawn-essence, contraindications, and preparation techniques for basic alchemical pills."

"By tomorrow?"

"Is that a problem?"

"Well, I would have liked another look at the scroll."

"I can't imagine why you'd need it—didn't you say you'd memorized far more than that in the palace? And as you spent all of your first day studying, I would have thought you knew it perfectly by now." He smirked. "But if you really haven't managed to retain such a simple thing, you can ask Master Koren. I lent the scroll to him last night."

Tori's lips tightened. There was no way she was asking Master Koren for anything.

"And remember, anything less than ninety-eight percent will prove you simply don't have what it takes," he said with a satisfied glint in his eye.

For the remainder of the afternoon, he demonstrated something he called "plant phytolyzation," where he made slow lifting motions with his fingertips that somehow caused the seedlings to grow. He said he was "streaming elixir."

But the test dominated her thoughts, and she made plans for how to pass. He was keeping her from studying simply so he could declare her unfit. She wasn't about to let that happen.

"The writings always talk about 'streaming essence,'" he said, "but for those of us in the Royal Tribe, our dawn-essence has been replaced with the elixir."

He made the seedlings sprout leaves. "Wielders do something similar, of course, except they bind their element to the elixir before streaming it outward. But I think I've proved one doesn't need to be a wielder to be successful." He sniffed, a look of self-satisfaction on his face.

The moment he dismissed her for the day, Tori went straight to the Pavilion of Honorable Logograms, which now shone golden-green in the light of the setting sun. Bronze candelabras illuminated a circular jade foyer where a young woman sat behind a desk.

"May I help you?" the woman said, smiling.

"I would like to see your books on—" Tori stopped herself. She had been about to say "plant alchemy," then thought better of it. She wouldn't risk word getting back to Master Kwai'le and giving him a reason to gloat. "On Antiquitals."

"Right this way."

The woman led her to another circular room, this one several times the size of the foyer, surrounded by three levels of balconies. Shelves stood along the jade walls, some filled with scroll bags, others with silk-bound volumes.

The librarian walked to a shelf with a metal plate labeled *Ancient Races*, and handed Tori a book made of bound palm-leaf pages.

Tori flipped through a few pages just for show. Inside, several chapters were dedicated to the Antiquital tongue.

"They had their own language?" Tori asked, genuinely surprised.

"They spoke the Old Speech, actually."

Tori saw that she was right: the Old Speech appeared on the next page. As was required of all royalty, Tori had been tutored in the basics of reading the Old Speech, which sometimes appeared in very ancient writings. The Old Speech was always written in glyphs—the oldest writing in Arizan, predating even the ancient logograms used for etched metal.

As Tori studied the pages, her surprise grew. One chapter was dedicated to a comprehensive study of glyphs. Each glyph had been labeled with a phonetic pronunciation, constructed using radicals from the logograms of the common tongue.

"This is incredible," Tori said. "I didn't know any record still existed on how the Old Speech was pronounced."

The woman smiled. "Well, there you have it." She indicated a small golden bell on the wall. "Take your time browsing—we're open all night. If you need any help, just ring."

Tori flipped through the book for a few moments more. If she had more time, she would study this out of sheer interest.

As she was about to close it, a picture made her pause: a drawing of an exquisitely beautiful person covered in leaves. The caption read: *Antiquital of the Wood Tribe*. Tori creased her brow. The picture bore no resemblance to the fearsome drawings of Antiquitals contained in the histories.

The thought of the histories brought back memories of the tests she had taken as a youth, which in turn reminded her of her present predicament—she needed to pass the alchemy test.

She slid the volume under her arm—she would need to make a show of borrowing something. And who knew? Maybe she would have time to study it.

Her search for anything on plants or alchemy in the shelves around her proved fruitless, so she climbed a jade staircase to the second floor. Nothing on plants here, either. How could there be no books on plants in a lush place like Peach Blossom Grove?

A flash of excitement fizzled into disappointment; the shelf labeled *Alchemy* was simply a collection of the life stories of famous alchemists. None of the other shelves were any better.

If she failed this test, the humiliation of it would be the least of her worries, she thought, dropping her head back onto her shoulders and blowing out a frustrated breath. Maybe she should go see Master Koren after all.

Just then, her eyes landed on something—leafy vines spilling over the balcony rail on the top floor. She straightened, stepping away for a better view. Groups of plants revealed themselves. Though the jade roof tiles above them now reflected lantern light, in the daytime they must have served as a sort of greenhouse.

Tori turned in a circle to take in the balcony from all angles and spotted what looked like the edge of a scrollshelf. Hope filled her. If there were writings on plants anywhere in this library, it would be there. She raced up the stairs.

At the top, draped in vines and surrounded by potted plants of all sizes, books and scrolls filled the space, interspersed with small, round tables. When she read the metal plates on the shelves, Tori almost cheered—every one of them related to plants, and though Master Kwai'le's scroll was nowhere in sight, several writings together covered everything she needed to learn—and more.

Fresh air flowed in from a small window in the roof, and Tori looked up at it, filling her lungs. A bright gibbous moon smiled back at her. Then she piled books and scrolls on a table between two trees and settled in for a long night.

Chapter Forty-One

ASHES IN THE WIND

The night had been fruitful. Still, the next morning when the light was still gray, Tori made her way to the alchemy cave. Getting there before the alchemy master would allow her to mentally relax before the test, something she always found helped her.

She opened the cave door, and her heart sank: Master Kwai'le was standing over the pill furnace. The smell of processed herbs hung in the air.

"Master," she said, remembering to bow.

He continued motioning with his hands at the furnace.

She straightened. If he expected her to bow until he deigned to acknowledge her, he'd be sadly disappointed. But her impending triumph lightened her mood. In the time of a stone's warming in the sun, she would have succeeded in proving him embarrassingly wrong about her.

The dark blue furnace eye pulsed with light, then, a breath later, three shiny black pills the size of blueberries floated from the furnace mouth and hovered in the air.

Master Kwai'le plucked them out one by one and dropped them into black porcelain pill bottles. While he sealed the tops with wax, the light of the dark blue spirit stone grew fainter until it had reached its residual, faint glow.

"Nice and early, I see," he said with a hint of sarcasm.

She couldn't think why. It *was* early. A glance out the door confirmed it: the sky was only now brightening.

He motioned to the table, where paper, ink, and brush had been set in front of a hardwood chair. Once she was seated, he handed her a thick bound volume with the stylized logograms *Plants of Greater Arizan Testing Manual Volume 1* written across the cover.

She scanned the first page. Like the bamboo scroll she had studied on the first day, the page contained a detailed drawing of one plant, along with close-ups of its seed, leaf, root, flower, and, if applicable, its fruit—he had grossly understated the scope of the test.

Master Kwai'le had said she needed to know the names of the plants, their characteristics, planting and harvest requirements, associated essences, contraindications, and preparation techniques for basic alchemical pills. But, in fact, each of these parts—seed, leaf, root, flower, and fruit—had different characteristics and associated essences. The techniques for crafting basic alchemical pills were therefore also different, depending on which part of the plant was being used. This meant that she wasn't required to know 350 items of information, but four times that number.

She attempted the mental calculation, then stopped—it didn't matter; she was more than prepared.

"You have until the third mark on the sundial," he said. "Begin."

She'd be done long before then.

First, she flipped through the entire volume, orienting herself, like she would in any new location. As she did, her studies from the night before came back easily. Then, she turned to the first page, dipped her brush, and wrote.

By the time the sun passed the second mark on the sundial, she was already finished, with a stack of heavily inked papers lying in front of her. Not only had she responded to everything the test required, she had also thrown in some extras for good measure. On top of that, she had taken care to use the flowing script of the court, just to drive home a point: she *was* a princess—and she still knew how to work.

Master Kwai'le was pruning one of the larger plants when he noticed her sitting with her hands in her lap. He glanced at the sundial, smirked, and sauntered in.

"Finished as much as you could?"

The smirk disappeared when his gaze fell on Tori's paper pile. She hid her own smirk by sipping water from her bottle-gourd, the warmth of vindication filling her.

He picked up the first sheet. "Humph," he said, and picked up the next one. When he had read that, he went on to the next. "A little too much extraneous detail," he said, looking annoyed.

Next page.

He finished the pile, then went to the counter without another word and started tidying.

She decided she could afford to be a gracious winner. Once he acknowledged his error, they could move on.

In these matters, polite conversation was usually a good method of easing the tension.

"Was that scroll nook designed for something specific?" she asked, pointing to the empty nook with the red silk lining.

"It was designed for a priceless treasure," he said, sweeping something invisible off the countertop. "A scroll handed down from my master's master. It would normally go to my own successor, but I've never found a worthy protégé, so it will probably stay here forever."

So, in his view, in all of Peach Blossom Grove—a place filled with immortals—no one was a worthy protégé. Why was she not surprised?

Polite conversation, she reminded herself.

"Why is the nook empty?"

"The elder borrows the scroll from time to time," he said.

"May I ask what the scroll contains?"

"Every alchemy technique ever known on the face of Arizan for melding spirit stones," he said, wiping the pill furnace with the edge of his sleeve. "A rare treasure, even for a master alchemist."

Tori tilted her head. "She's not an alchemist—why would she need that?"

"It is not my place to ask such questions, and neither is it yours."

He dusted his hands and walked toward the nursery, motioning to the ink and brushes on his way out. "You can clean that up later."

So much for polite conversation. Well, he asked for it.

"Could I have my score, please?" she said, entering the nursery behind him.

He cleared his throat. "Satisfactory. It appears we can finally move on to actually studying alchemy."

Nice try. He wasn't getting off that easily.

"I'd like my actual score. I take it I got at least ninety-eight percent?"

"There are more important things than book learning," he said, reaching into one of the boxes and shoving a seedling at her. "Today you will attempt to phytolyze this ubax seedling."

Tori folded her arms across her chest. "I'd like to know my score first, if it's all the same to you."

"It's not all the same to me, since I judge it useless. You, however, are clearly intent on wasting time instead of learning alchemy."

Tori clenched her jaw, holding back the outburst begging to erupt. If she insisted on receiving her score, it might give him the excuse he needed to declare her a time-waster, and terminate her apprenticeship.

"Fine," she said, taking the plant. She had passed his tedious test, and she would prevail over his silly seedling. One way or another, by the end of the day she would force him to acknowledge he was wrong.

"Close your eyes and see the elixir in your kernel to connect with it," he said, "then cycle it, and stream it outward."

This was ridiculous. How in the name of the Six was she supposed to see something she drank as a baby? She hadn't even seen it in Master Banfay's bottle.

But if she asked for clarification, she risked opening herself up to criticism and tainting her victory, so she closed her eyes and tried to remember everything she could about the stone kernel.

She had heard the kernel was somewhere around the navel, deep beneath the muscle. It was also the residence of her ketua—the six residual elements responsible for making her a sixfold wielder. Her mood darkened. She had felt sensations there long ago, when she had entered the Door of Golden Ash.

Her eyes opened involuntarily, and her master's sour face greeted her.

"See the elixir," he repeated unhelpfully.

She tried. After about half the time it would take to drain a cup, he sighed dramatically and headed inside.

"Continue," he said, calling over his shoulder.

There was nothing to continue. She first needed to figure out what he meant by "see the elixir."

He had instructed her to close her eyes, which must mean this was something to be felt, rather than seen. But the elixir was in the same place as her ketua; would this disrupt her seal? She absently pressed a palm to her navel.

No, Master Kwai'le had said wielders merge their element with the elixir, which sounded like a conscious act. But she had no access to the elements, her ketua was bound—she was safe. She relaxed, and instead of wasting her time trying to see the elixir, she tried to feel it.

It wasn't a quick process. Master Kwai'le had time to concoct two batches of pills, clean the pill furnace, brew tea, and drink it—twice—and read through half of a very long scroll.

The sight of him reading reminded her of the scroll with the stick figures she had found on his shelf the day before. After she remembered to sit in horse stance, some of the breathing techniques came back to her, and she tried them.

A faint warmth emerged where she believed her stone kernel to be. Her eyes flew open. "I felt something!"

Master Kwai'le looked up from his scroll and gave her a flat look. "That's the idea." He shook his head and went back to reading.

It took the better part of the afternoon for her to feel it again, and this time, it stayed. He seemed to sense this somehow, because at that very moment he looked up from something he had been writing and said, "Now cycle it, and stream it outward through your hands and into the seedling."

Now, she just needed to figure out how to do that. She held the plant outward, then stretched one hand out like she would embrace it, the way she had seen in the drawing. Nothing happened.

His instructions to "see the elixir" came back to her. She hadn't followed this because it had seemed absurd, but perhaps she was wrong; perhaps this wasn't something one actually saw, but rather something one imagined. If so, streaming the elixir would follow the same process.

She tried to visualize the warmth she had felt in her kernel, and decided it looked like a small yellow light. Then she pictured the light flowing through her palm and into the plant.

In the time it took to blink, the seedling withered. Tori gaped at the remains. "I think I need another."

Master Kwai'le added a final stroke to his paper, then set down his brush and came outside. He glanced at the withered plant, then jerked his head at the seedling box. "Try again."

With his critical eyes on her this time, she found it hard to remember what to do. She tried to imagine the yellow light, or the warmth, or anything, but nothing happened.

Do not let him see you fail.

She remembered to close her eyes then, shutting him out, and forced herself to refocus. The warmth returned, but this time, before she could summon the mental image, her mind's eye noticed a little golden ember, unfabricated by herself. She focused on it, then imagined it flowing outward through her palms.

A loud snap startled her. The plant in her hand was aflame. In the space of a breath, it burned to ash, which swirled in the wind, then blew away.

Master Kwai'le gave her a wry look. "Might as well get another." He walked back inside, mumbling, "I only hope I have enough."

Tori narrowed her eyes at his back, then trudged to the seedling box, cursing fluently under her breath.

Chapter Forty-Two

SISTERS AND BROTHERS

Tori was grateful for a break from alchemy—where her triumphant written test had been overshadowed by all the seedlings she had burned to ash—and therefore found herself looking forward to the group session in weapons training.

When she arrived at the second level of the training grounds, six other students were already waiting: four women and two men. The number of women was comforting; she wasn't the only one dabbling in men's activities. Though she found it impossible to imagine that any woman—apart from the weapons master, naturally—could take fighting too seriously.

As Master Maeli mounted the steps, the students rushed to form a line, which Tori managed to join just in time to bow.

"Master!" they said in unison.

Master Maeli walked past and stood opposite the steps.

She looked the group over, then gave a quick nod. "Begin."

The students separated into two horizontal lines facing her, one behind the other, then everyone moved through the basic dagger forms. They were faster than Tori and much more fluid, and by the third movement, Tori's steps had blurred into guesswork. It took all her concentration just to keep up.

They often ended their movements with an undignified grunt. Tori felt embarrassed for the women. How could a leader who degraded themselves in private command respect in public? She tried to imagine her mother's court ministers grunting like men, and couldn't.

"Pair off," Master Maeli said when they had finished. "Sadeera, I am counting on you to explain things to Tori."

"Yes, Master." A young, dark-skinned woman bounced over, and Tori hid her surprise. A yellow ring flickered around the pupils of her flame-blue eyes, and her tightly coiled hair had metallic silver strands running through it: Sadeera was an Ant. She greeted Tori with an artless smile. Tori liked her immediately.

Sadeera tipped a small gray bottle onto a rag. "Wipe this on your dagger. It'll dull the blade."

Tori wiped, then used her finger to test the edge. She nodded. "Not bad."

Sadeera then led her to a wooden crate sitting beside the medicine hut. She reached in, pulled out two cloth vests, and handed one to Tori.

"What's this?"

"It's so we don't kill each other," Sadeera said, slipping it over her head and tying it to her chest and torso.

"But the blades are dulled." Tori slipped on her own thickly padded vest.

"They're still sharp enough to break the skin if you thrust them hard enough. These are etched weapons, remember."

"I thought Master Maeli liked her students to fight realistically," Tori said.

Sadeera pointed to a single black stripe on her own lapel. "All of us are still one-bars. A realistic fight between one-bars would probably end in maiming." She giggled.

Sadeera and Tori found an empty space away from the other pairs, who had already begun sparring.

"When Master Maeli rings the gong, you'll move on to another partner," Sadeera said. "Everyone here has to spar with everyone else. Now, put your guard up, like this. Good. Let's start circling," she said, moving in a slow circle, facing Tori.

Before Tori could blink, Sadeera darted in, tapped Tori on the solar plexus, and jumped out of reach.

"I'm going to do it again," Sadeera said. "This time, try to parry."

Tori tried, but Sadeera was too fast. In three quick moves, she had touched Tori on her stomach, chest, and throat.

Embarrassment heated Tori's cheeks, and instead of feeling foolish for fighting, she felt embarrassed for not fighting better.

Master Maeli hit a small gong, and all the pairs stopped and bowed to each other.

"You're fast," Tori said.

Sadeera dimpled. "Time for the next one. See you later." She bounced away to another student.

"Remember," Master Maeli said. "Let your weapons become an extension of yourselves. Feeling this oneness is the path to obtaining Unity with the Sword."

A short man with a serious face met Tori next. The moment the gong sounded, he spun and jabbed with all the intensity of someone who had something to prove. Tori managed to parry a few strikes, but he always hit her somewhere else. A new bruise formed with every breath.

Typical man. Guarding his little domain like it meant something. She was sure he was fighting twice as hard as he would with another man—trying to prove fighting belonged to men. The thought had barely formed when his dagger jammed into her gut, driving the wind from her. As she caught her breath, he hopped back, guard raised, eyes trained on her like he expected her to suddenly revive and maul him.

This was ridiculous. She would not spend all day as a punching bag.

When the gong sounded, she attempted to catch Master Maeli's eye, but her next opponent blocked her view—a tall, skinny girl with an expressionless face.

"Just a moment," Tori said, leaving the girl with her guard up.

She approached the weapons master. "Master Maeli, this isn't working. You said I'd be learning speed and technique, but I'm not gaining ground with either."

"Quick progress should not be your focus. Doing things properly should. Sparring allows you to put your technique into practice."

"The others are certainly practicing, but I can't say I am. I'm more like their wooden dummy." She rubbed her bruised arm.

"And you will continue to be their wooden dummy until you learn to integrate the dagger forms. Look around. Everyone you see is a one-bar, which means they are only six moons more advanced than you. So focus on your technique, you will do fine." She strolled away then to observe a sparring pair.

Tori set her jaw. So much for that.

This, apparently, was how one trained a daughter. Her mother always showed the same kind of confidence—except, Tori realized, it wasn't the same at all. The empress believed Tori could serve a purpose. Master Maeli believed Tori could become something more.

She returned to her partner. The girl's crazy fighting style distracted her so much, Tori couldn't tell what to avoid. She beat Tori within the space of a breath, then did it again and again.

A short, stocky fellow was next, followed by two more women, the last of whom had cropped, straw-colored hair. She slashed Tori so hard, her vest stuffing fell out.

The woman apologized profusely.

"It's very important to guard your stomach," she said, snatching the fallen stuffing and trying to shove it back in.

Mercifully, the gong sounded before she could slash something more. It rang three times in succession, and the students fell in line.

Master Maeli faced the group. "Avoid overeating," she said. "We will train just as hard after the noonday meal."

"Yes, Master!"

Then, with a nod, she dismissed them, and everyone walked away, chatting like close friends.

Sadeera bounced over to Tori. "Want to join us? We take our meal over there, by the water." She pointed to the watercourse.

With a word of thanks, Tori followed her up to the third level, studiously avoiding the well with its irksome bell. They stopped at a gap in the stone wall. There, a staircase stretched to the bottom where the others were already lounging on a wide ledge by the water.

"The wall blocks the sun this time of day," Sadeera said, taking a peach from her pack, "so we can eat in the shade."

The kindness of the group disarmed her, particularly in how they treated Sadeera—no one spoke condescendingly, no one ignored her or shifted away—here, she was just like everyone else.

Though Ants weren't feared or hated like wielders, their residual Antiquital blood nonetheless relegated them to a class of slaves and beggars. The best any freeborn Ant could hope for was a job no one else wanted—an offal cleaner, or a profession contaminated by death, like a butcher, executioner, or funeral barge operator. Yet here Sadeera was, well-dressed, sociable, and acknowledged just as capable as anyone.

Most of the group had fruit or sweetbread, and everyone shared them around.

"I'm sorry about the stuffing," the girl with cropped, straw-colored hair said, handing Tori a sweetbread. She introduced herself as Suli.

Embarrassment at her own incompetence prickled Tori's skin, but she buried it under practiced indifference. "I was meaning to ask, how do you protect your stomach?"

Suli showed her a sweeping downward movement. "This will block an attack. Before we had the chest guards, one girl did get stabbed in the stomach, though."

Tori arched a brow; she had some idea of who might have done the stabbing.

"She spent three moons recovering," Suli continued. "You could hear her groans anytime you walked past the Houses of Healing. It was awful."

Tori grimaced. "What became of her?"

"She went on to earn her two-bar, so it all ended well. But still, you should practice the block a lot; in a real fight, a stomach injury could be fatal."

Tori would never be ready for a real fight at this rate. She wasn't even ready for a fake one—and she was beginning to suspect even that might be more dangerous than she had thought.

"Has anyone in class ever died?"

Sadeera giggled. "Everyone in Peach Blossom Grove eats the blue spirit-fruit, so no matter how bad the injury, you won't die."

With a glance at Suli's daggers, Tori made a mental note to try the blue fruits.

The serious man who had knocked out her breath leaned forward to look at Tori. "Unless you're decapitated," he said, then flashed a good-natured smile.

"Anyway," Suli said, "the chest guards do their job, and we'll be learning more blocks soon. You have to know several to pass the two-bar grading."

Tori's eyes fell on the black stripe on Suli's lapel, the same as Sadeera's. Though everyone here was dressed differently, they all wore the same stripe.

"How many bars are there?" Tori asked.

"For students, six. Masters have their own grades."

She remembered that Keya had worn six stripes, along with all the smugness that came with them. Irritation sparked briefly inside her. Tori didn't even have one stripe—yet.

"I forgot to mention," Sadeera joined in, brushing away a dragonfly, "when you block, try to connect with your daggers."

Tori nodded, hoping to look like she understood.

Sadeera's dimples appeared, her flame-blue eyes twinkling as though she had guessed Tori's secret. "Just try to sense them. You know, so they can sense you. Master Maeli says that's the first step to obtaining Unity with the Sword."

A strange and beautiful fish as long as Tori's arm, with scales shimmering in shifting hues of red, yellow, green, and violet, stopped in front of Tori and looked up at her with expectant, puppy-dog eyes. She wished she had some oats. When it realized she had nothing to offer, it drifted from one person to the next, wearing the same hopeful expression—unnoticed, because everyone was too caught up in conversation.

A tap on Tori's shoulder made her flinch, and she dropped her sweetbread into the water.

"I'm so sorry!" Sadeera said, the yellow around her pupils shrinking. "I just wanted to ask if you're coming to the play tonight."

This time, Tori did understand. Elnora had begged her to go.

"Yes, I'll be meeting my gentlewoman there."

Sadeera looked puzzled.

"My friend, I mean. Elnora." It felt odd calling Elnora a friend—yet at the same time, there wasn't another person whom the term fit better.

As the fish swam back in Tori's direction, its gaze fixed onto her floating sweetbread. All at once, the fish flew into the air, flapping its fins like wings. It did an impressive spin, then dove back down, gulping up the bread.

Soon, everyone was throwing bits of sweetbread, which in turn attracted a whole school of rainbow fish. Before long, the air was filled with them, spinning and diving.

The women and men laughed together like sisters and brothers, and Tori watched them curiously. There was no division between them—they were simply people, focused on their similarities instead of their differences. Even the man who had knocked out her wind talked amicably with two women, like it was the most natural thing in the world. Maybe he wasn't insecure after all.

Her mind went to Senrik and Ruvien, then to the ridiculous poems of her palace suitors. Things were so different in Peach Blossom Grove.

After the noonday meal, they continued sparring. Tori tried to sense her daggers the way Sadeera had advised, but in vain. She did, however, manage to get thrashed six more times.

The final gong rang, and everyone lined up.

"Train well on your own tomorrow," Master Maeli said. "Most of you want to be peacekeepers. You have much to learn before you can join their training group, so work hard." She gave a nod of dismissal.

Everyone bowed. "We honor you, Master!"

"Do not forget to spend time studying nature, too," she said, as people packed up their things. "There is much wisdom to be gleaned from the animals, for those patient enough to seek it."

Tori wasn't sure what wisdom animals could teach, but she knew one thing—if she didn't hurry home, she'd be late for the play. She rushed back to her cottage, managed a quick bath, and arrived at the playhouse just in time.

Chapter Forty-Three

AYENASHI AND ZARIEN

The shutters of the playhouse slammed closed the moment Tori stepped in, plunging her into darkness. She blinked, trying to make sense of the shadows.

Two points of candlelight flickered on the ends of poles as two boys rushed around lighting wall lanterns, and soon, dim lights outlined the playhouse guests.

People were seated on benches in snug groups of four. She scanned the crowd for Elnora and spotted her curly-haired silhouette, waving. Tori smiled and went over.

"Here," Elnora said, patting the empty seat beside her.

Tori was relieved to not have to share the bench; people never seemed to tire of touching her hands and clothes.

"How did you get this to yourself?"

Flute music interrupted the answer, and screens that had been blocking the stage slid apart. Floor lanterns resembling rocks lined both sides of the stage from front to rear, illuminating a beautifully painted backdrop of misty mountains. Murmurs of appreciation rippled through the crowd.

At that moment, a thin shaft of light spilled in through the playhouse door, then blinked out again as the door closed. Two masculine silhouettes stood inside the entrance: the taller one strong and straight, the other standing with an insouciant lean. Senrik and Ruvien.

As Tori scanned the space around them, hoping she had missed an empty bench by the entrance, Ruvien's silhouette seemed to lock eyes on her. He leaned over to Senrik as though whispering, and pointed in her direction. Tori glanced away—like that would somehow camouflage her.

A moment later, the men greeted them quietly, and sat on either end of the bench. Senrik, who was on her side, leaned forward to keep his shoulders from touching her, and his robes once again gave off their sensuous agarwood smell.

A narrator's voice rose above the flute. "In the Age before Ages, Suro spoke, and Ketuan was filled with reproducing power. Water gushed from her womb, and six children were born, each resembling one of the elements from which their mother had been created—one of water, one of wood, one of air, one of fire, one of earth, one of metal—each child's element speaking of their particular gifting."

The rippling of stringed instruments introduced six players, who drifted onstage wearing elaborate costumes.

"They were beautiful beyond imagining," the narrator continued. "And Ketuan made for them the sky and the sun and the stars and the moon, a gift for her six children, whom she loved."

At that, hanging lanterns shaped to look like the moon and stars flickered on by themselves, above the stage.

Impressive. Tori couldn't even see the stagehands who lighted them. The crowd applauded.

"Amazing," Elnora breathed.

"Then," the narrator said, "Ketuan desired that her children remain close to her a while longer, as when they had lived within her womb. So she petitioned Suro, requesting that she might return forever to the bones from whence she had been made, that her children might live upon her. And Suro granted her request. And so Ketuan became a great mountain, and her children built upon her six palaces."

At that, the players made hammering and sawing motions, as though building. Then all but two of them pointed to some imaginary place offstage and exited.

The two that remained were a man in a kingly costume that gave the impression of leaves, and a woman in gauzy blue robes that floated behind her as she walked. A child in the shadows fanned her with a palm branch, blowing her robes back. These two were obviously Zarien, the Wood Father, and Ayenashi, the Water Matron.

Something near the fanning child caught Tori's eye, and she stared in astonishment: a youth moved his hands in a breezy motion, fingertips extended toward the stage—he was wielding the wind! This was what allowed the child's fan to blow Ayenashi's robes so dramatically.

Tori's gaze flitted around to see if anyone noticed. Apparently they did: some people pointed, but instead of fear or disgust, she only saw delight at the wielding.

Of course, Tori thought, remembering where she was. They had never seen its ugly side.

The two players continued to hammer and build, stopping now and then to dance to the merry music of flute and strings. Two palaces that had evidently been lying flat were hoisted up behind them, in front of the mountain backdrop. They shimmered, as though their paint had been mixed with pearl dust.

"And so Ketuan's children lived upon her for innumerable years in the Age before Ages, happy and content upon their mother's bones."

"How macabre," Tori said, with a wry half-smile.

Senrik leaned in and whispered, "Actually, Ketwanen means 'mother's bones' in the Old Speech."

His breath smelled edible, like sweet licorice root. Tori leaned away. The Ghenz were a lawless bunch—even those with pretty faces. That knowledge should be enough for her.

She gave him a dignified nod. "Thank you."

He had, in fact, told her something she already knew. As a child, her nanny used to read stories to her from the old lore, which mentioned that *ketuan* meant "bone" in the Old Speech, because her bones were created from stone—the bones of Arizan.

The music changed, and Tori stiffened as a stream of water floated through the air, glimmering in the lantern light. Ayenashi wielded shamelessly, swirling it into a ball above her head, then drew it out like a ribbon and twirled it around her as she glided in a sinuous circle around Zarien.

Children's voices rose up in a haunting melody, and Zarien stepped backward into the shadows, while Ayenashi continued her water dance alone.

The children sang in an unfamiliar language. It reminded Tori of the pronunciations of the Old Speech she glanced at in the palm-leaf book on Antiquitals. She determined to study it properly—she would have enjoyed understanding the song.

Senrik said something, but because of the volume of the singing, he was obliged to lean in close—close enough to brush his arm against hers. Goose bumps rippled from her arm to her head.

"They're praising Ayenashi, the Water Matron," he whispered, "because we're in Ayenashi's Veil."

Hoping to pretend she already knew—and thus prevent more conversation—she gave him a knowing nod. He responded with a quick, almost nervous smile.

The narrator's voice resonated through the room. "In that time, the High Water-creatures, servants and companions of Ayenashi, teemed upon the face of the mountain."

Children appeared onstage then, holding up poles supporting two silk creatures. The children ran around Ayenashi, and whenever they crossed the path of the wind wielder, the creatures undulated, as though swimming.

Ruvien clapped. "Beautiful!"

The offstage singing reached a crescendo, but Tori could no longer fully enjoy it—ever since Senrik had brushed against her, all her focus had been turned toward trying not to notice the fragrance of agarwood, or the heat of his body beside her.

The play went downhill from there, turning into a full-blown love story. Though everyone knew that the two ancestors got married, Tori had for some reason not anticipated this. But Ayenashi and Zarien sang now, dancing with their faces so close, it looked at times like they would kiss.

Tori shifted as far as she could in Elnora's direction. Elnora gave her a puzzled look, then glanced at Senrik and hid a half-smile.

The screens slid together, once again hiding the stage, and someone plucked a cheerful melody on the pipa while they waited for the next act to start.

Tori's rebellious eyes flicked sideways. Senrik's arms were crossed on his chest, his sleeve hugging the contour of a well-formed bicep. Her pulse quickened.

She looked away, inwardly cursing her folly. How could she even entertain thoughts of a Ghenz? A commoner from Hanmar was one thing—but this? Even if she could somehow look past the lawless culture he came from, certainly no one else would.

Yumay had sent her a message by hawk just yesterday: Tori's secret rice donations to the Ant slums had been discovered, yet the ministers had voted to keep them. Taking a Ghenz intimate would cost her the credibility she'd fought hard to build—with the people, with the ministers. And how could one protect others when one had no influence of one's own?

A short while later, the screens slid apart again, and instead of the palaces, the backdrop depicted beautiful trees. More cutouts lined the stage, giving the impression of a grove. Round blue lanterns hung from the branches—spirit-fruit.

The trees blinked. Holes had been cut into them, and hidden stagehands had now opened their eyes. Everyone clapped.

The trees watched intently as children showered Ayenashi and Zarien with flower petals, evidently a wedding. The narrator's story confirmed it. Several long songs followed, accompanied by more of the embracing than any real dancing.

Of all the nights to be sitting next to Senrik, why did it have to be this one? Tori's gaze landed on his hands. They were firm and capable, with a raw, unpolished beauty she wanted to reach out and touch. Her jaw tensed with the realization.

When the dancing finally ended, Zarien took Ayenashi by the hand and led her toward the back of the stage. The rock lanterns went out one by one, darkening the path they left behind. Just before they came to the final tree, the couple stopped. Zarien threw a look over his shoulder, eyebrows waggling suggestively, then vanished into the dark with his bride.

Ruvien whistled and hooted as the screen closed. A few people chuckled. Senrik rubbed the back of his neck and sat up straighter.

This kind of tension could not be allowed to linger.

Tori looked at him, voice casual. "Why did the trees have eyes?"

He cleared his throat. "Zarien granted them sentience," he said. "They're spirit-fruit trees."

His blue eyes glimmered darkly in the torchlight, drawing her.

She pulled her gaze away. "I see."

The screens reopened onto a brightly lit grove where Ayenashi and Zarien danced around each other, stroking each other's faces.

Tori tried to distract herself by recalling any snippets of the mythology she could remember. According to her nanny's stories, everything had obeyed the Six when they walked the face of Arizan: earth, animal, plant, stone, and weather. And because the Six served Suro, their bidding was always good. The Six also produced forty-eight children, who themselves were the ancestors of humans and Antiquitals.

As Tori watched Ayenashi and Zarien, she wondered if the Six, ancestors of them all, had really looked like this. The way the vines wound through Zarien's hair brought to mind the metallic silver strands winding through Sadeera's. Tori pondered the similarity. If the people onstage resembled anyone, it was the Ants.

Why were Ants so rejected, then, when they looked more like the ancestors than anyone else?

Senrik leaned in and whispered, "Almost makes you think of the Ants, doesn't it?"

Tori swiveled to stare at him, but his eyes were on the players.

As her gaze trailed over his profile, her heart gave a traitorous kick. Was he truly as bad as the rest of his people? A more dangerous thought came: What if he wasn't?

He looked at her, and she glanced away awkwardly, pretending to be searching for something behind him. She felt like a fool—and also immensely grateful that darkness was hiding the flush on her cheeks.

The play ended with an elaborate display of wielding water and fire, and even vines that twisted along the floor like snakes. A dark cloth that had lain on the floor unnoticed until now, was whipped off suddenly, and a glowing path of spirit stones appeared. With the blinking eyes of the spirit-fruit trees, the moving vines, the flames, and the water, everything onstage looked alive.

"And so Mount Ketwanen remains to this day," the narrator said, "filled with Ketuan's life."

A quiet longing stirred inside Tori to see the mountain for herself.

In a final flourish, Ayenashi floated another stream of water through the air, then twirled, spinning it outward. Tori sucked in a sharp breath as water splashed her full in the face.

She wiped her eyes. Senrik's sleeve was soaked from shielding his own face, but Ruvien and Elnora were dry.

Ruvien held up a waxed cloth, grinning. "It pays to come prepared." He gave Elnora a wink. "It also pays to sit next to me."

In one sweeping movement, Ayenashi motioned to the water that had fallen, and it lifted off the wooden floor and undulated toward her.

Two girls hooked long poles onto the window shutters, swinging them open, and Tori squinted as evening light burst in.

She started to look around, but Senrik's gaze caught her mid-motion. His blue eyes sparkled now in the warmth of the sunset, and she stared into them, the flutter in her chest warning her that she was in danger of feeling more than she ought.

"Today's the twelfth," he said, his voice tinged with uncertainty. "Almost the full moon. The Veiled Forest will be filled with fireflies tonight. Do you want to come?" He glanced at Elnora. "Both of you, I mean. Ruvien and I are going to the Waterwall."

"I can't," Tori said. "I have a...commitment."

Senrik's gaze shifted to the floor and back, and he broke into a forced-looking smile. "Another time, then."

As she left the playhouse, regret twisted inside her, even though she had done the only reasonable thing.

The sun dipped behind the horizon, leaving the grass beneath her feet a dull gray-green.

She didn't slow her steps, didn't let herself look back.

I have to stay away from him, she thought. *There's no other way.*

Chapter Forty-Four

THE PERFECT JEWEL

Zinchen glided into her minor audience chamber, at the end of the Hall of Heavenly Fragrance. Today, instead of twelve low desks lining the gold-paneled room, there were fifteen—a situation that always predicted an unsatisfactory session.

The women kneeling behind the desks lowered their heads as Zinchen swept past and mounted the dais steps, placing herself on the tailu-bird seat in the center, where Lina was already waiting.

They prostrated themselves and presented their formal greeting. The usual twelve were her most powerful nobles, the countesses of her twelve provinces, matriarchs of their respective houses. If Zinchen won their agreement today, none of the lesser noble houses, or even her ministers, would dare oppose her plan. Every army in the Min Territories would march under her banner.

"Rise."

Only Countess Ellie was absent, due to an urgent matter with Ghenz raiders on her borders. *But Ellie's contribution has already been made*, Zinchen thought, feeling for the scroll hidden in her sleeve.

As the women shuffled back behind their desks, she glanced at the three extras. Lord Kai's mother was among them, but she was never a problem. Zinchen had recently promoted her to special counsel—not for her arguments, which were rare, but for her visibility. The court needed time to grow used to her, cooling their resistance and any resulting threat to Kai when he finally rose to royal consort. A slow game, but one worth playing, for his sake.

It was the other two who were a thorn in Zinchen's side. Including at least two Varanaken matriarchs was an ancestral obligation—military talks demanded their presence. She hoped they'd keep silent; their contributions were seldom courtly and never of value.

"As my foremothers intended," Zinchen said, "Min has for many long years been the most prosperous nation in Shudon. The Jeng Territories, despite their jewels and rice paddies, are impoverished. Their gross mismanagement of resources should be set right, for the benefit of all the people, and for the strengthening of the Min noble houses. I have summoned you here today to reveal my objectives to do just that."

The women visibly brightened, as she knew they would.

"My grandmother, Empress Zeyora, had the foresight to marry the daughters and sons of the lesser branches of the House of Min into the Jeng court, and her actions have borne fruit. As you all know, the Min-kezu—my extended family—are now the main civil servant class in the Jeng court, wielding almost as much power as the Shazori regents themselves. Which means that, in practical terms, the Jeng court is largely loyal to me."

Countess Sul of Vang Province peered at Zinchen with interest.

Zinchen smiled inwardly. Sul was a great intellectual, and, next to Ellie's, the House of Vang was the most powerful in Min. If Zinchen won Sul's support, she would have the backing of the two most powerful noble houses. The remainder could hardly oppose her then.

"Furthermore," Zinchen said, "as the Jeng court has for many years now awarded tax-free lands to their civil servants in lieu of gold, the Min-kezu are now some of the most significant landowners in Jeng. One could say I already own Jeng, in all but title."

Sul furrowed her brow. "What does Your Majesty mean by 'already'?"

Zinchen smoothed the cuff of her sleeve. "That at long last, the time has come to reunite the land of Shudon."

A murmur of uncertainty rippled through the hall.

"Your Majesty, is it feasible to assume control of the Jeng throne?" Sul said.

"The strength of your armies will assure that it is. That is why you are here today," Zinchen said. "I am, of course, unable to compel your houses to do this, since it is not a matter of defending the Min Territories, or even the palace. Still, I have every confidence that your wisdom and good sense will lead you to the inescapable conclusion that the time is ripe to unite Shudon under the Min banner."

She removed the scroll from her sleeve then, and handed it to Lina, who took it down to the matriarchs and rolled it open for them to read. Ellie's letter. Though Ellie's language was cryptic, every woman in the room would understand.

"As you can see," Zinchen said, "the House of Hanmar was the first to recognize the wisdom of this, and to pledge its unequivocal support."

The nobles studied the letter, muttering and nodding their heads.

Zinchen continued. "As Fuyel said: 'When the nobility stands as one, no blade can reach the land. Unity is invincibility—and before invincibility, even the proudest enemy bows.'"

Every matriarch knew the passage from *The Doctrine of Unified Arms.* Fuyel was a famed southern queen in the years after Ishairo. When the final queen of Ishairo's unified Shudon died, her daughters tore the land in two, and power-hungry nobles fractured it further: mostly royal daughters, or regional matriarchs—like the women kneeling here. Civil war followed, not settled by victory but by exhaustion. Trade collapsed, famine spread, and no faction could dominate. So the realm splintered—each queendom ruled by the woman ruthless enough to hold it. Fuyel's mother was one of them, and Fuyel was pushed into becoming a great military strategist.

"I now command legendary etched arms and armor," Zinchen said, sitting taller. "Pledge your forces to me, and they will be equipped with weapons so superior, victory will cease to be a question—it will be inevitable."

She listened with silent relish to the low voices of assent that hummed through the chamber and marked the moment as a success. This was her true strength: that her people desired to serve her. Any monarch could force obedience through fear—and many had, to their own detriment.

Zinchen steepled her fingers. Lasting power required more. It required that nobles and ministers not only kneel in court, but also align themselves in private. That kind of loyalty could not be extracted—it had to be cultivated.

Countess Amarin of Kiir Province spoke first. "If Countess Ellie is in support, then I can't very well refuse. Your Majesty's objective seems like an excellent one. It is high time to unite Shudon under the Min banner and put the wasted wealth of Jeng to use. All the people of Shudon would benefit from this move—not only Min, but Jeng also." She bowed. "Only the Empress Zinchen can bring true prosperity. She has done so in Min; now this prosperity will spread throughout the whole land."

Some of the women murmured their agreement.

But the Varanaken matriarchs both appeared unmoved. Though their tribes were rivals in everyday life, in Zinchen's court they always presented a united front.

Takren—matriarch of Lord Akiren's clan—wore her silver-streaked hair in a simple twist, her weathered face expressionless, her robes stiff with embroidery denoting rank. She held herself with the stillness of someone used to being obeyed.

"You speak of prospering the noble houses," Takren said, "but I have heard nothing of benefit to the Varanaken."

Zinchen suspected she knew which benefit Takren desired. Would she be brazen enough to say it outright, in the presence of the nobles?

Takren continued. "Our boys are elite, surpassing any of your armies. As any victory you win will be thanks to our boys, any talk of reward should mention us first. Even Jeng knows how to reward its most valuable people."

Amarin frowned. She wasn't the only one: every woman here understood Takren's meaning.

"We all know that Jeng rewards its people with land," Amarin said. "Whose land, exactly, were you hoping to steal?"

Zinchen had long suspected the matriarchs nursed quiet resentment over their ancient land allotments—but she hadn't expected them to voice it outright. That they now dared to speak so plainly meant one thing: they no longer feared her displeasure. A troubling omen.

"Do you suggest we risk our boys for nothing?" Takren said.

Amarin scowled. "You seem to believe the people's prosperity is only worthwhile when it benefits the Varanaken. And as for risk, you heard Her Majesty: the soldiers will be outfitted with etched weapons and armor. The only risk would be for those foolish enough to refuse them." This was a slight on the Varanaken warriors' well-known refusal to wear anything but their traditional armor.

"All battle involves risk," Takren said. "And unless the Jeng nobility is in support, battle there will be."

Sul's brow furrowed, apparently considering this, her intellectual mind turning the statement over, seemingly unfavorably. Zinchen lips tightened.

"Takren raises an important point," Sul said. "Everyone knows the Min-kezu are connected with Your Majesty; therefore, the Jeng people may not trust them wholeheartedly. Your Majesty needs the support of other Jeng nobles to ensure success, or the Jeng nobility will turn the people against you. As Fuyel also said, 'To rule a land, you must command its hearts. The blade conquers borders; only the will of the people secures them.'" She bowed low. "I am Your Majesty's humble servant and will wholeheartedly put the army of Vang Province at your service if Your Majesty can give us assurance that at least one major noble house in Jeng—one with the power to sway the others—supports your cause. This would put my mind at ease."

Every noble present, save Amarin, voiced their agreement.

In that moment, Zinchen saw her error: she should never have relied on Ellie's letter alone. However great Ellie's influence, her absence outweighed it. Presence, not rank, had won the moment.

Frustration clawed at her. Yan had warned her the Min-kezu were fractured; he was still untangling which of them could be trusted. In Jeng, the only ally she could unequivocally count on was Prince Filo's mother—but to approach her with such a request would reek of desperation, and jeopardize the terms of Tori's alliance.

She smoothed her expression, suppressing the flash of irritation. "I would have expected better judgment from all of you than to withhold your consent over such a trifle," Zinchen said, keeping her tone even. The nobles lowered their eyes. "But very well. I will grant your request and provide formal confirmation. Once this is done, however, I expect no further wavering."

She rose and left the audience chamber, tension coiling in her chest.

"Lina, contact Rozalia immediately. It is time to begin negotiations for Tori's alliance."

Tori would be angry—she had always insisted she would choose her own intimates. But indulgence in this matter was a luxury Zinchen could no longer afford to bestow.

Compensation would be required—something thoughtful, something to take away the sting. In time, the girl would see reason.

"How dare those Varanaken," Zinchen said to Lina, lips tight. "And Countess Sul tests my patience—if not for her former loyalty, I would not let her lack of cooperation today go unchecked." She let out a measured breath, laced with the irritation she didn't bother to hide. "But she will give her support, and once she does, everyone else will fall into line."

Lina dipped her head. "No one would oppose both the House of Hanmar and the House of Vang."

"This, however, puts me in a difficult situation with Rozalia. I had been purposely making her wait, as you know, to ensure the most advantageous terms for Tori's alliance. Now, though..."

She pondered the situation as they walked through the Hall of Heavenly Fragrance.

"What I need is some kind of gift—something that displays my might, something overwhelming. Rozalia must feel honored by the urgency of my request, not superior. I need something that reaffirms that, no matter what terms I might insist upon, this alliance is still to her advantage."

Lina's gaze fixed onto the floor in front of her, evidently considering possible options. "Your Majesty might accompany the letter with a treasure from Tey Zuben."

"Yes," Zinchen said slowly, the elegance of the idea unfurling. "Perfect."

A short time later, they arrived at her treasure room. Zinchen pricked her finger and smeared blood onto the lock, and it opened with an airy *toof*.

She walked across a golden insignia set into the marble floor while Lina lit the lanterns that stood waist-high beside polished columns.

A warm glow bathed the room, revealing groups of ornately carved chests. In the center of them sat a table with a black marble box on top, two handspans wide.

Zinchen opened it the same way she had opened the door lock, and colorful gems shimmered in the lantern light—her Tey Zuben jewels. Nestled among them was a simple gold scroll case, though it, too, belonged, for it contained a Tey Zuben stone more precious than the rest, one that had secured Zinchen's reign—Tori's birth charm.

The charm was kept in a small bone cylinder. Tori's Certificate of Belonging—the original, not the second one the midwife had made—was in there, too, hidden in a false bottom.

Shortly after the ceremony where Tori was publicly proved as an infant to be an heir of Zinchen's blood, symbols had appeared inside the birth charm. Those symbols, if seen by someone knowledgeable, had the power to shake Zinchen's reign—or even to end it.

But the second certificate was what she needed now, which Zinchen kept in the same gold scroll case. The scribes would need it to draw up the alliance with Prince Filo, since it detailed which moon and year Tori had been born under. Zinchen would tell them to begin this afternoon.

She set the scroll case on the table while she sifted through her jewels, searching for one that would produce the desired effect on Rozalia. Though Tey Zuben jewels did not glow like spirit stones, their intense colors moved dynamically within the stones, giving the impression of life. And though, unlike spirit stones, they could not also treat ailments, they did have various uses—for those who knew what they were.

Zinchen didn't know the purpose of even half the jewels here. They had been lavished on her with no explanation by the Tey Zuben queen twenty years before, a token of their wretched agreement. Zinchen set her jaw against the ache that always came with that memory—she would not think of it now.

Shades of blue moved in a lazy, liquid motion in one of the jewels, forming bubbles over and over that drifted to the stone's perimeter, popped, and disappeared. When placed in a bath, this jewel warmed the waters and made them gently roil.

She examined a bright yellow fire jewel next. Inside, was a pulsing starburst of red with a smaller blue starburst in its center, and in the center of that, a white one. Occasionally, one of the starbursts flared, shooting out in violent flashes, tendrils of color spiraling and twisting. Though different in design, it resembled the swirling red stone she had used at the Tailu Festival to try to control the wielder. Why hadn't it worked?

The yellow fire jewel she wasn't certain of either—or even if it had a function at all. It was probably safer not to give it away.

She sifted around until a pale purple gem caught her eye. Inside, swirls of deeper purple chased each other, like two snakes. She placed the gem on her finger and immediately it melted, stretching and sliding around her finger, wrapping like a ring.

She slid it off and held it to her collarbone. The ring flattened and stretched around her neck, fastening comfortably at the back. This stone had one purpose only: to display the power of its owner to possess rare, unfathomable things.

She gave a satisfied nod.

"This is it," she said, turning to Lina. "The perfect jewel."

As she picked up the gold scroll case to remove the cylinder with the birth charm, footsteps shuffled in the hall, followed by a murmuring exchange with the door guard. A moment later, the guard handed Lina a letter.

"From the princess, for Her Majesty."

Zinchen set the scroll case down and read: Tori would be away longer than expected. She would be making the Septad herself.

She studied the letter, eyes narrowed in contemplation.

"Lina, you've spent time with the loremasters. Can just anyone make a Septad?"

Something like the light of realization crossed Lina's face, but it faded, and she shook her head. "I'm sorry, Your Majesty, I don't know."

Zinchen waved the apology away. But something about Tori's letter seemed odd. As she processed the meaning of it, she absently picked up the scroll case and opened the top.

"Have the scribes draw up Tori's alliance this afternoon," she said.

"Should you perhaps wait, Your Majesty? Rozalia might wish to include special requests."

Zinchen paused, fingertips resting inside the rim. "Yes, of course," she said coolly. "My thoughts were occupied." She capped the case and returned it to the treasure box, her mind still circling the Septad.

The Arun clan could work with etched metal because their bloodline could nurture etching essence. And Midra had once mentioned that healers needed medicinal essence in order to do their work. Did Tori have some kind of special dawn-essence?

She pulled the purple gem from her neck, and it morphed once more into a ring. She spun it round and round her finger, brow knit.

What kind of person could make a Septad? Loremaster Jin would perhaps know, but she preferred not to consult him for now. The less people who knew her real plans, the better.

"I will entrust this jewel to you," Zinchen said, sliding the ring from her finger. "See that Rozalia gets it. Then bring me Loremaster Jin's glyph book on the Septad. I want to ensure there is nothing I missed."

Chapter Forty-Five

THE PROPHECY

Caliss hurried down the road with her two guards, the hood of her plain gray cloak pulled forward on her face.

She stopped abruptly, narrowing her eyes on her chief guard, Strond. "They *attacked* the Min Daughter?"

"They thought it would please you, Regent," Strond said, twisting the braids in his beard, "striking the House of Min. I didn't know they'd act alone. But some skilled person saved her. Left Skrem and the boys in a bad way."

"Dead?" she asked.

Strond shook his head. "Paralyzed."

A disgusted exhale escaped her, and she continued walking. "How did those dimwits divine where the Min Daughter would be?"

"Apparently they had help. Someone high up in Hanmar. A decipherer of clues or something."

Caliss considered this. This decipherer of clues was either a traitor, or a buffoon. Maybe both. "And the princess?"

"They don't know. When I saw them, they could barely form words. The others said the only ones who left the village were a master healer and two servants. Unless she was disguised."

"Well of course she'd be disguised if she were traveling on foot," Caliss said, motioning impatiently at her own disguise. "Tell the rest of those meddling fools to keep their distance. I can't afford to have it said that the Min Daughter was attacked on my orders. When I'm ready to eliminate the little flea, I'll do it my own way—discreetly. Right now, I have other things on my mind."

She had to be fast. If she didn't return to the Jeng Palace by nightfall, Loreshi would be suspicious. She only hoped that left her enough time to win the favor of the chief wise woman.

They arrived at last inside the mud walls of a village. Pretty huts filled the place, built of thatch and rocks in the Ghenz style. People tilled the ground or fed chickens with customary Ghenz indifference to any minor disagreements unfolding around them.

In one place, two youths argued with knives bared, while an old grandfather squatted beside them, calmly digging in a vegetable garden. Farther down the road, two women shouted, while a well-built man—clearly the object of their quarrel—watched with a sheepish cringe on his face. One of the women tackled the other suddenly, dropping her to the ground, then grabbed her neck and punched her, bloodying her nose. No one spared them more than a glance as they settled their differences.

The Ghenz were her mother's people, and this felt like home.

"That's Tuven's house," Strond said, pointing to a two-story building made of wood and river stone.

It sat on the other side of a small community plot, where people dug with hoes, singing a song to Yarin, the sea goddess, as the deep, haunting sound of the varglinn droned through the air. Caliss's heart ached. It reminded her of the songs her mother used to sing.

Poor Mama. Caliss took in the well-maintained houses, the lush vegetable gardens, the high-quality linen the people wore. If her mother had come from a prosperous clan like this, her father might have treated her better.

They arrived at the bottom step of the house, looking up. An old woman sat by an open door, wearing the feather necklace and red-tasseled shawl that designated her as the clan's chief wise woman. Tuven.

"Now, we wait," Strond said.

Tuven stared down, studying them. She tapped her staff once on the floor.

Strond dipped his head. "Let's go."

When they reached the top, he touched the backs of his fingers to his lips, then to his forehead, honoring the sea goddess. "Yarin keep you," he said. Caliss repeated the action.

Tuven did the same. Her face was deeply lined, and framed with a thick gray braid on either side of her head. Something in the woman's eyes reminded Caliss of her mother. If Mama hadn't died young, would she look like this now?

Without understanding why, she found herself yearning for the old woman's approval.

"What have you brought me, Strond?" Tuven said, keeping her gaze on Caliss.

"This is the one I told you about."

Tuven studied her a long while, gaze shifting from head to toe before finally pulling herself to her feet, gripping her staff for support. Even standing, she was deeply bent.

She shuffled through the open door and waved them forward without looking back.

Strond remained outside, while Caliss followed. Inside, tapestries and animal heads adorned the rough stone walls. Tuven passed a heavy oak table in the center of the room, supporting herself on it as she went, and headed toward a fireplace at the far end, bordered by a bookshelf. She eased herself into a chair beside it, then motioned at the chair on the other side of the fireplace. Caliss sat.

"Strond tells me you would seek the support of the clans to help you take command of Jeng," Tuven said, taking a brand from the fire to light a long pipe. "Why should I consider this?"

Caliss tensed. That loose-tongued fool. Strond was supposed to have mentioned who Caliss was, not what she wanted. She had intended to work up to her request, casting herself first in a favorable light. Now, everything was off-balance.

She had been certain she could persuade the old woman, given enough time, but now she saw not an old woman sitting before her, but a great leader of her mother's people. And before her, all Caliss's intentions had been laid bare.

Caliss looked at the floor, hoping there was still a chance to impress her. "I can do certain things. There's a goblet at the palace. I can make it light up."

Tuven's eyes narrowed. "Are you a wielder?"

"No," Caliss said quickly. "Nothing like that. I find them despicable."

Though it was her envy that made her despise them, their potential for power. If she had been a wielder, what power she could have harnessed with the *Dawn-Essence Manual* she now possessed. Thankfully wielders were a hunted, dying breed.

Tuven took a draw from her pipe. "Good. Tell me about this goblet." Her sharp eyes bored into Caliss, filling her with a sense of reverential fear. She had never been able to keep secrets from her mother, either.

"Its purpose is to separate dawn-essence from blood," Caliss said, suddenly afraid Tuven would ask her how she made it work. She was sure that whatever a Mattah was, they didn't do anything as simple as streaming their essence. It was cheating, and she knew it.

Tuven pointed to a stone pillar in the corner of the room, half hidden in shadow. "Do you know what that is?"

A golden chalice stood on the center of the pillar, its bowl half the size of a melon and covered in softly glowing spirit stones, supported by a thick gold stem.

Caliss's eyes widened. "The relic." She had heard stories of this as a child.

Tuven nodded. "Can you operate it?"

Caliss sent her spirit sense out to it, then streamed her essence, trying to lift it the way it was said the ancient Mattahs had done—the way she had sworn to her guards she could do. But the relic swallowed up everything she sent. Would someone even at the second stone kernel level be able to satisfy such a monster?

Uncertainty filled her. She had to win Tuven's favor.

She drained every drop of essence from her dawn channels and pooled it in her kernel, yet instinctively she knew she needed more. A passage from the *Dawn-Essence Manual* came to her: *Accumulate essence from air and ground, open the dawn channels and circulate.*

Caliss closed her eyes, sending her spirit sense into the air and ground. To her relief, she could sense the dawn-essence hovering there in minuscule clouds. She dragged at them, sweeping them in through her pores, gathering them into her kernel. Then she streamed every last bit of this essence into the relic. Two of its stones lit up.

Panic shook her. The Mattah would at the very least have been able to light them all.

She dropped to her knees. "Please. With a little more time, I know I could operate it." She looked up into Tuven's face and met her penetrating gaze.

"What makes you think more time would help you?" Tuven asked.

Caliss searched for a way to explain, without admitting she was cycling dawn-essence.

"Because my goblet at home works the same way. I send my"—she searched for the most impressive word—"my power into it, and it comes to life."

"Where do you get this power from?"

Caliss's chest tightened. She could never admit she had been using the forbidden Watani practice.

And yet something in Tuven's eyes told her the woman already knew.

"From the essence in men's blood," Caliss said, fearing to lie. "Living men," she added, pushing the memory of her previous lover from her mind. "When my goblet separates the dawn-essence from the blood, I drink it."

Tuven puffed thoughtfully on her pipe, her face shadowed with contemplation.

"This is something a Mattah can do," she said. "Nonetheless, the sacrifice must be made freely. A man's physical needs can sometimes make him weak, vulnerable to manipulation." She gave Caliss a warning look. "But the true Mattah will draw men's allegiance effortlessly. For her, men will willingly spill their blood."

The relic drew Caliss's gaze and she studied it, sensing its hunger now. One man's blood would never satisfy this creature—many would die to fill it.

"If you obtain the power to operate the relic," Tuven said, "you will not need my consent—all Ghenz will know and serve you."

The words hung in the air, filled with both a tantalizing promise and a crushing lack of certainty.

Tuven tapped out her pipe and tucked it away, then slid an ancient-looking book from the shelf beside her and placed it on her lap.

"This book has been passed down for generations. It contains the secret knowledge of our clans." She dragged a gnarled hand down each page, scanning it. Finally she came to a drawing of a circle made of interlocking spirals. "The great seal, forged in the Celestial City of Jade, realm of pure fire. It belonged to Ishairo, and was meant for his heir after him, the person who would one day rule the world in his place. It is an item of great power and will make its possessor invincible. No one, human or otherwise, can prevail against the possessor of the Celestial Seal."

The frightening image of the Watani messenger flashed in Caliss's mind. Not even the Watani?

Tuven nodded at the ground by her feet. "Kneel, my child."

Caliss obeyed.

"I have seen that the portents have appeared upon the face of Arizan—and now, at this very moment, you arrive. You came seeking support, seeking destiny, but destiny itself seeks you. Now, hear the words of the prophecy."

The firelight cast writhing shadows on Tuven's face as she traced a finger over the lines of the page.

"Birthed in fire, her reign will shake the empire. Cloaked in shadow, she gathers her power, serene. She alone will stand when blood like a river runs."

Chills skittered up her back. Was the prophecy referring to her?

Birthed in fire—her mother had suffered violence when Caliss was in the womb, and she had birthed her by the light of a campfire. Even her name fit: her mother had named her for the Old Ghenzan word that denoted both "intense heat" and "suffering": *Calissorg*.

Cloaked in shadow applied to her doubly—had she not been ruling from the shadows these past twenty years, gathering her power? Not to mention serenely nurturing her essence in secret.

Caliss's heart hammered in her chest.

Tuven's face was grave. "Many powerful longevitists travel far to consult me for my wisdom. And many, drawn by the power of the relic, have asked my consent to operate it." She held Caliss's gaze. "None have succeeded—not even in lighting one single stone." She paused, letting her meaning settle. "You, my child, are the one of whom the prophecy speaks, our long-awaited Mattah. You are fated to possess the Celestial Seal."

Caliss closed her eyes, letting the words settle like a balm over old wounds.

After all she had been through—after the pain, the trials, the indignities—her destiny was to triumph over those who had humiliated her.

The frightening face of the Watani messenger flashed in her mind, and a slow smile spread on her lips. She would no longer need to fear them. She was Ishairo's heir—she would rule over them all.

"I was afraid you would think me evil," Caliss said, with a lighthearted chuckle, "because of the blood."

"There is no good or evil," Tuven said, "only power and weakness. When the weak obtain favor from the powerful, they call it good, do they not? When they do not, they call it evil." She closed the book. "And people envy the powerful, dreaming of taking what's theirs. If they succeed, they become like those they once envied. Tell me—have they turned from good to evil, or are they simply the same, only with more power?"

Caliss nodded. "I have always seen it so, too."

"With the Celestial Seal, you will be beyond such petty notions as good or evil. There will only be your will, and those who obey it." She patted the book. "But for the prophecy to be fulfilled, the seal must be found and bestowed upon the heir. You must therefore find it. This is your destiny."

Caliss breathed in deeply, clothing herself with these words. "How?"

"There are signs, knowledge of the wise women passed down orally from chief to chief for generations." She pulled a yellowing parchment from the shelf and wrote on it with a quill. "I shall finally be unburdened of this task."

When she had finished writing, the paper contained four words.

"On this page are the portents that will lead you to the first clue. Once you decipher these portents, the clues will be revealed. Follow them, and you will find the seal. But be swift—you must decipher the portents before summer's end. If you miss them, there is no telling when they will appear again."

Tuven leaned heavily on her staff to push herself to her feet, then opened a chest that sat on floor behind her. "Our writings tell of the dangers of the seal, even to the heir. If someone handles it without the special implements, that person will be consumed with fire, and the seal will again be lost." She pulled out a black velvet bag and handed it to Caliss. A gold filigree casing in the shape of a flattened mandarin twinkled up at her, strange markings carved all along the border.

Tuven gave Caliss a knowing smile. "These are the implements you need. Your victory is assured."

As she left the village, Caliss glanced again at the yellowing parchment. The first words read *golden shadow*—cryptic nonsense, unless one understood the old ways.

She didn't. And worse, she couldn't afford to guess.

Someone would need to decipher it. But who could be trusted with knowledge like this?

Her mind turned, piece by piece, until the answer took shape. Risky—but perhaps it could work.

She turned to Strond without slowing her stride. "I need you to find someone," she said. "Fast."

Chapter Forty-Six

DECIPHERER OF PORTENTS

Lee pulled his cloak tighter in spite of the warm weather, continuing down the deserted path until he saw it: an old stone fortress, crumbling into shadows. Only thugs would think of meeting in a place like this.

"Protect me, Grandmother," he said, then walked forward, clasping the painted miniature that hung from his neck. He kissed his fingertips and tapped them first to his heart, then to the portrait, pretending his family matriarch was still alive. Perhaps she could hear him from the labyrinths.

A shuffling sound came out of nowhere, and something yanked his cloak. Lee spun, crying out in fear, then let out a little laugh: his cloak had tangled into the leafy shrubs lining the path. He twisted himself free and continued onward, heart pounding.

When he arrived at the fortress door—just a large, open space—a puddle of water inside the threshold stopped him. Several pools obstructed the ruined entrance hall, glistening dimly under the streams of light that fell through the roof. He climbed gingerly over piles of stones to avoid wetting his feet, until he finally reached a crumbling staircase: they had told him to come to the second floor.

He examined it dubiously. Stairs were missing on one side or the other, forcing him to walk up it in a careful zigzag, but he came at last to a dark, rubble-filled foyer.

He glanced at his instructions and dabbed his brow. "I wish to the Six I had never laid eyes on Hong and Druce." He glanced around nervously as he crept forward in the darkness, afraid to have been overheard.

A door finally greeted him, and he knocked. If he backed out now, they would kill him for sure. Or worse, they would tell Ellie he had betrayed her. He would lose everything then—his houses, his wealth, his clothes.

He gave a reassuring pat to the silk robes hidden beneath his old gray cloak. No, he had done the right thing. Best of all, Hanmar would finally be free of Ants.

A gruff voice sounded from inside. "It's open."

Lee peered into the dim room. A cloaked figure stood by an arched window, looking out onto the cliffs.

"Come in," the figure said in a woman's musical voice.

Lee squinted. A woman?

He gave her drab wool cloak a disapproving frown. So, they hadn't paid him the respect of coming themselves, they had sent a mere servant. He lifted his chin, his composure returning along with his indignance, but when the woman turned and stepped out of the shadows, Lee caught his breath.

"My lady."

Her gaze was a crystal light in the dingy room. "You recognize me. How gratifying."

"Who wouldn't recognize the imperial vice regent of Jeng?"

Vice Regent Caliss inclined her head, revealing a golden halo of hair beneath her cowl.

When he had deduced that Hong and Druce worked for her, he had assumed it was through a long chain of command. How could those Ghenz thugs be so closely connected to such an illustrious personage?

He dipped into his most elegant bow. "How may I be of service, my lady?"

"On the contrary, it is I who have something to interest you," she said. "I understand you want to rid Hanmar of the Ants."

His stomach clenched, aware that someone of her station could easily pass this information to Ellie.

But her soft blue eyes stilled him. They were heavily lined with kohl, something he normally found distasteful, but on her, it was elegance itself. Most of all, they expressed all the sincerity of someone who truly understood his heart.

"There's nothing wrong with wanting," she said. "It's what makes us human."

Her eyes held him, and all he could think to say was, "Thank you, my lady."

No, that wouldn't do; he wanted her to see him as knowledgeable, perhaps to admire him. He needed to impress her.

"The Ants are, as you say, my lady, a terrible problem. I would be happy to brief Your Ladyship on the history of the matter."

"What a curious thing to say," she said, unblinking. "But I have no need of history lessons."

Lee tensed. Was that displeasure in her eyes?

"Of course not," he said, with another elegant flourish. Then he somehow stepped on the edge of his inner robe and stumbled forward. He righted himself, face hot with embarrassment. To his relief, she had looked away.

"But I'll need your help, as it were, to help you," she said. "I understand you're a skilled decipherer of portents."

He puffed up a little. "I do have some skill in that area. Some might say *considerable* skill"—he smiled modestly—"though I would never presume to say so myself. Decipherer of Riddles and Enigmas was my official title."

"Clever *and* modest," she said, turning to face him. "The defining traits of a real man."

Lee straightened, a flush rising to his cheeks. She thought him impressive. She thought him a real man.

But of course she did—word of his brilliance had clearly preceded him. That was why she'd enlisted him. But perhaps—now that she'd glimpsed him in person—her motives had deepened. He was an attractive man, after all.

Steady on, you old rogue, he thought with an inward smirk.

"You certainly seem up to the task," she said. "There's an ancient item I require. It will help me eliminate the Ants once and for all, but I first need you to procure it for me."

He nodded quickly. "Of course, my lady."

"It's a magical item," she said, watching him closely. "Does that bother you? I would never ask you to do something you didn't want to."

He tried to hide his discomfort. Though he had always avoided magic—such things were often dangerous and unpredictable—he couldn't risk losing her good opinion. "Not at all. I would be honored to find this item for you, my lady."

She laughed softly. "I was sure danger would be nothing to someone as capable as yourself." She looked over her shoulder into the shadows. "Now, it can only be handled with implements made by the master smiths of old."

He tried not to fidget. She had just called him capable—he couldn't admit he didn't know where to obtain such items.

Before he could think of a suitable lie however, a massive blond brute stepped out from the shadows where she had been looking and shoved a black velvet bag into Lee's chest.

Inside was a gold, disk-shaped casing, perhaps the size of a plum, with a pair of matching tongs beside it. Both had strange engravings.

Lee stared, astonished. "Is this...etched metal?"

She nodded. "It was passed down to me from my people—the Ghenz. My mother was Ghenz, you know."

He wasn't sure how to respond. She was so disarmingly honest, unearthing her unenviable roots with such charming humility. Still, if he admitted he had suspected this fact about her mother, she might think he was looking down on her: assuming someone was Ghenz was akin to declaring them rough and ignoble.

"I had assumed Your Ladyship's mother was from Hanmar," he said.

"So you believed a half-Ghenz couldn't be imperial vice regent?"

Alarm coursed through him. "No, my lady, not at all. I—I only meant not to offend. One must never assume."

"So being half-Ghenz is an offensive thing, then?"

The blood drained from his face. What had he done?

He was about to drop to his knees when she gave a bright laugh.

"I'm teasing," she said, her eyes two twinkling blue pools. "And actually, my mother did tell everyone she was from Hanmar."

Lee sagged with relief. He chuckled, dabbing his brow. "Your Ladyship has quite the sense of humor."

What a woman. Power and delicacy rolled into one. He had never met anyone like her.

"What is the item you wish me to find, my lady?"

"A seal handed down from my ancestors, made especially to eliminate the plague of Ants in their lands. Isn't that beautiful?"

Lee tilted his head, trying to remember the histories. When had the Ghenz ever eliminated Ants?

Thankfully, she saved him the embarrassment of admitting his ignorance.

"The Ghenz were the original enemies of the Ants—though a man of your learning would already know this."

"Yes, I—I seem to remember reading that," he said.

"What you may not know—for it was never recorded—was that it was the Ghenz who first enslaved the Ants, back when our people arrived from Ghenzan."

The Ghenz suddenly rose in his estimation. He had never realized what a forward-thinking people they were.

But why had they never eliminated Ants completely? If he had this seal, he would eliminate the Ants not just in Hanmar, but also throughout all of Shudon. Perhaps he would do just that, once he found it—he would be a hero in his day.

She seemed to read his thoughts. "I must warn you, the seal will kill anyone who is not of Ghenz blood, so you must never try to use it. In fact, you must not even touch it without the tongs, and then only to slip it into the gold casing. Hide it away the moment you do, for even looking on it for too long could poison you." She slipped closer, her voice a caress. "You're not like the others...I would hate to endanger you."

He listened, entranced. Her words were pure music.

"No one else must even glimpse the seal. If the wrong person were to find it, there would be no getting rid of the Ants...ever." All the conviction he himself felt on the matter was reflected in her eyes.

By the Six, she was beautiful. For a moment, he allowed himself the pleasure of imagining those blue eyes gazing at him in admiration and love.

He pressed a hand to his chest. "I will follow Your Ladyship's command unwaveringly."

She removed a yellowing parchment from her sleeve. "To find the first clue, you must first, before summer's end, follow the portent written on this page. You will find it in Ma'yanar Forest."

He managed what he hoped was an elegant bow, but the mere mention of the haunted forest stiffened his spine.

"I know such a trifle won't concern a mind like yours," she said, "but I might as well mention that ghosts cannot harm anyone who carries etched metal."

Thanking the stars, he tucked the velvet pouch away, close to his chest.

"Does this seal have a name, my lady? A name is sometimes a clue in itself."

An unreadable look clouded her eyes, and for a moment, she didn't answer.

"It is called Antfall, or Ant Scourge. But some old texts refer to it as the Celestial Seal."

He shook his head slowly. "I've never heard of any of those names."

Oddly, she looked relieved. "That's not important, darling." She smiled. "Eliminating the Ants is what matters, after all."

Darling. Heat crept up his neck as he gazed at her lips. She was marvelously beautiful when she smiled.

"I am entirely at your service," Lee said with another polished bow, and she dismissed him with a smile as sweet as spring lilies.

By the time Lee climbed over the last rubble heap and exited the fortress, all thoughts of danger had left him, replaced forever by the caress of her voice and the memory of her beautiful kohl-rimmed eyes.

To have been received so graciously by the vice regent of Jeng!

He thought with scorn of the cold reception he had received from Empress Zinchen, who had failed to recognize his talents. But Vice Regent Caliss, the most powerful woman in Jeng, had done that, and more.

His mind wandered. What would life be like as the intimate of such a woman?

Though the time and place of their next meeting had not yet been set, he would insist on meeting in a place where she could see him in his elegant clothes and one-of-a-kind frogworm pin.

For now, he would use his talents to win her admiration. As for what might follow...who could say?

He smirked. *You old rogue, you.*

Now, on to Ma'yanar Forest.

Chapter Forty-Seven

TRAIL OF EMBERS

Alchemy continued along the same humiliating vein for the next three weeks: every seedling Tori touched either didn't respond or else blew away in a cloud of ash.

But that would all end tonight. After another excruciating day under Master Kwai'le's ridicule, she had devised a plan.

The hedge snagged her robes as she slipped through it into her garden, holding a wooden crate overhead. Her clothes had already been dirty from incinerating plants all day, but now, the hedge had positively spoiled them.

She crossed her small lawn, mounted two steps, and set the crate onto the floorboards of her back patio. She had bought the crate from Old Griff—the insufferable fruit seller had actually made her pay five skades, even though he had plenty of empty crates lying around. But since nobody else had a box, she had been forced to pay.

A glance through the latticework of her patio door confirmed that no lanterns burned inside, which meant Elnora must have still been assisting Master Banfay. Good. Tori didn't need any witnesses; she had suffered enough embarrassment for one day.

She lowered herself painfully onto a reed mat, her sore legs protesting every movement, thanks to yesterday's session with Master Maeli. When

Master Maeli had first told her she would spend entire days in horse stance, she had assumed it was hyperbole. Yesterday, she had learned differently. Her legs still felt as wobbly as a bowl of aspic.

She reached into the crate where ten seedlings sat in a scattered mess. Scooping carefully to avoid shaking the dirt from the roots, she lifted a plant, then rested her hand in her lap. Even if it meant staying up till dawn, she would master this technique tonight.

After only two rounds of breath—far less than it took in her lessons—she spotted the glow of elixir. As before, it was soft and misty, but now she could precisely sense its width: about the same as a strand of hair.

So that was all it took, she thought, exhaling in relief—a little time without that insufferable alchemy master breathing down her neck. Why hadn't she realized it sooner?

Eyes still closed, she focused on the elixir strand. From what she understood, phytolyzation worked by streaming the elixir through her arms down into her hands, then outward into the plant. She already knew she needed to visualize this before she could see it spontaneously, and did so during every alchemy session. But this time, she took it a step further: she imagined the plant in her hand growing and pushing out leaves, its roots sending new shoots.

Her palm tickled, and she opened her eyes to view her success.

Disappointment surged. The seedling looked exactly as it had before.

She tried again, this time keeping her eyes open while she imagined the glowing strand streaming into the plant. A breath later however, the plant shriveled into a thin brown string.

With an exasperated exhale, she dusted the string into the box. Maybe she needed to use more elixir.

Since it was difficult to stream elixir with a plant in her hand, she left the plants in the crate this time. When she closed her eyes, the glowing strand reappeared in her mind's eye, building gradually into a pleasant warmth. She focused her thoughts on it, imagining the strand of elixir rushing out like a torrent of molten gold.

She winced—instead of streaming outward, the strand tangled down the length of her arms. A moment later, her palms burned with the pain of hot needles. Desperate to expel the heat, she thrust her palms at the seedlings. The box split with a crack—but the plants looked the same.

A headache threatened. She took a deep breath, pushing down her frustration, then began again. Sweat beaded on her forehead. Before she could visualize anything, however, pain stabbed her midsection and searing heat shot through her palms, exploding with a loud pop. Plant parts lay everywhere, scattered on her arms, her robes, her hair.

Tori cursed in frustration. The thought of enduring Master Kwai'le's insults for another day was too much.

Lanterns flickered on inside the cottage, and a silhouette approached the patio door. Elnora stepped outside, her gaze falling first on Tori's robes, then on the mess around her. She bent forward, picking a leaf from Tori's hair.

"Clearly I have no idea what I'm doing," Tori muttered.

"The best fishers weren't born knowing knots. They just never stopped tying them."

Tori glanced at the darkening sky; she had been sitting here for about the time of a candle's burn. She rose, resisting the urge to kick the broken box.

Then something occurred to her. "Master Banfay works with plants. Has he ever mentioned phytolyzation?"

Elnora thought for a moment. "I think that's just for alchemy. But he does mention wielding forms sometimes."

"Why? Those are just for wielders."

"Actually," she said, looking hesitant, "if you look in the sitting room shelf, beside that palm-leaf book on Antiquitals you've been studying, there's a wielding scroll he lent me, one of Master Koren's. Apparently, the forms help him in his work. Something about controlling the flow of elixir."

Tori scrubbed a hand over her face. "Well, good for him." She wouldn't touch the thing. There had to be something else.

But as they ate fried noodles from the communal dining hall, Elnora's statement niggled at her. They treated the wielding forms so casually here, even Master Banfay. How could they not see wielding for the destructive thing it was?

And yet...

Her mind combed through every display of wielding she had seen since arriving in Peach Blossom Grove—none of it had been anything short of beautiful.

"You once asked me why wielders are so hated." Tori tapped her wine cup, sending circles through the liquid. "Honestly, I'm beginning to wonder."

"Master Banfay has a theory," Elnora said. "He says people in power always fear those who are different."

Her mother's face came to her, and a chill rippled over her scalp. Whatever the views were in Peach Blossom Grove, nothing had changed in the palace. There, she had to remain hidden—and for that, she needed the Septad. Unfortunately, she thought with a grim inward sigh, the Septad involved alchemy—and she still hadn't figured out how to control the flow of elixir.

"Has Master Banfay ever explained to you how he controls the flow of elixir?" Tori asked.

"He said you have to listen to it. I didn't understand, though. That's why he suggested the wielding forms; he said it would help when I'm working with plant remedies."

"I wonder if master healers and alchemists flow their elixir differently?"

"I'm not sure. I only know that an alchemist grows the plants, then uses them to make magical pills, whereas a master healer uses plant pills and powders to heal."

"Couldn't anybody use magical pills? People just have to swallow them," Tori said, helping herself to another bowl of noodles.

"A healer makes them more effective, especially master healers, because she or he is able to nurture medicinal essence—or, in our case, medicinal elixir." Elnora's cheeks reddened then, and she said quietly, "Master Banfay says I have it."

"Like I've said before, you have the gift."

Elnora looked away, unable to accept a compliment, as usual. "Actually, Master Banfay said *the gift* is something else. It's what alchemists have, and *the gift* is its actual name. Apparently, that's what makes alchemy so difficult to master—you have to have *the gift*. But don't ask me what it is. All I know is that for both master healers and alchemists, the wielding forms help control the flow of elixir."

Tori tensed.

Yet neither Master Banfay nor Master Kwai'le were wielders, so the forms must be able to act on the flow of elixir separate from wielding. And she desperately needed something to move her forward. Perhaps if she used them cautiously...

Tori tapped her heel, her nervousness finally showing. "Maybe I'll just look at the scroll briefly."

After dinner, Tori stepped outside, scroll in hand, and filled her lungs with the fresh night air, hoping it would calm her. The White River sat high in the sky now, a banner of diamonds and milk flowing over Ishairo's head.

She closed the door on Elnora, who was busy cleaning up after dinner. Even though no one else here thought so, doing this felt somehow dirty, and she desired privacy.

The thick scroll was labeled *Beginner's Wielding Forms*. Tori sat cross-legged on the mat and unrolled just the very first section—she refused to do more—and her lantern highlighted bold logograms at the top: *Anyone caught wielding outside Peach Blossom Grove will be banished.*

Well, that was no problem—she wouldn't be wielding anywhere.

Her eyes traveled farther along to a list of breathing techniques entitled: *Breathe the elixir. Connect with the elixir.* She closed her eyes, and began.

When the glowing strand appeared, she opened an eye and read the next step.

Move into horse stance and flow.

Ugh. Not again.

She stood on aching legs, then lowered into the stance with a groan. After a few rounds of breath, her legs trembled, which meant a painful spasm awaited her the moment she stood up.

Longer meditation equals greater connection. Deep desire elevates effectiveness even more, the scroll read.

It made no sense, of course, but as she expected nothing less from Master Koren, she went through the breathing and arm movements anyway, for about the time of a stone's warming in the sun.

The glow built slowly in her mind's eye—then, in a sudden flare, the elixir strand doubled in thickness. Her heart kicked with anticipation: for the first time, she felt she had truly connected with the elixir.

Without knowing how, she opened her dawn channels and circulated the newly thickened strand through her torso and limbs, just like the scroll said. She wasn't imagining it—she could feel it, a trail of embers gusting through her body.

Anticipation sharpened into fear. She stopped, braced her hands on her knees, then leaned into the patio wall, waiting for her legs to spasm. Nothing happened. She walked slowly inside the cottage, supporting herself on the furniture.

After a while, she stared at her legs in stunned amazement: not only had there been no spasm, but her legs also no longer even felt sore. Cycling the elixir had healed them.

Hope sparked in her chest. Now that she understood the technique, she'd never have to open that wretched wielding scroll again. She could circulate the elixir properly now—which meant alchemy was finally within reach.

She pursed her lips. At least, that was how she hoped it would work.

As she reached for the door to close it, the sight of the White River stopped her. Its stars, even in all their brightness, never strayed outside their confines. Surely it was the same with the elixir—surely the elixir wouldn't mix with her ketua simply because she was cycling it.

She gazed at the stars, a cautious thrill rising. In two days, she'd try alchemy again—and this time, things would be different.

Chapter Forty-Eight

MARTIAL SISTER

The next morning, Tori waited on the empty second level of the training grounds. As much as she didn't love horse stance, she was curious to see how cycling the elixir would affect her stamina.

"Tori."

She flinched, then cursed her jittery nerves. Despite Master Banfay's assurances, her mind had not yet healed from the attack at the Laughing Skunk, and she still found herself jumping at the slightest surprise—in a moment of inattention she had failed to notice the weapons master ascending the steps with Keya.

Tori faced Master Maeli and bowed.

"Your elder sister is here, too," Master Maeli said.

Irritation prickled her, but she directed another bow at Keya.

Keya reciprocated with a smug dip of the chin.

"I have some business to attend to," Master Maeli said, "so Keya will take over today. She is very experienced in helping new students. Keya, Tori's technique is good for a beginner, so I would like you to start teaching her how to use it in practice."

Keya placed a hand over her fist and lowered her head. "Yes, Master."

But something in Keya's eye made Tori uneasy, something that said being left alone with her wasn't the best idea.

"Could you stay a short while, Master, to ensure I'm fully grasping the lesson?"

"Keya is more than able to handle that," Master Maeli said.

"I also had questions about horse stance, something I wanted to show you." Hopefully she could invent something plausible.

"Show Keya, she will know how to help."

Tori bowed. "Thank you, Master. Still, it would mean a lot to have you witness my very first training session with a senior."

Master Maeli paused, evidently considering this.

"Very well. I could watch the first round."

A moment later, Senrik and Ruvien arrived at the bottom level and set down their things by the weapons racks. Good. They were doing their own training; there would be no time to notice her.

Keya took out a long ribbon and began wrapping her hair in a ponytail. As she did, Senrik and Ruvien moved away from the weapons racks and into the sparring circle, drawing a small crowd.

Suddenly there was a flash of steel, and the ringing of metal echoed through the air. Senrik moved far more lightly than his muscular build promised, fluid and feral. The heat of attraction prickled Tori's face.

Ruvien weaved around the circle, grinning, while Senrik watched him lazily, his golden hair catching the breeze. In a sudden movement, Ruvien sheathed his blades and jumped, drawing his bow and shooting it over and over in one smooth motion. Senrik batted away a shower of arrows, skipping backward, outside the circle. Ruvien landed lightly, then dropped and rolled, springing up again next to a weapons rack. Senrik pounced, covering the ground between them, sweeping his sword down effortlessly, cleaving the rack in two.

Tori cringed, but Ruvien had already ducked and slid away. He popped up on the other side of the broken rack, apparently unscathed.

But then, with a look of surprise, Ruvien glanced down—his sash dropped to the ground, severed, and his outer robe fluttered open. The crowd erupted in cheers.

Ruvien laughed and clapped Senrik on the back.

By some maddening instinct he looked up then, seeming to spot her, and pointed in her direction. Tori's stomach dropped—they were coming to watch.

Great. Senrik as an audience was all she needed.

Master Maeli stood off to one side. "Begin when you are ready."

Keya finished tying her ribbon, her eyes flicking almost imperceptibly toward the two men mounting the steps, a smile curling the edge of her lips. As they headed toward the back wall, however, Senrik gave Tori a nod, and Keya's face darkened.

She turned to Tori. "Ready?" Her voice was artificially warm. "Now remember to grip your daggers, like this." She demonstrated the basic grip anyone could master on the first day. "We're going to practice your spin-and-slash technique, except we'll do it while we move in a circle. Like this."

Keya crouched, circling Tori, then spun, wheeled her daggers overhead, and slashed to one side. "Now you try."

Tori blundered through a ridiculous imitation.

Keya gave a little laugh, eyes flicking toward Senrik. "Put some vigor into it. You're not made of water." She demonstrated again, whirling impressively.

Tori kept trying, each time feeling more and more foolish.

"Keep circling," Keya said. "Your opponent's not going to stay put for you."

Tori circled, then successfully stepped forward, spun, and slashed. Keya parried with her daggers, pushing so hard that Tori stumbled, off-balance.

Tori spun and slashed again, and again Keya pushed her off-balance.

"Now add the first part of the basic forms to that," Keya said. "Step forward, slap your daggers together, and thrust."

Tori did.

Keya laughed again, this time louder. "Are you hoping to slash me with your mind? You'll never touch an opponent like that. Come closer."

Tori circled, spun, and slashed, then stepped closer to Keya and thrust. Keya gave her a stinging smack in the face.

Tori stared, incredulous. "What was that for?"

"You were too close."

"You told me to get in close!"

"Dagger fighting is close contact. You can't cut your opponent unless you get in close. On the other hand," Keya said with a smile, "if you stick your neck out, you'll get it cut off. It's all about balance. Now, do it again."

Tori repeated the technique, careful to get close, but not as close as last time. Keya smacked her on the other cheek, her gaze flitting briefly toward Senrik.

Hot annoyance flashed up Tori's neck. Those slaps were for his benefit. Tori slashed again, trying to control her irritation.

Keya circled faster. Tori matched her pace. Then suddenly, Keya whirled her daggers in a flurry and stabbed them at Tori's neck, stopping less than a handspan away. Tori froze, breath caught in her chest.

How could Master Maeli let this maniac train people?

Keya's eyes were cold, but her voice remained pleasant. "Let's try that again."

Fine. If that's how she wants to play, let's see how she likes it when I draw blood.

Tori glanced at Senrik. He was leaning back on the wall, watching, arms folded, while Ruvien tossed nuts into the air and caught them in his mouth.

Tori darted in as fast as she could, determined to slash Keya's clothes. Keya stepped aside, then stuck a foot out and tripped her. Tori stumbled forward, but quickly regained her footing, feigning indifference even as humiliation burned her inside.

"Excellent balance, Tori," Master Maeli said.

"Now let's add more of the forms," Keya said sweetly. "I'll show you how they look with an opponent."

As Tori went through the forms, Keya softly struck and parried in perfect coordination with Tori's movements, and for the first time, Tori understood what the forms really meant.

But then, as Tori moved through the part where she jabbed at Keya, instead of parrying, Keya shifted aside and slapped her hard.

"Enough, Keya," Master Maeli said calmly.

"Yes, Master. I was just teaching Younger Sister not to get so close."

"You made that point already."

Keya bowed.

Keeping her gaze away from Senrik, Tori spun her daggers in her hand the way she'd been practicing for the past four weeks, the ease of the movement restoring some of her confidence.

As Keya moved faster and faster now, Tori struggled to patch her pace—she was determined to avoid more slaps.

"Stop," Master Maeli said. "Do not be too hasty, Tori. You must learn the basic forms properly before adding speed."

How can I not, when your star pupil is trying to thrash me? she wanted to say, but it sounded childish.

"The faster I go, the faster I'll get to Mount Ketwanen."

A faint frown crossed Master Maeli's face. "You will go to Ketwanen when you are ready, not before. Now begin again, and this time I want to see perfect forms, not meaningless speed."

They began again, but the instant the angle of their bodies blocked Master Maeli's line of sight, Keya jabbed the butt of her dagger at Tori. Tori twisted away, executing her forms as perfectly as she knew how. Keya tried to deal her another slap, but Tori ducked aside faster than she knew she could.

Keya's nose flared. With startling speed, she trapped Tori's hand under her armpit, twisted her arm behind her and slashed her cheek, drawing blood.

Tori stumbled, her weapons slipping from her hands, and touched a finger to the burning cut.

"Keya!" Master Maeli strode over. "What in the name of the Six has gotten into you?"

Keya quickly sheathed her daggers and bowed low, hand over fist. "Apologies, Master! Please punish me."

"Have you lost control of your weapons?" Master Maeli said, her voice sharp with disapproval. "Shall I give you a wooden one, like Master Koren's children?"

Keya bowed lower, eyes to the ground.

"You are dismissed. Go sit by the watercourse and contemplate your behavior."

Keya bowed again, then ran to pick up her things.

"Come with me, Tori," Master Maeli said, walking to the medicine hut. The moment her back was turned, however, satisfaction flashed behind Keya's eyes and she walked away.

Ruvien slunk off next, with Senrik following.

Master Maeli opened the hut's red door and handed Tori a piece of white cloth. "Apply pressure to your cheek," she said, pulling out a small porcelain jar. Once the blood flow was stemmed, she smeared ointment from the jar onto Tori's cheek with a tenderness that for some reason pained Tori's heart. She searched for memories of her mother tending to her wounds as a child, but found none.

The ointment stung.

"The wound will vanish faster than a soul in Black Valley," Master Maeli said, replacing the jar on the shelf. "Banfay's remedies are second to none. By the time you come back in two days, not even a scar will remain." She let out an exasperated breath then, and shook her head. "What in the name of the Six got into that girl?"

Just then, a messenger came running.

"Master," he said breathlessly, holding out a note. "It's from the peacekeepers. They said it's urgent."

She read it, then turned to Tori. "I have to see to this." She shook her head again. "I had hoped Keya would take over today, but you will have to train on your own. Practice horse stance for a hundred breaths, then go through the forms. You can leave at midday." To the messenger, she said, "Come, I will need to consult my map before I can give orders." Then she jogged down the stairs, robes fluttering behind her.

When the sun reached the top of the sky, Tori stopped and drank from her bottle-gourd. A smiling Elnora mounted the steps, carrying a bamboo box labeled *Medicine*. Her smile faded when she noticed Tori's cheek.

"Don't worry," Tori said. "It's been treated with Master's Banfay's ointment."

"What happened?"

Tori exhaled. "Long story."

Reluctantly, Elnora drew her eyes away and began transferring small porcelain jars from her box into the medicine hut.

A short while later, they were on the path home.

"I meant to tell you," Elnora said, "I saw Master Kwai'le."

"Lucky you."

Elnora smiled. "I went with Master Banfay to get spirit stones from him. He said to tell you he'll be busy tomorrow. He's buying a new messenger hawk."

"So he can only be bothered to train his apprentice when he's not at the markets? How responsible."

But she was relieved, actually. Even though she had been curious to see how her new understanding of the elixir would affect her alchemy, after her session with Keya, a break would be welcome.

Footsteps crunched on the gravel behind them, and Ruvien appeared suddenly next to Elnora. "Speaking of messenger hawks, you wanted to see the Greenstalk hawking post, didn't you?"

Elnora looked him over. "Where'd you come from?"

Ruvien winked.

Senrik fell into step beside Tori, in full view of her ugly cut. Tori lifted her chin, hiding the humiliation of knowing he had seen her get sliced.

"I thought I might check for messages myself if I knew where the hawking post was," Elnora explained to Tori. "We haven't heard from Yumay lately, so I wanted to be sure her notes weren't getting lost."

"Our hawks don't lose anything. You'll understand when you see them in action. And it just so happens that Senrik and I are going to Greenstalk tomorrow," Ruvien said. "People reported suspicions persons passing through recently. We're on local postings now for the peacekeepers, so Master Maeli commissioned us to keep an eye on the place. We'll take a quick look around, then show you the hawking post. After, we'll all go to the teahouse for the noonday meal. Better than any palace food." He grinned.

Elnora's brow creased. "I don't know, Princess. If there are suspicious people, maybe you shouldn't go."

Ruvien waved a dismissive hand. "Don't worry. Nothing exciting ever happens in Greenstalk."

"Better to be safe," Elnora said. "Like Granny used to say, smell the wind before you cast off. And even if Yumay already wrote, a letter takes five days to come."

"By rider, yes," Tori said. "Yumay would send a hawk for anything urgent. I'd have the message in half a day."

But even as she said it, an uncomfortable doubt crept into her mind.

Her gut tensed without reason. Everything was fine—so why did she feel like running?

"It's settled, then," Ruvien said cheerfully. "We'll all go to Greenstalk tomorrow."

Chapter Forty-Nine

GREENSTALK VILLAGE

Since Greenstalk Village was less than five fen away, the following morning they arrived at the village wall in about the time of a stone's warming in the sun. People carried baskets in and out of an arched passageway, or led donkeys pulling carts of vegetables and chickens.

The passageway stretched ten paces deep, ending in a gate that opened onto a street canopied with lanterns and lined with colorfully painted stalls. The aroma of smoked land crab filled the air, which vendors cooked inside giant steel drums.

"This is incredible," Elnora said, gazing at a stall where crystals dangled from the eaves, flashing in the sunlight.

As they passed it, a redhaired man sitting in the dirt caught Tori's attention. A donation plate lay at his feet, and he held a wooden board that read: *Will work for food.* Beside him sat a boy that could have been his twin, if not for the difference in their ages—around twenty years, by Tori's guess. Both looked up at her with reddish-brown eyes, the movement of looking up making the netlike scars on their cheeks and necks shine like molten copper. Ants, a father and son.

As they didn't have the haunting smile and glassy, bloodshot eyes of strangling smile addicts, Tori untied her money pouch and emptied it into their plate. One gold petal sat nestled among pink and blue skades—they would eat well for many days.

Senrik's gaze caught the donation plate, then flicked back at Tori with a look of respect. He dipped his chin. But Tori refused to feel gratified for something that was only natural. She kept walking.

When the Ants' effusive words of thanks finally died down behind her, the sound of music caught her attention: a woman sat off the main path, strumming a pipa.

"Listen, you have ears," she sang in a smooth alto, "and I will weave you a song of the stars—for stars whisper secrets of light and of hope."

She cradled the pear-shaped instrument and plucked its four strings in a liquid, rolling sound, like musical raindrops.

"Ishairo the Sunderer cleaved the land, and with his blade, he bound it anew."

Her fingers slid smoothly from note to note.

"Sunderer, unifier, rise to the heights! Climb the mountain, ascend your throne! From the heavens, let your radiance fall, a sovereign light from your celestial home."

It was a well-known tune, and an Ant servant in a nearby animal seller's stall hummed along as he wrung a goose's neck and handed it to a customer.

"Look at those," Elnora said, pointing to a stall filled with carved wooden boxes. "You've been wanting a box."

Tori went over and picked up a box smaller than her hand. No opening was visible anywhere, just intricate engravings of flowers. It would be perfect for Wan's game of Umbrage, which she had always kept in the black velvet pouch he had given her. But lately she had been wanting something to protect it.

"You all go on to the hawking post," she said. "It'll take me a while to choose."

"I'll stay with the prin—" Elnora caught herself. "I'll stay here."

"The whole point of you coming today was to see the messenger hawks," Ruvien said. "You're going to love it. Next to the regular birds, our Peach Blossom Grove hawks look like queens and kings, because of their fancy homing stones."

"What are homing stones?" Elnora asked.

"Spirit stones, except cut with facets, like jewels. They work alongside the bird's natural homing instinct. One stone stays with the bird, while the twin stone goes wherever you want the message delivered."

"So the first stone helps the bird home in on its twin?" Elnora asked.

Ruvien nodded.

"Why are there regular birds and Peach Blossom Grove hawks in Greenstalk?" Elnora asked.

"For situations like yours—other hawks arrive with messages for us, but they can't come through the Veil. So the Peach Blossom Grove hawks have to transfer the messages to their own legs and fly in with them."

"I just remembered Master Kwai'le is buying a new messenger hawk," Tori said. "I'm definitely staying here."

"No one in Greenstalk sells special hawks," Ruvien said. He thought about it, then squinted at Senrik. "Do they?"

"Not taking any chances. Elnora, you go." She indicated the gray hood that half covered her face—Elnora had insisted she wear a disguise. "I'll be fine. Anyway, I probably won't even be halfway through by the time you come back." She picked up another box.

With a reluctant nod, Elnora placed her money pouch in Tori's hand, and left. Tori remembered then that she had given all of her money away to the Ants, and she blessed Elnora inwardly. When they returned to the palace, Tori would repay her double.

For now, though, Elnora was the rich one, Tori thought with a wry chuckle. Whenever she helped Banfay with herbal mixtures, he paid her.

A box the color of coffee caught her eye. It was carved in a simple geometric pattern and inlaid with gold. The artistry was exquisite; the shopkeeper would no doubt want a fair price for this one.

She hefted Elnora's purse, trying to judge its contents; she didn't want to empty it. How long before Tori herself could start getting paid for alchemy?

She pressed her lips together, remembering the incinerated seedlings. Even with her newfound understanding of cycling the elixir, she might need to rely on Elnora for a while yet. She put the box down; she should probably find something cheaper.

She picked up a smooth, light-colored box with no adornments. Although this one was plain, that very fact made it more exquisite than the others, because whereas they had carvings that might conceal an opening, this one had nothing—and yet no opening was visible.

"Is this pine?" she asked the pot-bellied shopkeeper.

"It is. From the forests of Mizvale, in Jeng." He gave a proud nod. "Finest wood you can buy."

As she contemplated it, trying to puzzle out its construction, conversations drifted in and out around her.

"He said she had bark and vines instead of skin and hair." A group of young men strolled past, eating roasted meat skewers.

"Utter pig's breath. Your cousin must have been in his cups that day."

"That's the thing, my cousin barely touches a drop. And he said she appeared out of nowhere—or rather, she stepped out of a tree."

Laughter.

"Ain't no such thing ever existed," his friend said. He shook his head. "Tree people."

They continued to argue, their voices fading as they walked away.

Tori picked up the coffee-colored box again; the prices might all be the same. "I still prefer this one. How much?"

She didn't hear the shopkeeper's reply. A group of rough-looking men, with blond hair and braided beards just like her attackers, stalked in her direction. One of them locked eyes with her.

Suddenly, she was back in the deserted alleyway at the Laughing Skunk. She dropped to the ground, scrambling away from the road on hands and knees, breath coming in short bursts. Her eyes jerked left and right, looking for somewhere safe, a place where she couldn't be dragged away, but there was nothing. The men's heavy footsteps thudded—they had already reached the stall. She covered her mouth with her hands, whimpering, and huddled into a ball. One of them was demanding something from the shopkeeper.

Tori pressed her forehead to her knees, trembling.

The shopkeeper refused nicely, stating the quality of the boxes, but the thug lowered his voice menacingly. "We're just asking for a discount, friend. It would be a shame for this to get ugly." He tapped the knife at his waist, and the group had surrounded the stall. A boot touched Tori as they did, and she flinched and cried out.

The thug looked down and grinned. "Well, what do we have here?"

"Halt!" Senrik's voice thundered as he elbowed his way through the crowd.

The thug closest to Tori reached for his knife, but Senrik was on him in a flash, seizing him by collar. He shoved him against the stall post, cracking the wood. "I said, halt!"

Just then, Ruvien sauntered in, eating a bowl of crab. He paused mid-bite, glancing from man to man.

The thugs attacked. With his left hand, Senrik hurled the first man at them, making them stumble backward, while with his right hand he drew his sword. They rushed forward, slashing with their knives. Senrik spun his sword in an arc, pushing off all three at once. They rushed in again, but before their weapons could land, three arrows knocked the knives from the hands of two of them and pierced the hand of the third. He cried out. The thugs turned and ran.

The vendor slumped back against a stall rail, his face ashen.

Tori realized she was weeping. *This isn't the Laughing Skunk. I'm safe. I'm safe.*

Elnora emerged from the crowd, noticed Tori, and paled. She rushed to her side and wrapped a protective arm around her.

"What happened, Princess?"

Tori forced herself to stand on shaky legs. She pulled her hood forward and wiped her eyes with trembling hands.

Elnora took her arm, but Tori pulled away. "Thank you. I'm fine," Tori said, her voice breaking. "Let's just go."

All the way home, she walked far ahead of the others, and when she finally reached her cottage, she went straight to her room and sat on the bed, head in her hands.

She had shamed herself with tears. How could she face anyone again?

After some time—she didn't know how long—the door creaked open. She didn't bother to look up.

Elnora remained unusually quiet for a long time. But when the silence stretched on, Tori raised her head.

Heat flushed her face and neck. It wasn't Elnora.

Master Maeli watched her with calm, steady eyes. "Elnora told me what happened."

Tori gritted her teeth. She had already disgraced herself in front of Senrik and Ruvien—did Elnora have to tell the whole world?

Birdsong, cheerfully indifferent, filled the silence.

"What happened wasn't your fault," Master Maeli said, her voice soft. "You must not hide from your shame and humiliation. Instead, use it as fuel. If you do this, I promise you will never have to fear people like that again."

Tori's throat tightened. She wanted to believe her—to rise above her weakness. She just didn't know where to begin.

Master Maeli went to the door. "I expect to see you tomorrow as usual. Meet me at the peach trees at dawn. We are going to do something new."

Chapter Fifty

THE BEAR AND THE WOLVERINE

As instructed, Tori arrived at the peach trees at dawn. Master Maeli was already waiting. She motioned Tori to walk beside her down the petal-covered path toward the forest.

"What are we doing?" Tori asked.

"Today we are going to find a very dangerous animal."

They took an unfamiliar path, and before long arrived at an area filled with what looked like ordinary trees, apart from their red, orange, and yellow fruits, which glowed like party lanterns in the dim forest—spirit-fruit.

The lomi were quiet today, wafting slowly over the trunks and over plants in a sparkling mist.

A shadow shifted behind the trees, and yellow eyes flashed. Tori froze. But Master Maeli held out her hand and casually strolled toward it.

A tiger slinked into view, its massive head at eye level with Master Maeli. It lowered itself under her hand, and she stroked it.

She looked over her shoulder. "Come. Do not be afraid."

Tori crept closer.

"Put your hand out slowly," Master Maeli instructed, but Tori's limbs refused to move.

"It will not hurt you. This here is nothing but a big kitten," she said, scratching behind its ears. The tiger purred.

Tori's voice was barely audible. "I'm fairly certain I heard you use the words 'very dangerous.'"

Master Maeli smiled. "There are no dangerous animals inside the Veil."

Tori forced her trembling hand forward, and the tiger immediately nuzzled its head under it. Despite of her trepidation, she mimicked Master Maeli, stroking behind its ears. The fur was thick and velvety, and she found herself running her fingers through it.

The tiger let out a low purr that vibrated all the way into her chest. Tori grinned. Growing up, her interaction with animals had been limited, and she had always longed for it.

Suddenly, though, the tiger opened its eyes, stretched, and simply walked away.

Master Maeli chuckled. "Oh, you have had enough, have you? You old user."

The tiger looked back once, then slunk out of view.

Tori stared after it, breathless. "That was incredible."

Just then, one of the yellow spirit-fruits dropped to the ground beside her. Its inner light pulsed several times and slowly dimmed. Then little lights spread over the fruit, until the entire surface resembled a ball of fireflies. The lights floated upward toward the tree, then flew into the branches, as though being sucked.

Tori stared. "What just happened?"

"There is no death in the Veil," Master Maeli said. "If a fruit falls and is not eaten, it will simply be reabsorbed." She reached up and plucked a glowing red fruit from the bough above her. "Try one."

Tori bit into it. Instantly she was invigorated, as though she had woken up from a long, peaceful sleep and then plunged into bracing waters.

"Now I understand why people always head to the blue spirit-fruit trees in midafternoon," Tori said, taking another bite. Up till now, she had been too busy to try one.

Master Maeli gave a nod. "There is a difference, however, between the blue ones and these. These are regular spirit-fruits—they merely nourish one's dawn-essence, which, as you know, the body itself is partially made of. But we will talk more of this later."

Tori dropped the seed, and, just like the fallen fruit, it transformed into glowing sparkles that floated into the tree.

They walked to the exit of the Veil, passing through the familiar sensation of a water curtain and into Ma'yanar Forest on the other side, then came to a place with two tree stumps.

"Now watch," Master Maeli whispered, sitting down.

It was a long while before anything happened. Eventually, though, leaves and branches started to rustle.

An enormous black shadow loomed between the trees, and soon a black bear stepped into a beam of sunlight and sniffed the air.

Master Maeli put a finger to her lips, motioning for silence, as though Tori needed the reminder. She couldn't have made a sound, even had she wanted to.

The bear looked up at a beehive nestled in the branches of a tall tree. It climbed, stuck its paw into the hive, and ate, oblivious to swarming of angry bees.

What was the lesson here? That dangerous people can be mollified by sweetness? Sweet words? That certainly wouldn't work with her mother.

As the bear ate, a patter of tiny footsteps drew near, and a small brown creature with a pointed nose scurried out of nowhere.

"Wolverine," Master Maeli whispered. She motioned with two fingers for Tori to watch closely.

After a moment of sniffing, the wolverine's gaze locked on to the bear. Its fur spiked out peevishly. It let out a growl, then scurried forward like a street thug hankering for a fight and started climbing. To Tori's utter astonishment, the little creature darted in, bit the bear's leg, then scurried back down the tree.

Master Maeli pressed her lips together, half-smiling.

Tori grimaced. This wasn't funny at all. She hated the idea of watching it get torn in two.

The bear stopped, momentarily confused, a paw full of honey halfway to its mouth. Then, apparently unconcerned, it continued to eat.

The wolverine scurried up again and bit the bear a second time. This time the bear looked down and saw it.

Tori cringed, willing the little creature to run. Instead, it growled, spiked out its fur, then darted in a third time, biting the bear's other leg.

The bear stared at the wolverine, almost with a look of astonishment. It licked the honey off its paw, then casually climbed back down with the attitude of a bigger thug who was about to teach the first one a lesson.

Tori found herself making flicking motions with her hands, mentally telling the little creature to shoo. Master Maeli placed a hand on hers, stilling them.

The wolverine waited, in a posture of utter defiance. The moment the bear reached the ground, it slapped its mighty paw down at the creature.

But the wolverine avoided the strike, then launched into the air and nipped the bear on the nose.

The bear groaned and slapped its paw down again.

Again, the wolverine darted out of the way and jumped up, nipping the bear.

This time, the bear passed a paw over its nose in a painful motion, as though trying to massage an ache. The moment its nose was exposed, the wolverine nipped it again. The bear, furious, slapped its paw, but the wolverine was simply too fast.

After the fourth nip, the bear rubbed its nose again, turned, and lumbered out of sight. The wolverine stared after it, body rigid with irritation.

It shook itself once, smoothing its fur, then scurried back into the shadows.

As soon as it was gone, Master Maeli made a sign, and they reentered the Veil.

"Now, tell me," Master Maeli said, when they were back in Peach Blossom Grove, "what are the components to victory for a smaller person?"

They stood near the blue spirit-fruit trees, their silvery bark lit with rings of pale blue light.

"To be faster and have the better technique."

"Flawless technique, preferably, since you may not know how good your opponent is until it is too late. But there is one more thing I did not mention, because it is above your level. Also, it was better for you to see it in action first: a smaller person must fight with more intensity, and this must become her normal mode."

She sat cross-legged on the grass. "Now, I want you to go through your forms, but this time, meditate on the wolverine as you do. This, I hope, will more quickly bring you to the level you need to be."

"So I'll be able to go to Mount Ketwanen sooner?"

"No. Your grading will still be held five moons from now—you have been training for one moon, and six moons is the minimum required for passing the one-bar. But you will at least have the satisfaction of making faster progress until then."

"What happens if I don't pass?"

"You will train six moons more."

"I don't have that kind of time," Tori said. "I can't be absent from the palace for more than eight moons in one stretch. I need to go to Ketwanen after six moons, at the latest, whether I'm ready or not."

Master Maeli's expression hardened. "Your impatience concerns me. I will not send you out until I am certain you can survive."

She regretted the half-truth she had to tell. Though she had never thought twice about lying to her mother, deceiving Master Maeli felt wrong. "But if I miss the chance of creating the Septad, my mother's war will cost countless lives. By this time next year, I'm sure her armies will march."

"Meaningless loss of life is inevitable in any war."

Tori studied her master. Did she dare be honest, even after deceiving the elder? If Master Maeli knew the truth, she might never trust her again. And yet, she wasn't like the empress. She hadn't punished or coerced, only offered guidance. Didn't that deserve something more?

Tori met her master's gaze. "I haven't been entirely honest," she said. "I'm sorry." She drew a steadying breath. "The truth is...I need the Septad for myself. Without it, I'll become my mother's slave."

Master Maeli's eyes lost their sharpness, and she looked at Tori thoughtfully. "Enslavement is something I understand all too well. And I have realized there is more danger in trying to slow you down than in speeding you up, which is why I am training you above your current skill level. However, I would not do this if I did not believe you could succeed."

"But what if I fail?"

"Never set your mind on failure. Now, show me your forms again."

Slipping the Night Twins from her waist, Tori tried her best to execute the movements flawlessly.

"Again," Master Maeli said, when she had finished. "This time with more intensity."

Tori repeated the form, trying her best to make it more intense. Afterward, she stood panting.

"Again. This time, move in a circle, as though sparring."

The memory of Keya's slaps returned then, and suddenly she was the wolverine and Keya was the bear. Tori darted in and out, nipping with her daggers.

Keya vanished, replaced by the thugs at the Laughing Skunk. Anger surged through her, and she whirled in a fury, slashing them over and over till she finally slapped the Night Twins together and bowed, breathing hard.

Master Maeli gave a short nod, then plucked a blue spirit-fruit and threw it to her.

Tori bit into it. Her eyes widened. Energy rushed through her; it swirled in her stone kernel, shooting through her dawn channels, illuminating invisible pathways she hadn't even known existed. It was both ice and fire, breath and nourishment.

She took another bite, the juice tingling on her tongue. The fruit had the consistency of a juicy, ripe peach, but with the flavor of blueberries and raspberries and something indefinable.

"Regular spirit-fruits, like those in the Veiled Forest, nourish only dawn-essence," Master Maeli explained. "Though elixir now flows in our dawn channels, the body itself—flesh, bones, blood—is still made of essence and the six elements. This is why regular spirit-fruits invigorate the body. But blue spirit-fruits are something more: these trees drink from the crystal streamlet, which is a conduit of dawn-essence."

"So then, blue spirit-fruits nourish essence doubly?"

"Not merely essence, they work with the elixir itself, allowing it to exert its will over the body."

Tori glanced at the partially eaten fruit in her hand. The idea of the substance within her having its own will made her feel uneasy. She discreetly let the fruit drop. It burst into sparkles of light the moment it hit the ground, which in turn flew back into one of the silver trees.

Master Maeli smiled. "The elixir's will is always for good; following it always leads to life. It is the reason members of the Royal Tribe live on and on, when the world around them dies."

"So that's what immortals are, then."

"Some would call them that. But longevitists also have what they call 'immortals'—sect elders who have extended their lives by nurturing their dawn-essence. Still, the measure of immortality is greater for those in Peach Blossom Grove, those who continually eat the blue spirit-fruit; they age more slowly, and live longer." She turned slightly, and her star-jewel flashed in the sun. "Neither of these, however, are true immortals. Only those who have made the journey to Lake Kenjing can never die."

Tori tilted her head, trying to fit the pieces together. "So those who eat the blue spirit-fruit will die if they stop eating it?"

"Nothing really dies within the Veils, but yes, they would disappear forever. And sooner or later, many do, when they've had their fill of life. I've heard it described as the feeling one gets after a banquet. Though the food was good, and the company enjoyable, at some point, one is full, and ready to go home. Thankfully, this happens very slowly for our members," she said. "Master Kwai'le, for instance. He is one hundred seventy-five, yet he still looks like a man of sixty."

"He's not immortal?" Tori had never seen a star-jewel on the miserable alchemy master's forehead, but she had thought that was by choice.

Master Maeli shook her head. "True immortals all look young. Apart from white hair for some of us, we experience no aging, no subtle mental fatigue. We are always hungry for more, so to speak. And a true immortal can never be injured or killed. Although, in a sense, we have already died."

"Meaning?"

Master Maeli shook her head. "Another time. For now, all you need to know is that the elixir's will inhabits those who have tasted it. Follow it, and you will do well."

"You speak of it as though it's conscious," Tori said, hoping to be contradicted.

Master Maeli looked at her curiously. "You do know where the elixir comes from, do you not?"

Tori nodded. "Lake Kenjing."

"And you know how that lake came to be?"

"Yes, the elder told me. It was created by Ishairo's melted sword, which contained his stone kernel." She hesitated. "Though truthfully, I don't entirely understand the significance."

"One's kernel contains one's consciousness, one's spirit, one's life," Master Maeli said. "Therefore Ishairo and his sword were one. In a sense, then, Lake Kenjing *is* Ishairo—as is the elixir. Which means that yes, the elixir has a consciousness of its own. This is why we strive to obtain Unity with the Sword, as Ishairo did. It is the highest level of attainment anyone can achieve here at Peach Blossom Grove."

"What exactly is Unity with the Sword?" Tori asked.

Master Maeli looked thoughtful. "To different people, it means different things. But for me, it means becoming one with your weapon. With that in mind, begin your forms again. This time however, try to connect with your daggers, just as you would with the elixir; flow with them."

Tori focused on moving with precision, speed, and ferocity as she imagined fighting the bearlike thugs, and a sneering Keya.

But Master Maeli's voice broke through her thoughts. "Feel the blades, Tori. They are not separate from you—they are you."

The words struck something deep within her, and she closed her eyes. Instead of stumbling, her strikes came faster, her steps lighter.

By the end, Tori was drenched in sweat, her arms and legs trembling from the effort.

Master Maeli dipped her chin in approval.

The moment Tori had caught her breath, her master's gaze sharpened.

"Are you ready? Good. Again."

CHAPTER FIFTY-ONE

THE HARDEST THING

When Zinchen entered the loremaster's chamber again, Loremaster Jin was reaching for something on the top shelf.

"I have more questions about the Septad," Zinchen said, sweeping in. He turned suddenly, then winced, pressing a hand to his lower back.

She settled herself at the table and motioned him to do the same.

Two weeks had passed since she had begun her private study of Loremaster Jin's glyph book on the Septad, yet nothing was clearer.

"There is a matter of some sensitivity I would like your insight on," Zinchen said. "Can I rely on your absolute discretion?"

"You have my word, Your Majesty."

Zinchen dipped her head at Lina, who handed him Tori's letter. As he read it, a troubled look grew on his face.

"It appears," Zinchen said, folding her hands on the table, "that there are still people with the knowledge to make a Septad, and they are teaching the Min Daughter to do so. What do you make of that?"

He paused for several moments, as though carefully considering his response.

"Much knowledge has been lost on the creation of such things. But I can say that, with one exception, the Septad works similar to the Old Magic. Is Your Majesty familiar with how the Old Magic works?"

"Familiar enough," Zinchen said. It was something she had experienced all too closely in Tey Zuben. A half-buried memory floated into her mind of the Tey Zuben queen and the frightening things that had happened whenever she spoke. "What is the exception you speak of?"

He hesitated. "The queen who first made it was Ishairo's ancestor—a powerful wielder."

Zinchen lowered her brow. "I fail to see your point."

He lifted his rheumy eyes to hers. "I'm afraid that's what made it possible for her to create it, Your Majesty."

She let the implications of this sit with her. Tori was a wielder? The very idea was absurd. There had never been anything odd about Tori, apart from her naive sense of justice.

"Loremaster Jin, are you suggesting the Min Daughter might be a wielder?"

He lowered his eyes, but said nothing.

"I have seen my daughter almost daily since her birth. She would never have been able to hide her wielding from me."

"Hiding for that long would indeed be very difficult, Your Majesty. To a wielder, wielding is irresistible."

His words provided no comfort. She remembered then how Tori had rescued the wielders in the dungeon. Was it possible there was no lover, after all?

Her mind picked through any other odd things she might have witnessed, piecing them together, and the girl's odd movements at the Tailu Festival came back to her: she had pressed her hands to her stomach, as though trying to quiet it.

"Where does the wielding come from? Which part of the body, I mean."

"It comes from their stone kernel," the Loremaster said, "deep beneath the navel."

Zinchen forced her face to remain smooth, but anger simmered beneath the surface. How could her own heir be defective? She inwardly cursed the Tey Zuben midwife who had delivered Tori. The woman must have known.

No, it was Zinchen's own fault. She pressed her lips into a flat line. She should have expected something like this: How could anyone born in Tey Zuben not be tainted by the Old Magic?

And yet, wielding was not the same thing. The Old Magic, though sometimes frightening, had hummed through the fabric of the world since the beginning. Wielding elements, however, was inhuman; it was the very nature of Antiquitals. Her foremothers had identified it as a source of chaos, the enemy of civilization. It was the whole reason they had executed the Antiquitals, and had culled wielders till only the current remnant remained.

A thought struck her. Why did the crystal not ring at the naming ceremony, when Tori was named chief equitess-in-waiting? Zinchen's triumph that day would have been transformed into disaster; she would have been forced to act decisively against Tori, in order to save face.

A tender memory flickered in her mind of a little child stretching out her arms, calling her "mother." The thought of harming that child made her stomach sick.

Not to mention, the scenario would sabotage her plans. For one, Zinchen would be forced to ally with Prince Filo herself—which was courting disaster. His mother was the first complication: ambitious, possessive, and certain to demand influence over Jeng. The second was just as troubling. With Filo as intimate, Zinchen would have seventy-eight intimates instead of seventy-seven—an inauspicious number. If the people began to think her reign unlucky, the consequences could spiral quickly. And worst of all, the new Min Daughter would be her sister Ko-li's odious child. Ko-li had been a persistent burr under Zinchen's heel until the day she'd finally dealt with her, and her daughter, Yuchi, was cut from the same abrasive cloth.

Her temples throbbed, but she resisted the urge to rub them. She folded her hands on her lap. Her only hope—for Tori and for herself—was absolute control.

"Is there any way to stop wielding?" Zinchen asked. "A medicine, for instance."

"I've never heard of any, Your Majesty."

"What about controlling it, then? Or harnessing it; making it useful. Would the Old Magic perhaps work?"

He looked uncertain. "I suppose, in theory. If the Septad can control Antiquitals, certain Tey Zuben stones might perhaps control a wielder." He nodded slowly, considering this. "The stone would have to match the wielder's element. But if I may be so bold as to say so, I would caution Your Majesty to be careful with the Old Magic."

"Yes, yes," she said, waving a hand dismissively.

What he didn't know—few did—was that Zinchen could connect with the Old Magic. A residual gift, or curse, from her time in Tey Zuben. The power threading through her bones could bind with certain locks and keys she had acquired there, and until now, she had confined its use to this. But perhaps it could serve a broader purpose. She disliked the idea—but she disliked the alternative more.

Perhaps there was something in her box of Tey Zuben stones that would serve. She had failed to activate the one she had tried using during the Tailu Festival, but she was closer than ever to unlocking its function. If she could control Tori—bend her power into service—her legacy would be secured. And more than that, she might uncover a way to command all wielders. No more wasted potential. No more sawings befouling the town square. Instead, useful slaves.

Not to mention, she now knew there were people alive with the skill to create a Septad. Who knew what else they might be capable of?

The thought sent a quiet thrill through her.

"Lina, dispatch watchers to Greenstalk Village—no one the Min Daughter might recognize. I want eyes on her and those she is with. They are not to return until she is located."

Those teaching Tori this skill would have to be brought into Zinchen's service. Though the Septad would make her invincible in war, mastery of such craft could usher in a golden age, one to eclipse even the triumphs recorded in the *Chronicles of the Queens*.

But what if her plan for control failed?

She saw again the child with outstretched arms, and her chest tightened. She would be forced to do the hardest thing she had ever done—execute her own heir.

She pushed the thought away. Whatever came, she would face it—and, as always, she would use it to her advantage.

Chapter Fifty-Two

LETTERS AND REVELATIONS

When Tori arrived home the next night, Elnora met her at the door.

"I was thinking we could go to the communal dining hall tonight," she said.

Tori's heart sank; after a supplementary training session with Master Maeli, she was ravenous. "You didn't pick up dinner?"

"We've been here over one moon, Princess. Maybe we should start eating with everyone else."

"Everyone else lives here—we're visitors." Tori sighed. "Never mind. If you go now, I'll be dead from starvation by the time you get back. Give me a moment to change."

They walked along the watercourse, now lit up with glowing lotus flowers, passed the playhouse, and in ten paces more were standing in front of a white stone building with a brown-tiled roof.

Lanterns hanging from the roof's crescent-moon eaves swung lazily in the breeze, and light poured from the windows, illuminating the path outside.

Tori opened the door. Smells of scallions, ginger, and steamed bread made her mouth water. Though she had considered the food too plain only weeks before, now she couldn't wait for it.

The place was clean, well lit, and—despite the large number of tables—had a comforting, homey feel, as though everyone here was extended family.

Elnora pointed. "Look, there's Senrik and Ruvien."

The men were seated in the corner of the room. Tori searched for another table—she hadn't seen the men since her embarrassing display at Greenstalk, and couldn't bear the idea of them mentioning it—but Ruvien was already waving them over. Tori forced a smile.

"You're in luck," Ruvien said, scooting to make room for Elnora. "We just sat down." The table held enough food to feed ten people. How much did these men eat?

As he made space for Tori, Senrik greeted them with a nod. His hair was damp, and unlike her, he smelled fresh from a bath.

She discreetly scooted away, hoping his sense of smell wasn't as keen as hers, and thanked the Six she had taken the time to change out of her sweaty clothes.

Senrik lifted some fried roots from the main dish into his bowl. "I was impressed the other day," he said to her.

Tori stiffened.

"With your fighting. I've never seen someone come so far in such a short time."

She released a silent exhale. He was referring to her session with Keya, the lesser of her humiliations now.

"I have a long way to go," she said. "Five more moons before I can even take the one-bar."

"Five moons is a blink. Pour yourself into it, and you'll be surprised how far you come."

"Ruvien, could you pass the salt? We're all out." A girl at the next table had twisted around to look at them. "Oh, hi, Tori!" she said, smiling.

Ruvien passed her a small bowl that had been nestled between their food dishes. As she took it, she let her hand linger a moment on Tori's sleeve.

Tori tried not to react. *That's just how things are done here.* Even Elnora didn't object anymore.

Tori took a bite of pan-seared greens, and let her gaze drift around. People talked and laughed, some of them leaning over to speak to the people at the tables behind them, as though everyone was welcome in everyone else's conversation.

The door opened, and Master Maeli came in, then left a moment later with a basket. Tori thought of their recent conversation.

"What are your views on Unity with the Sword?" she asked, looking at Senrik and Ruvien.

Ruvien peered over the rim of his bowl as he shoveled noodles into his mouth. He jerked his head at Senrik. "Please don't ask him that," he said, chewing. "We'll be here all night."

Senrik ignored him. "Unity with the Sword means embracing your weapon fully, the way Ishairo did."

"I think that's Master Maeli's view, too," Tori said.

"It's the ideal, anyway."

"Your ideal, you mean," Ruvien said.

Senrik gave a small shrug. "Few ever get there."

"Have you?" Tori asked, remembering the ease with which he had sliced through the weapons rack.

"Some days it feels close. Other days, not so much. But when I train at the Waterwall—especially at night—it's different. Sometimes, it's like the sword and I understand each other." He gave a small nod toward the sword propped against the wall beside him.

Tori glanced around—was he the only one in the room with a weapon?

"What's the Waterwall?" Elnora asked.

Ruvien wiped his mouth, evidently surprised. "You haven't seen the Waterwall?" He looked at Senrik. "They haven't seen the Waterwall."

"They haven't been here long."

"It's the major feature of Ayenashi's Veil. You have to see it. They say it contains Ayenashi's treasure."

"Each of the Six hid a special treasure inside their Veil," Senrik explained.

"I've even heard it said that the treasure is an ancient being," Ruvien continued, "though I've never seen it. One of Ayenashi's High Water-creatures, her personal companion." He bit into a cloud bun. "Wouldn't surprise me, there's enough room for it; the wall goes on forever. Senrik and I once tried to find out where it ended. Walked all night."

"Did you find it?" Tori asked.

He shook his head. "Not sure it has one."

"Everything with a beginning has an end," Elnora said.

Ruvien shrugged.

"What's your view on Unity with the Sword?" Tori asked him. "I take it you don't agree with Senrik."

"Ruvien doesn't agree with anything that's good for him," Senrik said.

Ruvien leaned back easily against the wall and poured himself some wine. "Look, Ishairo was one with his sword. Literally. None of us can ever achieve that. I mean, my bow doesn't contain my stone kernel, right?" He took a drink. "And since we can never actually become one with our weapons, what's the point in even trying? Just live your best life, that's what I say. I mean, if you think about it, that's what Ishairo did."

Senrik gave him a long-suffering look and shook his head.

"So, what are your views?" Ruvien asked, eyes on Elnora.

"Don't ask me. I'm just a simple woman from a simple fishing village."

"There's no shame in humble beginnings," Senrik said. "Ishairo was the same."

Elnora shrugged. "Unity with the Sword is fine for immortals and wielders and whatnot. They can worry about all that kind of thing. Us regular people need to keep our hands on the net, as Granny used to say."

Ruvien raised his wine cup to her, then drank.

"The prophecies say Ishairo's heir will return someday," Senrik said, taking a sip of water. "We should all be ready."

Ruvien tsked. "Prophecies." Then a mischievous glint appeared in his eye. "They say the heir will be a sixfold wielder. Maybe one of your descendants, aye, Senrik?" he said, casting a meaningful grin in Tori's direction. Senrik choked mid-sip.

"Master Koren's a sixfold wielder," Elnora said.

"Too old," Ruvien said. "He's two hundred twenty-five. The Peach Blossom Grove prophecies say the heir will be two hundred—not that I believe any of that."

"Two hundred twenty-five years old," Elnora said, with the same wide-eyed, awestruck look that always crossed her face when immortals walked by.

"That's nothing," Ruvien said. "He and Master Maeli are the youngest ones on the council."

Tori tilted her head. "If they're the youngest, why does Master Maeli have white hair?"

"Her hair's been white most of her life. Story goes that she gave birth to a stillborn daughter when she was young—hair turned white overnight."

Tori pondered what level of grief could have had this effect on such a fierce, confident woman.

Muffled sounds from one corner of the room grew louder, then transformed into sobs. Everyone turned in that direction.

A young man stood between two immortals, sniffling and wiping his nose, while the immortals spoke in low voices, apparently trying to calm him.

As the immortals led him out the door, people from the young man's table pleaded with them not to take him.

The door closed, and a hush fell on the dining hall, leaving only a low hum of voices and the click of chopsticks.

"What's going on?" Tori whispered.

Ruvien's face had lost its cheer. "He wielded outside Peach Blossom Grove."

"What will they do with him?"

"Nothing. He's banished."

Tori remembered the warning at the top of the wielding scroll. "Why so extreme? I mean, why teach wielding and then banish someone for using it?"

"He's not banished for wielding," Senrik said. "He's banished for wielding outside Peach Blossom Grove. If he had been caught, it could have put the village at risk."

"That makes no sense at all," Elnora said. "Peach Blossom Grove is hidden."

"Wielders are criminals, by law," Senrik said. "That means they can be tortured. And under torture, anyone will talk—even about Peach Blossom Grove."

"What does it matter?" Elnora said. "We're the only ones who can get in."

"It matters because the forest would be patrolled. No one would be able to leave safely after."

Elnora nodded slowly. "Like master healers."

"Or peacekeepers," Senrik said.

"Plus, there's all those with relatives on the outside," Ruvien said. "Like Old Griff."

A prickle of irritation ran up Tori's neck at the mention of the loud, obnoxious fruit seller. "The one that's always screaming for money? Why doesn't somebody banish *him?*"

"I heard he needs money for his sick father," Senrik said.

"No, it's his mother," Ruvien said. He wrinkled his brow. "Or was it his aunt?"

Tori rolled her eyes. "See? He can't even get his story straight."

"Of course, if they did patrol the forest, I could always hide in the trees and shoot them," Ruvien said. "But I suspect the council may not like that."

"Hard to picture you sitting still long enough," Senrik said.

Ruvien drained his cup. "True. Didn't leave the Outlands to sit still."

"You're from the Outlands?" Elnora said, looking at Ruvien with interest.

He spread his arms and smiled. "Can't you tell?"

Tori finally placed his accent.

"I love Outlands herbs," Elnora said. "I've never met anyone from the Outlands before. Why did you leave?"

"Probably kicked out," Senrik said, with a quick smile.

Ruvien threw a cloud bun at Senrik's head, which he caught midair and finished in two big bites.

"I left because of my family's beast lore," Ruvien said, pouring himself another cup of wine.

"Your family are animal trackers?" Elnora asked.

He shook his head. "Papa makes bows, Mama made arrows—we sold them. But on her side, there's this old tradition to study magical beasts and record their habits in the lore book for whoever comes next. It meant something a few hundred years back, can't remember what. It was her passion, though. I'm hoping to finish it."

"How did you end up in Peach Blossom Grove?" Tori asked.

"I was going to ask you the same. When did you drink the elixir?"

"I had it as a baby, apparently, though I have no idea who gave it to me, or why. I can assure you no one at the palace knows about it. And you?"

"I heard rumors—beasts showing up around Ma'yanar. Figured I'd come take a look. Stumbled into Master Banfay in the middle of one of his trips. Senrik was with him, so he gave the elixir to both of us. The rest is history," he said, swirling his wine.

Elnora looked at Senrik. "Why were you traveling with Master Banfay?" Ruvien froze, wine cup to his lips.

Senrik ate in silence, eyes on the table. He finished chewing and swallowed. "He found me wandering. I killed some clansmen."

Chills rolled up Tori's spine, and all her dislike of the Ghenz came flooding back.

"They banished you?" Elnora asked.

"Ghenz don't get banished for killing clansmen," Senrik said with a mirthless laugh. "But families take revenge. It was better that I left."

He looked regretful. Tori almost felt sorry for him, but she checked herself—could any Ghenz truly be sorry for such a thing?

Her eyes drifted to his hands—large and menacing. She had wanted to believe he was different, but Senrik was just like the rest: a lawless, merciless killer.

"Why did you do it?" The words escaped before she could stop them.

"Raiding party gone wrong," he said, his voice heavy with what sounded like genuine sadness.

He drank his water, eyes downcast, so different from the confident fighter she had admired in the ring. She had known then that he was a warrior, but somehow hadn't thought of him as a killer. Was there a difference?

The door opened, and a boy walked through the hall, riffling through a basket that hung from his neck, then started handing out letters.

He approached Tori's table. "Letter for the sixfold wielder," he said, handing it to her with a flourish.

Tori thanked him and looked at the seal.

"It's from Yumay," she said, scanning the short page.

In typical Yumay fashion, the letter got straight to the point: her mother had met with the twelve countesses, but Yumay was unable to find out what had been discussed.

The letter boy stopped suddenly a few tables down, then came back to Tori. "Sorry," he said. "Missed this one."

Half expecting a postscript from Yumay, she eagerly took the new letter, but when her eyes fell on the seal, her stomach clenched. "It's from my mother."

As she unrolled the paper, a sense of unease set in. Was her mother writing to insist she return to the palace? Or was it some other demand?

She read slowly, sifting the lines for the unspoken message these letters always contained.

Unease turned to fear as she read it again, then rerolled the letter with trembling hands. It was heavier now, an iron bar instead of paper.

She took a slow breath, trying to convince herself she had misunderstood. But it had been painfully clear.

Her mother knew her secret.

Chapter Fifty-Three

BIRTH CHARM

A wave of nausea rolled through her, and Tori left the communal dining hall.

She soon found herself standing beneath a lantern on the floating gazebo, reading the letter again.

I trust by now you understand your mission fully—as do I. More importantly, I understand what makes it possible.

Let me be clear: the legacy of the foremothers is not to be gambled with for the sake of sentiment. Not even for the ones we cherish most. Pity weakens. Power sharpens.

Your duty therefore must be fulfilled without error. Finish your task quickly and return to the protection of the palace, before any misunderstandings arise.

You are my heir. It would be a sorrow to me if that were to change.

Anyone else who read the letter would think it spoke of inheritance. After all, the ancient laws—established in more perilous times—still held that an heir's claim could be challenged after eight moons of absence. Though Shudon was no longer a fractured land of warring queens, even now, in a unified Min, those old laws remained untouched.

Zinchen appeared to be urging her to return quickly, to protect her claims. But Tori read the message beneath the ink.

Footsteps creaked on the bridge, and a moment later, the gazebo shifted. Elnora leaned over the rail beside her, looking out onto the water.

Under the light of the gibbous moon, the lotus buds opened, petal by patient petal, until they glimmered like elegant lanterns, heartlessly serene.

"She knows," Tori said, handing Elnora the letter. "She wants me back under her protection—which, of course, means her control." Tori scrubbed a hand over her face. "She knows what the Septad is...what kind of people can make it. If I'm exposed as a wielder and bring shame to her name, she'll have me executed."

Elnora's brow creased.

"If I died, Cousin Yuchi would become Min Daughter. My mother hates her." Tori stared at the dark water. "Apparently she hates me more."

A face came to her: the wielder mother in the dungeon, begging on her knees to go to the saw instead of her son.

"I never expected my mother to be affectionate," Tori said, swallowing hard. "She is the empress, after all." She stopped talking—she must have sounded so weak.

Reaching into her pouch, she pulled out the smooth bone cylinder and tipped the birth charm into her hand. She absently passed the tube to Elnora, then gazed into the charm's swirling center.

The swirls had moved apart tonight, leaving a clear, undisturbed darkness that glowed faintly with little dots of light. It almost resembled its own sky, with its own tiny constellations.

Tori looked upward, and her eyes found Ishairo. A hundred tales of courage and honor flashed through her mind, tales that should have given her strength. But she was unable to find strength in any of them; all were meaningless in light of what she now faced.

The beating of wings sounded in the trees, and across the water, a crane soared into the sky, white against black.

Elnora suddenly caught her eye. Her face had turned pale, and her hands were tucked behind her, as though concealing something.

"What is it?" Tori asked.

Elnora's eyes were fixed on the charm. "There's something I need to tell you," she said, her voice soft and shaky. "About birth charms."

Tori waited.

"Back in Tenisha-ko, Granny was the midwife. One time, I helped her deliver a baby for the noble family over there. They paid her to get a birth charm, and when the baby was born, Granny pricked its heel and squeezed blood onto the stone. The blood disappeared, the stone glowed."

Tori nodded. "The charm glows when it fixes to a child."

"Granny tested it then, to make sure it was good. If the stone had been faulty, it would have absorbed her blood too, and then the light would have gone out. But Granny's blood rolled off, like when you drip water on wax. That's how she knew the stone was good, you see. When it's fixed to a baby, no one else's blood goes in."

"Except the mother's," Tori said.

"Right, because after that, Granny pricked the mother's finger. Since I'd never seen a birth charm before, I remember expecting her blood to roll off too, but the stone just sucked it in. Then it flashed."

"That's how they prove maternal lineage," Tori said, wondering where the story was going. "They do it a second time too, when a noble mother officially names her heir."

Elnora took a deep breath and held it, as though unsure she should say more. "Anyway, Granny linked the birth charm to a Certificate of Belonging. She said it's always done that way, so that you'll always know the original, since whenever the two come together, they both glow. That only happens if the charm and certificate were originally linked."

Finally something Tori didn't know. "Why are you telling me this?"

"You said the empress hid your birth charm because she wanted control," Elnora said, barely above a whisper. She licked her lips. "I don't think that's the reason." She hesitated—then finally brought her hands forward. "I don't know why I tapped the tube, I just did. There was a false bottom."

In her hands was a sheet of parchment, old, and sealed in one corner with a faded stamp. She held it beside the charm, and her face fell when they both pulsed with a soft, unmistakable glow.

Tori reached for the document, running her gaze over its swirling script, and an unexpected chill spread up her spine despite the warm summer air.

One line caught her eye:

Tori of Tey Zuben, a royal child...

The next line was blotted out entirely, replaced by words that made no sense: *...was adopted by Princess Zinchen of Min.*

The gazebo seemed to tilt, and Tori steadied herself against the rail. There had to be some mistake.

But the words were there, plain and unambiguous.

Denial turned to shock, shock to numbness. She gazed into the water, where fish shimmered beneath the circles of light cast by the floating flowers, as she sifted through the history of her birth.

Before Tori was born, it was known that her mother had been barren, and on that basis, her mother's sister had more than once attempted to take her place. But the sister's claims failed when her mother went to Tey Zuben on a diplomatic mission and returned with Tori nine moons later. People said it was the Old Magic in the Tey Zuben air that had changed things.

"My mother once said my birth secured her throne." Tori chuckled bitterly. "Now I know what she meant. I'm just another piece on her game board. After all, I'm not her daughter."

Her mother would do anything to sit on the Jeng throne, but if Tori's wielding were to be discovered, her mother would lose face, and possibly the people's support. Hence her mother's threat.

Yet something about this didn't quite fit. Tori's distaste for military strategy meant she had forgotten most of her mandatory lessons on the subject, but she did, however, recall one thing: when seizing a new land, the conquering queen should be present in order to maintain power. Her mother would know this—military strategy was one of her strengths.

But how could her mother possibly sit on the throne in Jeng? The Jeng people would never accept someone who had not descended from the Thana bloodline—that was a concept the Jeng held sacred.

Tori's mind returned to their last conversation at the palace, when she had warned her mother of triggering a revolt for this very reason. Yet her mother had been unperturbed, and had simply said Tori would help her. What could she have meant?

The answer came slowly. Tori rarely thought of her late father, Lord Tam; he had died when she was only three. But she remembered now that, though the family had since diverged into different branches, he had nonetheless descended from the first Thana empress.

She clenched her jaw, the realization bearing down on her like a leaden weight: though Tam was no more her father than Zinchen was her mother, it would be claimed that Tori had Thana blood. She would be Zinchen's puppet in Jeng, solidifying the rule of the House of Min.

If Tori refused, she would be executed. If she was revealed as a wielder, she would be executed. If she deviated in any way from her mother's control, she would be executed.

She stared into the black, empty horizon, letting this new reality sink in.

After all, I'm not her daughter.

Chapter Fifty-Four

A RARE SEED

The wall crystals seemed brighter in the dim, predawn light, bathing the alchemy cave the next morning in a soft green glow.

Tori paced the room.

I should able to push this aside. She was never really a mother to me anyway.

Instead, she hadn't slept because of the ache in her chest. The revelation of her birth along with the threat in her mother's letter made her feel like someone who had lived their whole life inside a scroll painting, thinking it was real, until a storm came, washing away the ink images, leaving nothing but ruined, sodden paper.

Never again would she take things as they appeared.

And yet, knowing she was expendable only made her want the Septad more, if only to beat her mother at her own game. If Tori was a game piece, she would at least be a piece that moved on its own—even if it was broken. And the Septad was the only thing that could possibly secure her win.

She would bring it to the palace, hidden, and let it disable every testing implement there. Then Tori would insist on being publicly tested by all of them.

She rubbed the spot between her brows, trying to think the steps through, but exhaustion engulfed her, and her eyes fell on Master Kwai'le's stuffed-silk chair.

As instructed, she had been at the cave at first light. He, on the other hand, probably wouldn't show up at all. She had heard he had spent the past three days trying to buy a messenger hawk.

She sank into the soft, welcoming silk and closed her eyes.

I'll set my own conditions. I'll refuse to be her puppet in Jeng. And I'll make sure she agrees, by refusing to hand over the Septad till she does. She will. She won't say no to that much power.

And the Septad really would save countless lives, Tori hadn't lied about that. No Ants would be slaughtered on the front lines. She really did want that, once her own life was secured.

"Nice to see you've made yourself comfortable."

Tori's eyes flew open, and she bolted to her feet.

Master Kwai'le stood in the doorway, eyeing her with unconcealed contempt.

She thought to apologize, but resentment stopped her. Why should she apologize for sitting down? He should be the one apologizing. He had kept her waiting, without even offering a decent place to wait.

She dipped her chin. "Good morning, Master."

He walked to the scrollshelf, muttering to himself. Then he bowed to the shelf, arms extended outward with an ornately carved scroll case on his open palms.

Tori had rarely seen anything so beautiful. It was snowy white, with gold engravings in the shapes of clouds and mythical creatures, and a gold cap at one end.

He slid it slowly into the padded cubicle. This had to be the priceless scroll he had spoken of.

"We'll be working on something unique today," he said, his voice still laced with irritation.

A rap sounded at the door, and the miller peered in, holding a silver-feathered hawk.

Master Kwai'le threw an exasperated glance at the rising sun. "Already?" He stalked forward, taking the bird, as well as the accompanying letter.

"Looks like he needs retraining," the miller said.

"I just bought him! Paid enough for him, too."

He set the bird on a perch beside the scrollshelf, then pointed to a bright blue homing stone on the counter. "See that? He was supposedly trained to home in on it, even if its twin gets lost." He lifted the identical stone hanging from the bird's neck. "Which it isn't."

The miller took his leave, and Master Kwai'le sat at the table, grumbling under his breath. "Best hawk you can buy, they said. Your troubles are over, they said. Charlatans. I've got a list of orders as long as my arm coming in from the Silver Cloud Mountain Sect—worth hundreds of gold petals—and the Bridge of Heaven Sect won't be far behind. I can't afford a bad hawk."

As he read his letter, Tori wandered over to the hawk stand. The bird regarded her with fleeting interest, then preened its silken plumage.

On the shelf beside her, the snowy-white scroll case they would be working on drew her eye. She slid it carefully from its cubicle, tracing her finger over a tiny gold lion with a fish's tail.

"Do not touch that!" Master Kwai'le's voice boomed from across the room. He rushed forward and grabbed the case from her hands. "This is not some palace toy."

Tori drew back, surprised. "I thought you said we'd be working on it."

"That's because you don't listen," he said, red with anger. "Now take your seat." He motioned pointedly to a hardwood chair. "*Your* seat."

Again he slid the scroll case into its cubicle. Then he reached into his pouch and produced a bright green seed the size of a pearl.

"*This* is what we'll be working on," he snapped. He took a deep breath, apparently trying to calm himself. "Master Koren believes it might be easier for someone with a hexatic ketua to begin with a seed."

Great. Master Koren again.

"This is from the Traveler's Vine, which you've no doubt noticed growing everywhere." His tone made it clear he had every confidence she hadn't noticed it. "In spite of its abundance, it rarely reproduces by seed, preferring instead to send shoots through the ground. Which makes this seed exceedingly rare. You will probably never find another. *I* have never found another. A lot of pains were taken to procure this one, which means I expect you to take extreme care with the way you handle it." He paused, eyes boring into her, then handed her the seed.

She took it carefully.

"The prolific nature of the Traveler's Vine makes its seed sensitive to the slightest touch of elixir, which means even someone with your"—he frowned—"*limitations* should be able to phytolyze it."

As though her inability to phytolyze plants was her fault.

And anyway, he shouldn't be wasting her time with seeds—she needed to learn about spirit stones.

He motioned to it. "Now remember, see in order to connect, then cycle it, and stream."

Ridiculous as this was, he obviously wasn't going to let her progress until she did it. She took a breath to center herself, sat in horse stance, then closed her eyes and tried to locate her elixir strand. But there was no trace of it, none of the ease she had felt when she had cycled it only days before.

He spoke, breaking her concentration. "No need to discern the element yet. Just see the elixir, cycle it, and stream it into the seed. This should be easy."

Discern the element? She could have sworn she read the term in Master Koren's wielding scroll.

The thought made her uneasy; the elements were connected with ketua. She took a breath, trying not to let this distract her.

"No, no." His voice dripped with impatience. "Were you not listening when I said this seed is rare? You'll drop it, holding it like that."

He plucked the seed off her palm and placed it in his own hand. "Like this," he said, and held it out to her again.

She arranged the seed in her palm precisely as he had done.

He furrowed his brow, removed it, then positioned it in the exact same spot. It wasn't even rotated. Irritation prickled her neck.

"Begin—and be careful this time. This is a rare seed. Do not to drop it."

She closed her eyes and tried once more to still her mind.

"Remember, see, cycle, stream," he said, breaking her concentration again.

As she searched again for the elixir strand, a loud exhale shattered her focus.

"Just see and trickle it, then. Even you should be able to manage that."

She gritted her teeth, pushing down her annoyance, and reached for the strand again.

"A trickle, I said. With a hexatic ketua, one would think you should be able to manage one trickle."

She rose out of horse stance, her sleep-deprived patience wearing thin. "Have you no respect for—"

"Respect?" His face grew dark, and his voice rose. "If you weren't the empress's daughter, you'd be nothing. Respect must be earned!"

Tori flinched as though she'd been slapped. She had been about to say, "respect for the fact that people learn differently."

"Now, stream!"

She kept her face placid, trying to find the elixir, pretending he hadn't struck her rawest nerve. But rejection constricted her chest, making it hard to breathe. She *wasn't* the empress's daughter.

Her hand shook, and in one horrifying moment, the seed fell and bounced several times on the floor. It rolled to a crevice in the wall, hovered on the edge, and disappeared.

Master Kwai'le threw up his hands and stormed out. She stared at the door, feeling bewildered and bruised and wronged.

Anger flared, and she clenched her fists, willing him to return so she could unleash her pent-up fury. But the moments passed, and her anger cooled, and soon all she felt was the bitterness of his insult.

A dark cloud seemed to cover the village as she walked home, in spite of the clear morning sky. What had she done to deserve this? Hadn't she deigned to submit, to bow, to call him master, even though he was so far beneath her?

The thought startled her. There it was: the pride he had implicitly accused her of.

But of course she had pride. She was the Min Daughter, for heaven's sake!

If you weren't the empress's daughter, you'd be nothing.

Her breath caught in her chest. She might be the Min Daughter—but that was all.

When she reached the cottages, two servants exited with a mop and a bucket, deep in conversation. They looked her straight in the eye as though they were her equals, smiled, and continued talking, without breaking stride. Her stomach churned oddly.

She lifted her chin—her pride was something innate; nothing could be done to change it. But she wasn't going to let his insults, or anything else, keep her from getting the Septad.

At her front door she halted, unwilling to go inside. Then she grabbed the handle and set her jaw, steeling herself for what had to be done.

CHAPTER FIFTY-FIVE

EUPHORIA

Tori leaned against the open door, staring into the dark sky outside her patio. She had been standing there since her alchemy lesson had been cut short, and had taken all day to build up her resolve.

Clouds obscured the stars, leaving the sky looking heavy and the air so oppressively thick that her robes clung to her humid skin. Though the smell of rain promised relief, no breeze stirred.

She mustered her courage at last, reminding herself that without the Septad, she had no bargaining piece, and she sat on the floor, unrolling the whole of Master Koren's scroll.

Laid horizontally, it stretched a surprising twelve handspans wide, obliging her to weight the ends down with stones. She skipped over the bold-lettered warning of banishment, quickly scanning the sections of script, drawings, and horizontal tables. She just needed to find enough to get herself started.

The first of the tables listed the five stone kernel levels, along with the abilities that could be expected at each. These differed depending on whether one was a wielder or merely a longevitist.

The section labeled *Stone Kernel Level 1* stated: *Can cycle the elixir to counteract certain poisons, and for minor self-healing of bruises, headaches, and sore muscles.*

Apparently, one didn't even need to be at kernel level one to do that. Her own leg soreness a few days ago had disappeared after cycling for only a short time.

A wielder can communicate with their sympathetic element to wield it according to their will, she read farther down. Gooseflesh rolled up her arms.

The next part, entitled *More on Communicating with the Elements,* was followed by notes about the sensations that indicated an approaching *kernel expansion*. She skipped it, along with the next few sections detailing stone kernel expansion itself.

At last, she came to the part she had been looking for—a full sequence of the wielding forms, with explanations. They were at the opposite end of the scroll from the initial drawings, as though Master Koren was deliberately trying to confuse matters.

She lowered herself into horse stance and tried to attain a state of calm, despite the persistent buzzing of gnats.

The instructions had said to find the strand of elixir and connect with it, then circulate it through her dawn channels. She forced herself to focus, trying to see or feel the elixir. The moment she glimpsed it, however, it disappeared.

She tried again, but again it eluded her, visible, yet intangible, like a warm breath in cold air.

The third time, in desperation she pleaded with it to stay, even though she knew that was pointless. But to her surprise, it worked. The elixir hovered, as though listening, and a hushed shiver of wonder traveled through her: the elixir could hear.

Circulating it came surprisingly easily after that. Once she began, the golden strand moved on its own, clear and strong, and much thicker than the last time. It was no longer the width of two hairs, but more like three or four. How was that possible?

As she flowed through the forms, the elixir flowed through her dawn channels, exhilarating her—until she sensed her *ketua*, the residual elements in her kernel that made her a wielder.

She set her jaw, determined to ignore it, but an odd sensation kept drawing her: it felt as though her ketua was feeding off the elements in her surroundings, sucking them in through her pores...and getting stronger. She knew she should resist, but an expansive joy filled her, a euphoria that lifted her, lightening her limbs and her heart, telling her all was well.

A distant image of Wan's face drifted by—serious, kind, cautioning.

I'll be careful, she thought, unworried, buoyed by the euphoria.

She continued, sweat soaking her robes, the euphoria strengthening her—along with her ketua.

An overfull feeling deep beneath her navel tugged on the edge of her mind. *What if I break Wan's seal?*

But her sense of euphoria answered: *All is well. Nothing else matters.*

Some far-off part of her felt dimly alarmed by this response, but a deep yearning silenced the protest before it could come—a yearning to touch the elements, to understand them, and to have them understand her. There was an inevitability about it all, like floating on a rushing river. The river would take her where it wished; struggling was pointless. There was nothing left but to yield.

A refreshing breeze blew through the house, and on the rooftop, rhythmic waves of rain pattered hard and soft, keeping time with her movements.

Suddenly, Veyli's little face appeared, smiling. The euphoria vanished.

A memory hovered, cutting and clear: Veyli's mother wiping dirt from the girl's body, weeping. She lovingly brushed off one of her little hands and crossed it over the girl's chest, then pulled up the other hand, doing the same, her grief blinding her to the shell that dropped out of the clenched fist, broken.

The memory faded, leaving Tori vibrating with a frustrated craving, hating herself for wanting more. How could she have allowed herself to enjoy wielding forms?

She pulled the broken shell from her pouch and stared at it, then buried her face in her hands.

What am I becoming?

A sharp tug in her belly produced a painful, frightening straining. She pressed a hand to her navel: she had almost broken the seal—she was sure of it.

The front door opened, and Tori kicked the stones off the scroll and threw herself into a chair.

The scroll rolled together as she grabbed the first thing she could find. It was the palm-leaf volume on the Antiquital tongue. She ran her eyes over the glyphs she had been studying, reading them effortlessly.

Elnora walked in with a basket smelling of wok-fire and garlic, her gaze drifting from the book to Tori's soaked robe, before raising an eyebrow. "Studying hard?"

"Au am ha ka hamakai," Tori said without thinking, fluent now in certain parts of the Old Speech.

"Wow. What does that mean?"

"It means, *I am as you see me.*"

Tori felt guilty for the deception, and for her instinct to hide from Elnora. She put the book back on the shelf. "Except it's not true. I was doing the forms," she said, unable to say *wielding* forms.

Elnora nodded as though that were perfectly normal, and lifted several covered bowls from her basket onto the table.

As they ate, the elements in her kernel seemed to nourish themselves as well, pulling from her surroundings at an alarming speed. Would Elnora have herbs that could stop it?

"Something odd happened while I was doing the forms," Tori said, but her words just wouldn't flow; she couldn't bring herself to voice her fear that the seal might be breaking. "I'm never doing them again," she said instead.

Elnora put down her chopsticks, looking thoughtful. "You know, Princess, I've come to realize wielding isn't what we thought."

Desire flared inside Tori, but Veyli's face returned, and guilt snuffed the craving out.

"I won't betray her memory," Tori said, then rose and went to her room, yearning for another taste of euphoria.

Chapter Fifty-Six

THE TRAVELER'S VINE

As the alchemy cave came into view, Tori's slatted bamboo lantern cast a soft glow onto the gravel path, and the first pink slivers of dawn appeared in the sky.

The heartsoreness she thought she had left behind the day before came flooding back as she reached for the door.

Perhaps he won't come, she thought. He didn't seem to like his new messenger hawk; he might spend the day buying another one.

Master Kwai'le's voice, however, drifted out before she could console herself further. "Home!" he said.

The sound of fluttering wings followed.

"No, not to the old stone. To this one!"

Inside, Master Kwai'le was adjusting a red homing stone around the hawk's neck, where the bright blue one used to hang. He set the bird on its perch, ignoring Tori's greeting, then picked up an identical red stone from the counter on the opposite side of the room.

"Home!"

The hawk flew to him and stood on his arm.

"Good, good," he said, feeding the hawk from a bowl. "I think we're finally getting it."

He shot Tori a brief glance and pointed to the table. "You can thank my hawk for that."

Sitting in the middle of a plate was a bright green seed. *The* seed. Her cheeks flushed.

"Next time, you'll be the one who digs it out of the cracks."

Servants' work.

If you weren't the empress's daughter, you'd be nothing.

She tightened her jaw—what if the wielding forms she had done the night before had all been for nothing?

"Well, don't just stand there, get on with it, " he said. "And this time, no sitting—the elixir sometimes circulates more effectively when we're on our feet."

He set the hawk on its perch, then returned to the counter and picked up the homing stone. "Go on," he said, with an impatient gesture, the moment she reached the table. "It's not like you have time to lose."

Tori kept her face smooth. She refused to give him the satisfaction of a reaction.

Once she was in horse stance, she located her elixir strand quickly. The size of it surprised her; it was now several hair strands thick.

She circulated it easily, like she had the night before, and just like the night before, it took off, moving on its own, filling the reservoir in her stone kernel with each cycle. In her mind's eye, she reached into her kernel to pull on it, then streamed it effortlessly through her hands. When she did, it seemed like the elixir itself reached for the seed, guided not by her, but by its own inner knowing.

Sharp cracking sounds snapped through the air, and a pale green point pushed out from the seed. It stretched upward, deepening in color as it grew, and several bright green leaves sprouted.

Master Kwai'le's head jerked up. He placed the homing stone on the counter and walked over, then picked up the plate with the seedling, clearly trying to hide his astonishment.

"I guess this wasn't a total waste of time," he said. "Continue."

She did. The plant fluttered, as though brushed by a breeze, then jerked once and shot up half a handspan high, branches pushing outward like little arms with tiny leaf-hands.

The thrill of success flooded her, and she smiled at the Traveler's Vine. A mouth-shaped crease in its upper leaf almost looked like it was returning the smile, like it was happy for her. She sent one more tiny stream of elixir to it, and the plant clapped its hands.

Master Kwai'le looked irritated. "If you don't take things seriously, you'll never make any progress."

"What? My proof of progress is sitting right here."

"You've barely grasped the basics—quite belatedly, I might add. We haven't even moved on to actual alchemy." He walked outside.

Tori followed. *Then why in the name of the Six aren't you teaching me?* she wanted to say.

"Any village healer can make medicines from plants and let the plants' natural elements do the work," he said. "Alchemy, however, is another skill entirely. It requires very specific ingredients grown to very specific ages." He clasped his hands behind his back. "Take the essence-building tablet, for instance. All of its plants must be phytolyzed to exactly five hundred fifty-five days." His expression made it clear he thought she would never manage this. "The silver dog-leaf pill requires plants to be seven hundred seventy-three days. And these pills are just the simple ones."

She hated how much the idea daunted her. Maybe it would be different with spirit stones.

"It's the same with spirit stones," he said, and leaned over a box. He lifted out a gray mushroom no bigger than the nail of her little finger, placing it in her hand. "This is Lion's Cap fungus. Phytolyze it to exactly nine days."

"How do I do that?" she said.

He gave her a long-suffering look, then folded his arms and waited.

Evidently she was expected to puzzle it out. Some teacher he was.

She sifted through all she had learned so far: her imagination had helped her stream the elixir, and she had also imagined the seed growing before it actually did. Maybe this worked the same way, and she just needed to imagine the mushroom nine days old.

She connected with the elixir, then stopped: What would it even look like at nine days?

You'll work it out, she told herself, closing her eyes. Master Banfay's words returned to her then: *We cycle—and are guided by—the elixir.* Only it wasn't his voice she remembered; the words rose from within her—a whisper, threaded with a deep knowing: the elixir needed to guide her.

She connected with the elixir again, cycling it till it moved on its own through her dawn channels. Then she streamed it outward and simply relaxed, following the elixir's lead, directing it however it willed her.

When she opened her eyes again, the mushroom had grown to the circumference of an apple, with a yellow ruffle around the edge.

Master Kwai'le furrowed his brow. "It's not a true skill till you can repeat it over and over with the same result."

He gave her another, and she repeated it. Then he gave her three more, each time instructing her to phytolyze the mushroom several days older than the one before it. She succeeded every single time.

"All unusable," he said, placing them in the box and dusting his hands.

A prickle of irritation sprouted up her neck. If they were unusable, why didn't he throw them away?

He reached into a red box that was set apart from all the others. "Bleeding pine, six moons old," he said, handing her a tiny pine tree no bigger than her hand. "Phytolyze to exactly eight years, three days." A smirk shifted on his lips.

Tori connected with the elixir, surrendering to its will. A steady stream flowed through her hands, then dwindled to a trickle and finally stopped.

She was now breathing heavily; she had used more elixir than she had thought, and the reservoir in her kernel was completely spent, apart from a few drifting embers. But the tiny pine looked exactly the same.

"Here we go again," Master Kwai'le mumbled, but before he could say more, the plant in her hand suddenly pushed up, sprouting so quickly Tori had to drop it.

Roots tunneled eagerly into the ground, while its trunk thickened moment by moment, reaching upward to the sky. In the time it would take a candlewick to catch, its mass overshadowed them both.

Master Kwai'le stared at it, no longer smirking.

Smugness stirred in her chest, and she smiled the smallest of smiles. "Satisfactory?"

"It's off-center."

"You didn't tell me to center it."

"Do you have to be told everything? Aren't nobles meant to exercise their judgment and take the initiative?"

"Is there a problem with me being noble?" Her neck heated.

"There's a problem with students who don't take things seriously, do subquality work, and then expect to be congratulated for it," he said, turning to walk inside.

She inhaled slowly through her nose, as though breath alone would keep her from snapping. "I did everything you told me," she said, following close behind. "And I don't need your congratulations. What I need is for you to teach me what I actually came here to learn. I'm supposed to be making the Septad."

"For that, you need top-grade spirit stones," he said, turning back to his counter. "You haven't even started the low-grade ones."

"Then why are you wasting my time with plants?"

"Think, Princess—think!" he said, spinning to face her, tapping a finger on his temple like she was an imbecile.

Pent-up frustration exploded inside her, and she was talking before she could stop herself.

"I've had enough of your insults. Like your lessons, they're clumsy and aimless. Now if you're going to teach me, do it. But I'm done being talked down to." She glared, her breath coming quick and shallow.

His mouth went tight. "You refuse to be taught because you think you know everything already. You're a sorry excuse for an apprentice. Just a spoiled, self-important princess."

Tori shook with anger. "And you're a pompous, condescending teaching disaster!"

His eyes blazed. Then, all at once, he strode to the hat peg, slapped on his hat, and flung open the door.

"You're finished here. I'm going to see to it that you never come near alchemy again."

The door slammed.

The hawk jerked up its head and threw her a questioning look. She stared at the closed door for a long moment, trembling with anger. In an effort to calm herself, she walked over to the hawk and held out a hand, which it immediately nuzzled.

As she stroked its head with a finger, her anger slowly waned, and nervousness took its place.

What had she done?

She should leave. But if he returned to find her gone, it could make matters worse.

Not knowing what else to do, she stood petting the hawk, mentally replaying the scene. What a fool she had been, losing control like that.

But with every self-reproach, fresh anger replaced remorse.

I had every reason to say what I did. He should apologize to me!

Yet a master would never be made to apologize to his student; she knew that as well as anyone. And now she had just jeopardized everything.

Her nervousness increased. He had threatened to keep her from studying alchemy—not just with him, but at all. She paced the room, petted the hawk, then paced the room again.

"He wouldn't really do that, would he?" she asked the hawk.

It nuzzled her hand.

A sharp knock rattled the door, and a man in a green messenger's tunic peered in. "Tori?"

She squared her shoulders and nodded.

"The elder has summoned you," he said. "She's waiting."

Chapter Fifty-Seven

GLORIUM

The messenger's words had been ice in her dawn channels. Who knew what Master Kwai'le had told the elder? As she walked along the cliffs toward the waterfall, she cursed him silently.

Then she cursed herself. She should be someone who could own up to her mistakes when she faced the elder; she should present clear motives for her actions, yet without evading responsibility. But Master Kwai'le was wrong—how could she take the blame?

I have to win over the elder, convince her I did the only possible thing. Except she wasn't sure it was true.

Tori clenched her jaw. Her position as Min Daughter was a sham, her influence in the world was tenuous, and now her success at Peach Blossom Grove dangled like an old leaf in autumn.

When she reached the waterfall, she stood for several breaths, trying to calm her nerves. The flowers trailing down the rockface shone warm and bright in the setting sun, and rainbows shimmered from the mist of the falls as it slipped into the turquoise pond.

She rounded the pond and studied the tall, narrow staircase. Although not as shaky as she had been the first time, she was by no means reassured, and pressed herself against the damp cliff as she climbed.

Mist sprayed her face when she reached the top, and she stood on the ledge, heart pounding from its narrowness and height. She glanced at the deepening blue sky, dreading the dark descent that awaited once her meeting was through, then took a breath and hurled herself through the falls.

As before, the cold force of it sent her stumbling into the darkness, shivering. She instinctively closed the neck of her drenched robes, blinking the green crystals into view. The arched entranceway showed itself, and she headed toward it.

An enormous, multiheaded shape moved toward her. Tori clapped a hand over her mouth to keep from crying out, but Theliane looked her over with benign disinterest.

Three deep voices spoke in unison. "Come. You must wait by the fire."

Tori followed the nine-headed dog past the statues of Ishairo guarding their porticoes and into the cavern, its multiple levels now dark with evening, apart from the fire that blazed in the fireplace that looked like a tiger's mouth.

Two of Theliane's heads picked up cushions and dropped them beside the fire, while another nodded at Tori to sit.

Her clothes were dry by the time the elder arrived and sat at the stone table. She motioned Tori over.

The elder looked into her face, and Tori's breath caught: her blind white irises had brightened into silver. As she peered across the table, no displeasure showed on her face, but her keen eyes seemed to note Tori's every thought and failure.

Tori looked away.

"Though you are one moon early," the elder said, "it appears I must now assess your progress."

Every coherent thought fled Tori's mind.

"Master Maeli is satisfied, though she fears you are too impatient at times," the elder said. "Yet I deem such a trait to be tolerable in the young. Though not ideal, it is, in truth, inevitable." Her silver eyes sharpened. "Master Kwai'le, however, finds you"—she paused—"unsuitable for the study of alchemy. And in this matter I must heed his counsel. You are therefore released from this discipline. If it is your will, you may continue your lessons with Master Maeli and train as a peacekeeper."

Disappointment sank like a stone inside her chest. The Septad was out of reach.

"Now you must go," the elder said. "As the night has fallen, and you are yet unpracticed in the descent from the falls, Theliane will bear you home upon her back."

Irritation flared inside her. Master Kwai'le was the one who had behaved wrongly—and now she was the one who was punished?

"Elder, I know I spoke out of place, and for this, I apologize, but Master Kwai'le put me in a position where I had no choice."

The elder frowned. "A quick temper is also common among the young—a trait I do not deem acceptable. As a student, you should have endured, rather than let your temper rule you, for no matter his faults, disrespect toward one's master shall not be suffered in Peach Blossom Grove. He has wisdom to impart, and you have much yet to learn."

He wasn't imparting anything—that was part of the problem.

Master Kwai'le had mentioned he had never found a worthy protégé, which must mean he had past apprentices. Though they may not be masters, if he had trained them, they were bound to be good enough.

"Can't someone else teach me? Surely there are other alchemists in Peach Blossom Grove?"

"That is beside the point. Even if there were others, they would first seek the counsel of Master Kwai'le, and who, pray, would wish to take on a pupil who shows no respect for their master?"

Tori dropped her gaze to her lap, her cheeks hot. How could she have been so foolish as to let him provoke her?

"But none in all of Arizan possesses his mastery," the elder said. "Nor is there another with the skill to impart such knowledge as you require. In truth, he alone is capable of teaching you." The elder's silver eyes were grave. "We must strive to understand the reasons behind another's manner, for only then may we respond with wisdom. Master Kwai'le bears a past most burdened on account of the nobility," she said. "I may not say more, for the tale is not mine to speak. But know this: because of this past, he shall never attain immortality, though he desired it above all else."

As much as she hated him, the injustice of it moved her. She tried not to care.

"But he's practically immortal anyway. As long as he eats the blue fruit, he'll live as long as he wants."

"Not as long as he wants. Every mortal body must, in time, wither and fade. And yet, for the very same price, he might have lived forever."

"What price?"

"The price that Suro herself did set, when she looked with favor upon Ishairo's sacrifice. For she remembered the intent of his heart and the longing of Ketuan, her daughter, that a Royal Tribe should ever endure to reign in Arizan. Thus did she give her assent to Ishairo's will and decreed that whosoever, being mortal, shall drink of the waters of the lake formed by the melting of his blade, and thereafter offer themselves upon the altar of Suro—as Ishairo once did—embracing death in the lake with his same fearless heart, shall be granted immortality in Ishairo's stead."

Tori furrowed her brow. "Isn't the whole point of immortality precisely so you *don't* have to die?"

The elder peered at her, silver eyes bright, silver hair gleaming in the firelight. "Only the one who dies shall truly live."

Gooseflesh rippled up Tori's arms.

"The wise know well that death is an end none may escape," the elder said. "Thus, it is but a small price to pay in exchange for immortality. Yet perhaps that is a discourse best left for another time. Now, you must go."

The words snapped Tori back to the present, and a sharp ache deepened within her. The elder was right: she was the one who needed Master Kwai'le, not the other way around.

She should have held her tongue until she got what she needed—she had done the same countless times in the palace. Had the fact that he wasn't a nobleman changed the way she had treated him? The thought shamed her.

And besides, his behavior—unacceptable as it was—had done nothing to diminish the total well-being she felt at Peach Blossom Grove.

"Please," she said, her voice hoarse with emotion, "it's the only thing that will stop my mother's war."

The elder's eyes settled back to bland white, and her gaze, thoughtful, drifted past Tori.

Tori waited, her throat tight.

"Before you lies a destiny of great weight," the elder said at last, "yet its full shape is shrouded from my sight." She lifted her voice. "Theliane."

The nine-headed dog padded in, one head carrying a purple pouch embroidered with gold, which she laid in the elder's hand.

The elder pulled out a smooth white stone with iridescent veins.

Tori's eyes widened. She had seen many treasures in her life, but never one like this. An opal was the closest comparison she could make, but its veins were many times more vibrant—and they glowed.

As the elder turned it over in her hand, the veins flashed. "This is a glorium, a spirit stone of the earth element."

She removed a gold chain then from the pouch. Hanging from its middle was something like a finely wrought gold net, and she slipped the stone into it.

"It is the last of its kind, most likely," the elder said. "Such stones were birthed in the hidden places of the world, in long ages past. This one I discovered myself upon Mount Ketwanen, three thousand years ago."

Three thousand years.

She struggled to grasp such a timespan.

The elder slid the glorium across the table. "Though your fate is shrouded, yet one thing I have clearly seen: you were meant to have this stone. Therefore take it now; it is my gift."

As Tori searched for words worthy of something so ancient, so priceless, hope and dread battled within her: Was this confirmation that she could keep training—or a signal of its end?

"Your desire to continue despite your discouragement," the elder said, "may perhaps be a sign of that which I cannot perceive."

Hope stirred briefly, but the elder's grave expression crushed it before it could rise.

"I shall not hinder you, yet Master Kwai'le is the one with whom the decision lies. If you wish to continue your alchemy, you must convince him to accept you once more."

Chapter Fifty-Eight

SPIRIT SENSE

The meeting with the elder had left Tori so distracted that Master Maeli canceled the next day's dagger lesson and sent her off to "contemplate nature."

The day after that, Tori stood at the door of Master Kwai'le's cave, fists curled to keep her hands from trembling. Would he throw her out the moment she stepped inside?

She took a breath and eased open the door to find Master Kwai'le standing at the hawk perch, his back to her.

"Master," she said, bowing low. The words came with difficulty, though she had rehearsed them more than once: "I acknowledge my mistake. With your permission, I'd like another chance to try."

He turned, features tightening with displeasure at the sight of her—but when his gaze landed on the glorium hanging from her neck, displeasure shifted to puzzlement, then to contemplation. Tori remained silent—he had the look of someone weighing a matter, and she feared saying more would tip the balance against her.

After a while, he glanced at the drizzle that had begun to fall outside the open door, then, without a word, he reached for the bamboo hat on its peg.

"Please, Master, I—"

"Well, don't just stand there," he said, putting on his hat and walking outside. "We have to move fast if we want to catch the ghost flowers." He raised a hand as though touching raindrops, then turned and strode away.

The rain misted her face as she hurried after him. He had not accepted her, or even acknowledged her apology—but he hadn't thrown her out, either; something about the glorium had apparently bought her time. She worked through the implications and saw this was a test: if she impressed him today, he might just let her stay on.

After about the time it would take a candle to burn, they arrived at part of the Veiled Forest Tori had never seen, where the ground was chalky white instead of black, and sloped upward toward a group of trees that looked like giant mushrooms with grassy tops. As they neared, the trees turned out to be over three hundred handspans tall, with black scales instead of bark, and trunks that split in two far above their heads.

"This is Dragon Blood Hill," he said, "and these here are dragon-blood trees."

"I've never heard of them," she said, hoping to impress him with her humility.

"And yet the species dates to ancient times when a dragon died in Outer Shudon. Trees sprang up from its blood, and the species was born. In time, some of their seeds were brought into the Veil."

As he spoke, they sheltered from the drizzle beside one of the long, straight trunks. Tori craned her neck to view the top; a network of narrow branches gave the impression of the underside of a mushroom, and the top was not covered in grass at all, but in long green needles.

"Fewer and fewer exist nowadays," Master Kwai'le said, running a hand down the black scales. "Their popularity as a medicine has worked to their detriment, because most lack the skill to use the trees without destroying them entirely. But those in the Veils are safe—this one, for instance, is over eight thousand years old."

He led her to another tree with a wide gash on its trunk that looked like a bloody, gaping wound. Tori ran her fingertips over it. Smooth red resin had dried on the surface, like clotted blood.

"What happened to this one?"

"That's part of our lesson today," he said. "But first, on to ghost flowers. To identify ghost flowers, you must first identify their element. Which is?" He clasped his hands behind his back.

"Air," she said.

"Correct. It is also the flower most closely connected with the Ghost Stone, which you would need in the unlikely event you were to advance enough to make the Septad."

"Yes, the elder mentioned it," she said, ignoring the slight and trying to showcase her knowledge. "It's one of the only stones needed for the Septad that isn't found in Ketuan's Veins."

"It's one of two," he corrected. "The glorium is the other." His eyes lingered on it for a beat.

She brushed her fingertips across the stone, its true worth finally coming into focus. Not only was it the last such stone in all of Arizan, but without it, making the Septad would have been impossible.

By making the gift, the elder had implied Tori was both worthy and capable: worthy to receive it, and capable of making the Septad. It was this quiet vote of confidence that had kept Master Kwai'le from rejecting her outright, for although the decision was ultimately his, if he meant to diverge from the elder, he would need to be certain of his reasons.

Tori tried to still her nerves. Everything really did depend on impressing him today.

"Because the Ghost Stone is of the air element," he continued, "its very nature causes it to disperse itself from Ketuan's Veins into the six Veils. Having said that, I don't think it's possible to find it. Not only would it require one to possess a more sensitive spirit sense than anyone I know—including Master Koren—but also, not unlike etched weapons, it is the stone that does the choosing. If it wishes to remain hidden, nothing will reveal it." He glanced at the glorium again. "However, we will see how you do with the flowers."

The drizzle turned into a shower, which rolled off his wide hat and surrounded his body in a circle of pouring water as he pulled a knife from his robe and examined the wounded tree. Though Tori stood close to the trunk, drips fell through the branches and soaked the crown of her head.

"Now, though ghost flowers are extremely difficult to identify on a rainy day, they are impossible to identify otherwise. With luck, however, I'll be able to find one so you can at least train your spirit sense to the air element."

"But if you can find the flower, doesn't that mean you're sensitive enough to find the stone? I mean, assuming it chose you."

He shook his head. "Though the ghost flowers feed on the dawn-essence of the stone, this is the air element we're talking about—its energy could emanate from anywhere within a five fen radius, sometimes far beneath the ground. Unlike with common spirit stones, digging up the plant would do no good—you'd have to dig up the entire forest. No, the point here is simply to train your spirit sense. Once you do, you can then learn to follow the meandering path of the air element to the point where it is strongest. Why?"

"Because the stronger it is, the closer you are to the stone?"

He gave a nod.

When he had sliced a strip from the wounded tree, something that looked like blood poured down the smooth black scales, puddling on the ground.

Suddenly, droves of scorpions swarmed in from every direction. Tori jumped aside, into the rain, but they still scuttled over the tips of her toes, feeding on the tree's blood. She shivered. Some were as big as her hand, with shells like metal shields and tails ending in vicious double stingers.

"Shield scorpions feed on the sap of the dragon-blood tree," Master Kwai'le said calmly, "also known as dragon's blood. And since the scorpions' shells are essence-reflective, it's impossible to use your spirit sense on the parts of the ground where they have made their homes. So this how we clear them."

"But why clear them here?"

"Ghost flowers tend to grow in the same areas as dragon-blood trees, but you can't sense their dawn-essence if the scorpions' shells are blocking them."

He pulled off a piece of dried resin and handed it to her. "Clotted dragon's blood will also do the trick in a pinch, though it takes longer. Incidentally, it's a good pain remedy. Keep it."

Rainwater from the branches blew into Tori's face, and she stepped back, wiping her eyes. Her gaze drifted to the ground as her foot landed beside a large scorpion. She jerked away, but it had already whipped its tail and pierced her shoe, burying its double stingers into her flesh before scuttling off.

She stumbled against a tree, pain radiating from her foot all the way to her knee. But when she slipped off her shoe, horror filled her: a large black hole had appeared on the flesh, surrounded by sickly green rot. She whimpered as the hole widened, the web of rot traveling to her ankle.

Master Kwai'le grabbed the creature that had stung her. It buried its stingers into his hand, but instead of leaving a rotting hole, green venom oozed from the wound, which closed and disappeared without a trace.

"Though they're not normally dangerous, once shield scorpions get a feel for stinging people, they never stop," he said, ripping off the scorpion's tail and claws, till only a shiny gray shield with twitching legs remained.

While Tori's body pulsed with pain, turning every raindrop into a burning lead weight, Master Kwai'le unhurriedly cut the belly open with his knife and plucked out a stone the size of a blueberry, only orange-colored, and glowing from within. He tossed aside the scorpion's body, which burst into sparkles that disappeared into the earth.

It was only after he had wiped the stone and tucked it away that he pulled out a porcelain bottle and tipped three shiny green pills into his hand.

"These will help," he said.

Grimacing with pain, she took the pills and swallowed them.

The rotting green web—which had now reached mid-leg—stopped its spread, then reluctantly shrank along with the hole as green venom oozed from the wound. A few breaths later, the wound had closed, leaving just a small circle of tender pink flesh.

She tested her foot.

"All better?" he asked.

Still sore, but nothing like before.

She nodded and thanked him. "What were those pills?"

"A simple formula made with shield scorpion venom. Not that you needed it, though; the elixir would have cleared your blood if you had bothered to cycle it."

How could she have possibly cycled elixir while suffering that kind of pain?

"Why didn't the venom affect you?" she asked, deflecting the focus away from herself.

"Blue spirit-fruit; I eat it every day." He lowered his brow. "As should you. The blue spirit-fruit allows the elixir to quickly eliminate sickness, disease, and, in this case, poison—not to mention extending your life," he said. "At my age, I'd die without it. Which is why I can never leave the Veil for more than a moon at a time."

He held up the orange stone he had taken from the scorpion. "Now, tell me what this is."

It was like nothing she had seen before, an orange stone that glowed with an odd bluish light.

Still, while humility was one thing, complete ignorance might ruin her chances with him entirely. She ventured a guess. "It appears to be a spirit stone," she said, then regretted it the moment she had spoken: spirit stones came from the earth.

But he said, "It is. Magical creatures—such as shield scorpions—have a stone kernel, like us. They feed on plankton and small plants, which in turn feed on the unseen particles of spirit stones that originate in Ketuan's Veins and run throughout Arizan. After many years, those particles accumulate in the kernels of magical creatures and form a special type of spirit stone. They are not useful for medicine, but they can be very useful for expanding one's kernel. Longevitist sect members, for instance, use them whenever they can."

Though the very idea of stone kernel expansion felt distasteful, she was determined to show an interest. "How do they work?"

"You swallow them. I'll sell this one at the next sect auction. Now, let's move on," he said. "We've wasted enough time already."

The clouds burst into a downpour, soaking Tori to her skin as she followed him through Dragon Blood Hill. His gaze roved back and forth, pausing now and then to squint at the empty air.

After they had been walking a while, he stopped abruptly, making a gesture for silence. He pointed between the trees a few paces away: an adorable white bunny with a pink nose and blue eyes sat between two patches of yellow flowers, nibbling at the empty air.

"Speaking of magical creatures," he said in a bare whisper, "that is a ghost rabbit."

The image of him ripping out the shield scorpion's spirit stone came to her. "Please tell me you're not going to kill it."

He gave her an odd look. "Killing magical creatures is forbidden in the Veil of Ayenashi, unless absolutely necessary. Now, if you're finished flaunting your ignorance, pay attention to that bunny; ghost rabbits feed on ghost flowers."

But it wasn't nibbling anymore; it had started cleaning its face with its paws.

"It's full," he said, letting out an impatient breath, and he threw a pebble at it. Tori froze: the bunny vanished like mist.

"Like ghost flowers, the ghost rabbit can become invisible," he said. "Unlike the flower, however, the animal may disappear at will."

He walked over to where the bunny had been, then stooped and studied the ground.

"Ghost flowers mimic many varieties of ordinary flowers," he said, brushing his hand slowly through the air. "They put up shoots among the ones they imitate, making them nearly impossible to distinguish. In the rain, however, the ghost flower disappears entirely, meaning that the first place to look is for bunches of flowers with chunks missing. Since the ghost rabbit was here, this would have been an excellent place to start," he said, "but it seems to have devoured everything. You'll need to find another. Use your spirit sense. First, you must connect with the elixir; then, while connected, reach out with it and try to sense the elements." He turned away, scanning the ground around him.

The thought of sensing the elements disturbed her—it sounded too much like wielding—but she couldn't risk him thinking her incapable.

She lowered into horse stance, connected with the elixir, and cycled it, but when it came time to reach out with her spirit sense, she realized with a sinking feeling that she had no idea how.

A shuffling noise approached and, fearful of more scorpions, Tori shifted her gaze to it. She let out a breath—just another ghost bunny, standing so close she could reach out and touch it.

Though its fur was wet, it still looked impossibly soft. It noticed her then, but instead of vanishing, it met her gaze with wide, dewy eyes. Tori's heart melted.

"Aw, look at you," she said, reaching out the way Master Maeli had taught her with the tiger, drifting a finger toward its fuzzy little head.

Suddenly, the bunny lunged, giving her a sharp bite. Blood welled continuously from her finger, despite the rain washing it away. The bunny darted off, turning invisible mid-run.

"Why in the world did you do that?" Master Kwai'le said, coming to peer at the hand she was now cradling.

Embarrassment burned her face. "It was cute."

"Magical creatures are dangerous. *Especially* the cute ones." He shook his head.

"But Master Maeli said there were no dangerous animals in the Veil," Tori said, feeling the need to justify herself.

"She was talking about *regular* animals. Magical creatures are not regular animals." He shot her a reproachful glance, then slid an ointment jar from his pouch. "Rub this on. It'll take longer to heal than the scorpion sting. When it closes, eat a pinch of the dragon-blood tree resin to remove the bruising; any part of the dragon-blood tree promotes blood circulation."

Though the ointment dulled the sting of the bite itself, her entire hand still throbbed. "Couldn't I eat some now? You mentioned it was a pain remedy," she said, smearing on more ointment because of the rain.

"Weren't you listening? I said it promotes blood circulation. If you eat it with an open wound, you could bleed out. This is going nowhere," he mumbled, his face betraying his nearly depleted store of patience.

If she didn't sense the ghost flower soon, he might end their lesson—and she would have failed the test.

She tried to puzzle out what it meant to reach out with her spirit sense, but thunder rolled, and he looked at the darkening clouds.

"Time's up," he said. "The weather's changing."

"No, wait! Just a little longer—I'm almost there."

He frowned, glancing at the glorium. "We leave in half a candle's burn," he said, then strolled away and started picking herbs.

Tori's mind raced, leaping from thought to thought until she landed uncomfortably on the wielding forms, and how they had activated the elements in her stone kernel. Could the forms help with this?

As she moved through the breath and arm movements, that loathsome sensitivity to the elements returned, but instead of trying to ignore it like before, she embraced it. Then she turned her mind toward the elixir, willing it to guide her. The loathsome sensitivity expanded.

All at once, not only could she feel the elements, but she instinctively identified them, one by one. Her chest felt light—she had discovered her spirit sense.

She pressed a hand to her navel then: nothing felt strained, no sign of kernel expansion. Her shoulders relaxed. So the wielding forms really were the way to increase her effectiveness. She would be careful not to do them all, of course, perhaps skipping every other one, to ensure she never activated her wielding.

Refocusing on her purpose, she reached out for the air element. A twinkle caught her eye—several paces away, raindrops bounced off the protruding roots of a tree, spraying in all directions, but instead of soaking into the ground, some of them landed midair, sparkling like morning dew on spider's silk.

She walked over and reached out a hand. Soft, invisible petals greeted her fingertips.

"I think I found one," she said.

Master Kwai'le stopped picking herbs and walked over. He ran a hand over the place she was touching, then looked at her with startled, if grudging, respect.

Before today, she might have gloated. Now, however, she bowed, hand over fist. "Please, Master, I'm asking you to keep me as your apprentice."

He glanced briefly at the glorium again, then made a show of rolling his eyes. "Do you think I'd be standing out here in the pouring rain otherwise?"

Tori sagged with relief.

Thunder cracked and lightning flashed.

"The summer showers have begun," he said. "Come on. There's a shortcut past the Waterwall."

They hurried off Dragon Blood Hill though the worsening rainstorm, until a cliff made entirely of water greeted them. Though its surface was rippled by wind and rain, it appeared translucent and dimly lit from within.

As they rounded its corner, Tori's breath caught: the Waterwall stretched on as far as her eye could see. A deep yearning arose within her then; she felt like the wall itself was calling to her, and her to it. In that moment she wanted nothing more than to stay. But they rushed past, and soon the Waterwall was behind them.

She scanned the forest, searching for a landmark that would help her find it again, but the rainstorm blurred every direction into the same watery green. So she scooped up handfuls of pebbles and mud as she hurried after Master Kwai'le, shaping them into small mounds to form a trail of markers that would lead her back to the Waterwall.

Sheets of rain hammered them, and thunder shook the ground. She flung her arms over her face and pushed through the storm till they came to the grove of peach trees, which were writhing in the wind, spraying petals everywhere.

As she stepped onto the petal-strewn path, she stole a glance over her shoulder to look at the trail she had laid.

Her chest fell. The torrent had devoured every last marker, leaving nothing behind but a streaming, flattened ground.

Chapter Fifty-Nine

THE WATERWALL

The moment she heard footsteps, Tori rushed to open the door.

"Did you get it?" she said, letting Elnora in.

Elnora handed her a paper. "Senrik and Ruvien would be happy to bring you to the Waterwall, you know. They've offered before."

"You didn't mention I was going tonight, though, right?" Tori said, glancing at Ruvien's messily drawn map.

"No, but wouldn't it be better if I had? They go there all the time; they know the way."

Tori stepped into the damp night air, holding up the map. "And now, so do I."

All along her path through the Veiled Forest, sparkling fountains of lomi spilled down silverly moonbeams. Though she had brought her slatted bamboo lantern, she didn't need it—flashing fireflies lit the air, and the light of the full moon illuminated not only Ruvien's drawings, but also everything around her. She could even see a vague notion of their colors.

None remained of the mounds she had left earlier today on her way out with Master Kwai'le, washed clean by the rainstorm, and she wondered now why she had felt compelled to leave them. Why had the Waterwall so captivated her?

Senrik and Ruvien had mentioned it, but that couldn't be the reason; they mentioned so many things.

Perhaps it was the mystery that drew her. When she had glimpsed it through the rain, she couldn't help feeling it held some enigma, waiting to be discovered. Or was it its endlessness that had moved her?

As she considered this, the noise of crickets and night birds ceased, leaving only the sound of her muted footfalls on the rain-softened ground.

Yes, endlessness—that was it. It seemed nonsensical, yet she felt that uncovering the end of something infinite might grant her the power to do the impossible...Perhaps to defeat her mother.

As she ventured deeper into the forest, it struck her how unafraid she felt here, in spite of her experience with shield scorpions and ghost rabbits. She glanced down at the rabbit bite, which was still red and sore. Oddly, the experience made her feel more secure—she finally understood how things worked: as long as she avoided odd-looking creatures, she was safe, and unlike at the palace, nothing lurked in secret, scheming.

A faint light appeared through the trees, brightening as she drew nearer, and she emerged into a clearing to find the Waterwall. Glowing softly from within, it lit up the space around it, and its soothing trickle filled the air.

She approached and looked up at the top, surprised at its height, which was more than twice her own. Rightward, it extended infinitely, continually flowing into the ground, yet without pooling. Its clarity amazed her, too; she could see far into its depths, despite the ripples created by downward streaming.

Colors flickered inside then, as though alerted to her presence, and the wall filled with creatures made of what appeared to be soft light. Most looked like fish, but some had forms unlike anything she had ever seen.

She started walking, searching for the end of the wall. The creatures followed, keeping pace alongside her, as though expecting her to throw oats or sweetbread. But their placid expressions told her they wanted nothing, and she realized then that anything she threw would simply be swept to the ground by the water's downward current.

At one point she almost thought she heard the creatures whisper. She stopped and looked at them. Were such things possible in the Veil?

While she considered this, a beautiful pink-and-blue creature appeared, the color of cloud-blush and mist. Like the others, it, too, looked soft and luminous, yet more splendid. And it was larger than the rest: its head was the same size as Tori's, and it extended into a body of about the same width.

It hovered at her eye level, swaying rhythmically as it peered at her with brown, near-human eyes. Those eyes made her pause; they were ancient and profound, and shone with such intelligence that she half expected it to speak. Tori stared back, captivated and disturbed.

The creature turned in the direction Tori had been headed, swam a few paces, then waited, as though willing Tori to follow. She did, and as they went, the creature kept to the outer edge of the wall where it was most visible. It was fast. Although it moved almost languidly through the water, Tori had to jog to keep pace.

Regardless of how far they went, the Waterwall's end eluded her. After a while, Tori's pace slowed, her breath coming in short bursts, and soon after, she stopped, panting. The blue-and-pink creature stopped, too.

The whispers returned then, and Tori darted her eyes to Waterwall, examining the creatures one by one, unable to find the source.

Suddenly she froze, fear spiking in her chest: the whispers were not coming from the Waterwall—they were coming from inside her.

The need to flee filled her, but the creature's soothing stare retained her, its eyes urging her not to run.

Tori took a long, slow breath, calming herself. Then a new feeling surprised her: a deep longing to understand Unity with the Sword.

The Night Twins suddenly felt heavy on her belt—maybe she should practice her dagger forms. Though she questioned how much weight she should give to the advice of a lawless Ghenz killer, Senrik had said he felt closest to achieving Unity with the Sword when he was at the Waterwall.

Master Maeli, too, believed one could achieve Unity with the Sword by becoming one with one's weapon. Perhaps she should try.

As though in answer, a silvery-white fish appeared, hovering sideways. Tori stilled; its shape—slender, sharp, disturbingly precise—looked exactly like a sword.

She pulled her daggers from her belt, then slapped them together and began.

A few more fish arrived, swimming in leisurely circles, stopping occasionally to watch her. Tori focused on the soothing sight of them as she whirled her daggers overhead, stepping, jabbing, turning, trying to connect with the weapons' consciousness.

But she felt nothing, except the shape of their hilts. What did it mean to become one with them? She pondered this as she moved through the forms.

As the pink-and-blue creature studied her with placid brown eyes, an identical, smaller creature swam to its side. Its baby.

Tori's chest ached at the sight, though she didn't know why.

Coming out of turn, Tori caught the adult creature's eye, and a profound peacefulness soaked the ache, stilling her heart, till it seemed almost not to beat. The stillness flowed deep into her stone kernel, and in her mind's eye she saw herself floating alongside the creature in the Waterwall. The stillness turned into whispers speaking from within. They told her not to strive, to relax and be inwardly silent.

Tori thought to resist, afraid of what was happening, yet she knew she must yield or lose the moment.

She calmed her turbulent thoughts and welcomed the stillness that transformed her mind into a glassy pond on a windless day. As she continued to moved through her dagger forms, wielding forms now flowed in and out, without her conscious effort.

Tingles rippled from her daggers into her hands, then seeped into her dawn channels, gently energizing them, like fireflies floating on a breeze.

She heard whispers again, but felt no more resistance, and although she couldn't make out their words, she somehow knew they were telling her to relax her grip. She had not noticed before, but her fists were clenched, and a flicker of wonder stirred inside her. Had she heard the elixir's voice?

The moment she obeyed, the Night Twins felt alive; they were anchored to her hands, yet light and airy; autonomous, yet connected, like parts of her body. The rhythm of her breathing synchronized with the rhythm of her blades, and the creature's brown eyes sparkled with something like approval.

She finished her forms, breathing heavily. The Waterwall teemed with creatures, every one of them watching as she slowly, reverently shifted her daggers into one hand again, her pulse thrumming with awe. She closed her eyes and bowed to whatever had spoken from deep within her.

Suddenly, the pink-and-blue creature darted away at a startling speed toward the end of the wall, leaving behind a trail of light.

Disappointment settled on her: no creature would swim that quickly if the end of the Waterwall was close. She stared in the direction she had been headed. The wall stretched on so far, it faded into the distance, endless.

Tori plodded away, dejected. She couldn't do the impossible after all.

It took a long while to reach her starting point at the clearing. She gave the wall one last, regretful look, then turned to leave for home.

Just then, however, the pink-and-blue creature returned.

Its eyes met hers, piercing her with a solemn, unbroken gaze. Then, out of nowhere, a series of images flashed through Tori's mind—ancient tales she had never heard of, or even imagined.

Tori's breath caught. This was one of the High Water-creatures, an ancient spirit being, the servant and companion of Ayenashi!

The moment the realization hit, a grave, unknown voice slipped into Tori's mind.

It has been an age since any have seen me. But I choose now to be seen by you.

Tori's mental question came spontaneously: *Why?*

An endless breath of time stretched on as she waited, both yearning for the answer, and dreading it.

Finally, the voice spoke again. *Because it is your destiny.*

Then, with one final look, the spirit being turned and slowly swam away.

The other creatures followed, their lights disappearing into the depths, until once again the Waterwall resembled a transparent, gently streaming cliff.

Tori stared into the glowing waters with a hammering heart, wondering who she really was.

Chapter Sixty

A HAPPY, HEALTHY EUNUCH

When Tori arrived at the training grounds the next morning, she found Ruvien waiting instead of Master Maeli.

He strolled over to her and held up two fingers. "Two things: one, Master Maeli's gone, and two—"

"Gone where?"

"Some urgent matter with the peacekeepers. And two—"

"Well when will she be back?"

"Tomorrow—can I finish?" He held up his fingers again. "Two, you promised to let me show you and Elnora the Greenstalk Teahouse as soon as you were free." He grinned. "Which apparently you are."

She gave him a tight smile. When she had made the promise via Elnora a few days prior, her intention had been to never be free. She had managed to put distance between herself and Senrik for nearly five days now, and had even succeeded in affecting a cold civility whenever they met on the training grounds. Going to the teahouse with him would ruin everything.

A thought occurred to her, lightening her mood: maybe Senrik wasn't coming.

Ruvien waved to someone behind her. "Ah, Senrik, right on time."

Tori blew out a breath.

He greeted Senrik with a slap on the back. "Did you find Elnora?"

"She's on her way."

A short while later, Tori found herself walking beside Senrik on the road to Greenstalk, while Elnora and Ruvien chatted up ahead.

She would have to make the best of this. And because it would have been rude not to respond to his attempts at conversation, she spent the entire walk looking everywhere except at him, so that she could pretend she was speaking to a homely, distant cousin, instead of an attractive, heavenly-smelling non-cousin—and lawless killer.

Thankfully, when they arrived in Greenstalk, Elnora expressed a desire to look at the fabric stalls, and the men left to do other things. So Tori made sure to point out everything Elnora might like, and they took the better part of the morning to fully appreciate the fabric choices. The fabric stalls at Greenstalk were filled now with an array of summer colors.

Tori rubbed a piece of cloth between her fingers. It was pink, with threads of other colors running through it. "What about this one?" Tori said.

Elnora shook her head as she sipped from a bottle-gourd of pear juice, her third that morning. "I've got three bolts already; that's more than enough." She glanced at the sky. "Anyway, we should probably get going. We promised the men we'd meet them at the teahouse at midday, latest."

Tori exhaled. "Then let's get this over with. The sooner we start, the sooner we finish."

Elnora smiled. "You know this is where they got your spring rolls from, right? I don't think you'll suffer too much." She placed the empty bottle-gourd into her basket of purchases. "Could we make a little detour first, though?" To illustrate her intentions, she pressed her knees together, making desperate bouncing movements.

"We'll be late," Tori said. Not that she minded. "And there'll be a privy at the teahouse."

"I can't walk in and go straight to the privy. I'd be mortified."

Tori scanned the area for a suitably secluded spot. A group of unused merchant stalls caught her eye, at the outer corner of the market, around fifty paces away. Behind them, she could just make out a deserted, grassy area with three dilapidated wooden shacks.

"So, how are you feeling about alchemy now that you found the ghost flowers?" Elnora said, as they headed toward the unused stalls.

"Like I need to bite my tongue from now on and just learn."

Elnora gave a regretful smile. "I know you'll do well. You're so good at everything. And if it's any consolation, you're not the only one he's a hogs bottom to. Master Kwai'le can't stand Keya, either."

"Not sure if being lumped together with her is a consolation, actually."

"Did you know she's a noble, from Jeng?"

Another reason not to become her mother's puppet in Jeng. Imagine dealing with a court populated with ministers like Keya.

"Which got me thinking," Elnora continued. "I may have figured out what his problem is."

"Enlighten me."

"Well, apparently when he was a boy, he and his family were servants of a very cruel noble lady. It was ages ago—did you know he's a hundred and seventy-five?"

"Yes, Master Maeli mentioned it."

"Well, they worked hard for little pay, and then his mother got sick. They couldn't afford a healer, and the noble lady refused to help, so his mother died. Then, because they had no one to take them in, he and his four younger siblings ended up as the woman's slaves, until Master Kwai'le escaped."

Tori felt sorry for him in spite of his behavior to her, especially when she remembered what the elder had said about losing his chance at immortality. "What became of his siblings?"

"He didn't know."

"Master Banfay?"

Elnora chuckled. "No, Ruvien. Who else?"

When they arrived at the deserted area, Tori took the basket, and Elnora went behind the first abandoned shack.

As Tori watched a beetle scuttle through the grass, the sound of muffled screams drew her attention to the third shack, several paces away.

Two broad, ill-kempt men—one with a ponytail, the other with a scraggly beard—were dragging a woman toward it, a hand covering her mouth. She was an Ant, with raven feathers in her messy black hair. She whimpered, struggling to pry herself free.

"You there! Let her go!" Tori said.

The man with the scraggly beard shoved the woman to the ground and straddled her, pinning her arms.

Before she could think, Tori was running toward them, swinging her basket at the man's head. She knocked him off. The woman scrambled away without looking back.

The man swayed, apparently stunned, but the one with the ponytail stalked toward Tori, his expression dark.

Elnora rushed to her side, grabbing her arm. "Quick, Princess. Run."

They bolted away, leaving the basket behind, but before they could reach the second shack, the men overtook them.

"Hey, pretty ladies, not so fast," the man with the ponytail said, blocking their way.

Elnora pulled Tori close. "Leave us alone."

The man snickered, exchanging glances with his scraggly friend, then stepped closer. "Don't think we will. You disrupted our party, so I'm guessing you must want to keep us company. What you think, Mushi?"

The memory of the thugs at the Laughing Skunk came back to her, and Tori frantically scanned the space, searching for a way out. They would need to reach the first shack before they were anywhere near the open village. No one would hear them from here if the men covered their mouths.

The men were long-legged and muscular; if she and Elnora ran, the men would simply catch them.

Mushi stared at them maliciously through his scraggly beard, then looked Elnora over, licking his lips. "I think you're right, Fang. They must want to keep us company. Everyone knows the only ones that come back here is vagrants and whores."

Tori felt for her daggers with trembling hands. "That woman was no whore. You abducted her."

"She weren't no woman," Mushi said. "She were an Ant. Even if we killed her, no one would care. Ain't that right, Fang?"

Fang gave a brown-toothed grin. "That's a fact. Ain't no one bothered us yet about killing a few Ant whores."

Mushi's arm whipped out suddenly, wrapping around Elnora. She screamed, but he slapped a hand over her mouth.

Fury raged through Tori, and the image of the wolverine flashed in her mind. In one smooth movement she gripped her daggers, lunged, and slashed, slicing the man from face to arm.

Mushi hollered, releasing his grip, and Elnora ran, screaming. The man went to follow, but Tori swept out her foot, tripping him. He fell with a heavy thud, cursing.

Fang lunged at her, but Master Maeli's lessons returned, and Tori spun out of reach—fast, perfect, intense.

Mushi lumbered upright again, his sleeve covered in blood. He punched at her, but she crouched as his fist passed over her head.

"You wanted company," Tori said, spinning on her heels in the dirt. "Here it is!"

She launched her dagger into Mushi's other arm.

With a curse, he yanked it out and hurled it down, his face contorting with pain as he tried to stem the flow of blood, his malicious gaze fixed on her.

Suddenly, realization crossed his face, and his eyes widened. "It's her," he said.

Fang's eyes widened too, then he spat and pulled out a massive knife. "They told us to find her. No one said we had to find her alive."

They recognize me?

He crouched and started circling Tori, but Tori did the same, her body buzzing with focus. She noted every shift of his eyes, every twitch in his muscles.

He slashed out with his right hand, so Tori dodged left. Then he did it again, and again she dodged, but this time his left fist smashed into her cheek. Stars exploded in her vision and her head whipped backward.

Tori crashed against the ground, robbed of breath. She blinked to clear her blurry vision and tried to move, but she was anchored to the ground by her own heavy limbs.

Fang spat again, then sauntered over. With all her might, she willed herself to move as he pulled back his booted foot, aiming at her side. His foot flew forward, but she rolled just in time, grabbing her second dagger along the way.

The force of the kick threw him off-balance, and he stumbled, enraged.

Tori pushed to her feet, trying to remember her forms, but her whole head throbbed, and she couldn't think. So she seized on the only memory she could: the eyes of the High Water-creature at the Waterwall. A faint whisper passed through her then, like a sigh on a breeze, and a deep, incomprehensible peace engulfed her.

Though she didn't know what awakened it, she sensed the air element activate in the Night Twins, and she knew a blade of air had formed, subtly extending their reach.

Deeply calm now, she spun her daggers as she circled Fang, her composure seeming to enrage him more.

"I'll kill you, whore!"

He rushed her, but this time, instead of dodging, Tori dropped to the dirt, then arched backward, sliding through his legs, daggers thrusting up.

"Wrong on both counts." Though she was marginally too low to reach him, the air blade connected as she passed through, and she felt flesh tear.

With a roar, Fang dropped to the ground, hands between his thighs, a red patch blossoming on his trousers. Mushi took off running, cradling his blood-soaked arm.

Footsteps thudded behind her, and Tori spun to find Senrik bounding forward, sword drawn, but he checked his pace to a walk when his eyes fell on Fang, rocking himself and groaning on the ground.

When he reached Tori, Senrik's gaze lingered on the cheek Fang had punched. The spot throbbed and burned now, as though split.

Fang groaned, and Senrik cast him a dismissive glance. "You're lucky it wasn't me, man," he said, sheathing his sword.

A moment later, Elnora and Ruvien ran to their sides.

Elnora scanned Tori's cheek with a frown, but appeared satisfied enough with its condition to start picking up the spilled contents of their basket.

At the sight of Fang's bloodstained trousers, Ruvien dipped his head at Tori with a look that said he was impressed.

"We'd better go," he said, "before people start asking questions. Peacekeepers can kill if necessary, but not too sure we can castrate."

They slid behind the shacks as Fang's cries grew loader. Tori hardened her heart. He was a rapist—he deserved castration.

His groans turned into pathetic sobs. Tori set her jaw. He was a murderer—he deserved death.

But though she tried to ignore him, she couldn't.

"Will he die?" she asked.

Senrik shrugged. "Maybe."

His casual disdain for life chilled her, and once again, she struggled to reconcile the image of the heroic figure running to her rescue a few moments prior with a person who would murder his own clansmen in cold blood.

"He'll bleed out if he doesn't get help soon," Elnora said as they hastened to the exit.

The thought of Fang's death brought Tori no satisfaction, which surprised her. It felt wrong somehow, dealing out death by her own hand.

"With the way he's carrying on, the whole village will be here in no time to bandage him up," Ruvien said. "Don't worry about him."

Elnora gave him a flat look. "Did I say I was worried?"

A moment later, a crowd of people streamed into the area on the other side of the shacks, obviously following the noise.

Ruvien gestured with his head and grinned. "See? He'll soon be a happy, healthy eunuch."

They slipped into the main village, then back on the road to Peach Blossom Grove. Though Ruvien thought the teahouse was a better way to end the day, Tori just wanted to go home. She had almost taken lives and wasn't sure how to feel.

After they stepped through the familiar sensation of the water curtain and entered the Veil, Elnora glanced at Tori, squinted, then wiped something from Tori's forehead with the edge of her sleeve. A moment later, she wiped a different place.

Heat coursed through Tori's body, sending out a burst of perspiration. She dabbed her face with her own sleeve now, then stared at it, confused: it was covered in a sheen of black, oily sludge. Elnora frowned.

More black sludge beaded on the back of her hand. Alarm flared, but she tried to tamp it down. She had just been in a fight—of course she would be dirty.

Then another wave of heat surged, and beads of the same oily substance rolled off her arms and dripped to the ground in thick black circles.

The fear was hard to hold back now; whatever this was, it wasn't from the fight—it was coming from inside her.

Elnora insisted she see Master Banfay, but by the time they reached Peach Blossom Grove, the internal heat wave had cooled, and the black sludge had vanished completely off her skin.

Chapter Sixty-One

STONE MELDING

Tori convinced herself the black sludge had been a rare mishap, one of those unexplainable things in life you need to forget and move on, so she continued as before in Peach Blossom Grove.

Over the next four moons, her alchemy slowly improved. Though Master Kwai'le was rarely satisfied with anything, she, at least, felt plant phytolyzation was becoming easier.

Early one morning, she arrived at the cave to find Master Kwai'le lining up pairs of spirit stones beside the pill furnace. Each pair consisted of two colors in varying shades of the six elements—gray, blue, green, brown, white; red or orange or yellow; and a few clear, colorless ones—all of them smooth and round, and emitting a faint glow.

When he finished, she expected him to move to the plant nursery for her usual lesson. Instead, he stayed where he was and cleared his throat, like he was about to say something he'd rather not.

"Lessons with spirit stones require a certain aptitude for using one's spirit sense, which it appears—at long last—you have begun to grasp."

It took her a moment to puzzle out his meaning—she would finally be working with spirit stones! A smile tugged at her lips.

"Having said that, you must still proceed with caution. Your spirit sense is adequate, nothing more; your common sense, however, leaves much to be desired—as your encounter with the ghost rabbit several moons ago proved. If you had tried petting a magical creature in Ketuan's Veins, it would not have ended so well."

The jab should have stung—instead, her chest lifted, and she fought back a grin. He actually thought she might make it to Ketuan's Veins.

He handed her four white jade slips separated by shiny blue beads and bound together with string. Carved lengthwise along the strips were glyphs of the Old Speech. Thankfully, her time studying the palm-leaf volume on the Antiquitals allowed her to read them easily.

"These, of course, were not written with a Septad in mind," he said, "so they merely contain instructions for healing stones—the ones master healers use, like these." He indicated the stone shelf above the counter. "As such, they only deal with the melding of two elements. But whether it's two elements or six, the principles are the same."

He pushed a pair of spirit stones toward her, one red and one gray. "The fire and metal combination is a common choice in treating disease. You must activate the stones by connecting with elixir, letting it flow through you, then streaming it outward, like with plant phytolyzation. Here, however, you will need to direct two streams of elixir, one toward each stone."

She began. A few moments later, she realized something: she had connected with the elixir and cycled it without closing her eyes, or even lowering into horse stance.

As she continued, her spirit sense picked up the fire and metal elements in the stones. She instinctively pulled twice on the elixir, streaming once toward the red firestone, then again toward the gray metalstone. The ease with which she did this surprised her.

Ever since she had found the ghost flowers, she had been practicing parts of the wielding forms each night—never in sequence, of course, and sometimes doing them backward; she didn't know exactly how it worked, but suspected the uninterrupted sequence was what would lead to a stone kernel expansion. Yet although the practice had made plant phytolyzation easier, she hadn't realized till now just how much four moons of this had benefited her.

"No, no," he said. "You have to direct the elixir into both stones at once."

She did.

"Now direct a third stream between the stones to link them. This will keep them together and help each stone to reach into the other once they get into the furnace."

Tori did this, too. He made her stop and start over. Then he made her stop and start again and again for what seemed like a very long while, before allowing her to take a break.

She found she was panting.

"You'll need more stamina than that to make the Septad," he said. He nodded at her bottle-gourd, indicating that she could drink.

A question came to her from something she had seen in the palm-leaf volume. "Why is it called the Septad?" she asked. "I know it comes from the word for seven in the Old Speech—*septuma*—but there are only six elements."

"A lesson for another day." He indicated the stones with his chin. "Now gather your elixir and practice rationing it. The stones must be propelled forward four thousand years to form a metamorphic stone that would otherwise not exist."

"Propelled?"

He waved his hand impatiently. "Phytolyzed. Except, plants are phytolyzed, spirit stones are propelled. Once they're in the furnace, the additional heat and pressure will finish melding them, but first they must be properly propelled if they are to emerge as anything useful."

"How will we know it's useful?"

"The new, melded stone must retain the same intensity of light as the originals, as well as retaining their original shades of color, each of which must also send veins into the other. And," he said, holding up a small hammer, "it must be indestructible." He clasped his hands behind his back. "Begin."

Though she had never before phytolyzed anything to four thousand years, much less sent two elixir streams at once, she did her best. But she was already tired, and every time she streamed into one stone, the other stream dried up.

"Both at once," he said. "Don't tell me you've forgotten that already?"

She cycled elixir till it moved on its own through her dawn channels, then gathered it in her stone kernel, pulled up two streams, and pushed them both outward at the same time. Then she added a third stream, linking them. This time the stones slid together, as though pulled by an imaginary golden string.

The light inside the stones shifted to form several smaller lights, as though the components inside were changing shape. The stones looked like they were melting together at the place where they connected.

"This is where it gets delicate," he said. "A spirit stone in the process of metamorphosis cannot be touched by any implement—not even the hand—so you must hover it very carefully into the furnace."

Tori struggled to keep the elixir streaming as she spoke. "How?"

But speaking proved too much of a strain—the stones' inner lights blinked out, leaving them abnormally dull. Tiny cracks appeared on their surface.

Master Kwai'le's mouth twisted. "You've seen me make magical pills before. How did you think the pills hovered in the air?"

"I assumed it had something to do with the pill furnace," Tori said.

He exhaled impatiently. "Then, for the avoidance of doubt, hover the stones using elixir."

He slid another pair toward her, this time red and green. "The metal element was perhaps too heavy to start. We'll replace it with wood. Do the same as before, only this time"—he frowned at her—"hover them into the furnace."

Tori managed to get the stones to melt together, then sent a fourth stream of elixir into them, but still had no idea how to use it to hover them.

Remembering the importance of imagination, she tried something: she formed a mental picture of them hovering into the furnace.

To her amazement, the linked stones actually floated above the counter, but the elixir in her kernel was almost dry, and she feared it might run out entirely before she could get the stones into the furnace. What was more, she couldn't cycle elixir now to fill her kernel.

Remembering what he said about rationing elixir, she pulled back the stream slightly. The stones, now hovering in midair, fell to the floor and cracked.

Master Kwai'le made a wry face. "There goes six silver drams."

He pointed to the next pair and watched her closely. These cracked while still in midair. After her third failure, he handed her the jade slips.

"Study these thoroughly," he said. "Begin again when you're ready—and *only* then."

The heat of embarrassment crept up her neck.

As she studied, something about the jade slips bothered her: she couldn't help feeling she was missing something in the glyphs, even as she easily read them.

"May I borrow these slips tonight?"

"No," he said sharply. His eyes flicked to the glorium, and his tone softened. "But you can study them here as much as you like."

Just then, a knock sounded at the door. Master Koren stood in the doorway with a messenger hawk on his shoulder and held out a paper. The hawk glided to its perch and started preening.

Master Kwai'le threw up his hands. "Again?"

"My apologies, I'm afraid I read it," Master Koren said. "I assumed it was for me."

"There's nothing in my business everyone else can't know," Master Kwai'le said, taking the paper and looking it over. "I just wish I knew it first."

"An extra three hundred pills at the next sect fair," Master Koren said. "Impressive."

"A lot of new recruits," Master Kwai'le replied. "The essence-building tablets are always popular with them."

When they were alone again, Master Kwai'le removed the red homing stone from around the hawk's neck, then muttered to himself as he examined it with a magnifying glass. He was still doing this when Tori finished studying the jade slips, leaving her nothing to do but go pet the hawk.

The hawk nuzzled her hand, and she scratched the top of his soft, feathery head.

"What's your name?" she whispered. "Wings? No, Glider. You always glide straight to your perch, like something's driving you there."

The hawk closed its eyes, luxuriating under her caress.

"No, Glider's too mundane for someone like you. What about Driven?"

He opened an eye and tilted his head at her.

"This isn't an animal-care lesson, and we don't have all day," Master Kwai'le said peevishly.

Tori breathed in slowly through her nose, pressing her lips together to keep from responding. Then she walked back to the furnace and began again.

This time, she managed to hover the stones into the furnace, but they cracked the moment they went in.

Master Kwai'le rolled his eyes. He unhelpfully told her to look more closely at the instructions on the jade slips and start again, but she was already doing everything written there.

The tenth and final pair of blue and red made it into the furnace without dropping or cracking. Though she was exhausted, she also felt hopeful—she was finally understanding. If the stone came out even remotely resembling the ones on the shelves, she would consider it a wild success.

When the furnace eye pulsed with light, indicating the melding was done, Tori streamed her elixir to grab hold of the new stone and hover it out of the furnace.

The stones had melded oddly, and had lost all their luminosity. Tori noted with dismay that the original blue and red now looked like a misshapen lump of dull-colored clay.

Hoping to discover some redeeming quality, she reached out to grab it, then jerked her hand back with a cry. The stone fell to the floor and shattered into tiny shards, while on her hand, a searing red circle throbbed.

Master Kwai'le let out an exasperated exhale. "That's enough for to-day. Get that burn treated, and come back in the morning. If by the end of tomorrow you can't manage basic stone melding, we'll have to go back to phytolyzing plants."

Chapter Sixty-Two

BIRTHING A STONE

The following morning, after a glance at Tori's hand—now healed, thanks to Elnora's ointments—Master Kwai'le once again passed her the jade slips.

As she read, she finally understood what had been bothering her about them the day before.

"Master, this says, 'Let the method of heat and pressure be joined to the furnace stage, when the stones are within,'" she said, running a finger down the glyphs. "I had assumed the heat and pressurizing technique was something the pill furnace did, but now I'm wondering: Is this something I have to do?"

"It took you long enough to ask," he said, with a smirk. "Yes, the heat and pressurizing technique is what will merge the stones fully, to send their veins into one another, if you will. And although the pill furnace applies heat and pressure, the heat and pressurizing technique referred to here is something the alchemist controls."

Tori's jaw tensed. "Would it have been so hard to tell me that yesterday?"

"A student without the wits to raise the question isn't worthy of the answer. I will say, however, that if you can grasp this technique, then you can begin preparing for your final alchemy test—the one the elder requires."

Her irritation cooled; she was closer to her goal than she had realized. And she refused to go back to phytolyzing plants.

He pointed to the spirit stone pairs lined up on the counter. "Apply the technique detailed in the jade slips while propelling these stones forward exactly seven thousand years, six months, and anywhere from two hundred twenty-four to two hundred twenty-five days—no need to be too exact."

It was exact enough. Worse, she had no idea how to apply the technique.

She didn't want to ask. In spite of his pronouncement that only students who ask questions are worthy of answers, she knew from experience that he was being disingenuous; he was much more likely to make some cutting remark when she asked a foolish question, then stand back and let her figure it out anyway.

Leaning over the glyphs, she rested her fingers lightly on her temple, thinking. The glyphs describing the heat and pressurizing technique resembled figures making different motions with their bodies. Were they giving a demonstration of the forms she had to use?

She decided to imitate them. Beginning with the first pair of stones—a light blue and a pale gray, stones of the water and metal elements—she drew them together as before. This time, however, just before hovering them into the furnace, she adjusted her stance to mimic the glyphs, slowly changing the position of her arms and hands as the glyphs changed. A sheen of sweat rose on her brow.

Once they were inside the furnace, she continued the movements of her arms and feet shown by the glyphs. But her elixir was quickly draining, as were her energy levels. When the dark blue furnace eye flashed, it took all her focus just to hover the stone out without dropping it.

The stone was lit from within, and had a vibrant color.

Master Kwai'le shook his head. "No good."

"But they're melded."

He picked it up with a small pair of tongs, holding it to the light to show her. "There are no veins, which means the two elements have canceled each other out, instead of creating something new. The unique function of each stone has been transformed into completely useless."

He tossed it in the bin, then slid her a white stone and a pale green one—air and wood.

She poured all her strength into it. This one came out of the furnace lumpy, with several opaque spots, but otherwise its light was good, and it had veins of color mixed throughout.

He pursed his lips. "Maybe."

Tori tensed as he examined it. He held it up over the floor and dropped it—it shattered on impact. No explanation needed.

The same thing happened again with a blue and a green stone.

Master Kwai'le gave an exasperated exhale. "Stop rushing through everything. Focus."

He nodded toward a transparent, light brown stone and a colorless one, earth and air. But the fatigue that had been slowly creeping in finally seized her, and Tori could only stare at the stones, trying to regain her strength.

She couldn't afford to fail. When she had phytolyzed plants, the elixir had seemed to know what to do; she would have to trust it again.

She connected with the elixir, then cycled it and streamed it out, drawing the stones together. Sweat beaded on her forehead as she applied the heat and pressurizing technique and hovered them into the pill furnace.

By the time she hovered out the result, she was trembling with fatigue and lost hold of the stream of elixir. Tori froze as the stone plummeted to the floor.

But it didn't shatter. She wiped the sweat from her forehead, breathing heavily.

Master Kwai'le looked her up and down, frowning. "In order to create the Septad, you will need to propel not two, but *six* stones forward at once—to forty-four thousand years, four months, forty-five days. What you've just done is a mere trifle by comparison." He looked like he would say more, but his eyes fell on the glorium, and he simply shook his head.

He picked up the melded stone with his tongs and held it to the light, then he placed it on the counter and brought his hammer down on it. The stone didn't break, or even crack. Instead, it emitted a gentle, crystalline ring that rippled through the air.

He held the stone up again, tilting it from side to side, mumbling, "Crystals have grown together at the same rate." He spun it, examining it from various angles. "Veins appeared to have intensified in color. Interesting."

His eyes darted to her then, as though he were only just remembering she was there, and he cleared his throat. "Unsightly, but functional."

Tori gazed at the stone, feeling all the exhaustion and exhilaration and pride of a mother who had just birthed a girl child. The stone was lopsided, but it was also rich, and luminous, and beautiful beyond all imagining.

When he placed it on the shelf beside his own stones—her chest swelled. Her offspring wasn't merely functional—it was good.

"You will require a great deal more precision and stamina to succeed in the final test," Master Kwai'le said.

Tori held back a smile—she would be taking the test!

She dipped her head. "Yes, Master."

"The test consists of thirty-two stones; your stamina will be pulled on more than tenfold. You will need one moon to prepare—intensely. Working with spirit stones is no small feat."

Considering how wrung out she felt, she couldn't help wondering if twenty-eight days would be enough.

"What's the passing grade?"

"One hundred percent," he said.

She sagged. Then she caught herself—she had just done something incredible; she would hold on to that.

"But afterward, I'll be able to make the Septad, right?"

"That is the hope—there's no other skill I can impart, at least. Which is why I must ensure you have fully grasped what I am teaching. Though a Septad hasn't been made in the memory of anyone living today—including the elder—one thing I do know for sure: attempting it without the requisite skill would be more than simply a waste of precious spirit stones—it could very well be deadly."

He let the words hang in the air.

"I'll examine your stone further to ensure it isn't harmful when used for healing," he said. "After that, Master Banfay will assess its usefulness on a patient. Only once these two requirements have been met can I be certain you're ready."

He turned his back on her and started arranging the counter. "Tomorrow is the Greenstalk Autumn Festival, which most of Peach Blossom Grove will attend, but I should have your results after that. I'll let you know then whether you can begin preparation for the final test."

Chapter Sixty-Three

GREENSTALK FESTIVAL

The Greenstalk Autumn Festival had been the talk of Peach Blossom Grove for weeks. So the next day, Tori and Elnora entered Greenstalk Village alongside Senrik and Ruvien, who had insisted on taking them.

The crisp air buzzed with excitement. Everyone was dressed to celebrate autumn—as giant radishes, sweet potatoes, and more pumpkins and mushrooms than Tori could count—milling through stalls of candied nuts and roasted meats on sticks, their costumes' varying degrees of success giving the atmosphere a jovial, jesting feel.

The members of her group—apart from Tori herself—were the only exceptions: Elnora's radish costume actually flattered her, Senrik hadn't disguised himself at all, and Ruvien looked almost elegant in a cape made of leaves.

Tori, however, had opted to blend in. The thugs she had encountered here four moons prior seemed to have recognized her; she couldn't take any chances. And since she still had to make good on her promise to Ruvien, nothing would be allowed to spoil today's fun.

Tori adjusted the cloth winter-squash stem on her head.

"You look beautiful," Elnora said, her eyes warm with admiration.

Tori shot her wry look.

"You do! Everything suits you, Princess."

Even without Elnora's laughably generous praise, Tori would have chosen the same outfit. Apart from a small hole for the face and openings for her arms, she was entirely covered, the green-striped cloth ballooning out around her before tapering again at the knees. As she couldn't reach her waist, she had left her daggers behind; dressed like this, however, she wouldn't need them.

"I've never been part of the crowd at a festival before," Tori said, the novelty of the situation exciting her. "Look: I can buy my own elloku." Yet this also reminded her just how exposed she was.

They ordered several of the fried dough balls, then headed toward a candied hawthorn stand—Ruvien's goal of the day was to order every food available. She watched the people around them carefully. Despite her excitement, she felt a tiny bit on edge, not wanting anything to catch her off guard.

All along the stand, skewers with balls of shiny, red hawthorn fruit stuck out of wooden poles, like the fruit-laden branches of trees. Without asking, Ruvien ordered for all of them. When Senrik declined, Ruvien shrugged, a skewer in both hands, and took a bite of each.

"Crispy hops!" Elnora said, pointing to stall where heaps of the reddish-brown snacks sat piled on enormous plates. The seller used a small shovel to scoop them into paper bags for customers.

Ruvien handed her his candied hawthorn skewers, went to the crispy hop vendor, and, moments later, presented her with a bag. Elnora rewarded him with a wider smile than Tori would have imagined yet another snack could provoke—Elnora really did love those.

They spent the day eating and watching the festivities: jugglers, players, mask painters; leaf races down water channels; people biting at dangling fruit; judges weighing gourds; and communal cloth dyeing with walnut husks, onion skins, and madder root, where people dyed handkerchiefs and tunics, then hung them like a canopy of brown, yellow, and rosy orange leaves.

"Next order of business: the hawking post," Ruvien said, clutching a bag of roasted nuts in one hand while eating a meat skewer with the other. "Tori hasn't seen the birds yet."

Since the hawking post was on the opposite end of the village, they passed various stalls selling trinkets and toys along the way. The final row of stalls displayed an array of small paper kites on sticks, in the form of mythical animals. Some weren't kites, but lanterns, which glowed faintly now as evening drew near.

Each stall sold a different mythical creature, many of the kites with tails that lifted and fluttered in the breeze. They were of lemon and bright raspberry hues, sour apple and blueberry, all painted with the logograms for fifteen and ten to signify the fifteenth day of the tenth moon—the date of the annual autumn festival.

The luminous blues and pinks of one of the lanterns reminded Tori of Ayenashi's High Water-creature, and she noticed then that many of the creations resembled the strange fishes in the Waterwall. It struck her as regrettable, how close these vendors lived to the real-life versions of these creatures while believing they didn't exist. She mused on how limited her life had been before coming to Peach Blossom Grove, how little she had known of the world. Before, she would have dismissed these kites as amusing nonsense.

Nodding toward a yellow paper fish, Senrik said, "Reminds me of something I saw at the Waterwall."

Tori glanced up sharply—it was like he had read her thoughts.

His gaze settled on her mouth, and Tori realized that she was biting into a meat skewer. She dabbed her lips, feeling self-conscious.

"Don't stop," Senrik said, with a crooked half-smile. "I was thinking of getting one myself."

He waved over a food seller carrying a basket around his neck and, noticing that Tori had finished hers, bought one meat skewer for himself and another for her. Tori thanked him. It was glazed in a sweet, spicy sauce she couldn't seem to get enough of.

Halfway through, however, her stomach gave a warning twist—too sharp for simple spice.

"You know, I should probably stop here."

Ruvien took the half-empty skewer and bit into it. "Can't let good food go to waste."

When they arrived at the hawking post moments later, several hawks sat preening on their perches. Most were ordinary looking, but a few had shimmering plumage and sharp black eyes and wore bright, jeweled pendants.

A silver-feathered hawk with a dazzling red stone around his neck tilted his head, cocking an eye at Tori.

"Driven!" Tori said, rushing forward.

As Driven hopped down to meet her, Tori raised an arm, which dipped under the bird's weight. Its sharp claws slid through her sleeve, yet rested harmlessly against her skin. Driven nuzzled her, making her chuckle.

"He's got a message on his leg," Ruvien said, and looked at the sky. "And it's almost sunset. Shouldn't he have gone to Master Kwai'le?"

"Aw, don't make him feel bad. He's still learning," Tori said, stroking his soft head.

Driven closed his eyes and rubbed against her finger.

"You're learning, aren't you?" she cooed. "You're the perfect messenger hawk, yes you are."

Ruvien raised an eyebrow.

"She likes animals," Elnora said.

"But it's just a hawk."

"Driven's not just a hawk," Tori said, lifting her arm to release him. "Go on to Master Kwai'le," she said, pointing in the direction of Peach Blossom Grove. "Go on, now."

But Driven sailed in a circle around the hawking post, landed right back on the perch, and gazed at her intently, like he was trying to communicate something she didn't know.

"He'll figure it out eventually," Ruvien said with a shrug. "Come on—those play actors that were setting up along the way should be ready by now."

As Tori turned to leave, the discomfort in her stomach sharpened.

"I think I ate too much," she said, wincing.

Suddenly, a dizzy feeling took her and sweat streamed down her face. She leaned forward, a hand on her knee.

"What's wrong, Princess?" Elnora asked.

"I'm not sure."

A black, oily bead dripped onto the ground near Tori's feet. Then another.

Voices approached the post, laughing and talking. Tori recognized them: Suli and Sadeera. She looked up to see both girls dressed as cabbages.

Sadeera's flame-blue eyes met Tori's, and her smile froze. She glanced around nervously, then whispered, "You need to leave! Now!" She grabbed Suli's arm. "We have to tell the others to go back."

With one last glance at Tori, the girls broke into a run.

Elnora held Tori's wrist and took her pulse. "I can't figure out what's causing this."

Another wave of dizziness hit, and more sludge rolled down her face. It soaked through her sleeves.

"We have to get her home," Elnora said, lifting Tori under the arm. "Come, lean on me."

Tori dragged her feet, feeling sick. She was thankful the winter-squash costume hid most of her skin, but black circles had become visible even on her dark green sleeves.

As they passed the paper animals, something inside her started cracking, like an overfull wineskin ready to burst.

Her ketua reached for the elements around her—earth, metal, wood; water in jugs, fire in lanterns, air all around. Alarm coursed through her.

She grabbed Elnora. "The seal broke."

Tori limped along more quickly, but her stone kernel split, and every muscle in her body spasmed. Her kernel shed its outer layer, expanding, and she instinctively understood then the meaning of the black, oily sludge—her kernel was pushing out impurities.

Against her will, she touched the fire in the lanterns. Elnora jumped back just in time as fire leaped from Tori's hands and onto the stall with the beautiful paper creatures, sending it ablaze. Half a breath later, the next stall burst into flames, then the next.

Villagers screamed and pointed. A few people Tori recognized from Peach Blossom Grove raced away.

The stalls tumbled as they burned, each one pushing over the one beside it, till the last stall fell onto the hawking post, sending hawks screeching into the air.

Tori stared in horror as Driven struggled, flapping burning wings, then plummeted to the ground like a stone. Somebody dumped a bucket of water on him, but he remained on the ground, unmoving and charred.

Tori spasmed again, her muscles completely frozen.

Ruvien and Elnora lifted her under the armpits, dragging her like a dead weight, while Senrik guarded her, holding his arms out protectively, trying to block her from view.

"Guards! Get the guards!" people screamed, pointing at her. "It's a wielder!"

Senrik's hand flew to the pommel of his sword. "Get her out, quick," he told Ruvien.

More black sludge poured out, and she spasmed again, almost dragging Elnora down.

Elnora looked at Senrik, frantic. "The guards are coming."

Senrik bent to scoop Tori up, but she unwillingly touched the elements again.

"No!" she shouted, twisting free of him just in time before more fire blasted from her hands. Senrik leaped away.

Then a flood of water rushed in out of nowhere, soaking their feet and causing more shouts from the crowd. She had caused that too, somehow.

Guards appeared, running toward her.

Senrik drew his sword, but Ruvien gripped his arm. "There are too many."

"I'm seeing six," he said. "We can take them."

"Not guards—people." Ruvien motioned to the people, arming themselves now with sticks and rocks. "We'd have to hurt them."

"Leave me," Tori said to Elnora, gasping between spasms. She convulsed again, and the stalls once again blazed. "Now! Go tell Master Banfay."

Ruvien pulled Senrik away. "Let's not make it worse. The council will know what to do."

Sludge streamed into Tori's eyes, darkening her vision. The last thing she saw was Elnora, looking at Tori over her shoulder as she ran away, weeping.

Guards surrounded Tori, shoving her to the ground and quickly tying her hands with atha rope before yanking her up by the collar.

As they hauled her away, her ketua quieted, and all her strength drained, causing her legs to give out beneath her. Tori fell forward, limp. The guards didn't pull her to her feet, they simply dragged her through the dirt by the scruff of her costume. With her hands bound behind her as they were, if the guards dropped her, she would break her nose.

The image of a motionless Driven came to her, and she spasmed one last time, sending a final stream of black sludge dripping off her face.

They dumped her in a dirt cell with iron bars and walked away, grumbling about not missing the sunset dancers because of a filthy wielder. Tori lay there, hands bound, strength gone, face pressed into the dirt—until long after the sun had gone down.

After dark, the cell door opened, and Tori felt herself being dragged up by the collar again.

"The jail house is too good for the likes of you," one of the guards said, his voice sharp with disgust. "You'll rot in the hold. Filthy wielder."

He spat, the glob of saliva shining sickeningly in the light of the full moon. Tori squeezed her eyes shut as they dragged her over it.

When they came to a grassy area filled with weeds, a circle of stones appeared, low on the ground and covered with an iron grate. They pushed the grate aside and hauled her to her feet to reveal a hole. Terror seized her, but before she could react, they shoved her, screaming, into the darkness.

Tori plummeted, hitting her head and scraping her skin, then landed hard on her side, pain shooting through her body.

The fall had somehow loosened her bonds, so she freed her hands and pushed painfully into a sitting position. She seemed to be in a dry well. The air was sour and stale, like something long dead, making it hard to breathe, and she tried in vain to pull the neck of her costume over her nose.

Sharp points dug into her thigh and she shifted, trying to see what it was. Groping in the dark, she tapped her hand along several long, hard pieces.

When her eyes adjusted to the darkness at last, thin white shapes took form.

She jerked back her hand, cold rippling through her limbs: she had broken her fall on a skeleton.

Chapter Sixty-Four

THE HOLD

Tori slumped against the rough stone wall, too weak from grief, thirst, and the kernel expansion itself, to even to move away from the bones beside her.

Although a patch of moonlight glimmered off the rim of the well, everything else lay in shadow, and Tori strained her eyes to see into the pitch-black. She lifted her eyes to heaven, hoping to find Ishairo, but clouds concealed him.

Shivering despite her layered costume, she drew her knees in and huddled against the grainy, crumbling wall, but the cold stone only made it worse. Tears stung her eyes as she remembered how she had endangered the lives of her friends. She squeezed her eyes shut, whispering a silent prayer for Elnora.

How long before the Greenstalk guards found out who she was? Did they know already? Her mother would send for her, to be publicly disowned and executed.

When she opened her eyes again, she was astonished to find that she could see in the dark. Instinctively she knew this was a result of the kernel expansion.

As she scanned the well—dug deep into limestone—her vision continued to sharpen, as though the very act of looking was refining it. Another skeleton, fully clothed, sat across from her, hugging its knees…just like her.

Greenstalk villagers apparently had no taste for public executions. Here, wielders were simply left to rot.

More compassionate than in Silver Fox Springs, she thought darkly.

And a dry well made perfect sense: there was no water they could wield to lift them, and though wielding metal might remove the grate, the well was too smooth and deep to climb. If they tried wielding earth, the well would simply collapse, burying them alive.

Not that she could do any of these things. Though she had broken through, she knew nothing more than how to use her spirit sense to touch the limestone.

As her gaze drifted across the uneven wall, five faint grooves caught her eye, vertical and jagged. A little farther up, she noticed more.

Claw marks—someone had been trying to claw their way to the top.

She lowered her gaze, hoping the person had died quickly.

How long would it take for her?

That thought engendered another: a public execution would bring her mother too much shame. No, her mother would claim Tori had died on her travels, like Shelan, and order a grand funeral of state to be conducted in her honor.

Overcome with weariness, Tori leaned her head against the wall, gratefully accepting the bare cushion her costume provided.

Gratitude gave way to guilt. *I don't deserve even this comfort.*

As her eyes grew heavy with sleep, she saw Old Griff, raising money for his ailing parent by selling fruit. Stabbing regret filled her. She wished that, just once, she had bought fruit from him.

She drifted off slowly, glancing one last time into the cloud-covered sky. The image came of Driven sailing majestically through the air, and a tear rolled down her cheek.

Can you forgive me? The hazy thought floated away as sleep overpowered her.

Tori woke up retching. Pain shot from her newly expanded stone kernel, which bubbled and churned, as though filled with burning lava.

She groaned as it seared a hundred burning pathways through her dawn channels, threads of pain shooting from her armpits, wrists, and chest. She was on fire.

Trembling, she held her arms out in front of her. Filth from her kernel expansion still caked them, but beneath it, black lines appeared one by one, darkening. They snaked up her arms and hands, searing pathways along her neck, face, back, and legs.

Fear gripped her. *Wielder's venom.*

Master Koren had warned that when a wielder's kernel was sealed—as hers had been—their natural immunity to their own venom weakened a hundredfold, and for someone with a hexatic ketua like Tori, it could be fatal.

She gritted her teeth against the pain, seeking relief wherever she could—trying to visualize the pitiful claw marks being made, breathing in the smell of death—anything to distract her, but everything else faded into her suffering.

It was just what she deserved.

Veyli's face, gray with death, came to her, and she squeezed her eyes shut as waves of pain washed over her, again and again.

When she opened them, she didn't know whether she had been in agony for a few breaths, or an eternity. Her mind was hazy; had she been here several nights, or only one?

Metal ground against stone above her head. The grate was moving.

It slid away, and the silhouette of a man appeared, looking down.

He threw down a rope. "Grab it."

She huddled against the wall, terrified.

"Do it now!" the voice commanded. Her addled mind almost recognized the speaker.

Then a cloud shifted, and Ishairo the Sunderer twinkled once again in the sky, sword raised in triumph beside the full moon. Silvery light revealed Master Koren's face, beautiful and stern.

A rush of gratitude flooded her, and she curled herself around the rope, gripping it with all her strength.

Tori sailed upward through the air, and at the top, Master Koren hauled her out. His eyes fell immediately on her arms and face, and his eyebrows drew together.

"Come quickly," he said, replacing the grate. He motioned toward the bushes.

"Where are we going?"

He quieted her with a gesture, then shifted aside the brush to reveal a narrow, single-file path. Twigs snagged her clothes as she followed him, her pace quickening and slowing, according to the ebb and flow of her pain.

After about half the time of a candle's burn, the bushes thinned and a moonlit forest took its place.

Master Koren reached into his waist pouch and pulled out a round black pill the size of a blueberry.

"This will not last," he said, holding it out to her. "But it will at least get you there."

She swallowed it. The pain eased at once.

"Where are we going?"

"We are at the outer edge of Ma'yanar," he said.

Rather than relief, a mounting disquiet arose in Tori as the implications of his words sank in.

"I'm taking you back to Peach Blossom Grove," he said, but the tone of his voice stirred dread instead of joy.

Chapter Sixty-Five

BURNING WORDS

Peach Blossom Grove lay peacefully asleep. The only sounds were the trickle of the watercourse and the rhythmic rasp of frogs beneath a downward-slipping moon.

At the base of Council's Rise, Tori shed the winter-squash costume—her dignity preferring soiled robes to facing the council dressed as a vegetable.

The venom flared once more as she stepped onto the barge, and she gripped the rail, groaning. Master Koren rushed to support her.

He motioned to the barge operators. "Move quickly."

They did, though their faces didn't register understanding of Tori's problem. Or perhaps they were too tired to care.

At the top, the trellis canopy loomed over her accusingly. She leaned on Master Koren's arm as they walked beneath it and down the pathway of overarching trees.

Apart from the elder, the entire council was seated, even Master Maeli. When they reached the table, Master Koren released her arm and took his place. Pain from her venom surged, and she gritted her teeth, doubling over, leaning her hands on her thighs for support. Master Maeli observed her with a pained expression.

The elder glided in, silver hair flowing behind her, and all members of the council rose. But before she took her seat, her white eyes shifted to Tori's bent form, and her brow furrowed with concern.

"Hers is the worst case I have seen," Master Koren said.

The elder drew near, laid a hand on Tori's shoulder, and turned her so that she faced away. Hands pressed on Tori's back, spreading warmth through her body, enveloping the venom's fire. When the pain had calmed, a refreshing coolness came, like a mountain spring bubbling from the elder's hands.

The elder turned Tori to face her then and placed three fingers below her neck, just above the glorium. The same cool spring trickled through her dawn channels until she felt healed and whole, and no black venom lines marred her hands. All that remained was the dirty residue of her kernel expansion.

Overwhelmed with gratitude, Tori bowed low, but the elder had already turned away.

"Were there no signs of venom before now?" the elder asked, taking her seat in the middle of the table.

Tori dropped her eyes. Master Koren's warnings had been made before this very council; she doubted the elder had forgotten.

"Both Master Koren and Master Banfay warned me," Tori said. "I ignored the signs. But I tried to be careful—I only ever practiced the wielding forms in a broken sequence, never all together."

An angry light flashed in Master Koren's eyes. "This did not happen to you because you practiced the forms; it is because of your lopsided practice of them! If you had trained properly, as I instructed you to, you would have recognized the signs of an imminent kernel expansion for days before it came."

Tori hung her head.

His voice softened. "Practicing out of sequence was the very thing that made you connect unwillingly with the elements. A stone kernel expansion should not result in destruction, only the expansion of the kernel and the elimination of impurities. And your venom could have been corrected."

"Be that as it may," the elder said, "you must now bear the consequences. Henceforth, you can control your venom only by cycling the elixir."

Tori glanced up, alarmed. "I thought you healed me."

"Once a wielder's own venom has turned against them, there is no cure," the elder said, "save for immortality. Yet though your venom is more potent than most, it would also prove more perilous to your enemies, were you to master the technique of using it. Yet here you must tread with great caution, for you have no means to learn its mastery from a teacher now. Therefore, proceed slowly, for the venom could swiftly turn against you whenever you wield."

She would be sure never to wield again.

The elder pointed to the glorium. "That, too, clears venom. I suspect it was the very thing that saved your life."

The glorium felt heavy around her neck, as though weighed down by her unworthiness. Clearly she could no longer keep it.

She started removing the chain, but the elder stopped her.

"I do not desire it again," the elder said. "It was a gift. And you need it now more than ever, for it may only control the venom if worn upon your person. In this regard, it may be best that you did not succeed in going to Mount Ketwanen, for had you melded that stone into a Septad, the glorium's effects would be lost to you. Now, to matters at hand: Is there anything you would speak in your defense?"

The elder's words burned more than the venom ever had. She could've borne the pain—would have, gladly—if only she had succeeded in making the Septad. But she had failed. The weight of it crushed her, robbing her of speech.

The council members turned their solemn eyes on her—apart from Master Maeli, who looked at her with compassion, and Master Koren, who refused to look at her at all.

"Perhaps an exception could be made—" Master Maeli began, but Zanda, the hard-faced woman with the purple ribbon around her forehead, cut her off.

"No exceptions. Everyone knows the consequences." Zanda looked at Tori, frowning.

"This was not a case of willful disobedience," Master Maeli said. "You heard Master Koren—her only error was in failing to properly study the scrolls."

Tori blinked hard as tears pricked her eyes. Even now, Master Maeli refused to turn against her. It was a kind of loyalty she didn't deserve.

The elder stared ahead, expression stern. "Her intentions may have been without fault, yet her actions were not. Tori, as you offered no final words, I now make my pronouncement: you are hereby banished forthwith from Peach Blossom Grove."

Tori's legs grew weak, and a vise seemed to clamp around her chest. Though she had been expecting them, hearing the words aloud somehow made them unbearable.

"But where will she go?" Master Maeli asked. "She cannot very well go back to the palace. We all know the empress's penalty for wielders."

Tori tried to imagine surviving in the wild, eating herbs and hunting animals. The thought was utterly ridiculous; she was as helpless as an infant without someone else around—she had never even made tea.

But apart from Peach Blossom Grove, there was nowhere her mother wouldn't find her. No noble family would resist the prestige that came from making it known that the Min Daughter was their guest; no commoners either, for that matter. And if she hid her identity, it wouldn't last—her mother's people would scour the land until they rooted her out. She had to return to the palace and face whatever awaited her; there was no other choice.

The elder addressed the council members. "What rumors have you heard? Any talk that would put Tori's life at risk?"

"Nothing in Greenstalk," kind-faced Yeibe said, fingering her purple bracelet. "There were many winter-squash costumes, so people only know one of them was a wielder who was apprehended—no one recognized her as the Min Daughter." She gave Tori a gentle nod. "Your secret is safe."

"There," Zanda said. "No need to trouble ourselves further. She'll go back where she belongs."

"Zanda is right," Tori said, swallowing hard. "Though I'll secretly be her prisoner, I won't lose my life for now. As long as no one knows, my mother will pretend in public that nothing happened."

She had not meant it for sympathy, but pain shadowed Master Maeli's eyes. Master Koren furrowed his brows and looked down at his thumbs, circling them.

"Then you have cheated death," the elder said. "It is more than most wielders can expect."

"What of my friends? Are they safe?"

The elder said they were; her banishment wouldn't affect them.

Reassured, Tori considered then how she would travel home alone. Though it shamed her to make requests, she didn't know what else to do. "Is there...a carriage I might take?"

"A farmer's carriage awaits you even now," the elder said. "It will convey you safely to the palace."

Relief wrestled with sadness. It hurt more, somehow, knowing her banishment had already been so thoroughly prepared.

"I will accompany her," Master Maeli said, rising, but the elder held up a hand.

"Given your soft spot for Tori, prolonging the parting will only increase your pain, and hers. Big Gao shall suffice."

Master Maeli frowned, but sat.

"Big Gao awaits you at the entrance to the Veiled Forest," the elder said. And with that, Tori was dismissed.

As the ferry drifted down to the first pool, the weight of her isolation pressed in, and she was unable to keep the tears from falling.

But when she arrived at the bottom of Council's Rise, a curly-haired silhouette came into view.

Elnora rushed forward and wrapped her arms around her. "Oh, Princess," she said, sniffling. "I should never have left you."

"I'm banished, Elnora."

Elnora wiped her eyes and nodded. "I'm ready."

Beside Tori's discarded winter-squash costume, two packs lay at Elnora's feet—the ones they had brought from Min Palace. She handed Tori her daggers and waist pouch.

A wave of gratitude enveloped her. Elnora truly was the best person in all of Arizan, far better than any servant she could have imagined—or even any friend.

When they reached the end of the peach grove, a broad figure stood waiting at the forest entrance. Big Gao. Though the light in his eyes showed him to be an immortal, everything else—clothing, hair, body language—resembled a common thug, and a dangerous one, at that. She understood now why the elder had chosen him to accompany her: no one in their right mind would trouble any carriage he was driving.

He spoke to Elnora in a gruff voice. "Go home. Only one of you is banished."

Elnora lifted her chin and met his gaze. "I'm going all the same."

Big Gao shrugged. Then, with a jerk of his head, he motioned for them to follow.

"You don't have to do this," Tori said, as they walked into the forest. She should want Elnora to stay behind for her own good—yet her stomach tightened as she waited for her answer.

Elnora squeezed her hand. "Nothing's going to keep me from standing by you ever again, you hear? That's a promise, sure as the tide."

Then they sat together inside the rough farmer's carriage that would take her face her mother.

Chapter Sixty-Six

EMPTY-HANDED

Traveling as they did through hidden trails unmarked on any map, the Min Palace was only six hundred fen away. So, eight days later, they rolled up the slope toward the palace grounds.

Tori's muscles ached from the cramped farmer's carriage, and her stomach rumbled. Her last full meal had been at Greenstalk Festival. The few dried provisions Elnora had been sensible enough to bring, plus whatever small game Big Gao had managed to scrounge up, never amounted to much. And now, she was thirsty as well, having finished her water earlier that morning.

A messenger hawk swooped past her window, reminding her of Driven. She bowed her head. But a moment later, Big Gao rapped on the door and barked, "It's confirmed. No one at the palace knows what happened in Greenstalk."

It should have been good news, but a dismal sense of inevitability settled over her as they arrived at the main palace gate—once she entered, she would never leave again. No more Kazani, no secret charitable projects. From now on, she was her mother's prisoner, in all but appearances.

Eventually, she would become her mother's voiceless pawn on the Jeng throne, and since she had failed to provide the Septad and prevent the war, the blood of her own people would also be on her hands.

She drooped, suddenly feeling very tired. Her only comfort was the thought of her bed—she would throw herself into it and sleep her life away.

The carriage rolled to a stop, and outside, a murmured conversation followed. The gate guards glanced through the windows, then refused to let the carriage pass.

Elnora cracked the door, and spoke sharply. "Do you not recognize the Min Daughter?"

The guards had to take a second look before recognizing her. She wasn't surprised. Profuse apologies followed, however, and soon they were riding through the lower circle.

The palace grounds seemed to have a shadow hanging over them, even though it was a bright autumn day. The familiar sights felt oppressive, but when they entered the upper circle, oppression deepened to a feeling of suffocation.

She asked Big Gao to take her to her mother's residence. Her mother would either be in her personal chamber preparing for court, or in her private receiving room. Either way, if her mother learned Tori had arrived without visiting her first, it would only make matters worse.

They stepped out, and Big Gao rolled away.

"Wait at my residence," she said to Elnora. "Tell Yumay and Anlin I'm fine."

Elnora folded her arms. "They'll see that for themselves when we go back together. I said I wasn't leaving you again, and I meant it."

Warmth filled Tori's chest. She might not be free, but at least she wasn't alone.

The faces of her mother's eunuchs' showed that they, too, were surprised by Tori's appearance, though they hid it by bowing extra low.

They led her and Elnora to her mother's private receiving room, announcing her arrival in a loud voice.

Her mother was sitting at a large desk, looking into a wooden box with the gold-leaf logograms for *Zinchen* embossed on the lid.

When she saw Tori, her gaze swept her from head to foot—sharp, assessing, and laced with disgust. Lina, who stood behind her mother, bowed her head in greeting.

"Fetch decent attire for the Min Daughter," her mother said, addressing the head eunuch. "Her things were lost in her travels. And take this maid to the scullery, as befits her rank and birth."

Elnora shot Tori a worried look.

"Lady Elnora is a gentlewoman," Tori said, guiding Elnora behind her. "You promoted her yourself."

"And she is hereby demoted to the scullery," her mother said, with a dismissive glance. She spoke then in a voice Tori knew was for the benefit of any eavesdropping servants. "This lowborn woman is to blame for the trials the Min Daughter endured on her travels, as well as her current unpresentable state." She flicked her fingers, and the door guards rushed in, grabbing Elnora's arms.

"Take your hands off her!" Tori said.

The guards hesitated, looking at her mother.

"The scullery is a kindness she scarcely deserves, given the gravity of her offenses. But I am merciful. Should more serious charges surface, however, I will not be so indulgent."

Tori froze. Her mother was threatening to accuse Elnora of wielding.

With a wave of her mother's hand, the guards dragged Elnora away, just as maids bustled in with fresh clothes for Tori.

Helpless and angry, Tori let them dress her in clean outer robes.

When they had taken her filthy ones away, her mother said, "Lina, ensure no servants are within listening distance." Lina dipped her head and left.

Her mother looked at her then, excitement flickering behind her calm eyes. "Bring it to me."

Tori dropped her gaze to the floor. Her mother was asking for the Septad.

"I don't have it," she said, her failure at Peach Blossom Grove dragging on her like an iron chain.

"Explain yourself."

When Tori remained silent, a shadow darkened her mother's face.

"You deceived me. Defied me. And now you return empty-handed?" Her voice dropped, cold and measured. "You are a disgrace."

Tori's head pounded. She *was* a disgrace. And a fool. She had destroyed her only chance of freedom.

Feeling shaky, she went to her usual chair.

"I did not give you leave to sit," her mother snapped.

Tori remained standing, head bowed.

Her mother drew a bright yellow stone from her desk drawer, the spiraling, flashing reds and blues inside revealing it to be from Tey Zuben. When she held it up, a strange weakness washed through Tori, like at the onset of a cold.

"Your defects must be redeemed," her mother said. "But you will be happy to know that, in so doing, you might also save those like you, which was your goal, after all. It is foolish—*wasteful*, I believe you once said—to destroy something that can be put to good use."

Her words left Tori uneasy. "What are you talking about?"

"Wielders," she said simply. "I intend to make them useful, and you will help me do it. They will have to remain in the dungeons, however—that is not negotiable."

"You're going to enslave them?"

"I suspect that would be their preference, when compared with the saw."

"You can't cage people just to use their magic."

Her mother raised an eyebrow.

"What are you going to use them for?" Tori said.

"Does it matter?" Her mother tapped the yellow stone with a finger, and a jolt went through Tori's legs, forcing her to lean on a chair. Her mother gave a slow, satisfied nod. "Moving on to other matters, starting today, you will attend court with me as usual, only from now on, we will discuss in advance which views you will express."

Tori stared at her, stunned.

"In addition to this, you will wear your equitess collar to all court proceedings, to reinforce the gravity of your words in the ministers' minds." When she dropped the stone into her drawer, Tori's stomach lurched.

"We are due at court shortly for the morning session. Instruct the maids to bathe and dress you at once, then return—there are matters of consequence to discuss. I have secured the nobles' support to unify Shudon under the Min banner, but now, we must speak of logistics. Today, the ministers will debate the merits of deploying Ants to the front lines."

The words sank in slowly, chilling her.

"They will, of course, conclude that this must be done," her mother said, calm as ever, "once you explain to them how equitable a solution it is."

"No." Tori's hands curled into fists at her side. "You might as well just execute me now."

"I have no wish for your death—you must believe this. Furthermore, your cooperation is far more useful to me." Her gaze didn't waver. "But do not be mistaken, I would not hesitate to send a scullery maid to the saw."

Chapter Sixty-Seven

A SINGLE HAIR FROM NINE OXEN

Tori sat immobile on her throne, her neck throbbing under the feathered equitess collar her mother's maids had adjusted too tightly.

"Your report mentioned an oversupply on the Ant farms," her mother said, addressing a black-robed minister. She folded her hands serenely on her desk. "How many Ants could be spared?"

"Many triple births have been documented lately, Your Majesty," the woman replied. "This increase would easily allow two hundred thousand Ants to be drafted."

Tori clenched her jaw.

The Minister of the Right frowned. "Untrained slaves can contribute nothing to the cause, Your Majesty. The wisdom of the ancients would advise rather to strengthen your primary army, those who are properly armed with etched weapons and armor."

A red-robed scholar stepped forward. "Ancient wisdom must not be disregarded, but the bamboo that bends is stronger than the oak that resists: adaptability and flexibility are essential for the strength of a kingdom. Your Majesty should adapt to the changing needs by using unconventional methods."

"Ants play an important role in society," the Minister of the Right returned. "Who else would touch the jobs contaminated by death, if the Ants are all killed in battle?"

Her supporters voiced their agreement.

The Minister of the Left smirked. "Two hundred thousand Ants is like a single hair from nine oxen. Who will notice they're gone?"

Murmurs of agreement rippled around her.

Veyli's smiling face flashed in Tori's mind, and she squeezed her eyes shut. She knew she could persuade the court to see reason; she could sway them in two breaths.

The Minister of the Left faced the empress. "If you made use of Ant vagabonds as well, Your Majesty's vanguard would double in number. The people would bless you for ridding them of the beggars and strangling smile addicts fouling the streets."

The empress nodded thoughtfully, fingertips pressed together. Tori gripped the arms of her throne, stomach churning; any moment she would be called upon to speak.

Her mother's gaze wandered to the queens painted on the wall panels, pausing there, as though giving the matter full consideration. Then finally, she looked at Tori. "What does the Min Daughter think?"

Tori gritted her teeth and, with leaden steps, she forced herself down the dais stairs.

But as she stood among the ministers, anger flared inside her, and she changed her mind. She would end this madness now.

"Ants will make poor fighters," Tori said. "They have no military training, and many are malnourished. Beggars and addicts are worse. A vanguard of Ants might delay the conflict long enough for only a marginal advantage, if that. They would be nothing but an easy slaughter."

Her mother gave Tori a slow, cold look. "Is that how the eyes of equity see it? Like"—she paused—"an execution?"

She stared at Tori meaningfully, and Tori read the unspoken words: *I would not hesitate to send a scullery maid to the saw.*

Her mind filled with the image of Elnora being dragged away between two guards.

"No, Your Majesty," she said with a lump in her throat, then recited the lines her mother had given her. "Ants are a prolific race. Their species propagates far more quickly than humans. They will spring back from any"—she swallowed against the tightness of her collar—"from any reduction in population. Those who can be most easily spared must be willing to sacrifice themselves first. This is what equity demands."

"The Min Daughter speaks sense," the Minister of the Left joined in quickly. "Aggressively cutting back robust herbs doesn't harm the garden, it strengthens it. And even a small advantage is still an advantage."

Other officials praised the wisdom of this, and before long, the majority was in agreement.

"Very well," her mother said. "It will be done as the Min Daughter suggests."

She gave Tori a final lingering look, then casually dropped her gaze to other reports on her desk.

Chapter Sixty-Eight

INTO THE SUNLIGHT

Something inside Tori had fractured.

"I need to return to my residence," she said, as they entered her mother's receiving room after court. "I want to see my gentlewomen." She had to make sure they were well, and to find out whether Yumay's people could somehow help Elnora.

"Requests will be considered when you have proved you are ready to be useful."

"Isn't that what I just did? What more do you want?"

"Willful submission," her mother said calmly, fingering the yellow Tey Zuben stone again. "From all of your kind. Complete control is what is needed."

Tori shook her head in disgust. "You think keeping them locked in the dungeon will achieve that?"

"Yes, I expect it will. As for you, a room has been prepared for you below where you can reflect on your current situation. Until you find yourself feeling more cooperative, you will stay there at all times, unless your great-grandmother calls you for chief-equitess training, or unless I summon you."

The eunuch announced the arrival of Bokoon.

"Do not worry about losing face," her mother said. "All that is known is that the Min Daughter has returned from a long trip and will be conducting intense studies for me in my palace residence."

"Losing face? People's opinions are the least of my concerns!"

"You should reconsider that. Empires are not built upon truth, but on belief. Even the course of a war does not obey fact, but opinion." Her mother inclined her head. "As we saw in court today."

Bokoon entered, bowing low to the empress, while shooting Tori a contemptuous glance from under his brows.

"Bokoon, you will accompany Princess Tori to her new study. Bolt the door behind her and stand guard. Her work is of the utmost importance; she must not be disturbed."

Spiteful satisfaction flickered in his eyes. "Yes, Your Majesty."

"Tori, you will be summoned here tomorrow to report on your progress."

"Am I at least allowed to return to my residence to eat," Tori asked, "or am I meant to starve my way through my studies?"

"A meal will be brought to you after dark." Her mother unlocked the box with the gold-leaf logograms for *Zinchen*, removed a stack of papers, and began reading—Tori was dismissed.

Outside the receiving room, a long hall led them to a door that had remained locked for as long as Tori could remember. Bokoon pushed it open to reveal a staircase descending into darkness. Holding out a torch, he led the way to a stone landing, then down another hall that ended in a door with an iron bolt.

He opened it and stepped aside. "Princess." Though he dipped his head to her, he couldn't hide the loathing in his eyes.

Tori looked in. A small, dimly lit study peered back at her, with a haggard table and chair hunched over a washed-out rug, and a frail bookcase sagging against the stone wall. On the shelves, books and scrolls on policy lay in stacks, obviously for show. Who was meant to see them, Tori couldn't guess.

A clay pitcher and cup sat on the table alongside a lighted reading candle, the only other light coming from a narrow window less than one handspan wide, and a chimney corner with a struggling fire. A thin mattress lay on the floor beside it, presumably her bed.

Most servant's quarters were less austere. And yet, it was so much better than what other wielders would get.

The moment she stepped inside, Bokoon bolted the door behind her with a sharp click.

Her mind turned to the Ants and to her betrayal of them, how she had doomed them to be slaughtered.

Those who can most easily be spared must be willing to sacrifice themselves first.

She slumped at the table and dropped her head into her hands. What had she done? Tears came despite her efforts to stop them.

What would Master Maeli advise?

While the light outside her narrow window changed from white, to yellow, to deep orange, she sat inert, contemplating her failure. Her role as equitess was now a farce. She tugged at the feathered collar, shaking the clasp, but it wouldn't budge, and since someone else had always fastened it, she had no idea how it worked.

Its pressure against her throat reminded her how parched she was—she had drunk nothing since early that morning and was starting to feel dizzy. The pitcher contained barely enough water to fill the small clay cup. She grabbed it and poured.

Trembling now from dizziness, she spilled it; then, trying to steady the cup, she knocked it to the floor. Tori cursed as a water stain spread on the rug.

"Bokoon?"

No response.

"I spilled my water," she said, her head spinning from thirst. "Bring me some more."

"Your meal will be brought later," came the muffled reply.

"I'm not asking for a meal. I'm asking for water."

Silence.

She tightened her fists. "I am the Min Daughter, and I'm speaking to you!"

"And I'm a guard, not a food server."

She glared at the door, but dizziness overcame her. Aware then of how uncomfortably cool and damp the room had grown, she sat by the dwindling flame that persevered in the chimney among a pile of ashes.

The dizziness passed, and Tori moved to the window slit, hoping for sunlight, tiptoeing so her chin rested in the narrow opening. The smell of the cool autumn air filled her lungs, along with a painful longing for freedom. She moved away.

"At least bring me some more wood," she said to the door. "The fire has gone out."

No answer.

An image of Master Koren wielding fire came to her, and she pushed it away.

She banged on the door. "I said I need more wood!"

Her voice hitched from the dryness in her throat, and she started coughing, desperately eyeing the empty pitcher, then the water stain on the rug. She noticed few drops next to the pitcher, and she rushed to suck them up, barely wetting the tip of her tongue, which only increased her desperation.

The dizziness returned—worse this time—and she found she could no longer stand. She huddled on her mattress.

Whispers drifted through her, like a barely perceptible breath: *Quench your thirst.*

As she stared at the ashes, her thirst-muddled thoughts drifted to the playactor of Ayenashi in Peach Blossom Grove, wielding spilled water from the floor. In her mind, the water transformed into a maelstrom with a little girl thrashing around inside. She squeezed her eyes shut.

She tried to swallow again, but found her throat was simply too dry. Fixing her mind's eye on the elixir, she connected with it, cycling it through her dawn channels. She streamed it toward the rug, willing the water to rise up into the cup, even as she fought the fear of losing control. Elixir streamed freely from her newly expanded stone kernel, a reservoir so much deeper than she had remembered.

But nothing else happened.

She tried again, then again, each time meeting the same result.

What had the wielding scroll said? She tried to get her mind lucid enough to visualize it. She seemed to remember wielding was different from phytolyzing plants or propelling spirit stones, and words from the scroll came back to her: *First, touch the element. Then, stream.*

She instinctively identified the elements in her ketua—water, air, earth, wood, fire, metal—and reached for the water element, but it evaded her like a slippery fish.

In her mind's eye she lunged at it, gripping it fiercely, then tried streaming it outward. It pushed against the confines of her stone kernel, like steam in a firmly closed pot.

She gazed at the water stain, licking her dry lips. What had she missed? With regret she thought of how many times she had skimmed the wielding scroll, disdaining its words. Now, though, she closed her eyes and strained to recall any detail she could.

A few moments later, her eyes opened. "That's it."

Once again, she connected with the deep reservoir of elixir in her stone kernel, and, in her mind's eye, lunged at the water element, except this time, she willed water and elixir to bind together before streaming them outward.

She felt when the stream connected to the water in the rug, like two puzzle pieces snapping into place, and knew she could command the water outside her using the water element within.

Just as she had done when phytolyzing plants, she visualized the water in the rug rising into the cup. It floated out, hovered precariously for a moment, then drifted, trembling, to the clay cup and poured inside.

Tori gulped down its musty contents, tipping back her head to suck out every last drop. It was enough. As her headache eased, and some of her strength returned, immense gratitude filled her, tempered by a lingering fear of what she had unleashed. If she could do this out of thirst, what might she do out of anger?

Suddenly, dark lines appeared her arms, searing them. Wielding always had a cost.

The elder had said the glorium had preserved Tori's life before, yet though she felt it humming on her chest, it did nothing to ease the pain. But the elder had also spoken of cycling elixir.

With hissing breaths through clenched teeth, every movement an agony, Tori cycled elixir until it rushed through her dawn channels at will. As it overpowered the venom, indecipherable whispers blew through her, until the pain finally ceased, leaving Tori spent and shivering.

A shaft of evening sun now fell through the window slit, and Tori dragged her mattress beneath it, positioning herself so that it fell first on her face, then on one arm at a time, then on parts of her torso. But the patch of warmth was too narrow, and she grew colder.

Did her mother think a window was too great a luxury? Or perhaps a means of escape? It was ridiculous; Tori was under her complete control, there was nowhere she could go. If she had been given a room with a real window, she could have at least warmed herself in the sun. She steeled herself against what she would do next.

Cycling elixir once more, she reached out and touched the earth element. It was solid and difficult to move, yet once she did, it bound easily to the elixir, and she streamed it toward one of the bricks that framed the window slit. The brick slid out with a crash.

Her eyes flew to the door, dread rising—but no sound followed, no sign that Bokoon had heard.

Relief surged through her, then anger. What if she herself had just crashed to the floor, having fainted from thirst?

More easily this time, she pushed out another brick, careful to make it land outside on the grass. The shaft of light had doubled in width, measuring around two handspans wide.

She returned to the mat, comforted by the warmth as she cycled elixir to clear her venom, her mind turning over what she had just done.

Her mother had spoken of controlling wielders, yet in Peach Blossom Grove, no such control was ever necessary. There, they saw wielding as good, and everything wielders did reflected that, unlike in the outside world, where wielding was seen as seditious and dangerous.

Her mind went to the wielder at the Tailu Festival, then, more reluctantly, to her own past. Those tragedies would never have happened in Peach Blossom Grove.

She mused on this. *Wielding warms and wounds. It heals and harms. It's not evil; it just is.*

Her mother was wrong. Tori didn't need controlling, she just needed to master herself.

Power is never clean—but if I never wield it, I can't save anyone.

She let out a bitter sigh. Who could she save? She was a prisoner.

Her thoughts drifted to Elnora—her only real friend—buried in the scullery because of her.

She wiped her eyes, then pulled the birth charm from her pouch, staring into it. *Was I born to save, or to destroy?*

The birth charm swirled energetically, and an intense longing stirred within her to know the circumstances of her birth. Then, as she gazed at the strange symbols inside it, twisting and changing, a slow realization began to dawn.

When the full implications of it seized her, she bolted to her feet, pulse hammering.

"Bokoon," she said, banging on the door. "Open immediately."

Silence.

She cursed—she needed to get back to receiving room immediately, before her mother left for the night to see one of her intimates.

Her mother had said she would summon Tori tomorrow...should she wait?

As she paced back and forth through the shaft of reddening light, her steps grew slower, a thought taking shape, frightening and inevitable.

Eyes on the window, she stopped, shoulders squared. She was done waiting on her mother's whim.

Tori curled both hands around her feathered ruff and yanked, shattering the clasp, and flung it down, sending it skidding across the floor.

Then she wielded earth. In twice the time it would take to drain a cup, she had dislodged enough bricks to transform the window slit into a woman-sized hole.

She gripped the new ledge and hauled herself onto the raw stone frame. Then she wiggled, squeezing through the narrow opening, and fresh, new air rushed into her lungs as she tumbled out into the sunlight.

Chapter Sixty-Nine

A PRECIOUS REQUEST

Tori circled the outside of the building until she came to its wide entrance, then raced inside all the way to her mother's receiving room. She finally had what she needed to set things right; her mother would have no choice but to agree. And her most precious request, she would save for last.

"I'm afraid she's not here, Your Highness," the eunuch said.

Tori frowned. "This early?"

Then she remembered today was a full court day. Though Tori only ever attended morning sessions, some days court ran in the afternoon as well. Her mother might still be there.

She exited her mother's residence, hurrying through its private gardens, then up the steps of Her Majesty's court building and down the Hall of Heavenly Fragrance.

At the door, eunuchs waited alongside two Varanaken, who had temporarily replaced the door guards on account of a suspected wielder being recently spotted nearby. Tori swept past them and into the Royal Court Hall.

Except for her mother, the hall was empty. The empress sat at her desk on the dais surrounded by a stack of reports, writing. She looked up, surprised, and set her brush down between an incense burner and two silver bells, one for Lina, the other for the eunuchs.

"I told Bokoon you were not to be disturbed. Send him in."

"He's not here," Tori said, mounting the dais steps and casually leaning back in her throne. "I'm dismissing him from my service."

Her mother raised an eyebrow. "Except that Bokoon serves me."

Tori shrugged. "Then you can keep him. Now, we need to talk."

"You will return to your room immediately. No defiance will be tolerated, least of all from my defective daughter."

The comment stung.

"Except I'm not your daughter, am I?" Tori said, feigning cool indifference. "The moment Granny Nuwang died, the ministers voted your sister to be crowned in your place—she had an heir; you didn't."

Her mother's face was a mask of calm.

Tori continued. "But then you showed up with me, convincing them all that you had birthed an heir in Tey Zuben, that their vote was invalid. But you never gave birth, did you? It was all a lie."

"A bold accusation from one with so much to hide. Are you not ashamed, considering what you are?"

Tori reached into her stone kernel and touched the fire element, then bound it to elixir and streamed it outward. She gave a mental command to the standing lanterns at the end of the hall, then opened her palm. The flame from the lantern leaped into it.

"I'm not ashamed," Tori said, forcing a relaxed posture, even as the effort of wielding drained her.

Her mother pulled out the same bright yellow stone she had been holding earlier. "I suspected fire," she murmured. "This simplifies matters."

She whispered something into the stone, too low for Tori to hear, but it sounded like the Old Speech. Tori's limbs weakened, and she shivered with the feeling of the onset of a cold.

Her mother held the stone toward Tori, and the fire element dropped back into her kernel, confined once again to her ketua instead of streaming out, the elixir churning uneasily around it. With another word from her mother, the fire element leaped up again, binding with elixir, then shot from Tori's palm, burning it.

The horrible realization struck: her mother not only wished to control wielders, she had found a practical way to do it.

Weakening moment by moment, Tori tried in vain to regain control. The elixir swirled insistently, as though urging her to act, yet Tori found she could no longer even connect with it.

As though responding to her acknowledged helplessness, the elixir rushed through her dawn channels on its own, gathering mass, pooling itself in her stone kernel. The moment her kernel was full, the elixir hovered expectantly, like a person waiting to speak.

Tori wanted to listen, but was too weak to try. The only thing she had strength enough to do was to give mental assent to anything the elixir willed.

This was enough.

The power of her mother's stone shattered like a broken chain. Then the elixir split six ways, binding all six elements at once, and six streams flew from Tori's palms, connecting with the elements all around. Through the windows lining the tops of walls came the sound of a watery rush as a fountain exploded outside. An unexpected wind gusted through the hall then, and the marble floor rippled like water.

Her mother observed it all calmly. But when the golden headpiece she wore trembled, she stiffened. A moment later, she dropped the stone, shaking her hand as though cooling a burn.

Tori rushed off the dais, breathless, the stream of elements and elixir finally drying up. She felt the hum of the glorium as dark venom lines seared pathways along her arms and hands. She cycled elixir, cooling them, then locked eyes with her mother.

"If you ever use that stone again—or anything like it—I'll make sure the world sees this." Tori held up her birth charm.

Color drained from Zinchen's face. "Bring that to me. Now."

"I swear by the Six, unless you give me what I want, I'll show it to the ministers. You'll never get your war or a united Shudon. And if the *Chronicles of the Queens* records you at all, it'll be as a fraud."

Zinchen rose, taut as a drawn bow. "Guards!"

The Varanaken burst in—only to halt midstride when they saw Tori standing alone beneath the dais.

Zinchen's voice rang out. "Seize that charm."

Tori panicked—if they took the charm, she would once again be powerless. She wielded earth and air, sending the birth charm flying through the window, mentally commanding it to go to Peach Blossom Grove.

The Varanaken's eyes widened with rage: "She's a wielder!" They rushed her.

Tori slid the Night Twins into her hands.

"Stand down!" her mother shouted, but her voice was swallowed up in the clash of weapons as Tori blocked their strikes.

One swung his sword at her head. She dropped to her knees and slid, arching backward, wind skimming her face as the sword swung past.

She jumped to her feet and blocked a heavy blow, the force of it jarring her arm to the shoulder. They were too strong.

Her mother's voice drifted in and out of the clash of weapons, but the guards' hatred for wielders deafened them to her commands. As Tori blocked another strike, she saw her mother rushing down the dais steps.

With cold clarity she knew she would be dead before her mother reached her.

The elixir rose up within her, and she wielded earth and air. Ash flew from her mother's incense burner into both men's eyes, but this would buy her mere moments against trained Varanaken. She had to make a choice: them, or her.

As they cursed and wiped their faces, Tori leaped into the air, Night Twins raised. She plunged a dagger into one man's throat, then launched the remaining dagger toward the other man's head. It planted in his eye. He collapsed with a thump, just as her mother rushed up beside her.

Venom scorched Tori's wrists as she yanked the blades out again with a sickening squelch. She heaved, the sight of the bloody daggers in her hands bringing on a wave of nausea.

Her mother stared—not at the bodies, but at Tori. Then she took a breath, smoothing her expression, and without a word returned to her throne and rang the bell for Lina.

Tori turned away, trembling, just as Lina walked in.

"Lina, the guards were giving a demonstration and became careless," her mother said. "Have this cleaned up."

In the time it would take a candlewick to catch, Lina returned with servants, who mopped up the blood and dragged out the bodies. Tori forced herself not to watch. Did these men have children waiting for them at home? Self-loathing filled her.

When they were alone again, her mother said, "No one must see your birth charm. The symbols inside it will betray us both—there are some at court who know how to read such things." She studied her then, sorrow flickering behind her composed expression. "The symbols are not, as you guessed, those created by Min blood. And in the future, be more careful not to be seen wielding. Do not force my hand."

"That you can even say that," Tori said, struggling to mask her hurt. "I'm just another expendable piece on your gameboard."

Her mother's eyes took on a far-off look. "There is sorrow in duty. It is agony to give up your child for love of country. Yet I would do it again." She paused, as though considering whether to continue. "Just as I did with my son."

Tori knit her brow—her mother had always been called barren.

"You were wrong, you know," her mother said quietly. "I did give birth in Tey Zuben." A weary smile touched her lips. "The Tey Zuben queen gave me a choice—keep my son and forfeit the throne, or give him up and receive..." She gestured to Tori. "An heir. I chose to save Shudon."

Tori reeled. A brother—sacrificed for her.

"Where is he now?" she asked.

"In the place where he was born—the Hidden Realm, where time stands still. He will remain there forever as he was...an infant. And Min will forever be bound to Tey Zuben because of it."

What in the name of the Six did that mean?

Her mother seemed to contemplate the place where the guards had fallen, then the window the birth charm had flown through. She exhaled softly and folded her hands. "You said you wished to speak."

Tori straightened. Her time had come.

"I have six requests," she said, though her mother would understand they were really demands. "First, give up this plan of yours to enslave wielders."

Her mother glanced at the bright yellow stone on the floor by her feet, then at the hand it had obviously burned.

She picked it up, gazing at it as though weighing her chances of success, then slid it into her sleeve. "Very well."

"And no wielder should be executed until they are tested publicly at the palace."

Her mother gave her a dubious look.

"This will reaffirm your greatness in the people's eyes," Tori said, repeating the argument she had rehearsed. "It will establish you as a ruler who never punishes unjustly, even those most hated, which in turn will increase the people's trust and devotion."

Her mother seemed to consider this. She dipped her chin.

Tori breathed a silent sigh of relief. Now the next part had meaning.

"And I told you I would bring you the Septad. I still intend to." But even as she said it, a doubt nagged her: *How?* "You, in turn, must promise to protect the Ants from the front line."

Her mother arched a brow. "I was not aware you held the Ants in such high regard." She pursed her lips, evidently turning this revelation over in her mind. Then, after a beat, she inclined her head in agreement.

"Finally, until I return with the Septad, do not take any more action to advance this war."

"That will depend on when you expect to return. What is your estimate?"

Tori hesitated. She didn't know. Even if she somehow convinced the elder to give her the map to Mount Ketwanen, she still had to travel there. And before that, she needed to find the Ghost Stone. Not to mention that she actually had to make the Septad, which—according to Master Kwai'le—at her current skill level, could kill her. She might not return at all.

"Six moons. Furthermore—" Tori said, keeping her momentum, "if you want to take the Jeng throne, you'll have to sit on it yourself."

Her mother gave Tori a knowing half-smile, as if to say, *I knew you would piece it together*. "Your father, Lord Tam, was well loved in Jeng. Many there still consider his family's branch the true Thana line."

"Except he wasn't my father," Tori said, unable to keep the edge from her voice.

"He would have loved you regardless. That is the sort of man he was. He would have wanted you to claim the throne."

Tori folded her arms. "Even if you take down the Jeng emperor, I'm still only third in line. Did you forget the emperor has a son? And a half brother, Prince Filo?"

Her mother tsked. "Nobody wants a man to rule. And his son is two years old. As for Filo, his claim will vanish the moment he becomes your lawful intimate."

Tori narrowed her eyes. "I'm not taking an intimate I don't even know. And as I said, I won't be your puppet in Jeng."

Her mother's gaze cooled. "You were not born to follow your own will, but to uphold a greater one. If you will not rule in Jeng, your cousin Yuchi might as well be heir."

The words landed like a blade. So that was it. The only reason she was still breathing was because of her tenuous claim to Jeng's throne.

She shoved the thought aside, refusing to let the pain take hold. She'd find a way out later. For now, there was only one move left.

Tori nodded. "Fine. I'll sit on the throne, but I won't ally with Prince Filo."

Her mother's eyes glinted, just as they did when she planned her moves on a game board. She nodded slowly—was she merely contemplating, or giving her assent? It must be the latter.

"And the Jeng takeover must be done peacefully," Tori said.

"If this Septad is all it promises to be, that will be an easy thing. Make it quickly. I will issue a notice today that the Min Daughter is traveling on the empress's business. You have three moons."

"No, I said I needed—"

"Three moons is the most I can allow. Events have progressed too far to delay longer than that. You will be provided with a carriage and enough gold petals to travel in a manner that befits my heir. And of course, an adequate guard will ensure you arrive safely at Greenstalk Village."

"The gold is all I need," Tori said. "I can hire my own carriage. And I travel alone."

"Hire one if you wish, but I will not risk the journey going wrong. My guards will accompany you."

Tori lifted her chin. "They may not return."

Her mother's gaze flicked to the floor where the Varanaken had fallen, and she hesitated.

"Very well. Just remember, nothing is more important than the unification of Shudon. If you were ever seen wielding, the damage would be irreparable." Regret clouded her face. "I would have no choice but to enforce the law."

A sharp knot twisted in Tori's chest. *I'm not her daughter.*

Her mother studied her thoughtfully for a long moment.

"Someday you will make a strong empress," she said softly, almost affectionately. "I only hope you live to see it."

She placed a hand on the eunuch's bell, and Tori's stomach tightened—she hadn't made her most precious request.

"Wait," Tori said, as the bell chimed through the hall. "There's one more thing."

She fixed her mother with a hard stare. “Give me back my gentlewoman.”

Chapter Seventy

GHOST STONE

Gray skies greeted them when Tori and Elnora passed through the Veil of Ayenashi, and the air in the Veiled Forest smelled of rain. Lomi shifted gently around the bases of plants and trees, as though preparing their roots for the coming water.

"Are you sure, Princess?" Elnora said. "I'm sure Master Banfay would put in a good word for you."

Elnora was as solicitous as ever. Thankfully, her time in the scullery had been too short to embitter her—though Tori wondered if anything could really embitter so sweet a soul.

"I'd better do this on my own," Tori said. "I don't want to put Master Banfay in an awkward position with the council."

But the closer they came to Peach Blossom Grove, the more Tori's worry grew. Would the mere act of returning be seen by the council as an act of defiance, even if she was just there to talk? She might not even make it to the council, actually. After what she had done, the villagers themselves might throw her out.

Still, she had to try. There would be no chance of turning things around for the Ants and wielders without the Septad, and for that, she needed the elder's map—or rather, permission to copy it.

They hadn't been walking for long before a light drizzle misted the air, and soon after, a gentle rain fell.

"Something just occurred to me," Tori said, stopping on the path. "If the council sends me away, they might ban me from entering this forest again. This could be my last chance to find the Ghost Stone."

"But if they do that, I can't see them giving you the map either. What good would the Ghost Stone be?"

Tori paused, thinking it through. "I'll figure that out later. Right now, I need take my chances before the rain stops."

"All right, Princess. You know best." She huddled under the branches of an oak, hood raised, tucking back her curls.

"You should go to Peach Blossom Grove," Tori said. "This could take a while."

"Then I'll wait a while," Elnora said, and folded her arms.

Tori looked at her fondly. "Don't worry, I'm safer here than anywhere else on Arizan. Go say hello to"—the image of Senrik came to her, hand resting on the hilt of his sword, and heat rose to her cheeks—"to Ruvien and the others."

With a reluctant nod, Elnora left.

Alone in the rain, Tori turned in a slow circle, searching for dragon-blood trees. Though she was far from Dragon Blood Hill, a few of the trees had scattered throughout the Veiled Forest, and it made sense to her to eliminate the smaller number before moving on to the bulk of them.

She eventually found two, but after she had let down their sap to draw out the shield scorpions, her spirit sense revealed no air element along the ground, and the rain, instead of getting stronger, appeared to be letting up. She cursed. She should have started with Dragon Blood Hill.

As she headed toward the giant, grassy-topped mushroom shapes, she scanned the ground with her spirit sense. Just before arriving at the hill, however, something shifted in the corner of her eye. She turned to look.

Nothing.

A few steps later, the same thing happened: the moment she turned, she could no longer find what she thought she had seen.

When she saw something shift a third time, Tori continued staring straight ahead, keeping sight of it in her peripheral vision. Something red vanished, then a patch of blue.

Flowers were disappearing...ghost flowers.

Still looking straight ahead, she kept the blue in her sight, then tried to sense the air element around it—but she didn't have the skill to send her spirit sense sideways. She focused on the patch of blue in her side vision, and slowly turned.

Instead of blue flowers, a shimmering tree stump caught her eye. It was in the process of disappearing, consumed by points of light, but although its bark was no longer visible, something like a trail of clotted blood ran down one side—a dragon-blood tree.

Though nothing visible grew beside it, after searching the ground for shield scorpions she stepped closer, leaning in.

Raindrops splashed off the stump, then hovered above the ground beside it, about one handspan high. Tori smiled.

She reached out, brushing her fingertips on soft, invisible petals, then sent her spirit sense into the ground beneath them, scanning for the air element. A feeling of lightness touched her senses, and she latched on, scanning farther and farther around the plant, trying to figure out which direction the element was spreading.

She found a pathway at last. As she followed it, she noticed more and more drops of water hovering above the ground—she had found the vein of the air element the ghost flowers were feeding on.

Crouching low, she searched with her spirit sense, trying to find the place where the air element would grow stronger. But instead, the element suddenly disappeared.

She stood, a bitter smile on her lips—this was pointless; she didn't have the skill.

The rain, which had dwindled to a sprinkle, started lashing down once more, plastering her hair to her face. This might be the last time she ever stood in the Veil of Ayenashi; how could she consider quitting?

She retraced her steps back to the stump and found the ghost flowers again. As she scanned the ground with her spirit sense, a new vein appeared, veering in a different direction.

Following it on a meandering path, she rushed forward as she felt the buoyancy of the air element increase, past one of the dragon-blood trees she had bled earlier.

As she crossed, a shield scorpion turned and struck at Tori's foot. She jumped back just in time, but now an army of them surrounded her, tails raised. No more sap remained; they had cleaned the tree.

She fumbled in her pouch for the clotted dragon's blood, then threw it straight at them. They rushed to it, piling on top of each other in a greedy, writhing mass.

Tori slowly backed away, feeling shaky from the near disaster. As she did, whispers drifted through her and she tilted her head, straining to hear. But all she could hear was the downpour. She leaned against a tree, frustrated and exhausted.

The whispers came again, but her agitated mind couldn't understand them. Then the trickling sound of water streaming from the branches overhead reminded her of the Waterwall, and a sense of peace filled her.

She stilled her mind, remembering the glowing waters and the ancient spirit being who had spoken. Frustration left her, and she simply yielded to her desire to understand the whispers.

A knowing came on her then, just as when she connected with her daggers at the Waterwall, and she perceived she must connect with the elixir.

The moment she did, a *pop* sounded in her ears, making her wince, but instead of deafening her to the outside world, the voice whispering within her became clear: it was telling her to wield.

Because her mind was still on the ghost flowers, she reached into her stone kernel for the air element—but the whispers stopped her.

Not air, they said. *Water.*

It made no sense. She stood still, wondering if she had heard right.

She touched the water element inside, bound it to elixir, and streamed it out. The thrill of unlimited power filled her: water was in everything! But the whispers warned her sternly to let it go; she must reach out only to the rainwater that soaked the ground.

As she obeyed, more instructions came: she was not to command the water, as she had with the water in the rug, but simply to allow her spirit sense to travel with it over everything it touched.

Her spirit sense flowed over it and she listened, strolling along the path it took, rain beating on her head and back.

Air and water converged, soaking her spirit sense while lifting it up, telling her this was the place. She dropped to her knees and started digging with her hands.

Though the earth was soft and wet, it was slow work, and her fingers soon felt sore. Worse, the discouraging understanding eventually came that she had for some time been digging in the wrong direction; she would have to start again.

A glance at her dirt-caked fingernails confirmed she needed a tool. But she had brought nothing, and any sticks she could find now would be rain-soaked and break easily.

With an inward cringe, she remembered the Night Twins. She hated the idea of using those precious weapons for such crude work, but saw no other choice. So, she slid one of them from her belt and started digging.

The rain continued pouring while she dug, and she clumsily wielded rainwater, commanding it into the surrounding soil to keep her deepening trench from filling.

After about the time of a stone's warming in the sun, she sat back on her heels, surveying the hole she had made. It was the size of a watermelon, and deep enough to reach her elbows.

As she went to continue digging, her dagger suddenly shifted aside, away from the soil, throwing Tori off-balance. Perplexed, she started again, but again the same thing happened, her dagger shifting away as though it were a magnet repelled by its own kind.

She experimented with other spots in the hole and found that, while some areas allowed her to dig, others repelled her dagger entirely, leading her to surmise that the air element in the Night Twins was reacting in some way to the air element below.

Then her spirit sense snapped into focus, locking on to something. She sheathed her dagger and carefully dug with her fingers. When she felt a hard spot in the ground, she stopped wielding water, letting the rain fall into the hole, washing away the soil. Gradually, something that looked like a fragile soap bubble emerged, poking through the dirt. Her breath caught—the Ghost Stone!

Fearful of popping it, Tori gently coaxed it free, then scooped it into her hand. Its solidity and weight surprised her; although lighter than most stones of the same size, it was anything but fragile.

When the rain had washed the last of the dirt away, she held it up, transfixed by its smooth, perfectly round shape and delicate iridescent sheen.

She gave a short, bright laugh.

Warmth radiated through her even as the cool autumn rain beat down, and she broke into a run, heading for Peach Blossom Grove.

But as she left the forest and stepped onto the path lined by peach trees, she stopped for a moment, her excitement fading, heaviness taking its place. She plodded toward the blurry, rain-soaked village, her pulse throbbing languidly in her throat, trying to prepare herself for the moment when she would once again be cast out.

Chapter Seventy-One

THE PATH REVEALED

Zinchen's private war chamber stilled, like a caged beast ready to spring.

"Those are serious words," Zinchen said. "Can they be trusted?"

Joktan and Javan stood across the table, faces grave.

"Lord Akiren's matriarch visited while I was training at his villa," Joktan said. "I heard Lady Takren say it myself: she claimed to have seen a Watani come ashore in Jeng."

The Watani shouldn't exist, Zinchen thought, gaze falling to the carved pieces of a war board spread out on the table.

"And no report has been made to me," Zinchen said, exchanging a glance with Lina, who stood off to the side. "Can you shed light on that?"

Joktan dipped his head. "Some of the Varanaken matriarchs are grumbling about deserving more lands, Your Majesty. I believe they plan to use this knowledge as leverage to get it."

A carved horse on the table strained its neck forward, frozen in a gallop. Zinchen slid it across the board. "Send a rider to the coast. I want a quiet investigation to find out the truth. And you two keep your ears open. I require a full report on which of the Varanaken tribes are loyal."

Joktan beat one fist on his chest and bowed.

"And continue your secret training of my soldiers in the Varanaken ways." She gave him a significant look. "They must be able to defeat the Varanaken, should that day come."

As the men left the War Room, a messenger entered, delivering a wax-sealed missive. Yan's latest letter, lined with the coded warnings only she and he could read—*The Min-kezu are slipping, their loyalties uncertain.*

Through the window, pale light streaming onto the board fell on a game piece carved like a scholar, with hands tucked into her wide sleeves as though contemplating her next move.

"Are the arrangements complete?" she asked Lina.

"Nearly," Lina said. "It will be an unprecedented boon for the Ants, Your Majesty; a thoughtful incentive for the princess."

"More importantly, one she cannot refuse," Zinchen replied. "Very well, the moment circumstances permit, summon Rozalia to the palace to complete the negotiations. Yan's letter does not reassure me; Tori's alliance with Prince Filo must come sooner than planned." She moved the carved scholar and set it down with a click.

"The lomi's enigma has been fulfilled," the elder said, gazing on the five black-and-white stones scattered before her. She had summoned Koren much earlier than the time the council was set to meet.

Koren glanced at the stones, their glyphs now alight.

"'When six fingers shall grasp the wind,'" she said, "'the veil shall part, and the path be revealed.' Such were the lomi's words. And though I do not how such a thing is possible, Tori has taken the wind into her hands; the stones have revealed it."

She looked at him intently. "The veil is parting; the Celestial Seal once again chooses its place of appearing. Even now it is calling out to the wise, revealing its clues. The first clue will already be visible."

Suddenly the glyphs on the elder's stones blazed, then rippled across the stones' surfaces, like tiny embers blowing in the wind.

The elder sprang up, eyes fixed on the stones. "Others search for it, even at this very moment," she said, her tone edged with urgency. "You must reach it first, for the instant a clue is discovered, it disappears. Go quickly. I will inform the council. We await your report."

Koren rushed out, heading for Ma'yanar Forest.

Lee searched Ma'yanar Forest, guided by the flawless compass of his own intuition. The parchment Vice Regent Caliss had given him had referred to "golden shadow"—which he had easily found—and since sparkling ghosts had been hovering around it, he had concluded the two were somehow connected. He was therefore searching the forest for a greater congregation of the beings.

He patted the etched metal implements the vice regent had so graciously given him. Though their abominable giggles raised chills down his spine, the ghosts couldn't seem to harm him.

After following ghost trails a short while, something that looked like a curtain of sparkles slowly shimmered into view, as though appearing for the first time, just for him. The air around it rippled, like heat waves over a stone road.

"And here we are," Lee said, with a smile. He had evidently arrived at precisely the right time. Though he had not doubted his instincts—clues were, after all, his specialty—it was always satisfying when the world aligned with his brilliance.

A crack appeared in the sparkling curtain, widening, and the scene before him split—trees and leaves and yellow-and-green ghost-light—like a painted wall parting in the middle to reveal a secret room. He felt the blood drain from his face.

"Grandmother, save me," he murmured, kissing the portrait hanging from his neck.

The split widened, and a small forest alcove appeared, with a stone altar inside, crumbling on the ground. Lee skirted the sparkling curtain, walking a few paces beyond it to look at it from different angles. From behind, there was nothing, and from the side all he saw was a shimmering vertical line. Some kind of portal, then.

He hesitated, but the kohl-rimmed eyes of Vice Regent Caliss came to him, and he gathered his nerve, stepping into the alcove gingerly. He brushed sand from the altar's top till an ancient-looking mosaic came clear, its blue-and-white tiles emitting brief pulses of light in different hues, revealing hidden glyphs that had been etched inside. He smirked. Glyphs were child's play to a Decipherer of Riddles and Enigmas.

Following their instructions, he pushed two fingers into a small depression in the stone. The altar groaned open, revealing a hidden compartment just big enough for the scroll it contained—the first clue. He lifted it with a flourish, blowing off the dust, then quickly stepped away: lifting out items in such circumstances always triggered some kind of defense mechanism. As expected, the altar quaked behind him as he dashed for his carriage.

Once inside, he exhaled victoriously, glancing at the sealed scroll. Hanmar would soon be free of Ants. This "Antfall Seal," or "Ant Scourge," or whatever it was called, would give him everything—the vice regent's face came to him again, and his heart swelled. Yes, everything.

As his carriage rolled away, he broke the scroll's seal and spread it across his lap. Then, with the satisfaction that came from knowing success was inevitable, he set to work deciphering the next clue.

Koren arrived in Ma'yanar to find Henzan pacing, his eyes flicking between the slip of paper in his hand and the surrounding forest. Henzan had been spending a great deal of time here recently with copied sections of the ancient scroll, hoping the forest itself would aid his interpretations.

Koren greeted him briefly, explained the situation, and asked for help, but before they had taken two steps, a confusion of lomi circled Koren several times, then streaked away into the trees—they were urging him to follow.

They soon arrived at a place where the air shimmered in two ragged, vertical sections, like a torn curtain, with an alcove barely visible behind. Inside, dust hung around a collapsed pile of rubble. Someone had beaten them here, by mere moments.

For the first time, the possibility of a rival sank in, and Koren fervidly searched the pile. Lying beneath a rock was a hollow stone rectangle—just the right size for a scroll.

Koren's heart shrank. "We are too late."

"Maybe not," Henzan said, motioning him over. He pointed to a blue mosaic tile, then brushed his finger over it. A brief pulse of green light revealed the glyph for *press*. "Once we find the others, we might still piece together..." But when he brushed it again, the glyph was gone.

Henzan bent, shifting rocks aside, and picked out a white tile. He passed a finger over it, and though it lit up with a faint violet light, no glyph appeared.

Koren stood very still, contemplating the tiles. What might they still reveal? He had come across this particular type of mosaic tile in his youth. The technique used to make them was very ancient, even back then.

"All may not be lost," Henzan murmured. "Second clues usually take several days longer to decipher than first clues. We've still got a chance—if we use a different kind of knowledge."

Koren turned to him. "Do you have such knowledge?"

"Possibly." Henzan held up the tile. "These were etched with vanishing glyphs. I read about them once; it's a technique that only activates in certain places in Shudon—though I don't recall where. The glyphs always come in pairs, so if they were used for the first clue, they'll be used for the second. But here's the trouble...both sets of glyphs must be etched on the same kind of surface, whatever it is. Which means that, since this clue was etched on these tiles, the next clue will be, too. But I've never seen anything like these tiles before today." He rubbed the tile, making it light up. "If I only knew how it worked..."

"They're inlaid with fossilized bioluminescent lichen," Koren said. "It reacts to body heat. Artisans preserve the lichen with a special mineral paste that keeps the reaction stable, even after the lichen dies."

Henzan looked impressed.

"I traveled widely in my youth," Koren said, and shrugged. "Once, I met a supplier of these tiles. She told me the technique had existed for millennia, and that her family kept it alive in just five places across Shudon—places where the lichen thrives. Places I know."

Henzan's eyes lit up.

"You said vanishing glyphs only activate in certain environments," Koren said. "If we can cross-reference those with the supplier bases, we'll have our destination. The next clue will be where the two overlap."

Henzan stroked his long, white beard. "Give me three days. I know of a scroll collection—one that covers both glyphs and ancient mosaics. Now I know why." He chuckled. "Let me send word to find out which longevitist sect holds it now. Someone there will send me a list of which regions can activate vanishing glyphs."

"Then I'll meet you at Greenstalk in three days," Koren said. "We will travel together from there."

Chapter Seventy-Two

VOICE OF DOUBT

The rain stopped and the sky cleared as Tori made her way into Peach Blossom Grove, where the petal-strewn path glistened in the autumn sun.

She stood for a moment by the peach trees, gaze drifting across the village: the Pavilion of Honorable Logograms on one end, topped by its roof of sea-foam green; the watercourse in the middle, its gazebo floating among pink lotus blossoms, and beside it, the training grounds in three stories of towering stone; and at the other end of the village, the playhouse, with the communal dining hall just beyond, where people ate meals as one big family.

She tried to memorize the scene, taking in its arched bridges, its colors. Then, if they sent her away, she could still gaze at it in her mind's eye and feel closer to home.

Home. The word startled her, even as it made perfect sense: she had never before felt such a sense of belonging as she had here.

Her heart ached with the desire to remain, but she immediately stuffed the feeling down. She was here to convince the elder to let her copy the map, nothing more. If she could accomplish that, she would have to be thankful.

As she arrived at the fruit market, people buying and selling under colorful umbrellas still dripping with rainwater smiled at her as usual. Gratefully, she smiled back—did no one realize she had been banished?

Just then, a loud, grating voice crashed through the hum of easy, happy commerce.

"Ripe red apples for sale! Just two skades apiece. Ripe red apples!"

Old Griff caught sight of Tori and quickly swerved, walking in the opposite direction.

"Wait," Tori said, catching up with him.

He stopped in his tracks, his posture stiff.

She reached for her money pouch. "Did you say two skades apiece?"

He hesitated, as though anticipating a reprimand. "One or two."

"I'll take the whole box," she said, pulling out a handful of skades and dropping them into his hand.

He stared at the little pink and blue stones, then back at her again, uncomprehending. She had paid him more than double.

"I'm in a hurry," she said. "Could you leave the box outside my cottage?" Someone would find and eat them, most likely Ruvien.

Griff nodded, momentarily robbed, it seemed, of his ability to speak. He quickly recovered. "I'll have pears tomorrow. Plump, juicy ones. You like pears?"

"Perfect. I'll take a box of those, too."

As she started walking away, however, Tori reconsidered her words—tomorrow she might be gone. She opened her bulging money pouch. Even after repaying Elnora more than twice what she had spent over the past few moons, Tori still had a great deal of money.

"If I'm not here, let this buy pears for someone else," she said, pressing a gold petal into his hand.

Griff's eyes widened, then filled with tears. He clutched the gold petal in his fist, then bowed, his words of thanks following her long after she left.

When she arrived at the lower pond at Council's Rise, she steeled herself against the probable rejection that awaited. As it was the third morning of the week, the council would be in session, and they had no doubt informed the barge workers of her banishment.

But instead of being turned away as she had feared, Tori was asked to wait.

"No one is to ascend until Master Koren returns," the woman at the booth called over. "Council's orders."

Tori noticed then that there was no barge.

A short while later, Master Koren came sprinting up the cliff. He rushed past, apparently without seeing her. When she had waited again for about the time it would take to eat a meal, growing increasingly nervous, the barge finally floated downstream and let her in.

Soon she was at the top.

The trellis of lacy vines twinkled at her with its ever-present dewdrops, its fragrance enveloping her. Her pulse thumped with nerves as she passed under it, then down the path of overarching branches. Up ahead, the council sat, heads together, as though deep in conversation.

Though Tori was still a long way off, the elder looked up suddenly, meeting Tori's eye. Everyone at the table followed her gaze. A mix of curiosity and concern showed in Master Maeli's face.

Tori stopped where she was. "May I approach?"

The elder gave a nod. But when Tori reached the table, Zanda was the first to speak.

"Weren't you banished?" Zanda said, her face hard with disapproval.

Tori didn't look at her, choosing instead to bow low before the elder.

"Elder, I was hoping you would grant me an audience."

The elder dipped her chin. Zanda frowned.

"First, I want to say that my time at Peach Blossom Grove was—" Her voice caught. "It was the happiest of my life. I truly feel that the people here are my family."

Master Maeli's eyes softened.

"I never told you how sorry I am for what I did. For how I misused the wielding scroll. It was a rare treasure, and I didn't treat it that way. I was utterly ungrateful."

Master Koren looked up.

"What is it you now desire?" the elder asked.

Tori hesitated. With her mother, she had always had to scheme, to fight and manipulate for anything she wanted. But here? Here, that would only dishonor everything this place meant to her.

She knelt on the ground and lowered her head.

"Since you ask what I want, I'll tell you. More than anything, I want to be accepted back into Peach Blossom Grove." She raised her head to meet the elder's eyes. "But that's not why I returned. I only ask to borrow your map. One day at most—just long enough to make a copy—so I can find my own way to Mount Ketwanen and complete the Septad."

"You claim to realize your wrong," Zanda said, "and yet here you are, in defiance of the council's orders. Not only that, but you are also, by your own admission, still harboring the desire to return. And now you ask for one of the elder's treasures? If you were truly sorry, you wouldn't dare to permit yourself even to think such thoughts."

"If anything, her desire proves the opposite," Master Maeli said. "A truly repentant person always desires the chance to repair their error."

"So says the impartial judge."

Master Maeli started to respond, but the elder held up a hand.

"Maeli, we know well where you stand. Yet I must also disagree with Zanda on this point. The mere desire to return proves nothing, save the longing to return, and Tori has accepted that such a course is now beyond her."

Zanda dipped her head respectfully, and the elder returned her gaze to Tori.

"As to your request, possession of this map may only be granted to a resident of Peach Blossom Grove."

"I understand, Elder," Tori said quickly. "I don't ask that you give it to me. I only need to copy it—in your presence, if you wish."

"The map cannot be copied, for reasons I shall not delve into here. Suffice it to say, the map must be borne to Mount Ketwanen in order to serve its purpose, and thus, I cannot grant it to you."

Tori remembered Senrik and Ruvien. "What if someone else borrowed it? They could accompany me."

The elder shook her head. "I cannot allow one so clearly lacking in judgment to lead our people to a place such as Mount Ketwanen," she said, her voice gentler than her words.

"Couldn't you make an exception?" The desperation pressed in on her. "You once said my interests aligned with yours. That must still be true."

Zanda furrowed her brow. "You endangered every member of the Royal Tribe, and yet you ask for an exception?"

But the elder spoke with patience. "I cannot give you the map. Nor can I lend it. And as for whether our interests yet converge—fate alone will decide."

The words crushed her, the weight of it all settling over her—her mistake, her exile, her failure.

So that was it. She would have to leave Peach Blossom Grove, this time for good. And once again, she would come away with nothing.

The consciousness of her total ingratitude rose within her. From the time she had first arrived here, she had done nothing but take: information, training, the priceless glorium. Now, here she was again, asking for more.

If she was going to leave for good, she didn't want to leave as just a taker. She wanted, for once, to give—something of value—as a token of her gratitude for so many things, not least of which was simple kindness.

Her mother had provided her with a small fortune for her travels: fifty gold petals. But what was fifty gold petals in a place that could afford a building of solid jade?

Then she remembered the Ghost Stone.

Her mind fought with her, calling her a fool. If she gave it away, how would she ever find another? Yet it was the only gift grand enough to express everything she meant.

If she found another way to Mount Ketwanen, she would have to believe she could also find another Veil, and another Ghost Stone.

Tori rose to her feet. "Then I'll take my leave. But before I go, please accept this as a token of my gratitude for all I've received here," she said. "It comes from the Veil of Ayenashi—so really, it's rightfully yours." She held out the Ghost Stone with both hands. Now dry, it had transformed into a solid white sphere, indistinguishable from any common rock, apart from its perfectly round, smooth form.

Zanda glanced at it disdainfully. The other council members squinted, confused.

"Could I have some water?" Tori said.

Master Koren motioned to a cup sitting on the table beside him.

She stepped forward to get it, but stopped herself. Instead, she concentrated, cycling elixir and binding it with the slippery water element in her stone kernel. She wielded water, making it rise from the cup in a thin, trembling stream that dripped terribly as it undulated toward her. But she managed to control it long enough to release it in a splash over the stone in her hand.

Instantly, the stone transformed into what looked like a translucent soap bubble.

Master Koren leaned in, eyes fastened on it. "The Ghost Stone," he murmured.

Astonishment crossed every council member's face. Master Koren came to study it up close. He picked it up, his gaze flicking between the stone and Tori.

"It takes both tremendous wielding potential and spirit sense to find such a thing," he said to the elder, setting it on the table before her. "Not only that, but the stone chose her...no one else."

The elder's brow furrowed thoughtfully.

"Then it's a pity she had no regard for her training when she had the chance," Zanda said.

"I should have," Tori said, with a heavy heart, then bowed one last time, and began walking back through the path of overarching branches.

"Wait." It was Master Koren.

She turned.

"Would you embrace wielding now, if you could?" he asked, looking at her intently.

Tori nodded. "If I could."

"Then I must join with Master Maeli in recommending she be given another chance, Elder. An ability this rare must be fostered."

The council leaned their heads together, speaking in low murmurs. Tori picked up some of the words; it was the Old Speech. She heard "impossible" and "return," among other things, and her mind spun these in a dozen different directions, most of them negative.

They switched back to the common tongue, going over her disaster in Greenstalk, debating why she should be let back, and why she shouldn't.

"If she wants exceptional treatment," Zanda said, time and again, "she should be required to overcome exceptional circumstances."

Finally, the elder spoke. "I am in accord with Zanda. We will therefore proceed thus: Tori shall take the final test in alchemy and her grading in the use of daggers. Should she pass, it shall serve as proof that she has valued her time here beyond what is ordinarily expected. This, combined with her rare ability, will suffice to warrant my granting her the exception of a second chance."

Concern shone in Master Maeli's eyes. "But she is still missing her last moon of training—the most crucial stage of preparation. No one who has missed this stage has ever passed the test."

"Then this would indeed qualify as overcoming an exceptional obstacle, would it not?"

"With respect, Elder," Master Maeli said, "Tori is simply not ready."

"I have made my decision," the elder said. She looked at Tori. "Master Kwai'le shall be informed that you will take your alchemy test on the morrow. Should you pass, you may proceed to your dagger grading."

She nodded her dismissal.

At the lower pond of Council's Rise, three people waited. Tori's heart warmed at the sight of them.

Ruvien grinned. "See? I knew they wouldn't kick her out."

"Don't celebrate yet," Tori said, stepping out of the barge.

Elnora hugged her; Senrik dipped his head. Though he didn't smile, happiness flickered in his eyes.

"If I want to stay, I have to pass my alchemy and dagger tests," Tori said. "Tomorrow."

At that, every face grew somber.

They walked along in silence, but Tori's mind raced noisily. Over and over, the voice of doubt came, recounting a torturing truth:

She's not ready.

Chapter Seventy-Three

TESTING

Thirty-two spirit stones lined the counter of the alchemy cave—more than Tori had ever seen in one place—their soft, florid scent filling the air.

"Master, where did you find all these?" she asked, setting down her gourd. She hoped he wouldn't say "Ayenashi's Veil." Wherever he'd found them would be a perfect place to begin her search for another Ghost Stone.

"These are seed-grown," he said, "like all the stones you've worked with so far. You could say I grew them."

He picked one up. "They're on par with any standard-grade stones found in nature, but a seed-grown stone can never reach top-grade, regardless of the skill of the alchemist who grows them."

"I thought spirit stones were always found in nature."

"And I suppose you think I dug all my seedlings from the forest, too," he said, with a long-suffering shake of the head. "I grew these spirit stones by propelling the seeds forward twenty thousand years. The crystals multiply till the seed grows to a full-sized stone. This is the exact technique you've been learning, in fact. And if you pass today, you'll use the same technique again for the Septad."

"Where can you find spirit stone seeds?"

"Anywhere there's dirt, of course. They look like ordinary crystals, except with a faint glow."

He clasped his hands behind his back. "But we're wasting time. Your alchemy test is made up of two parts. The first is a preliminary assessment consisting of thirty-two stones. You must meld each pair of seed-grown stones and propel them forward exactly ten thousand years and one day. If you succeed, you'll be ready for the main test, in which you will meld one pair of natural, top-grade spirit stones."

She remembered how exhausted she had been the last time, having melded only six stones. She wouldn't have the stamina for thirty-two.

"Couldn't I go straight to the main test?"

He shook his head. "I can't risk it. A pair of natural spirit stones costs upward of twenty-six gold petals—twenty thousand skades. I have to be absolutely sure you're ready."

Tori picked up her bottle-gourd, filled with water from the crystal streamlet. She hoped it would work like the blue spirit-fruits, since this is what they drank—and because whenever she had tried to carry the fruits away, they vanished the moment they left her hand.

In the time of a candle's burn, she produced the first melded stone and hovered it out of the pill furnace.

Master Kwai'le examined it, then brought his hammer down. A crystalline ring filled the air. Tori released a breath.

The second stone took longer, but it, too, passed.

After the third stone, however, she realized Master Kwai'le had lined them up according to their level of difficulty, which seemed to depend on their shade of color—the darker the stone, the harder to meld.

With every stone her strength diminished more, and her melding time increased. She did her best to ration the elixir; at this rate, she would be here till sunset.

Strangely, her alchemical ability improved. It was as though her basic skills were feeding off the rising difficulty, like muscles bearing increasingly heavier weights.

So this was why Master Kwai'le had refused to let her take the main test; she had needed the preparation. Her gaze landed on him. He really was a wise teacher.

After every stone she melded, she cycled elixir just long enough to replace a bare minimum in her stone kernel, then took a sip of the crystal water. Though its effects came nowhere near those of the spirit-fruits, it was at least more invigorating than normal water.

By dark, she had successfully melded all thirty-two stones. As Master Kwai'le performed his final checks on them, Tori slumped into a chair, exhausted, and tipped her head back to empty her gourd.

She let out a long, tired sigh. Only one more pair to go—her final test. Trying to gather her strength, she cycled elixir.

"Hoping someone will finish the test for you while you wait to be served tea?" Master Kwai'le said, taking two more spirit stones from the shelf.

Then he took down another two. Tori's brow knit together as he lined up sixteen more pairs.

Her hands dropped to her sides. When he had said the preliminary consisted of thirty-two spirit stones, he had been talking about making thirty-two new ones!

She dragged herself back to the counter.

The preliminary lasted through the night. Tori grew wearier with every pair, and her elixir barely trickled in when she stopped to cycle it.

Unwearied himself, apparently, Master Kwai'le tested each new stone she melded. Tori would hold her breath whenever the hammer fell, then let out a silent exhale when he set the stone onto the shelf, signaling that it had passed. Twice, when he examined a new stone, he had leaned into it slightly and raised a brow, then glanced at Tori with a strange, almost respectful look before placing her stone on a shelf with black velvet lining. The shelf's label read: *Special. Multi-ailment.*

By the time the sun rose, she felt like a wilted flower. Master Kwai'le, who glanced up from examining her most recent stone, caught sight of her and frowned.

"They always overdo it at the end," he mumbled to himself, shaking his head. He looked at her and jerked his chin at a chair. "Sit, before you fall over," he said, then refilled her bottle-gourd from the rain barrel outside. She finished it in one long draught, and he brought her another. "Continue when you're ready."

He returned to her melded stone, which he seemed to be handling with special care as he placed it on the velvet-lined shelf.

As she drank, her eyes wandered over the stones glowing against the black velvet, among which three of her own now sat. Hers were misshapen in comparison to the others, but their veins were more brilliant, and the fact they were sitting there at all seemed a very good sign.

She continued melding throughout the morning, and by midday, the final two seed-grown stones of the preliminary test sat on the counter alone. But her elixir had dried up, and she felt too tired to even cycle it. She stared at the stones in a daze, vision blurred from exhaustion.

"One more to go," he said. "Finish this, and you're ready for the main test."

Tori squared her shoulders, took a breath, and cycled elixir. Though the strand was as wide as before, her parched dawn channels soaked it in, leaving nothing extra for her stone kernel. It took a long while before enough elixir had trickled in to allow her to continue stone melding, but the moment she could, she used all her force of will to finish. By the end, she was so tired she could barely see.

The hammer fell on final stone, whose crystalline ringing declared its own success. But as Tori stared at it, darkness closed in around her, narrowing her vision, until at last she saw nothing at all and collapsed.

When Tori opened her eyes, she was lying on the ground with a pillow beneath her head. She propped herself up on an elbow, head spinning.

Master Kwai'le nodded at the bottle-gourd in front of her. "Drink." She did. Though less parched, she felt no less depleted.

"Couldn't I do the main test another day?" She glanced at Master Kwai'le and was surprised to find genuine disappointment on his face.

"The Elder has given you today only," he said. "If you don't meld the final stones now, you will fail."

But she knew she couldn't go on, and her consequent, impending failure now loomed over her. She squeezed her eyes shut.

"You've just melded sixty-four stones," Master Kwai'le said. "Not only has your skill increased, but your stamina has as well. Now pick yourself up off the floor. You have a test to do."

He opened a porcelain box lined with blue silk and brought out two glowing stones, one green, one yellow—wood and fire—brilliant and sparkling. Top-grade spirit stones.

"The Septad is within reach," he said, setting the stones beside the pill furnace. "Succeed with these, and you'll be on your way to Ketwanen."

She pushed herself to her feet.

"The main test," he said, "is to propel these forward twenty thousand years, three months, and three days—precisely. Any deviation, and the stone will be nonfunctioning."

Tori connected with the elixir, but no matter how many times she cycled, she simply couldn't gather enough of it in her stone kernel to meld top-grade stones to twenty thousand years.

Help me, she thought, not knowing if the elixir would hear.

Suddenly, the elements buzzed within her, and an idea came.

Though uncertain, she touched the wood and fire elements in her stone kernel, and, as though wielding, bound each of them to her paltry pool of elixir, streaming each element into the corresponding stone, along with a tiny stream of pure elixir connecting the two.

It worked.

The difficulty level of the melding was so high it required all of her strength and the remainder of the afternoon to accomplish her goal—but she did. She leaned against the counter, utterly spent, and stared at the new melded stone.

Though somewhat lumpy, the green-and-yellow stone was smoother than any she had created so far. Master Kwai'le held it up to the light, then placed it on the counter and raised his hammer. Tori held her breath. The stone rang like a chime.

A moment later, burning veins snaked over Tori's arms and hands. While Master Kwai'le studied her stone under a magnifying glass, Tori cycled elixir, clearing the venom and pushing it back into the font that bubbled viciously now inside her ketua, but it spilled out again and shot through her dawn channels—except this time, she felt too tired to fight it. She slumped into a chair.

The voice of a child spoke in the distance, and Tori looked out the door to see who was walking by. The path outside was empty.

Pain urged her to try cycling again, and the venom receded to her fingertips. But again it flared, spreading like a web up her arms, and she sucked in hissing breaths through her teeth.

The child's voice spoke again. "Shall I?"

A different child responded in the Old Speech: *"Zhangni chui shan."* Give the command. As Tori breathed through her pain, she wondered idly why children were using the Old Speech.

Then she froze—the voices were not outside at all, nor were they distant: the second voice was coming from her pendant. The venom was affecting her mind!

"Please, Master," she said. "Something's wrong."

Master Kwai'le looked up from his magnifying glass. "No, no. I merely wanted to examine the crystals more closely."

"Not with the stone, with me. I'm hearing...voices."

A curious expression crossed his face. "Where?"

Realizing now that the first child's voice was coming from the stone she had just melded, she pointed first to the counter. "And here," she said, holding up the glorium. Her dawn channels burned, and she dropped it, gritting her teeth. "It's wielder's venom," she said. "It's gone to my brain. Please, call Master Banfay."

Give the command, the child's voice said again.

"Venom can't affect the mind." He looked at the glorium. "Did the elder tell you what that stone can do?"

"She said it cleared venom, but it's not working."

"What is the voice saying?"

"It's a child's voice. It's saying 'give the command,'" she said, aware of how foolish it sounded. "In the Old Speech."

A look of amazement crossed his face for a beat, then disappeared. "Pick up the stone and speak to it. Say, *ji heng chui.* It means 'heal' in the Old Speech."

"Why?"

"The nature of the glorium is to clear venom. That command will help it function."

She picked up the pendant and whispered to it. The stone buzzed, then flashed.

"Now put it down," he said.

The moment she let it drop to her chest, the glorium's iridescent veins glowed and dimmed back and forth, alternating between warmth and cold, while the venom grew lighter and less painful, then finally disappeared.

Tori sagged onto the table, feeling as though she were recovering from a long convalescence.

"Tell me what you know of spirit stones," Master Kwai'le said. "Apart from what I taught you, obviously."

She hesitated, and a shadow of disapproval crossed his face.

"You've done no wider reading? In nearly six moons?" He exhaled and clasped his hands behind his back. "Never mind. Suffice it to say that both natural and seed-grown stones will heal according to their nature—to a greater or lesser extent, depending on their grade. The principal difference between the two, however, is that natural spirit stones are sentient."

Tori went still, gaze dropping to the glorium.

"Those two stones—the glorium and the one you just melded—were speaking to you. All sentient things seek to communicate, but only those with the gift will be able to hear them. Still, the gift takes decades to develop, if it develops at all. Never in all my life have I met a student who had it."

"What is the gift?"

"For now, all you need to know is that you have it. That pendant has been steadily healing you, but now that you can command it, you have access to a much more powerful cure when you need it."

He told her to sit and recover, while he went back to studying the melded stone.

A short while later, a hawk with a bandaged head soared in and landed on Tori's shoulder, sinking it.

"Driven!" Tears stung her eyes. "How is this possible?" She stroked him over and over.

"Oh, good," Master Kwai'le said. "Master Banfay normally doesn't do animals, but I convinced him it would be a waste of a good messenger hawk otherwise."

He held out his arm for Driven, but the hawk looked away and nuzzled against Tori. Master Kwai'le lifted him from her shoulder and set him on his perch, but the moment he did, Driven flew back to her.

"You both need to recover," Master Kwai'le said, returning the hawk to his perch again, this time attaching him with a string.

Tori stood by Driven, running a hand over his silver feathers, while Master Kwai'le bent over the final melded stone again, using a number of implements to weigh and measure it in various ways. Doubt crossed her mind. When the stone had chimed under the hammer blow, she had assumed it had passed the test, but she realized now that he had never actually said it.

"Is the stone acceptable?"

"I'll tell the elder you're ready," he said, without looking up, "and that you'll need a day to recover. Dismissed."

Tori sagged with relief, and for the first time she felt grateful for her teacher. She owed him so much. All the books and scrolls in the world could never have transmitted the things he had taught her.

She bowed. "Thank you, Master."

As usual, he didn't bother to respond. A faint smile tugged her lips. She would miss his odd ways, now that her training was through.

As she gathered her things, her body felt slow and heavy, and her mind turned to the dagger grading. Even if she slept an entire day, would it be enough? She exhaled wearily and made her way to the door.

When she stepped into the sunset however, Master Kwai'le spoke.

"Tori." He looked up from his counter, meeting her eye, and gave a short nod. "Good luck."

Chapter Seventy-Four

AIR BLADES

When Tori reached the gate of the training grounds two days later, the buzz of conversation greeted her. People sat in groups on the grassy triangles surrounding the sparring circle, obviously waiting for a match to start. The second level of the grounds, where Tori's dagger training always took place, was mercifully free of spectators.

Master Maeli came walking toward her, her gaze sweeping over Tori's eyes and face. She furrowed her brow. "How are you feeling?"

Despite the fact that Tori had taken the day before plus better part of today to rest, her mind and body felt drained.

"All right, I think." But the autumn air felt cold instead of crisp, and she wrapped the fur-lined collar of her cloak more tightly. A metallic taste lingered in her mouth as if she hadn't eaten, and though she'd already consumed six blue spirit-fruits today, her body had absorbed the energy so quickly that the effects had lasted for only the space of a breath.

Her only hope was that Master Maeli wouldn't go too hard on her in the grading. She had never sparred with her master before.

Tori indicated the crowd with her chin. "Is something happening today?"

Master Maeli gave her a strange look. "Your grading. Those are my students. They are here to watch."

Tori's stomach tightened. She was about to be scrutinized by a whole group of experienced fighters.

"I always encourage my students to attend gradings," Master Maeli said. "Even senior students can learn something. Usually there is not such a big turnout, though. I think they are curious about sixfold wielders."

Tori recognized very few people in the crowd. Locked in conversation with Ruvien and Elnora, Senrik sat on the grass, hair blown back by a gentle breeze. Her stomach jittered nervously. A few paces away, Keya lounged on her side, eating an apple. *Great.*

Keya took one last bite, then threw the apple core on the grass, where it shimmered and disappeared. She rose and walked over to Master Maeli.

"I'm here, Master," she said, bowing.

"Tori, go to the center and stretch," Master Maeli said. "Keya's ready for your grading."

Tori froze. "I thought you were doing my grading."

Keya smirked and strolled away to the sparring ring.

"I am grading you," Master Maeli said, "and for this, I must be able to watch you from various angles. Now, your only object today is to keep from getting hit, nothing more. No need to attack Keya; she is many levels above you, and you will only waste your strength. Effective avoidance is the only goal in the one-bar grading. In a real fight, the first to deal a decisive blow wins—better to avoid it, at your level. Naturally, you will not be able to avoid all her strikes, but three cuts or less, and you pass."

Cuts? Tori looked around for the boxes of dulling lotion and torso guards they normally used in training. There were none.

"If she gets in four cuts, however," Master Maeli said, "you will fail." Though she stated it matter-of-factly, concern flickered behind her eyes, as if she were silently pleading with Tori not to let this happen.

She pointed to a sandglass sitting on a table beside a gong. "When the sandglass runs out, the gong will sound, ending the match."

"How long is the sandglass?"

"About the time it takes to drain a cup."

Tori's heart plummeted. So long?

It must have shown on her face, because Master Maeli said, "This is a minimum level. A lack of stamina could be the difference between life and death."

As Master Maeli took her place near the sandglass, Tori walked toward the sparring ring with the crowd's eyes boring into her. Keya was stretching lazily, like someone waking from a nap. When she noticed Tori taking off her cloak, her eyes creased with amusement.

She sauntered over, clapping a hand on Tori's shoulder, then leaned in, like a senior student encouraging her junior.

"I hear this is your last chance to stay at Peach Blossom Grove," Keya whispered, and smiled. "I'll send someone to help you pack."

She stepped back then, spinning her daggers in her hands. Tori's stomach knotted.

Master Maeli raised a hand, and the gong sounded.

When Keya slapped her daggers together and bowed, Tori did the same.

Then every thought vanished except of Keya's crouching form and the sound of her steps scuffling the dirt. They moved in a circle, daggers raised, eyes locked on each other.

Before Tori could avoid her, Keya darted in and struck.

Tori leaped backward, pain shooting through her arm as a patch of blood blossomed on her sleeve.

A fierce, self-satisfied look shone in the woman's eye. They had only just begun, and she had already proved Tori was hopelessly outmatched.

Humiliation flooded her, then indignation.

We'll see about that.

Their weapons clanged as Tori blocked a two-handed attack, pushing against Keya, dagger on dagger. Her wounded arm trembled and burned, as though it had been seared by a hot poker.

But her dagger forms returned instinctively, and she drew her arms around in a circle, throwing Keya off. Fueled by anger, Tori flipped the Night Twins to a back grip, then dipped, striking at Keya's leg.

Keya jumped easily away, ponytail fluttering. Tori panted, her exhaustion now compounded by pain and blood loss.

A breeze cooled the sweat on her neck as her eyes darted to the sandglass. It had barely moved—she would never make it.

With dizzying speed, Keya dropped to one knee and smashed the hilt of her dagger into Tori's shin. Tori heard it crack as bursts of light exploded behind her eyes.

She stumbled to catch her balance. Keya's blade flashed in the sunlight, and she struck again, slicing Tori's leg. The second cut. Keya leaped back, then lunged again.

Tori blocked, stopping Keya's blades a hair's breadth from Tori's face. It took all her strength just to keep the Night Twins in her grip.

Keya leaned in so close Tori could smell her breath. "I almost feel guilty," she said in a low voice. "It's like fighting a child."

Sweat ran down Tori's temples. One more cut, and she would be at her limit.

With a grunt, she thrust Keya off and jumped out of reach, groaning in pain as she landed on her wounded leg.

A succession of attacks and parries followed. She tried to find the sandglass, but Keya dipped forward, forcing Tori to dodge.

The woman flipped her daggers, a smile on the edge of her lips. It had been a feint. She was playing, a cat with her mouse.

In desperation, Tori lunged in a frenzy of slashing. Keya skipped backward, eyes cold with annoyance at her mouse's audacity. Playtime was over.

Now I've done it, Tori thought.

With that, the peace of inevitability overcame her, and she subtly loosened her grip.

The Night Twins hummed in her hands, and she felt their air element activate, forming invisible blades around them. Time slowed.

Keya flew at her, poised for a double strike that would take Tori to four cuts. She felt the air shift as Keya neared, and she knew instinctively where the blades would land, even as she knew she couldn't avoid them.

Daggers ripped through Tori's right side and left cheek, clean into the gums. Blood filled her mouth. She spun, and a blade of razor-sharp air spiked around the Night Twins as she swiped at Keya's arm, but the woman was already leaping away.

But when Keya landed, gasps erupted through the crowd: blood was spreading on her upper sleeve.

She looked down at her arm, astonished, just in time to hear the ringing of the gong.

Chapter Seventy-Five

THREE GIFTS

Tori spat blood onto the dirt. A moment later, Elnora was at her side, dabbing her face with herb-soaked gauze that stung like fire. Its bitterness leaked through her cheek into her mouth, but soon the only feeling that remained was a dull tug as Elnora sewed the gash together with silk thread.

Master Maeli walked into the sparring ring, her gaze flicking quickly over Tori's wounds, then over the red patch on Keya's sleeve.

"Keya has cut you four times," she said.

A gleam shone in Keya's eyes, and Tori's stomach knotted.

"But you did the unexpected. I count, therefore, that your cut on Keya nullifies her last one against you."

Tori's eyebrows shot up.

"But, Master," Keya said, stepping forward, "her weapons—she would never have struck me with another pair of knives."

Master Maeli frowned. "You were touched by a one-bar, Keya. Do not add to your shame by being a dishonorable loser."

Keya's cheeks reddened. She bowed, then left, avoiding the crowd as the training grounds cleared.

People cast respectful nods in Tori's direction as they went. Sadeera and Suli, who were filing out with the rest, smiled and held up their thumbs.

"I will speak to Master Koren now about your next steps," Master Maeli said. "Come see me when Elnora is finished tending to you."

As soon as she was gone, Ruvien and Senrik arrived.

Ruvien grinned. "Did you see Keya's face? She looked like she wanted to spit." He laughed.

Senrik gave her a nod, but there was something different in his eyes. Admiration?

As Master Maeli spoke with Master Koren near the gate, she tilted her head at him and smiled. Then, out of nowhere, she reached up and stroked his face.

Tori raised an eyebrow.

Elnora, who was wrapping a bandage on Tori's arm, stopped to follow Tori's gaze.

"Is that normal?" she asked, nudging Ruvien.

Ruvien blinked. "You didn't know? They've been together for over two hundred years."

"Then Master Banfay is her son?"

Ruvien nodded. "They adopted him as a newborn, a few days after she gave birth to their stillborn daughter."

As though on cue, Master Banfay arrived and started speaking to his parents. Master Maeli placed a hand on his shoulder and said something with a smile.

A spark of jealousy surprised Tori. She forced it down. She would be happy for him; he had a mother who loved him.

He dipped his head to his mother, kissing his fingertips and touching them to his heart. Then he bowed to both parents and left.

Master Maeli caught Tori looking, and beckoned her over.

"Meet us at the blue spirit-fruit trees at dusk," Ruvien called after her as she headed to Master Maeli. "We've got important matters to attend to." Then he, Elnora, and Senrik left.

Master Koren turned his penetrating gaze on her. "Congratulations," he said, sliding a rectangular object from his sleeve.

A teak lacquer box. It was inlaid with gold-foil flowers—chrysanthemums and narcissus, symbols of death and immortality.

Tori opened it. Inside lay a piece of folded cream-colored silk. A thrill shot through her—the elder's map.

"The elder says you must study this tonight and memorize it within three days; otherwise, you will have to wait till the next new moon before you can read it properly again."

Unsure of what he meant, Tori merely thanked him. Then, with a tender nod at Master Maeli, he was gone.

Tori slipped the box into her shoulder bag. She couldn't wait to study it. She would say goodbye to Master Maeli, then resist the urge to run, laughing, all the way to the spirit-fruit trees where the others were waiting for her.

Just as she turned to say goodbye, however, Master Kwai'le walked up the stairs and greeted them. The sight of a perfectly healed Driven on his shoulder compounded the happiness Tori already felt.

As the two masters started talking, Driven sat calmly, his silver feathers ruffling in the breeze.

Tori glanced at the sinking sun, hoping the conversation wouldn't take long.

It did. The two masters dragged it on and on, and furthermore spoke back and forth in such rapid succession it left no room for Tori to break in and excuse herself.

Eventually, Master Kwai'le turned to her. "Looks like it all worked out, then." There was no hint of sarcasm in his voice. He sounded...friendly—an unsettling thought.

"When do you leave?"

"As soon as we can," she said, then added, "I'm going to talk with the others about it now."

"Good, good. Just make sure you're well supplied." He jerked his chin at the medicine hut. "You never know what you'll need out there. Good cloaks, too. It's the first day of the eleventh moon. Harsh weather will be here before we know it."

"Yes, Master." She realized then that she was angled forward, like someone preparing to sprint. She straightened herself and forced her shoulders to relax.

"But you're in good company, where healers are concerned," he said. "By all accounts, Master Banfay is pleased with Elnora's progress."

"She has a good knowledge of herbs," Tori said, with a sense of pride.

Master Maeli raised an eyebrow. "Good isn't quite the word. Banfay tells me she has the makings of a master healer."

Tori stared. "I had no idea," she said, feeling guilty. She had been so absorbed with her own concerns that she had never once asked Elnora to elaborate on her training.

"Plus, you've got a gifted archer," Master Kwai'le continued, "and hero. You're in safe hands."

Tori cast a questioning look at Master Maeli. "A hero?"

"Senrik."

"But I thought Senrik—" Tori stopped herself. She thought what? *I thought he was a lawless Ghenz killer?*

"You should ask him to tell his story sometime." Master Maeli glanced at the sky. "But I must be off. I have matters to attend to that cannot wait. I will be around for the next few days, however." She smiled and laid a hand on Tori's shoulder, the way she had done with Master Banfay.

Warm gratitude poured into Tori's chest, healing parts of her she hadn't known were broken.

A master for a day, a mother for life. She, too, now had a mother who loved her.

"Be sure to come see me before you go," Master Maeli said. Then she jogged down the steps and out of sight.

Master Kwai'le, however, just stood there. He looked at the ground, the weapons racks, the stone wall. An insect caught his attention, and he squinted, leaning forward to study it, too.

The sun sank below the horizon, and Tori shifted, wondering how to break the awkward silence and leave.

"Well, Master..."

He nodded. "Yes, of course. I just wanted to wish you luck on your journey." He said this with the same ill-fitting friendliness as before.

Then he reached into his robes and pulled out a snowy-white scroll case with a gold cap. The precious alchemy scroll. The gold clouds and mythical creatures engraved on it had taken on a rosy hue in the fading light.

Tori glanced at it, then back at him.

"Well, don't just stand there like a stump," he said. "Take it."

She bowed respectfully and held out her hands, palms up, and the cool, heavy scroll case met her skin.

Unsure of what else was expected, she stayed frozen in position.

"It's yours," he said.

Tori glanced up sharply. He had been saving this treasure for a worthy protégé. *She* was that protégé!

A tangle of emotion welled up inside her. The fact that he valued her enough to give his most precious possession meant more than any praise.

"Thank you, Master. I—" Her voice hitched. "I will treasure it."

He gave a nod, his eyes moist. The act had been momentous for him, too. "That scroll will tell you everything you need to know about making the Septad," he said.

He reached into his robe and pulled out a black velvet pouch. "This is my second gift."

She looked inside—a tiny bronze ladle whose bowl was no bigger than a grape, sat alongside a bronze mold with six round depressions, each roughly the same size as the ladle's bowl. Ancient logograms had been carved into everything.

"Etched metal," Tori said. She tried to guess what it was for.

He nodded, looking pleased. "You'll need this to form the spirit stones from the streams at Ketuan's Veins."

She hadn't even thought of that. She knew how to propel spirit stones forward to age them, but those stones were already formed. What would she have done with molten stone?

"Thank you, Master. Truly."

"It's one of a kind," he said, nodding at it. "To activate them, send in a stream of elixir, then scoop the molten stone and pour it into the mold. The mold will cool the crystals perfectly."

The absolute certainty in his voice brought forward the doubts that had been hiding in her mind—what if she didn't succeed?

She pushed the doubts away. She would make the Septad, and stop the war before it began. She would save the Ants—for Veyli.

Before she could say more, he lifted his arm and Driven hopped down onto it. Master Kwai'le held out the hawk. "My third and final gift."

The moment he had spoken the words, Driven flapped his wings and landed on Tori's shoulder, which sank under his weight, his sharp claws tickling her skin through her robes.

Master Kwai'le sighed. "Just finished training him, too. But I might as well give him to you. You're the only one he seems to like."

She hoped she hadn't misunderstood. "I can keep him? As a pet?" Driven nuzzled her cheek.

Master Kwai'le shrugged. "If that's what you want."

He gave her a homing stone to match the one around Driven's neck, then slipped a paper from his sleeve and looked it over. "Though my reasons for giving him to you might not be entirely selfless," he said, handing her the paper. "This is the formula for Pixie Mint pills. I'm running low. I've made a third homing stone to guide him, so send word by Driven if you come across any Pixie Mint plants along the way. I'm hoping to find another supply."

"Yes, Master," she said, trying to match his matter-of-fact tone while holding a priceless treasure in each hand, her first alchemical formula, and a nuzzling, sharp-clawed hawk on her shoulder.

He riffled through his pouch. "Otherwise just get them on Mount Ketwanen. There are bound to be loads there. Then make the pills while the herbs are fresh, as many as you can."

There was that utter confidence again. He had no doubt she could do everything he asked.

"Cut them at the base of the stalks, mind you," he said, finally finding what he was looking for in his pouch. He took out a folded paper and handed it to her. "I'll also require the items on this list. They'll be harder to come by, so just get what you can."

The list was long, but instead of annoying her, it made her feel strangely warmed. She really was his protégé.

"Now, remember—the Septad requires precision, just like when you meld spirit stones, so be sure to concentrate."

She bowed again. "Thank you, Master, sincerely."

And with that, he walked away.

Halfway down the steps, he stopped and turned. "By the way, well done with Keya—she had it coming." He chuckled and left.

She stared at his back, her heart full, then turned the scroll over gently in her hands before carefully tucking everything into her bag.

The last lights disappeared from the horizon. The others would be waiting in the dark.

"Come on, Driven," she said, tying her cloak around her neck. "We've got important matters to attend to."

Chapter Seventy-Six

HOPE

Driven took off into the air, glided through the cloudy night sky, then circled once around three dark shapes sitting beneath the silver trees.

Ruvien and Elnora were unloading food from a wicker basket onto a blanket where blue circles of light from the spirit-fruit illuminated various dishes. Driven swooped down, snatching a cloud bun.

"Hey!" Ruvien swatted at him, but the hawk tilted easily to the side, then soared to the treetop with his prize. "Where'd he come from?"

"Master Kwai'le," Tori said, taking a seat on the blanket across from Senrik.

She showed them the snowy scroll case, the etched items for casting spirit stones, and the herb list.

"I think he just named me his protégé, though I'm not entirely sure what that means."

Ruvien looked at the list. "Apparently, it means you're his errand girl."

"More importantly," Tori said, taking out the lacquer box, "I have this." She opened it to reveal the folded map. "Let's study it and plan our route."

"What's the rush?" Ruvien said.

Tori raised an eyebrow. "Weren't you the one who just told me we had important matters to attend to?"

"I was talking about food," he replied with a laugh. "We'll look at your map. But first, let's eat." He made a sweeping gesture over the blanket. "Since we couldn't bring you to Greenstalk Teahouse, we brought the teahouse to you: cloud buns, fried curd puffs, yam cakes, folded egg-leaf. Here." He held out a cloud bun. "Pepper pork cloud. Careful, they're spicy."

The food was all Ruvien had promised it would be—every bit of it better than any palace food. As they ate, their conversation rolled easily from one topic to another.

"Let's all say what we want, or what we're looking forward to," Ruvien said. "I'll go first. I'm looking forward to being away from this place and seeing the sights."

Tori turned to him, surprised. "You don't like it here?"

"Sure I do. But you have to admit, Peach Blossom Grove is sorely in need of excitement. And I can't complete my family's beast lore sitting around on my hands."

"Are you looking for specific beasts, or just any magical creatures?" Elnora asked.

"To start, any creatures I can find," Ruvien said. "But the beast lore will only truly be complete when I find the Dither Beast."

"It lives on Mount Ketwanen?" Tori asked.

"Not sure. That page in my family's lore book is damaged. But by all accounts, there's nothing like it in all of Arizan, so I'm willing to bet on Ketwanen. In any case, it's the only place left to search, apart from Black Valley. But a few of my uncles went there years back—never heard from again."

"Nobody returns from Black Valley," Elnora said.

Senrik nodded his agreement. The spirit-fruit cast a glow on his face and hair as he ate, transforming him into a splendid god under the light of an otherworldly moon. Was he really a hero?

He stopped in the middle of chewing and looked at her, catching her off guard.

"What is it you want?" she asked quickly, feeling foolish for staring.

Ruvien chuckled and slapped Senrik on the back. "Don't ask him that. He'll dampen the mood with talk of honor. Let's hear what Elnora wants." He gave her a smile.

"Truthfully? I want us to all get back here in one piece. And if we ever do, I want to never leave again."

Ruvien's gaze flickered from her to Senrik. "Well, this is a fun group."

Elnora shrugged unapologetically.

Tori wondered how to bring the conversation back around to Senrik, and get him to tell his story. She had to know what Master Maeli had meant.

He caught her staring again. "Are you all ready to go?" he asked, popping a fried tofu pouch into his mouth.

The play of Ayenashi and Zarien came back to her, and she thought uncomfortably about the things that might be waiting at Mount Ketwanen. Could anyone be ready for that?

"As ready as I'll ever be," she said. "The main thing is that we have to go there and back in three moons. How soon can everyone leave?"

"I'm ready to leave tonight," Ruvien said, slipping his silver flask from his robe and taking a swig. He offered it to Senrik, who waved it away.

"Give me time to gather provisions," Elnora said. "A day or two."

Senrik nodded. "It's best to make sure we're prepared. Anything we forget here, we won't see for a long time."

When they had finished eating, Tori unfolded the map on the blanket, moving it closer to the spirit-fruit trees to let the lights shine down on it.

Ruvien took another swig of his flask. "This is in excellent shape, considering its age."

"How old is it?" Tori asked.

"It's from the elder's treasury," Senrik said. "Old."

A circle with drawings and notations filled the center of the cloth, and in each of the four corners, lines marked off an empty square. It took Tori a moment to understand what she was looking at. The circle was Mount Ketwanen, but several areas inside were missing, not like they were faded, but rather like they had never been drawn.

Ruvien noticed, too. "Are you sure this is the right map?"

"I can't see Master Koren making a mistake like that," Tori said. "I guess I'll have to ask him to explain it."

"He left on an errand for the elder," Ruvien said. "I saw him go just before dusk."

Tori cursed. "How long will he be gone?"

Ruvien shook his head.

"Should I go see Master Banfay?" Elnora asked. "He's Master Koren's son, after all. He might know something."

"Good idea." Tori handed her the map, and Elnora left.

In about the time it would take to drain a cup, she reappeared, holding the map box in the air. "I met him on his way to the Houses of Healing. Come."

She waved them over as she sat beside the crystal streamlet, out in the open, away from the shadow of trees. Then she spread the map on the grass. "He said we have to wait till the sky clears."

Eventually, a few solitary stars began to shine, and Tori's breath caught: glowing white glyphs appeared on the map one by one, as though responding to the starlight.

"Of course," Senrik said. "Star glyphs. They can only be read under starlight, in the darkness of a new moon."

As the White River lit up the sky, glowing white lines appeared on three of the blank squares in the corners of the map. These were soon recognizable as mini maps.

The top right square said *Ketuan's Veins* and was filled with wavy lines, as though indicating streams of water. Evidently, this was a close-up of the place, which had featured on the main map as a simple annotation.

The top left square contained a map with a dotted path stretching from the Ma'yanar Forest up to the border of Jeng. As she didn't recognize the third square, she glanced at the various other annotations glowing on the mountain itself.

Elnora pointed to an area of the mountain that had remained curiously blank. The only markings on it were the words *Kimezaiya's Palace*, evidently referring to Kimezaiya the Earth Maiden, one of the Six.

"Do you think they really know where Kimezaiya's palace was?" Elnora asked. But Senrik and Ruvien were too transfixed by the map to respond.

Tori studied it bit by bit. As she did, whispers blew through her, like a sigh on a breeze, and she stopped, listening intently. Instead of hearing something, however, a terrible image flashed in her mind: a woman with black lines on her face, walking into a wall of roaring fire until it consumed her. The picture frightened her.

She shivered and drew her cloak tighter.

"Well, it all looks fairly straightforward," Ruvien said.

"Looks can be deceiving," Senrik said. "See this here?" He pointed to an innocent-looking mountain range where the dotted path passed through. "It's a dangerous pass, better avoided."

"Aw, what's a journey to a mythical mountain without some excitement?" Ruvien said, drinking from his flask again.

Elnora squinted at the remaining square on the bottom left corner of the map. "Why is this one still empty?"

At that moment, the last of the clouds shifted aside, and Ishairo the Sunderer appeared. The final square lit up with glyphs and another dotted path, leading to a tiny Mount Ketwanen.

Then, on either side of the mountain, two more mountain ranges came into view, sloping downward to form the shape of an arrowhead, with Ketwanen at its tip.

"What is this?" Tori said.

Glyphs popped up over the mountains, labeling them. Tori's pulse skipped—the path to Ketwanen went straight through Black Valley.

Everyone exchanged glances.

"Maybe there's another way?" Ruvien said, looking less eager now.

"Master Banfay will know," Elnora said. "He's traveled all the lands of Shudon."

Tori nodded. "Ask him." She refused to worry until they were sure.

Elnora rose, map in hand, and Ruvien fell in step beside her, leaving Tori and Senrik alone.

A ridiculous uneasiness hit her. Shouldn't she be more concerned about traveling through the deadliest valley in all of Shudon than with being alone with Senrik?

Yet all she could think about was what the two masters had said about him. Were they right?

She glanced at him through the corner of her eye. Whatever he was, she would deal with it. But she needed to know the truth.

"I was speaking with Master Maeli earlier," Tori said, keeping her tone light. "She mentioned you have a story to tell. She and Master Kwai'le both said you're a hero."

Senrik dragged a hand through his hair, looking exhausted. "Is that what they call it?"

As he stared at the crystal streamlet, a symphony of crickets and hooting owls went on so long Tori was about to change the subject, just to save face. But then he let out a long, tired sigh.

"We were doing a raid on the northeast border of Min," he said. "It was supposed to be a clean job. In and out. That's how our wise woman liked it—no fires, no killing unless we had to.

"On our way back, we came across a village we hadn't marked. We went in, made lots of noise. Figured people would run and hide like they always did, and we'd take what we wanted. But the village matriarch surprised us. She rallied her people, and they came at us with sticks and farming tools. My clansmen killed her." He paused. "Everyone scattered—except her daughter. Pretty. My clansmen wanted to take her as plunder."

He glanced at Tori, eyes apologetic. "Clans do that, sometimes. Even ours. The wise women say mixing with outsiders is good for clan blood." He looked away. "I argued. She had just lost her mother, you know? I got them to agree to leave her. But when it was time to go, two of my clansmen were missing, and I just knew." His jaw flexed and he shook his head. "I found them at the matriarch's house. The girl was still fighting. They were going to kill her. The others came then and backed them up, said the girl would be trouble, that it was better to finish it. They refused to leave her alive." Senrik clenched his fists. "So I did what I had to."

Tori sat with this revelation, letting the weight of it sink in. When he had said he killed his clansmen, she had been thinking two or three. How many had there been?

And he had done it all to save an innocent.

She looked at him for a beat, taking in his profile. "What happened to the girl?"

"Went free. But what kind of life will she live?"

"You never know what kind of life a person will live," she said gently. "It's having the choice that matters."

He slowly unclenched his hands and stared at them. They were strong and elegant, hands made for heroic deeds—and, perhaps, for tenderness.

He looked at her, eyes filled with gratitude.

Tori smiled. "I never got to hear what you wanted out of this trip."

He stared straight ahead again, and for a breath or two seemed to be thinking. Tori followed his gaze to the crystal streamlet.

"Ruvien was right," he said at last. "I want honor." He paused. "I want to join a righteous cause. I want to obtain Unity with the Sword. I want—" He stopped short, the wistful call of a night bird filling the silence.

Tori turned from the water to find him gazing at her; the look in his eye sent flutters up her spine.

As she held his gaze, the soft, breathless words escaped her: "What else do you want?"

His eyes lingered on hers a moment longer. Then he smiled, shook his head, and looked away. "I want too many things."

Feathery shivers rippled on her skin, and she rubbed her arms.

"What about you?" Senrik said. "What are you looking forward to?"

The question caught her by surprise. She knew what she wanted—the Septad. But was she looking forward to something?

As she searched for her answer, a cool autumn breeze ruffled her fur-lined collar. She absently reached for the broken shell, brushing a fingertip over its worn edge. A fleeting doubt crossed her mind, and she briefly closed her eyes.

Then she hid the shell away and exhaled, releasing a burden she had carried for too long.

"I'm looking forward to finally doing something right."

The crystal streamlet reflected the sky like a looking glass, twinkling with starlight. Tori took in the water, the stars, the blue lights of the spirit-fruits, inhaling their fragrance, memorizing the moment.

Then a new scent drifted in, stirring something from the depths of her childhood, vaguely familiar, like a long-forgotten dream. She closed her eyes, filling her lungs, trying to place it.

Finally, she did. It swathed her now, invigorating her, soft like rose petals, crisp like pine—it was the smell of hope.

The Closing of the Scroll

I lift up my eyes from the scroll in my hands
After long study through fleeting time,
And memories rush back of sunny woodlands
When cheerful winds ruffled through the wild thyme;
All was pleasurable in my youthful prime.
My heart filled with joy at every new dawn
To read the words of my foremothers, long gone.

I lift up my eyes from the scroll in my hands
And writings like loyal kin surround me,
Within them many a prophecy spans
Over years I will never live to see.
And though I have studied them fervently,
Pouring my soul into them long ago,
Still they conceal things that I will never know.

I lift up my eyes from the scroll in my hands
And wonder if my foremothers once knew
These deep, hidden truths so few understand.
Will those who follow behind me see true,
And fathom these solemn winds that blow through?
Will they discern prophecy's silent drums,
And will they recognize her when she comes?

I lower my eyes back down to the scroll
Which is rolled up again, as though it knows
That to someone else I must leave the whole
Of these hopes as my time draws to its close;
My heart prepared for its final repose.
Yet tonight, my single solemn desire
Is to rest my old bones beside the fire.

The Closing of the Scroll
—from the writings of Loremaster Jin

ACKNOWLEDGEMENTS

It feels surreal to write this page—an epic novel finished at last. But I didn't do it alone.

To my daughters, Eva and Sylvia: you're my original fans, always eager to hear wild ideas. Eva, your sharp ear rescued me from many awkward phrases. Sylvia, your mapwork turned rough sketches into something beautiful. And thank you both for the tailu-bird chapter ornament.

To Erin Healy, writing coach extraordinaire and developmental editor: your wisdom shaped tangled notions into a real story. I'm deeply grateful for your guidance.

To Shawna Hampton, my editor: thank you for refining with care and catching what I missed. (One day I'll master those tricky hyphens.)

Thanks to beta readers Joanne Staunton and Anna Tan, and to critique partners Uma Rajasingam and Alyssa Rose for critiques, brainstorms, and friendship.

My niece, Alexi Colburn: thank you for always reading and encouraging.

To my parents and stepparents: your steady faith and love made me who I am.

Finally, my beloved Luc: your steadfast encouragement gave me the strength to persevere. This book is your doing, more than you know.

ABOUT THE AUTHOR

C.P. Silver didn't set out to write epic fantasy—but the stories wouldn't leave her alone. She grew up in the Cayman Islands, practiced law for ten years, became a French national, and even studied Chinese medicine. Through all those twists, writing remained her quiet constant.

Her debut, *Whispers of the Elixir*, is set in a matriarchal empire where secrets, sentient forests, and forbidden magic collide. Called "lush" and "evocative" by readers, it's a story of identity, rebellion, and women's power in all its forms.

These days, C.P. Silver lives in Europe. When she's not weaving fantasy worlds, she's usually reading in a sunlit corner or walking somewhere green.

Find her on Instagram at @cpsilver_author, on Facebook at /cpsilver-author, or on her website at www.cpsilver.com.

Printed in Dunstable, United Kingdom